4

HINTS

You Love

YOUR
BEST
FRIEND

Also by Kelly Siskind

Bower Boys Series:

50 Ways to Win Back Your Lover

10 Signs You Need to Grovel

6 Clues Your Nemesis Loves You

4 Hints You Love Your Best Friend

7 Steps to Seducing Your Fake Fiancé

One Wild Wish Series:

He's Going Down

Off-Limits Crush

36 Hour Date

Showmen Series:

New Orleans Rush

Don't Go Stealing My Heart

The Beat Match

The Knockout Rule

Over the Top Series:

My Perfect Mistake

A Fine Mess

Hooked on Trouble

Stand-Alone: Chasing Crazy

Visit Kelly's website and join her newsletter for great giveaways and never miss an update!

www.kellysiskind.com

4 HINTS
You Love
YOUR
BEST
FRIEND

A Bower Boys Novel
Kelly Siskind

CHAPTER

One

(Also appears as the epilogue in
6 CLUES YOUR NEMESIS LOVES YOU)

Callahan

All I've ever wanted is to give my brothers the happiness they deserve. There's nothing more important than ensuring they find love and success in life, but I've encountered a problem. A troublesome hitch I can't control. Specifically, the fact that every fiber of my being is highly attuned to my former best friend: Jolene Daniels, Ruiner of My Serenity.

I sense her the second she's near, like this precise moment. It's not just the telltale tingling up my neck when she enters the art gallery or my knee-jerk instinct to flee. My oldest brother's sharp intake of breath is a dead giveaway to her presence, followed by his I-want-my-ex-girlfriend-back sigh.

"Jolene's here," Jake says, like I don't know. "She brought drinks."

I keep my back to her. Pretend my heart hasn't turned into a jackhammer. I carefully lift another painting off the wall and lean it with the others.

Her appearance here isn't odd. A number of townsfolk turned up to help the Yard Goat Gallery owners clean up after last night's spring storm. It was a doozy, blowing through Windfall with a decisive hand, but the Yard Goat sustained the only real damage. An old tree came down on the train-station-turned-artist co-op, shattering windows and puncturing the roof. Some art was damaged beyond repair. Water seeped in, which means new floors are needed, along with new windows and drywall and a fresh coat of paint.

Since Jake and I run our own construction business, and I'm friends with one of the artists, we volunteered our help. Everyone else is here because this is Windfall. A close-knit community that helps when others are in need, sweeping, lugging, gossiping, arguing good-naturedly over what should be done next, or, in Jolene's case, bringing refreshments.

"I should go talk to her," Jake says, but my oldest brother doesn't move. "I still can't get over how great she looks. Even more beautiful than when she was younger, don't you think?"

I clench my jaw. If I don't turn around and participate in this painful conversation, Jake will wonder why I'm acting weird. He won't know *why* I'd like to demo the brick wall in front of me and sprint through the wreckage, but the wondering is just as bad. Wondering leads to questions. Questions lead to uncertainty, which eventually leads to mistrust. For twelve years, I've successfully hidden my role in his breakup with his ex-girlfriend, who happens to be my ex-best friend. Neither of them knows what I did, and I plan to keep it that way.

Unfortunately, there's no avoiding Jolene in this shoebox town.

Steeling my nerves, I turn around and, *Christ*. There goes my body again—*reacting*—like last night's storm is blowing through my chest.

Jo may appear innocent enough, with her country-girl charm, flirty brown hair, and warm chestnut eyes, but the beauty mark on her right cheek is the first clue she'll mesmerize—a dash of sensual mixed with sweet purity. Dangerous without even trying.

All this time later, my insides go chaotic around her. I still sense when she's in a room. She was my best friend for nine years, two of which she spent dating my oldest brother. We've been apart for twelve years since then, but my forced absence hasn't changed the facts—what I did to her and Jake was *bad* and *wrong*, and the guilt is even worse now.

"She does look great," I tell Jake, forcing a placid expression. "Have you asked her out yet?"

"Not on a proper date. The way things ended with us was messy."

Because I'm an asshole, and Jolene thinks Jake cheated, when he did no such thing. "That was just the town rumor mill."

"I know. I think she knows it too. When it all went down, she said that wasn't why she wanted to break up. But I'm not sure that was true, and doubts can linger."

Forget asshole. Just label me traitor and toss me to the wolves. "Give it time. You two were meant to be together."

Townsfolk are busy, moving easels and art supplies, carefully navigating the glass on the floor.

Jake leans on his broom and shrugs. "I know she's happy I'm back. We've hung out at her bar a few times, but people are always around, and I get weird vibes from her."

"Well, we did vanish for over a decade."

He smirks. "I survived witness protection, and all I got was this lousy life?"

"We should make T-shirts."

"Or kill our father," he grumbles.

"There will be no killing." I refuse to let anything bad happen to my brothers, even if murdering Raymond S. Bower would be justice served.

But yeah, WITSEC. Talk about a hellish shock. Ten years of fear and uncertainty, all thanks to our money laundering dad. No one, including Jolene, knew why we left town or where we went. The cartel who'd had a hit on us was wiped out by their rivals two years ago. We're now in the clear, but we all have lingering scars.

Jake and I stayed in Houston afterward, living together and building our construction business, unsure if we wanted to return to our hometown. He said there were too many unpleasant memories. I didn't want to face the mistakes I made.

Yet, here we are. Back in Windfall, because the rest of our brothers returned.

And my mistakes are smack-dab in my face.

"Hey, you two!" Jolene grabs a couple of sodas and brings them our way.

She's wearing cowboy boots and a jean skirt that shows off her shapely legs. Her fitted blue T-shirt reads *Fishing for Trouble*. Isn't that the God's honest truth? This woman never fails to inspire anarchy.

I accept her drink and nod at my brother. "Jake was just saying how great it is to have you back in his life."

For a second, her gaze seems to slide down my body. The perusal isn't interest. Jolene never looked at me the way she looked at Jake. She's likely surprised by my bulk now that I hit the gym daily on top of my construction work, but I instantly feel flushed.

Expectedly, she blinks and looks at Jake. "It has been great having your family back. I missed you *both* a lot." Her attention slides back to me. "I've tried calling you a few times, Cal. You're never around."

I shrug. "Been busy."

"What he's doing," Jake says, his tone hard, "is taking on extra work he doesn't need to do."

I crack open my can and take a long gulp of fizzy lemon soda. Anything to cool me down when around Jo. Unfortunately, nothing douses the fond memories she inspires—us competing in Monopoly or Sorry until the person losing upended the board in a dramatic fury. Playing touch football after a hard rain, diving into mud puddles, cracking up as muck covered us head to toe. We studied together, often ate dinner at each other's houses. Helped each other when needed, like the time she broke her arm jumping out of our tree house.

I was at her house daily while she was healing. Wrote her assignments, even brushed her hair and helped her get dressed. I could barely breathe those days, holding out her jeans, feeling the drag of my thumbs up her thighs, the sharp dig of her fingers into my shoulders as she used me for balance. Teenage hormones were not my friends back then.

Adult hormones aren't much kinder.

"There's nothing wrong with helping townsfolk," I tell Jake, forcing my focus on him. "Mr. Elroy needs a new back deck. The Liangs need a fence for their puppy."

His nostrils flare. "You're doing too much."

This is typical Jake. Our stand-in dad who kept us together when our worlds fell apart. I love that he cares so much, except his thoughtfulness enflames my guilt. "After being gone so long, it feels important to help where I can and reconnect with people. Like you two are reconnecting," I say emphatically.

Jolene glances at her cowboy boots. Jake scratches his chest, his intense focus shifting to her beautiful face. Their reconnection might take time, but I'm a patient man. I'll do my damnedest to give Jake everything he deserves. Namely, Jolene.

"What you're doing," he says to me, back on my case, "is working yourself into an early grave."

"The only person going into an early grave is our father,"

Lennon says, joining us. The second youngest Bower boy and the biggest pain in my ass.

"Again, no one's being killed." It's amazing how many times I've uttered that sentence in my life.

"Death is a natural part of existence," Lennon says, smirking through his hipster beard. "Speeding it up is simply helping Mother Nature." His smug expression passes over our awkward group, then settles on me. He raises an eyebrow brimming with know-it-all condescension. "How is everything these days, dear brother?"

I clack my teeth together. "Great, thank you."

"Like, *really* great?"

"As great as great gets."

"So you're *great*?"

"Absolutely," I say with a forced smile, refusing to look at Jo.

Here's the thing with Lennon. My meddling brother thinks he knows my secret. He thinks I'm as far from great as great gets because I'm in *love* with Jolene. I may be guilt-ridden over what I did—and there's no denying I'm still attracted to her sensual-innocent-siren self—but that's pure chemistry. I haven't spent time with Jolene in twelve long years. I no longer obsess over her, dream about her, wish we could be together.

As long as I keep our friendship minimized, I won't revert to my old pining ways. Plus, I have a plan to reunite her with Jake and fix the mistakes I made.

"If you'll all excuse me," I say as I inch away from the group, "I think they need help with the tree carnage outside."

This is my life these days. Making quick exits from coffee shops, family gatherings, bars, get-togethers. Anything to avoid Jolene and keep my family from learning too much.

I make haste and march toward the exit, but I feel Jo's attention on me as I move. She's probably confused as to why her former best friend is avoiding her like it's his job.

Once outside, I spot Ben standing over the fallen tree. He squints at its girth and rubs a hand over his shaved head.

"We'll need an arborist for that," I say, strutting toward him. A much easier task to focus on than righting my wrongs. "They can cut it up and turn it into wood chips."

"Sure, but..." Ben gets a hazy look in his dark eyes. "It's a great shape—the way it protrudes in sections. I could carve a bear in the top half."

"Or just a portrait of me."

His lips quirk. Ben is a built Black man who would look at home on a sports field, but he's a sculptor who started this artist co-op with other like-minded creators. "Too bad the gallery has investors, and I promised them we wouldn't create anything terrifying."

I attempt not to grin too wide.

At the start of WITSEC, I dwelled on what my old friends were doing, worried our disappearance knocked them for a loop. I obsessed over Jolene plenty, even though we were estranged by then, unsure if losing Jake and me in one night devastated her. Eventually, I decided worrying was for the weak.

I'm good with money and investing. Over the years, I built my savings, made discreet contacts in Houston. Found ways to keep tabs on the people I love. Ben has no idea I'm the silent partner financing his art gallery. My family doesn't know I hired a woman living in Windfall to do my bidding as needed. Why stress over the happiness of those you love when you can use a spy to ensure their success?

"I'm glad your investors are keeping you on your toes," I tell Ben, pleased my shell company has helped him realize his dreams. "Plus, people love a good story. When this is carved, tell prospective buyers the tree was about to crash down and you saved a child stuck in the branches before it fell. It'll cause a bidding war."

"That would be lying."

"Or just a creator creating."

"Or lying," he says on a laugh and slaps my back. "If I haven't said it enough, it's great having you home."

I'm not sure Windfall feels quite like home yet, but my old friends have welcomed me back into their fold, and the beauty of this area is undeniable. From our vantage point, I can see the Rough Ridge Mountains in the distance. Corner Creek meanders behind the former train station, with a tranquil forest on the far side. A welcome contrast to the polluted hustle of Houston, but it's not the landscape and quaintness that gives me this sense of peace I haven't felt in twelve years.

It's watching Lennon, who's outside now with his girlfriend, Maggie, the two of them laughing as they toss broken branches at each other. My youngest brother, E, has shown up with Delilah, and I swear I never thought I'd see him smile this wide again. Even Desmond is here. He's still snarly and grumbly, but the spark of affection in his eyes as he tosses his son over his shoulder and holds his soon-to-be-wife, Sadie's, hand like he can't live without her…well, I'm downright moved.

This is my purpose—securing my family's happiness. This is why I don't leave life to chance. And why I plan to do everything in my power to reunite Jake and Jolene.

"Javier's moving later this week." Ben grabs lopping shears to cut a longer branch. "If you're free, we could use another hand."

I mentally review my commitments—building Mr. Elroy's new deck, the Liang fence, renovating the Rosen kitchen with Jake, adding a garage and granny suite for the Whites with him too. There won't be much sleep in my future, but Javier was part of our posse back in the day. I haven't seen much of him since my return. "Count me in."

"Sweet. I should see if Jolene can come too."

"Nope," I blurt and launch a branch sideways.

Dammit.

Ben straightens and leans on his shears. "You don't want Jolene there, or Jolene's busy?"

"The latter, I assume. She's busy running her bar."

"Why do you assume?"

"Because it makes an ass out of U and Me?"

He huffs out an I'm-not-buying-what-you're-selling laugh. "Amusing, but you two used to be inseparable. I *assumed* you picked up where you left off."

We left off with me shutting Jolene out through no fault of her own. So, he's not wrong. Things are as uncomfortable as ever. "We're fine. Some friendships just don't last the test of time. Not that we're *not* friends. We just aren't as close as we were."

He stares at me like I'm that tree trunk, my true form hidden under layers of gnarled bark.

When his unwavering attention gets too much, I punch his shoulder. "I should check on the other helpers. Send me Javier's moving details."

I swivel before he replies, unsure where it's safe to work. I need a Jolene-free zone. Somewhere I can focus without everyone getting in my business. I spot a couple of older ladies attempting to pick up the heavy Yard Goat Gallery sign and march toward them.

But Jolene Daniels, Ruiner of My Serenity, steps in my way.

"You're avoiding me," she says pointedly and blows a wayward strand of hair from her eyes. She was never one to beat around the bush.

Unlike me, who excels at evading. "Like Jake said, I've been busy."

"Too busy for me?"

"Nope. Just"—I wave a vague hand around—"life. Work. It's not easy starting fresh somewhere."

"Exactly." Her brown eyes go soft. "I totally get it. At least, I want to try to get it. I know things were strained between us before you left. I'm not really sure why, not that it matters.

You're home now, and I want to help you adjust. I want my best friend back," she says more quietly.

My heart feels like it's in a vise clamp, pressure slowly squeezing the uncooperative organ.

There was a time I wouldn't hesitate to open my arms. Beckon her in. Hug and console this woman who used to be my other half. But the urge to run my nose up her ear strikes, to splay my hand on her lower back, feel her soft body molded to mine, my thigh pushing between hers as I—

"We'll go for drinks soon," I say and stalk away.

We won't. I don't trust myself around Jolene. I have no clue why, all these years later, she still makes me feel ravenous yet tender. Discombobulated. Having one-on-one time with her won't help my plan to reunite her and Jake. Which is fine. Operation Jake Wins Back Jolene goes into high gear tomorrow. Once they're in love and happy, my body will remember where it belongs—far away from my former best friend.

CHAPTER
Two

Callahan

Keeping secrets in Windfall is akin to hiding a fireworks show. The first year we moved here, I was ten, and my youngest brother, Edgar—or, as we call him, E—was seven. That fall, he was the only person not invited to his classmate Leo Whitaker's birthday party. Kids can be cruel, and I believed in justice served. As such, Leo's celebration ended with shrieks and screams when several black racer snakes mysteriously slithered through the gathering.

Afterward, I told one guy in the gym locker room I was responsible for the bedlam. I'm not sure which classmate overheard us or who took it upon himself to widely blab my heroics. Whoever snitched, by the time school was out, my mother was standing outside the front doors, her arms crossed, indignation clear as she said, "No son of mine pulls a prank and gets away with it."

Chelsea Bower is as solid as moms get.

My punishment was to make dinner every night for a month,

which wasn't as arduous as she assumed. Mom hated cooking for her five hungry boys, but I didn't mind chopping and frying. So I learned how to make chili and tacos and different kinds of pasta.

I also learned this town can't be trusted.

People in Windfall ingest more gossip than coffee. They'd rather spread I-heard-it-first bombshells than win the lottery. So, I'm meeting my hired spy in plain sight. It's our first face-to-face meeting since we started working together. Trying for covertness today will only draw scrutiny. As far as anyone in the town square is concerned, I'm sharing a bench with a random lady, while I read a copy of *The Bourne Identity* and she reads Windfall's local paper, *The Jangler*.

I hold my book in front of my face. "I trust you're well."

She doesn't glance my way. Just snaps her paper, lifting it higher. "I am."

"Thank you for helping organize Lennon's first date with Maggie. The rose and free dessert helped set the mood."

"Of course."

"And for finding E when he ran off on Delilah. None of us expected my father's autobiography news. That was excellent last-minute work."

"It's my job."

Honestly, Sandra was a find. When I decided to hire someone, I did research on the recent transplants to Windfall. Not only had she worked at a security firm for forty-plus years, she was unattached and had a reputation for discretion and hard work. Her eighties perm was a bit conspicuous, but she was an average-looking white woman who didn't stand out in a crowd.

Through her, I helped fund Ben's gallery. Jolene has no clue how many times I've eased her burdens and given her a moral boost. As each of my brothers returned to town, Sandra was my eyes and ears on the ground, allowing me to ensure their mistakes didn't derail their plans to woo their former flames.

Except with Desmond. Shockingly, he handled himself fine on his own.

Even though I'm back in town, her assistance remains invaluable. "Jolene needs some gentle prodding to open up to Jake," I tell Sandra.

She flips a page of *The Jangler*, awaiting further instruction.

"Too much force doesn't work with her," I go on. "She's stubborn and independent and doesn't take kindly to others forcing her hand." Like the time she was too nervous to try out for our school track team, and I secretly signed her up. She recognized my writing and punched me in the kidney. "We need to use subtlety," I add.

Sandra flips another page, angling away from me. "I could break something at her bar. Jake would have to go in and fix it."

That scheme would force their proximity, but I could never purposely cause Jo stress. "A rumor is the better angle. Find key people and let it slip that Jolene has been caught staring at Jake. Then suggest to others that Jake won't look at any woman but her."

"That could be too subtle."

"Not for the Windfall rumor mill."

Our local paper is called *The Jangler* for a reason. Jangling is the backbone of this town—chin-wagging, schmoozing, chattering. The less detail in a rumor, the better. The hens and rattling roosters of this town will pass the information along. Each person will tweak the story, tiny embellishments added until Jolene's stare is a full-on confession of love and Jake is crying himself to sleep at night, desperate to win back his lost love.

I know this because I used one such subtle rumor to break up Jake and Jo twelve years ago. It's only fitting I use the same tactic to bring them back together.

"Also," I add, "you need to let it leak that the ancient Jake-cheating rumor is false. Hint that Mary Ackerman was interested in Jake at the time and started it to break him and Jo up." Except that Traitor of the Year prize goes to me.

"Consider it done." Sandra methodically folds her paper in half. She stands and walks toward Delilah's coffee shop, Sugar and Sips, without sparing me a second glance.

Seriously. Sandra is indispensable.

A little kid runs by me, flying a small kite through the grassy town square. A teenage boy at the mermaid fountain reaches into the water and flicks droplets at a girl. She shrieks and smacks him lightly, laughing. For some reason, my shoulders tense. It's a beautiful spring Sunday. Townsfolk meander down the wide cobblestone sidewalks. Flower displays enliven the shop facades, but those teens are a reminder of Jo and me—the fun we had together, messing around and laughing. All of it gone when I vanished into WITSEC.

I take a deep breath, try to absorb the serenity, but my lats bunch toward my ears.

My phone chimes.

I glance down. A note from my calendar glows up at me:

Measure Mr. Liang's yard.

I swipe off the reminder and blink hard. I scroll through the rest of today's commitments—ordering wood from the lumberyard, deck construction planning, helping Javier move. I stand, eager to get to work. I'm clearly not built to uselessly lounge around on a sunny Sunday. I'm a get-busy and get-things-done kind of man.

CHAPTER
Three

Callahan

Measuring Mr. Liang's yard for his fence is actually fun. His new puppy, Sprocket, is a hilarious bloodhound. She has Dumbo ears that nearly reach the grass, and she loves nipping at the rough hems of my jeans. I spend half my time playing with her and the other half whipping out my tape measure and jotting down measurements.

"She likes you," Mr. Liang calls.

I look down at Sprocket's droopy face and massive ears. "If she mysteriously goes missing, I swear it wasn't me who took her."

He laughs. My phone chimes again. No rest for the organized.

"I'll be back Thursday afternoon," I tell Mr. Liang. "Is it okay if I work into the early evening?"

"Whenever is good. We're just thrilled you could fit us in."

I give Sprocket a final rub, then spend time in my truck reviewing my other side job—the Elroys' deck and its measurements. I check the notes I jotted down yesterday and calculate how much wood I'll need. When my phone chimes with my next commitment, I have just enough time to order my supplies and meet my friends for Javier's move. Not only does Javier run his own refrigeration repair business, he's moving to the other side of town, into his first purchased home. Being here to help him feels good.

Unfortunately, when I park my truck, I see two of my brothers, not my friends.

Lennon and E are standing on the street curb, the former always in everybody's business, the latter too intuitive for my liking. They're loitering beside a large moving truck outside Javier's rented house. Apparently, my brothers were also roped into moving duties.

I shut my truck door and head their way. "Wasn't expecting to see you two."

E salutes me. "Javier was in Delilah's shop and mentioned the move. I offered to help."

"I eavesdropped," Lennon adds. "Since E can't lift anything heavier than a pencil, thought it would be prudent to assist."

E punches his arm. Lennon flicks his elbow.

Mature adult men, we are not—an aftereffect of WITSEC.

Our family may have spent ten years in a big city, but we lived in relative isolation, mainly hanging out socially with one another. E's twenty-nine now, taller than all of us at six-foot-four, and an insanely talented illustrator. He's not as bulky as me, but he's fit from running and *can* lift things heavier than his pencil. Lennon, however, rarely speaks without sneaking in a jab. He hikes and rock climbs and works with our brother Desmond, running their outdoor recreation programs, cracking jokes twenty-four seven. All three of them are happy and in love with the women from their pasts. These two, in particular, also love tormenting me.

"So," I say, aiming to keep us from veering into unwelcome topics, "we should—"

"Lennon says you're avoiding Jolene." E looks down at me from his inch-and-a-half of height advantage.

Ignoring him, I smile at Lennon. From my experience, smiles and placid expressions are the best ways to distract and defuse. Any hint of weakness and my brothers pounce. "I talked to Jolene at the Yard Goat yesterday," I tell Lennon evenly. "You were there. I wouldn't call that avoiding."

"Except every time she's around, you find a reason to disappear as quickly as Desmond's patience."

I swallow a curse and try again. "I think you're—"

"Ooh." E points at me. "Like when she walked into Sugar and Sips last week. You left before you ordered your coffee."

Goddamn my attentive family. "I simply realized I was late for a job."

"And the day we had everyone out to test our new ropes courses," Lennon unhelpfully adds. "The second Jo showed up for the barbecue, you split."

"I was tired from working," I force out.

"He has been tired a lot lately." Lennon angles his broad shoulders, effectively cutting me out of their conversation. "He hasn't come out for beers with me in ages. Has he gone out with you?"

"Nope," E says, completing their body barricade. "Shoots me down every time."

Lennon nods thoughtfully. "And the only cool place for beers in town is the Barrel House."

E's eyes widen. "The bar Jolene owns."

Lennon unleashes his lackadaisical hipster smirk. "Coincidence? I think not."

"Look," I say, shoving their body barricade apart, "you're both being ridiculous. I'm not avoiding Jolene. It's just awkward seeing her again after all this time."

Lennon raises an eyebrow. "Awkward because you hooked up with her before WITSEC and you're terrified Jake will find out?"

"No!" I shout, quickly realizing my error. Shouting draws attention. Emotional outbursts encourage more scrutiny, and Lennon has been digging for dirt on Jolene and me for weeks.

My brothers wear matching expressions of I-knew-it indignation.

I take a calming breath. "I did *not* hook up with Jolene. There was just this *thing* that happened before I left, not of the romantic variety. Being around her makes me a bit uncomfortable."

Lennon snorts. "A bit."

E cocks his head. "What kind of *thing*?"

"I bet it was a schemy thing," Lennon says.

Damn it all to hell. "There's no *thing*. Forget I said *thing*. Just..." I glance around wildly. "Aren't we here to help Javier move?"

"The Bower boys!" Javier's deep voice rings out, *thank Christ*, ending this painful inquisition. He and Ben join us on the curb. "What are you three gabbing about?"

"Nothing," I say forcefully.

My brothers, thankfully, don't mention Jolene, but I don't like how they're scrutinizing me. Meddlesome troublemakers, the both of them.

Javier gestures to the house. "All the small stuff has been moved. I just need help with the larger furniture. It shouldn't take us too long."

We're five big, strong guys, all of us dressed for grunt work in worn T-shirts and jeans—my typical attire. Even Lennon has swapped his usual plaid for a T-shirt that says *Ironic* across the front. Moving should be easy, if my brothers quit badgering me.

We get to work, lifting and lugging. Lennon and E take turns casting raised eyebrows my way, which I studiously ignore. We shoot the shit about the good old days: the time we dared Javier to streak through cheerleading practice, Ben drinking at the Spring Fair and puking off the Ferris wheel, all of us cliff jumping at Bear Lake. Javier tells me about his new girlfriend, Simone, who lives in nearby Ruby Grove. Ben attempts to glare at me when I ask how his fiancée, Kiyana, puts up with his bad breath.

"Pepperoni sticks and Cheetos, dude." He points accusingly at the snacks Javier brought. "I have no control over my breath."

We're finished our moving duties, sitting on the steps of Javier's new porch, chatting and stuffing our faces with salty snacks.

"What was I supposed to provide?" Javier asks while licking his orange fingers. "*Fruit?*"

We all make gagging noises.

"Fruit is for suckers," Lennon says. "Bring on the meat sticks and fake cheese."

"I can do better than that." Javier wipes his orange fingers on one of the moving blankets. "If you all suck back some mouthwash, beers are on me at the Barrel. A thank-you for your help."

He doesn't wait for our reply. Just heads inside to grab his wallet, because why would we say no to free beers? Except the Barrel is slang for Jolene's establishment—the Barrel House. The one place I want to avoid.

"I'll call Kiyana. Let her know I'm heading out." Ben pulls out his cell and leaves the porch.

I scratch my neck and look everywhere but at my brothers.

"So, Callahan." Lennon's tone is pure patronization. "I assume you'll be joining us at the Barrel?"

"Since you're not avoiding Jolene," E adds, reading my face for clues.

I want to growl or tear off in my truck, but I keep it contained. I have no one to blame for this painful situation but myself. By feigning nonchalance where Jolene is concerned, I have no choice but to join these nitwits, where they'll no doubt analyze my every move.

"Beers at the Barrel sounds absolutely perfect," I say evenly. "There's nowhere else I'd rather be." Unless you count getting tortured in the Nine Circles of Hell.

CHAPTER

Four

Callahan

I spend the drive to the Barrel House stewing in regret over my past mistakes. And over the fact that I *have been* avoiding Jolene, when I truly miss my best friend.

It's an odd thing, losing the person closest to you, when she's alive and well. Especially when that person is Jolene Daniels. We met during our awkward preteen years. I was ten and she was a much older eleven. I'd just moved to Windfall and was apprehensive about starting school. I was a scrawny kid, more of an observer than a talker. It was the early fall. School was already underway. Jake and Desmond were at Windfall High. Lennon and E were at my school, but Lennon has always been a chameleon, friends with everyone, quick to camouflage and fit in. E is his own man—an artist who's happy blocking out the world while he sketches.

Back then, I had social anxiety.

That first day of school, I stood on the sidewalk, gripping my backpack straps like they were life preservers. Groups of boys walked by, joking and laughing and horsing around. Girls moved in small cliques, swishing their hair and talking over one another. I stood by myself, a lone rock damming the social stream, happiness flowing around me.

My breathing became more labored. Sweat gathered under my armpits.

"Hi," came a small voice.

Nearing hyperventilation, I hadn't noticed the girl standing beside me. She was thin and short, with long brown hair and bangs so thick I could barely see her eyes. But there was no missing her beauty mark. A single, intriguing spot at the edge of her curved cheek. She held a couple of books tight to her chest, and when she tipped her head and smiled at me, I breathed easier.

"Hey," I said. Or at least, I tried to speak. My anxiety-ridden voice barely squeaked out.

"I'm Jolene Daniels. You're Callahan, right? My mom said to say hi to you, because you're new and all. And I don't really have friends. So we could be friends, if you want. Unless you don't like being friends with girls? But I'm not girly. Not like them." She jutted her chin to the hair-swishers. "I like sports and stuff. And adventuring. Do you like adventuring?"

I didn't know what adventuring was. I didn't like hearing that this nice girl was a loner like me. But my death grip on my backpack suddenly wasn't so tight. "Adventuring sounds fun."

She made a small, excited sound that had me smiling. "We can start at lunch. Meet me at the cafeteria doors."

She waved at me and walked ahead. I watched her intently, feeling less anxious and less alone, so damn thankful for this chatterbox girl. Then some asshole smacked into her side.

Her books fell. The guy didn't apologize or bend down to help. He laughed at her, nudged his buddy, and kicked her books farther away.

That's when it happened. My first flare of protectiveness

toward Jolene—a rush of anger blasting up my neck, demanding action.

Being new in town and scrawny, I didn't launch myself at the bully. I hurried over and helped Jolene with her books, but I took a mental snapshot of the jerk, who was still laughing and pointing at us on the ground.

Then I made a plan.

I kept tabs on him for a few days, learned his name was Lane Ternent. I figured out which bicycle was his and what time he left school. I also learned what adventuring was.

Jolene was a grade above me, but every day after school, we went out hunting frogs and snakes. We pretended we were knights while traipsing through patches of forest, dueling with branches, and balancing on fallen logs. A bit immature for ten and eleven, maybe. Neither of us cared. With Jolene, everything was *fun*.

"You'll never breach my castle walls!" I yelled one afternoon, brandishing my branch with flair.

She roared in my face and bared her teeth. "My dragon just incinerated your head."

I clawed at my cheeks, moaning and groaning until I tripped over my feet and landed nose-first in a pile of leaves. Jo was on me in seconds, shoving leaves down my shirt and in my face. I smashed a handful into her hair. We were choking from laughing so hard, barely able to breathe.

When we were done, starfished on the ground, exhausted and smiling, she rolled her head toward me. "I'm really glad you moved here. Other kids don't know how to have fun."

I don't think I knew what fun was until I met Jolene. Or what it meant to want to avenge a person's honor.

My plan to give Lane Ternent a taste of his own medicine hadn't abated. Two weeks after the book-kicking incident— patience was key when avenging—I put cement glue on his bicycle seat. The front schoolyard was busy, but I was discreet in the application. I met up with Jolene as Lane came outside, ensuring we stopped to talk before he swung his leg over his bike.

The second he sat down, he frowned and tried to stand back up. His shorts didn't move with him. They were yanked down, and he mooned half the school.

People pointed and gasped. Jolene laughed so hard she tipped into me and cackled on my shoulder. It was a fantastic day.

As I park my truck outside Jo's bar, I feel decidedly less fantastic. I rub my chest, hating the tightness behind my ribs and my inability to quit thinking about Jo. Soon, everything will be easier. Once she's back together with Jake, she'll be too busy to worry about reconnecting with me. I'll maintain the necessary distance from her to keep my emotions in check.

Tired of stalling, I leave my truck and head into the Barrel House. It's not overly busy. One of the two pool tables at the back is being used, and a quarter of the booths and wooden tables are full with townsfolk enjoying drinks and greasy snacks. The dance floor is empty, but country tunes have people bopping their heads and tapping their heels.

I spot Jo right away, everything in me zinging at the sight of her. Flirty hair. Soft mouth. Tight tank top. *Puckered brow?* She's behind the bar, rushing around, and she looks stressed. The intense kind of stressed that makes Jo's brown eyes go hard.

I immediately tense. Debate going over and finding out what's wrong, but we're not friends like that any longer.

Blowing out a rough breath, I tear my gaze away and find the guys crowded around a table. The second I'm in speaking distance, Lennon nods at me. "Last one here buys drinks."

"I'm buying the drinks," Javier says, pulling out his credit card. "Payment for helping me move, and"—he looks at me with a full-teeth grin—"for helping me remodel the outdated bathroom in my new house? Any chance you're free to give me a hand?"

Chuckling, I mentally review my jam-packed days. Try to think of when I can fit him in. "Maybe in a few months. Not sure I can swing it right now."

"I'll take what I can get. We'll add nachos as a down payment."

He starts to stand, but Lennon puts his hand on Javier's shoulder. "You may be paying, but the last one here does the ordering." He flutters his fingers at me in a goodbye motion, knowing Jolene is at the bar.

"Move your ass," E says brightly. "And say hi to Jo for us."

Goddamn my brothers.

Refusing to admit they're getting to me, I pluck the card from Javier's hand. "No problem. Nachos, a regular pitcher of beer for the table, and something shitty and obscure for the hipster."

The guys laugh. Lennon glowers.

I march toward the bar, hoping Jo is busy with another customer. Luck, however, is not on my side. Aside from one man nursing his beer at the end of the bar, it's just her and me and my ever-present guilt.

When she spots me, she doesn't smile or wave or look less stressed. She flinches and flattens her lips.

Something compresses in my chest, like a wrecking ball has landed on my ribs. I should slap the card on the counter and order our drinks. Pull out my phone and pretend to read an important text while I wait, but I find myself leaning my elbows on the bar, closing the distance between us. "Everything okay?"

"Fine," she says coldly. "What can I get you?"

A new chest, for starters. Maybe better self-preservation instincts. "You're not fine, Jo. What's up?"

Her glare verges on hostile. "Like you care."

I rear back. "Of course I care."

Her expression shifts to incredulous with a side of *fuck off*.

"You don't pick up my calls or return them. You avoid me around town. You were my best friend for a decade, and now you want nothing to do with me. So, yeah, all evidence points to you *not caring*." She breathes hard, her face flushed with anger.

I'm struggling to breathe, period. Devasted I've hurt Jo this much.

As kids, she had no idea I was responsible for that mooning prank on Lane Ternent. Present-day Jolene doesn't know I'm the one who helped her find her current apartment, after her roommate got engaged. Or that I'm responsible for having her truck fixed last year. Malcolm Boyd of Boyd's Service Center couldn't access the part she needed. Sandra, being the exceptional spy she is, texted me the issue from her burner phone. I found the part at a random garage across the country, had it expedited to one of Malcolm's suppliers, who then forwarded it to the mechanic, with no mention of how it suddenly appeared. Jolene's happiness has always been more important than praise.

Except she's not happy, is she? She thinks I've written her off. That I don't care, when the problem is I care too much.

I scrub my hand over my mouth, leaning heavier on the bar. "I'm sorry."

"For what, exactly?"

"For avoiding you."

"But…why?" The plaintiveness in her voice flays me, as does the sad slant of her eyes. "Why can't you talk to me?"

"It's complicated." An old mistake I can't erase and a heart that might still be vulnerable to her mysterious charms.

She stares at me a beat, then deflates. "Just order your drinks, Cal. Go sit with the guys. You clearly don't want to talk to me."

I should do exactly that. Order. Pay. Go. But the wrecking ball on my sternum presses down harder, grinding painfully. I can't live with Jolene thinking I wouldn't move heaven and earth for her.

"When I'm with you, Jo..." I put the credit card on the bar and pick at a splinter in the wood, trying to find a middle ground between *my heart misbehaves around you* and a flat-out lie. "A lot of memories come back."

"Bad memories?"

"Hard memories."

"Like what?"

I look up at her gorgeous face. Her cheekbones are more angular than when we were teens. Her nose is still slender but more defined. Even with those changes, I still see the girl who'd pick up a snake bare-handed and act like a goof to make me laugh. My fellow adventurer.

"Remember our Cool List?" I ask.

She seems to startle, a small smile tilting her lips. "I think Loser List would have been a better title."

I huff out a laugh, because *yeah*. The two of us didn't hang out with the cool crowd back then, but Jo was determined to be different in high school. To morph into the popular butterfly she became. Before that, we'd built a ramshackle tree house together —my first taste of construction and working with my hands— where we'd often lie side by side, grumbling about the annoying cliques at school, or we'd play board games or pretend we were jungle people hollering up to the sky.

"I was so nervous to start high school without you," she says.

"I hated that I wouldn't be there for you if things were rough."

"The list we made was hilarious."

It was. The year was 2005, and I remember every line of it.

1. Sit at the back of classes.
2. Laugh at everyone's stupid jokes.
3. Flip your hair (Jo).
4. Only listen to Bow Wow and Snoop Dog (Cal).
5. Wear oversized belts and low-rise jeans (Jo).

6. Streak my hair and wear a wallet chain (Cal).
7. Strut instead of walk.

We actually practiced that—our cool struts.

"We were hopeless," I say, missing those days.

She shrugs a shoulder, seeming to search my face. "At least we were hopeless together."

"Except…" I tap my chin. "If I remember correctly, you were more hopeless than me."

"Me?" She balks and presses her hand to her chest. "Which one of us tried to lean back in his chair during English, going for cool, and fell flat on his back?"

Yep. I was that pitiful. But telling Jo about the incident afterward made her laugh, and I wasn't the only one who invited ridicule. "Which one of us insisted on wearing a daffodil corsage to seventh-grade graduation, because all the cool girls were wearing them, even though she was allergic?"

"Oh my God." She slaps her hand over her mouth. "I totally forgot about that."

I wasn't there to witness that disaster. A year younger, I sat at home, edgy and bored, while Jolene attended the party. I lay in bed, glaring up at my ceiling, unable to sleep. Then Jo turned up, mascara staining her cheeks, as she cried on my shoulder about the disastrous night.

"You sneezed in Tvisha Shah's face," I tell her now, glad we can joke about how embarrassed she was.

She cringes. "And in Eric Ackerman's punch."

"Which, according to you, he still drank."

She snorts, her eyes bright.

Bar staff mill around her. Country music and chatter fill the beer-tinged air, but we're in some kind of time warp. A bubble of history, with just Jo and me and the easiness we once shared. But Jo's brown eyes seem to shift, morphing from espresso to a richer mocha. Thick with intent I can't decipher.

She blinks and twists the bar cloth in her hand. "I can't believe you remember that."

"Jo." I swallow hard, wanting to end this trip down memory lane. Order beers like I planned, return to the guys. Instead, I say, "I remember every single thing we did together, which is why hanging out with you is tough. When the good moments rush back, I get upset about all the years I lived without you."

She sucks in a sharp breath. "So seeing me makes you angry?" she asks softly.

"In a way." Although for more complicated reasons. I rub the back of my neck. "Before WITSEC, you were the best part of my life. I know things got weird before I left. There were reasons for that I'd rather not discuss, but being forced to leave Windfall—to leave *you*—gutted me. Seeing you now reminds me of all I lost, which tends to make me mad. Furious over what my father stole from all of us." Desmond losing the chance to raise the son he didn't know he had. E and Lennon having to wait a decade to win back the women they loved. Jolene ripped out of my life. "It all sits heavily on me."

"I'm sorry. I didn't realize." She curves her shoulders forward, shrinking smaller. "I don't want to make things harder for you. I'll stop reaching out."

"Don't," I blurt, suddenly anxious. I'm tired of my past having power over my present. As hard as being around Jo is, maybe this time will be different. Maybe being closer friends won't cause another avalanche of affection to swamp me. The other option, never hanging out again, has my lungs constricting. "As tough as some days are, avoiding you isn't feeling like the right choice."

Slowly, she fits her hand into mine and intertwines our fingers. "Not talking to you doesn't feel right to me either."

The simple contact sends a shiver through me. Goddamn body, forever misbehaving.

"I get it," I say, trying to lighten the mood and regain control. "Without me, you have no one to show you how to be cool."

Eyes twinkling, she squeezes my hand. "Come with me to the Broccoli Showdown."

"The *what* showdown?"

"Broccoli." She releases my hand and grabs an empty pitcher. "Beer for the table?"

I nod. "Plus, a plate of nachos and your shittiest hipster beer for Lennon."

She laughs. "It's so fun tormenting him with hipster jokes."

"You have no idea. But back to the broccoli shindig—what is it, and why does it exist?"

"Maggie helps run town events and has been trying to promote the agricultural side of Windfall." Jo moves as she talks, pouring beer from the tap, bending over to grab Lennon's bottle. The prominent view of her lush bottom has me snapping my eyes to the bar top. "There was a beet festival last fall that you should never mention to her. It was a minor disaster. But since it's broccoli growing season, she's organized a broccoli showdown, which involves different broccoli cook-offs."

Gotta love Windfall's many wild and wacky festivals. Except attending those is more of a couple's day out.

"You should go with Jake," I say, but the words feel hard to force out. "I know he'd love to take you," I add for good measure. It's the perfect event for them to rekindle their romance and get to know each other again.

"I want to go with my former best friend," she says, firm, and plunks down the pitcher and beer.

Before I can reply, she takes Javier's credit card from the bar top and walks toward the cash register. She stops to talk with one of her bartenders and frowns, looking as stressed as when I first walked in. I silently stew over the festival we'll be attending, unsure an afternoon together is smart. Already, I feel a pull to open up to Jolene in a way that's hard to resist.

"Sorry that took so long," she says, handing me Javier's credit card. "Staff drama."

"No problem." I want to ask about said drama. Figure out why she's been stressed about work, but too many old feelings are swirling inside me. I give her a stiff nod.

"But we'll chat," she says before I turn. "Plan next weekend's broccoli outing."

This nod is more of an edgy jerk. Next weekend is only six days away. That gives me 144 hours to figure out how to be friends with Jo again without letting my irrational jealousy resurface and ruin everything a second time.

CHAPTER
Five

Callahan

I've never seen so much broccoli in my life. Flower bouquets with broccoli centerpieces are affixed to the old-fashioned lampposts. Stores have broccoli wreaths hanging on their doors. The town square is filled with booths, all decorated with broccoli pictures. Each team is cooking broccoli-inspired dishes like chocolate-covered broccoli, bacon-wrapped broccoli, broccoli cheese pie, broccoli pizza crusts topped with...more broccoli.

Townsfolk and tourists have pens and cards to rank the broccoli-inspired food. At the end of the day, "professional broccoli judges"—aka, town restaurateurs—will be doing more thorough evaluations, after which the Broccoli Showdown winner is announced. Rumor has it there's a broccoli crown involved. The whole thing is kind of ridiculous, but also fun. *Not* because Jolene has been grinning up a storm, shoving me from booth to booth.

"The chocolate-covered broccoli is shockingly good," she says after taking another bite. She licks her lips as she swallows.

I can't help zeroing in on the slow swipe of her tongue.

I shove a piece of chocolate broccoli into my mouth and wince at the taste. "I'd rather eat chocolate-covered worms."

She rolls her eyes. "You once screamed like a B-movie actress when I tossed a worm at you."

"And you never used to eat green vegetables," I shoot back.

"Tastes change."

A nearby boy shouts, "I hate broccoli!" making me chuckle. A number of couples hover intently over their rating cards, like they're scoring an Olympic event.

Jo lifts up her last chocolate-covered floret. "I'm a chocolate-covered strawberry addict. These are obviously a bit eccentric by comparison, but my sister's kids hate anything veggie-related, like I used to. Since her divorce—"

"Bailey's divorced?" I ask, frowning.

"Last year, yeah. Nothing dramatic. They just drifted apart. She's living with my parents now, so they can help with the kids. I go over and cook for them from time to time. Always hide puréed vegetables into dishes—spaghetti sauce, chocolate pudding, mashed potatoes."

"You cook?" First her sister's divorce, now cooking. I assumed I had the lowdown on all things Windfall, but I thought Bailey was happily married. And the Jo I knew was a picky eater who could barely boil pasta.

Jo beams, so brightly I find myself smiling with her. "I love cooking."

"Consider me surprised. What got you into it?"

We meander through the throngs of kids and broccoli-eaters, our arms brushing when we have to dodge people. And yeah... there goes my body again, *misbehaving*.

"You wouldn't know," she says, loud enough to be heard over the nearby busker, "but my father had a bad car accident a while back. He was pretty banged up and couldn't do much for a month or so. Even cook, which he loved."

I actually do know about the accident. Sandra's text informing me about it had me sleepless for several nights. I had Sandra send them ready-made meals, along with a cookbook I knew Mr. Daniels would enjoy. "I'm sorry," I say, glad I can finally speak the words in person.

"Thanks." She shoots me a soft look as we stroll. "He's fine now, but Mom had just started her flower shop and wasn't one for being a caretaker. My sister was too busy managing the Rousseaus' equestrian program. I didn't want him eating tons of fast food, so I started cooking. Anyway…" She stops walking and glances up at the cloud-dotted sky. "Someone from town sent over this amazing cookbook. Middle Eastern-inspired foods, with a lot of vegetarian dishes. Different stuff I wasn't used to, and the author wove in fascinating personal stories. When I was at my folks' place, I found myself reading it, getting curious. I have no clue who sent it, but that book changed food for me."

Warmth invades my chest, spreading so wide I almost admit the anonymous person was me. I gave her father that gift. Hoped it would bring him a bit of joy. But admitting the book came from me is the opposite of smart. Confessing how much Jo has consumed my thoughts over the years won't help me rebuild our platonic friendship.

Mrs. Jackson, who runs quilting classes in town, stops when she sees us. "Lovely to have you back in town, Callahan. Is your mother moving soon?"

"She's finalizing things in Houston, so hopefully, yeah. We'll all be happier once she's here." Our whole family back together in Windfall where we belong, proving my father's carelessness didn't ruin our lives.

She pats my shoulder, then slants a knowing look at Jolene. "It also sounds like Jake has been lost without you, dear. An amazing thing, for love to last the test of time." She winks at Jo and walks toward the bacon-wrapped broccoli booth.

Jo frowns after her but doesn't speak. I mentally high-five myself.

Seems Sandra's rumors have taken hold. Over the coming days, more people will suggest to Jo that Jake and she are fated soul mates. Jo will forget the messy end of their relationship. She'll remember how much she loved my brother and finally give him the second chance he deserves.

And I can do *this*. Be friends with Jo. Hang out and chat easily. Manage my attraction to her, which is only surface chemistry.

Needing a break from broccoli, I lead us toward one of the picnic tables set up for the event. Jolene seems pensive, likely thinking about Mrs. Jackson's love comment. It's best if I change topics. My grand plan will only succeed through subtlety. "Tell me more about that great cookbook."

We sit at the picnic bench, side by side, facing the broccoli booths and milling tourists. Delilah and E are at the broccoli Popsicle booth. Desmond is at the craft table with Sadie and their son, Max, making broccoli wreaths. All of them seem relaxed and happy, which makes me happy.

"The book was filled with gorgeous pictures," Jo says, perking back up. "I can't get into cookbooks without pictures, and I started experimenting with food more after that. Even thought about becoming a chef, which was silly."

"If you loved cooking, it wasn't silly. But I always assumed you'd get a job as a dragon slayer."

She throws her head back and laughs. "I would've killed it as a dragon slayer, but no. My aunt started the Barrel. She was struggling a bit when she brought me on, and I was at loose ends, unsure what I wanted to do for work. Being a chef seemed daunting, and my aunt made it clear she'd love for me to take over the bar eventually since she never married or had kids."

I think back to our youth, how kind her aunt was. More

present than her hot-and-cold mother. "I always thought it was sweet that she came to all your track meets."

Jo smiles. "She and my dad, yeah."

"Are things still strained with your mom?"

"Yes and no." She traces a carving in the picnic bench: *Sam + Lily.* "My mother still doesn't have a real maternal gene, but we don't fight like when I was a teen. We're just not super close. And I had Aunt Becca," she says with fondness. "If I was sick, she was the one who'd come over and bring me soup. She talked me through sad breakups and work stress and celebrated my small victories, like buying my first car."

"She was always the cool aunt."

"The coolest." She blinks, her pensive expression both sad and happy. "Anyway, she started training me on the business side of the bar. I wasn't sure if it was my calling, but then she got sick. Passed away from cancer a couple years ago. She wanted me to have the Barrel, and it's been mine ever since." Her voice dips at the end, filled with the weight of loss.

"I'm so sorry about your aunt, Jo. Hate that I wasn't here to support you when she passed."

She nods. "It was hard."

A sad silence settles between us. History we can't change.

"At least you have the bar," I say. "A piece of her to keep alive."

Like with her father's accident, it feels good to offer my sympathies in person. I sent flowers and made a donation in Rebecca's honor back then, but this means more. Unfortunately, the strained creases bracketing Jo's mouth hint at a different stress.

"You don't love running the bar?" I ask.

"Oh, no. I do." She flashes me a grin. "It's great. Her leaving it to me meant everything, and having the kitchen allows me to work with food in a roundabout way. What about you? I wasn't surprised you got into construction, even though I had to take the lead when building our tree house." She nudges me with her elbow, being cheeky.

Anyone else might buy her quick mood shift, but I know Jo's false positivity. I saw how stressed she was at her bar. Something's up with her at work.

I add *Find out what's stressing Jo* to my to-do list.

"You and I both know hammers and nails are not your friends," I say, sticking to her subject change. "Without me, you'd have four fewer fingers and a nail permanently lodged in your hand."

"Sure, but without me, who would've lip-synced to 'Shake Ya Tailfeather' while we worked, making you crack up so hard you nearly peed?"

I laugh at the memory. Watching Jolene attempt to shake her booty while singing into a hammer was too damn funny. But as much fun as we had building that tree house, she wasn't the one who gave me the gift of my job.

"The start of WITSEC was obviously rough," I say, getting back on topic. "I struggled a lot emotionally, but somehow graduated with a BA from a college in Houston. Lennon and E ditched the idea of school completely, and Jake never planned to go the college route. Des obviously flamed out of law school, but I got my degree, then I had no drive to do anything with it. Couldn't fathom planning for a future with a fake name. Jake knew I was low. Came to me one day and told me we had to build a new dining table for Mom, even though she didn't need one."

"He knew the work would get you out of your head?"

I nod, so damn thankful for my oldest brother. "He took charge with all of us. Must've been wading through his own mental swamp, but he made sure we didn't drown. Told Desmond to look after Mom emotionally, made sure E was drawing. Even came to me one day and shoved a newspaper in my hand. He'd circled an ad for camp counselors and told me to give it to Lennon, hoping it would get him out of the house."

"Why didn't he just give it to Lennon himself?"

"Lennon was pretty down, barricading himself in his room. Didn't always respond well to Jake's pushiness. Jake knew I'd go in with a softer touch."

He also somehow knew Lennon would be a natural leader and would thrive working outside. With me, he understood I needed the outlet of a physical job. He gave me a place where I could smash things productively and let out my angst. Use my analytical mind to plan projects. At his urging, I started working construction. We eventually began building a business together. Shared an apartment in Houston, even though I think he'd have rather lived alone.

For ten years, the oldest Bower took care of his family, clueless to the pain I caused him before our father ruined our lives. Now I can finally do something concrete for Jake and help him win Jolene back.

Silence descends between Jo and me. My right side tingles from our proximity on the bench—too much body heat to think straight. I shift away, clench and stretch my fingers.

She angles toward me, takes a breath like she's about to speak, but she shakes her head and rubs her palms down her thighs. A second later, she lifts her chin. "I probably shouldn't ask this, but have you ever—"

"Jo!" At the sound of Jake's booming voice, Jo startles and scoots away from me.

I have no clue what she was about to say. The vulnerability in her hesitant tone felt important, but she was probably just going to ask, *Have you ever eaten chocolate-covered snails?*

"Glad I caught you before the festival was over." Jake gives Jo his signature smolder. "I heard you were looking for me."

She squints at him. "You did?"

As far as I know, Jo hasn't been looking for him. My instigated rumor mill has likely taken on a life of its own.

"Guess my timing was good," he goes on. "Now we can hang out without me having to ingest broccoli."

"You could use the nutrients," I say a little too loudly. I stand from the table and cross my arms. "When Jake and I lived together," I tell Jo, "he only ate foods in the animal or beer food groups."

He hooks his thumb toward me. "This from the guy who had a list of rules on how I had to tidy the bathroom after I shaved or showered."

I blink at him. "Because you left the place looking like a chaotic flea market."

"Or you're just *anal*."

Jo quirks an eyebrow at me. "You didn't use to be a clean freak."

I didn't. WITSEC changed us all in different ways. "Like I said, this guy gives Pig-Pen a run for his money."

I offer Jake a placid expression. No point getting worked up. It's not like I need to impress Jolene, and this conversation makes me extra thankful Jake didn't want to move in to my two-bedroom duplex here. "Now that you live in your own bachelor pad, you can be as big of a slob as you want."

"I'm not a slob," he tells Jo. "I'm just relaxed, and my apartment is small but nice. I was actually wondering if you wanted to come over for dinner tonight."

A weird pain cramps my stomach. Probably too much broccoli.

Jo's attention darts to me, her brows puckered. She for sure feels badly about ditching me to hang out with Jake. A problem I can solve for her.

"Wow," I say, glancing at the time on my phone. "Turns out I need to leave. Promised the Liangs I'd get started on their fence."

"On a Saturday?" Jake asks, always in my face about working too much.

"Yep." I give Jo a strained smile. "Thanks for a fun day."

Two steps away, Jake grabs my arm and forces me to face him, keeping our backs to Jo. "Are you working this hard because you need money? If you do, all you have to do is ask. I'll help you out."

A slick of guilt coats my gut.

Before WITSEC, Jake was a solid guy, but also cocksure and sometimes arrogant. Friends came easy for him. Everything in life went his way. He was quick with a smile and was good to his family, but his needs often came first.

Then our worlds got turned upside down.

Over the past twelve years, Jake has grown into a steadfast man. He's selfless and compassionate—a take-charge guy, who is direct and upfront.

Unlike me, who's been less forthright.

He doesn't know about my padded savings account, because he doesn't know I use that money to secretly help my family and friends. He doesn't know I ruined his relationship years ago or that I'm still attracted to Jo. He's just being the good guy he's become, always putting me first, doing right by his family.

I fit my most reassuring smile on to my stiff face. "I'm good financially. I just like staying busy, but you'll be happy to hear I told Javier I'm too slammed to help him remodel his bathroom right now. And if I haven't said it enough, thanks for being a great brother." I pull him into a one-armed hug and pound his back. "Now go sweep Jolene off her feet with a romantic dinner."

"Not a hardship."

I give him a curt nod, then leave the happy couple, more determined than ever to reunite him with the woman he loves.

CHAPTER
Six

Callahan

I don't normally linger with my coffee before work, but I have time to kill. Sleep eluded me last night, so I hit the twenty-four-hour gym earlier than my usual crack-of-dawn time. I pushed through my sets like a man possessed. Muscle strain. Sweat pouring down my back. With another half hour before I have to head to the Elroys' for my Sunday work, I order a pastry with my coffee.

"You're never here this early," Delilah says, grabbing a to-go bag for my cinnamon bun.

"I was up early, and I'll take the bun on a plate today."

Her curly hair is tied back with a bright bandanna, and her apron reads, *Life's short. Eat more cupcakes.* Her expression, however, reads, *nosy meddler.* "You also never order a treat or stay to eat in."

"Do you make a habit of discouraging your customers from buying things?"

"Only when they act like their Bizarro selves."

"Bizarro *what*?"

She waves me off and takes my money. "It's a comic book thing. You're acting like the Anti-Callahan. And"—she smiles at someone behind me—"you're not the only one. Jolene, what are you doing awake before eleven?"

I swivel, only to find the source of last night's sleeplessness. Jo jolts at the sight of me, looking like her head never hit the pillow either. I guess her dinner with Jake went late.

My muscles tense and flex, that gym workout clearly pushing me too hard. Jo glances at the door, as though she plans to leave. Then she heaves out a sigh and comes up to the counter.

"I had trouble sleeping," she tells Delilah. "I'll take a coffee to go."

"Or you could sit with Cal since you two are never here at the same time. I actually put that bench seat in because of you guys." She nods to the cute blue table in the corner. Unlike the other tables, it has one long bench on the far side only. "I always loved that you'd sit side by side as kids, people watching and cracking up. Thought the one-sided bench would encourage others to do the same, but people usually drag extra chairs over."

That was exactly how we sat at the Broccoli Showdown yesterday. A way to enjoy each other's company while observing the crowd. Growing up, it was even more fun. We'd add a game to the dynamic, guessing what people were saying at other tables. We'd also go to flea markets and invent stories about the origin of old knickknacks. This morning, I don't feel like reenacting those fun days.

I debate taking my order to go, but Delilah hands me my plate.

I guess that's that.

"Meet me over there?" I ask Jo.

She nods, seeming as unenthused about our morning run-in as me. Jake must've really worn her out last night.

Decidedly less hungry, I wander over to the bench and pick at my cinnamon bun.

Jolene smiles tentatively and scoots in beside me. "You look exhausted."

"So do you."

She balks. "Did you just say I look like shit?"

"Whoa now." I hold up my hands. "You said the same to me."

"I'm a woman, Cal. You never tell a woman she looks tired. Did your mother teach you nothing?"

"Aren't you the girl who told me she wasn't *girly*? Figured you didn't count."

She elbows my ribs. "Next insult ends with this hot coffee in your crotch."

I clamp my hand on her mug. "I apologize profusely, Jolene. You look incredibly well rested. And feminine," I add.

She rolls her eyes and extricates the mug from my hand. A sip later, she says, "Don't make a sound, and give me all your money."

I almost check her forehead for a fever, but I see an old man leaning over a little girl in pigtails, and he's holding out his hand. Jolene's playing an impromptu round of our "What are they saying?" game.

The pigtail kid crosses her arms, but my brain's too tired for creativity.

"One more move," I say in a horrible high-pitched voice, scrambling for an idea, "and I'll...stick my tongue out at you?"

Jolene scrunches her nose. "That was subpar."

"I'm out of practice."

"Me too," she says quietly, fiddling with her mug handle. "Do you still play football?"

"That's a random question."

She shrugs. "There are so many years of blanks to fill in."

"Too many," I say and sip my coffee. Twelve unbelievably

long years. "No, I don't play football. Gave it up when we left here."

"But you loved it so much."

I nod, feeling a pinch against my Adam's apple.

Jolene stares at my profile, waiting for me to go on. When I don't, she says a stern "Callahan."

I almost laugh.

This was always her thing growing up. If we were hanging out and I'd get quiet, she'd look at me and say, "Callahan." That was it. Just my name. She'd fold her arms and stare holes into my forehead until I'd break and tell her I got a bad grade on an English paper or a bully was picking on E or I was frustrated with my father for barely acknowledging me when he'd spend loads of time with Lennon.

Her unwavering stare has the same effect on me now, knocking my vocal cords loose. "At the start of WITSEC, I avoided situations that made me uncomfortable, which was most of them. I didn't like lying to people. Making friends felt phony and uncomfortable, so I quit all team sports."

"You must have missed it a lot."

"Yeah."

"I play in a soccer league," she says, shifting even closer. "Nothing serious. Just a bunch of adults out for exercise and a good time, usually followed by drinks at the bar. You should join us."

I like that she plays soccer. I really like that she invited me along. I can picture Jo and me on a field, getting competitive the way we did during my family football games. Plus, there's no avoiding Jolene in this town. I'll see her at festivals, coffee shops, art galleries.

I nod. "Sounds fun. Hopefully I can fit it in."

"You two look cozy," Maggie says, heading toward us. She's dragging Lennon by the hand. Seeing his T-shirt lifts my mood exponentially. The cotton is bright pink and reads, *I'm so hipster, even I've never heard of my favorite beer.*

I smirk. "Who do I have to thank for this amazingness?"

Maggie bats her eyelashes. "Me, of course. Your brother lost a bet."

I gesture to the table. "Join us. I need all the details, please."

Maggie has red hair, a face full of freckles, and a personality full of sass. She eagerly pulls a chair over, while Lennon stays standing and crosses his arms, attempting to cover the shirt's slogan.

"As you know, we're renovating our house," Maggie says. "Turns out the wiring is from the dark ages, so we need to bring it up to code. Until we figure things out, we're not supposed to use the kitchen appliances, and Lennon keeps bragging, saying he can cook anything outside on an open fire. I bet him he couldn't bake a soufflé. He claimed otherwise and sweated over his fire with a Dutch oven. Lo and behold"—she fans her hand to his shirt, grinning her face off—"the soufflé was as light as a rock."

"The pink really works for you," Jo tells him, trying to keep a straight face. "Brings out the red in your beard."

Lennon purses his lips. "I have no issues with the pink. I'm a real man. Real men love pink. The slogan is the issue."

As amusing as his shirt is, I don't like hearing Lennon's having wiring problems. Old wiring can overload and shut down. In dangerous cases, it can heat up and cause a fire. "You're not using any appliances until the electrical is fixed, right?"

"Only in emergencies," Maggie says. "Like when Lennon makes us soufflé rocks for dinner."

Lennon huffs. "They weren't that bad, and we're being safe. It'll take a while before we can fix the wires, but we'll do more takeout. Support town restaurants. So don't you dare offer to help. I'm aware you're working yourself to the bone these days."

I maintain a controlled expression. Yes, my free minutes have been dwindling, but Lennon's been using that kitchen without a second thought for close to a year. It's easy to think one night of cooking won't matter, but all it takes is one bad wire to heat and spark. If he won't accept my assistance, I'll simply find a covert way of helping out.

For now, I turn to Maggie. Although I'd do anything to see my brothers safe, riling them up is another favorite pastime. "How long does he have to wear the hipster shirt?"

"Three days."

"If I can get you a new one, is there anything in the bet that would disallow a swapping of the shirt?" I have several ideas on how best to mess with Lennon. The leading candidate is the simple slogan: *Slap My Back if I'm a Hipster.*

Maggie's green eyes gleam with mischief. "No, sir. There is not."

Lennon slams his hands on the table. "I didn't agree to a new shirt."

Maggie studies her nails as though blasé, like she's not loving every second of his discomfort. "You didn't stipulate that you *wouldn't* wear a second shirt."

Lennon straightens. He looks about to throw a tantrum, then his attention darts to Jolene. His eyes shift back to me, then they dart to the far end of our bench. Without saying a word, Lennon slides in beside Jolene and scoots so close she gets jammed into my side.

Instinctively, I slide my arm around Jolene's back. She grips my thigh to keep from toppling farther into me, and my body becomes one of those faulty wires, verging on combustion.

"Between yesterday's festival and this morning's coffee, looks like you two have finally had time to catch up." Lennon's comment is mundane, but there's nothing subtle about his guess-who-has-the-upper-hand-now look. And yeah. I get his intent. If I mess with him by making a new shirt, he'll find ways to make my life with Jo difficult. Like shoving her against me at a table. Not that having her pressed against me is hard. But *I'm* suddenly hard and breathing too damn fast.

"The festival was great," Jo says and angles herself to smile at Maggie. Her hand moves slightly, sliding up my jeans. "You did an amazing job planning it."

Maggie says something back. I think Lennon speaks too. Fuck if I know. My nerve endings have become a swarm of bees, all of them buzzing at once. Even worse, my hand develops a mind of its own, flexing on Jo's soft hip. She leans harder into me, or maybe Lennon's shoving her over. I'm honestly not sure if I'm in Windfall or on Mars.

All I am is *sensation*. And dumb.

I tilt my head slightly, feel the drag of Jo's silky hair along my nose. I don't mean to inhale—swear to *God*, I don't mean to—but Jolene has always had this scent about her, a musky femininity that is devastatingly alluring. I'm dying to know if it's changed.

Bad news: it has not.

She still smells like the perfect blend of casual and mysterious. Like her country style and sensual beauty mark have a signature scent of lightning storms and wild flowers.

"It has been nice," Jo says, her quiet voice breaking me out of my lusty haze. "Finally catching up," she adds.

Maggie and Lennon are surprisingly gone, but we're still pressed together with my arm around Jo's back. Her hand is on my thigh. I should move—always *should* around Jo—but want takes over. "Yeah, it has been."

A soft sigh escapes her. "We didn't do this enough our last years together."

"Do what?" I say, but my voice sounds too rough. Strangled. *It's just attraction,* I remind myself. A surface reaction to Jolene's undeniable appeal.

She adjusts her position, rubbing her outer thigh against mine. "Before your family left, there was this weird distance between us. We spent time together, but there were always other people around."

Because spending time alone with Jolene made me want her more. Made me worry I'd do something insane like kiss my brother's girlfriend. She also never looked at me, her younger *friend*, like she looked at Jake. "You had more fun hanging out with the oldest Bower."

She ducks her head, her layered hair cascading in front of her face. "I was pretty insecure back then."

"Not in high school."

She flicks her hair back, revealing intense eyes. "I was picked on for *years*, Cal. Shedding my awkwardness and getting prettier didn't magically reverse that damage."

She got breathtakingly beautiful, not pretty. But hearing she felt insecure in high school is a shock. As far as I knew, Jolene blossomed during that time. Walked with confidence. Suddenly made friends easily. "If you were feeling insecure during those years, you hid it well."

"Did you share all your innermost fears with me back then?"

I most certainly did not, the biggest one being my feelings for her. "Not everything needs to be shared, I guess." But my mind is stuck on the fact that younger Jo kept secrets from me. "What else?" I ask, unable to drop the topic. "Were there other things I didn't know about you?"

She nibbles her lip as a rush of color rises to her cheeks. She drops her gaze a moment, then slowly looks up, but my phone chimes with a calendar alert:

Work on the Elroys' deck.

I blink at the screen, unsure how I lost track of time. Except time isn't the only thing I lost track of, considering how close I'm still sitting to Jo. Around her, I have a tendency to forget my place in her life.

"Gotta head out," I say as I quickly stand. "Hope you get some sleep, even though you look incredibly well rested."

She doesn't smile at my joke. Just frowns slightly. "I'll send you the soccer info. Please try to come."

A cocktail of feelings bubbles through me. Gratefulness for her offer, stirred with apprehension and a hit of excitement. I do want to play. I love being active and haven't played with a team in too long. Being outside with Jolene and a group might be less intense than talking with her one-on-one. We'd just be a couple of old pals mucking around on the soccer field.

I nod, unable to help the smile that creeps across my face. "I'll be there."

CHAPTER
Seven

Callahan

"She's our biggest threat." Javier stares at Jolene, who's huddled with her team on the other side of the soccer field. "If we don't neutralize her, she'll be insufferable at the bar."

"Agreed," Delilah says, fixing the messy bun on top of her head. "Last time they won, she passed me my beer after the match and said, 'To help wash down the bitter taste of defeat.'"

Ben huffs. "After the last game, Jo asked Kiyana if I also have trouble scoring at home."

I muffle my laugh. Growing up, watching Jo take my brothers down a peg with her ballbusting jabs was always a blast, as long as I wasn't on the receiving end. "We definitely have to steal the ball from her."

"Yeah," Javier says and knocks my shoulder, "*you* do."

"Whoa, no." I hold up my hands. "I'm not the right person for the job. I'm the new guy. One of you should do it."

We're a smaller group than a full soccer match. Eight on each side, with an extra player who subs in as needed. Some of the participants I know, like Ben, Javier, Delilah, Jolene, Lennon, and E's pal Ricky. Some I remember vaguely from high school, like Tvisha Shah, who Jolene sneezed on while trying to be cool with her daffodil corsage, and some are residents who moved here while I was hiding from cartel hit men.

Friends or not, they all welcomed me with enthusiastic handshakes and haven't hesitated to pass me the ball. I've run my ass off, loving sweating it out on the field and feeling part of a team, but I'm far from a soccer pro. If I get up in Jo's space and fumble, Poor Sportswoman Jolene will be unleashed.

"It has to be you." Javier grips my shoulder, looking like an army general about to send his troops into battle. He flicks his dark hair out of his eyes. "Accept your fate."

"Why me?"

"You distract her."

"No, I don't." But my gaze slides to the opposing team. Jolene is listening as Lennon speaks. She looks adorable in her striped high socks, short shorts, and old-school soccer T-shirt.

Her focus snaps to me, like she senses my attention or she wants to keep tabs on our team.

I mouth, *You're gonna lose.*

This game is bringing out my inner thirteen-year-old.

A smirk tilts the corner of her mouth, then she mimes slicing her neck.

I chuckle.

"Yep." Tvisha's attention ping-pongs between Jo and me. "It's gotta be Cal."

More sweat gathers along my forehead. "Once again, no, it does not. I can't lose to Jo like that. She'll be unbearable."

A chorus of *yeps* rings through the group.

Tvisha gives me a reassuring nod. "You can do it, Cal. She's off her game when you're near her. She nearly tripped over the ball once."

She did, but I didn't see the full fumble. I was on the sidelines while another player subbed in. Dripping sweat, I wiped my forehead with the hem of my T-shirt. When I dropped my shirt, I saw the near spill. She was focused on the ball at the moment, not me. Clearly, these folks are messing with my head. They don't want to be the ones in Jo's crosshairs.

Ben slaps my back. "Take one for the team, bro. Just don't go rushing in on her. She'll expect it and dodge you."

"That," Javier says, pointing at Ben then at me. "When you're closer to her, get into her space with smaller steps."

"Crowd her and get her head down," another teammate adds.

"Be patient and dare her to move," Tvisha says. "But watch her for fakes and feints. She loves mind games."

Like miming my death before we return to play.

"Get your butts on the field!" Lennon calls.

He's our unofficial referee, even though he's playing on the other team. Jolene wasn't lying when she said this group is only out for a fun time. The competitiveness is good-natured. People smile and laugh when they screw up. They're a nice bunch of laid-back people, getting outside and being active, but they seem intent on throwing me to the wolf, otherwise known as Jolene Daniels.

"I'll do it," I say, "but you all owe me beers."

"That's the spirit! Hands in." Tvisha shoves her hand into the center of our circle. We all follow suit, stacking our hands on top of one another's. She counts down and calls, "Operation Break Jo!"

We cheer. I shake my head, knowing I'm about to be in big trouble.

The game resumes. I replay everyone's advice while keeping my focus on Jo. Her expression is intense, her body loose but nimble as she waits to nab the ball. Single-minded is the best way to describe her right now. As kids, whether playing sports or board games or adventuring in the woods, Jo always embodied the dedication of an Olympic athlete. My only saving grace was trash-talking to distract her. A skill I'll need to resurrect.

The second she gets the ball, I follow my team's advice and encroach on her with smaller steps. "Your shoelace is undone," I say.

She feints left, not missing a beat. "Your fly is undone."

I almost look down, only to remember I don't have a zipper on my workout shorts.

Time to take off the proverbial gloves. "I hope you don't cry when you lose the ball," I say, mirroring her moves.

"The only balls you can handle, Bower, are your own."

My face gets hotter. Her smile is pure evil as she tries to blow past me.

I block her way. "When you lose," I huff, breathing harder, "I'll make sure they report it in *The Jangler*."

"The only thing I'll be losing," she says, keeping in control, "is your too-slow shadow."

"Arrogance doesn't become you."

"I'm not arrogant. I'm good."

"Cocky."

"Confident," she says as she fakes right.

"Shit, Jo." I drop my voice. "Did you just get your period?"

Eyes suddenly wild, she looks down, and I steal the ball.

I spot Javier, open and ready for a pass. I kick the ball to him and watch with a pounding pulse as he bears down on the goalie and scores. I whoop. My team erupts, everyone sharing high fives and back slaps. Swear to God, I haven't had this much carefree fun in years.

Jo saunters up to me and crosses her arms. "Proud of yourself, are you?"

I bow. "Extremely."

"I can't believe I fell for the period stunt."

"Don't go blaming your defeat on some words I uttered. I beat you because I'm better."

"At trash-talking."

"Better is better, Jo." I lean down, getting up in her space. "Just admit I'm a superior soccer player."

"Okay," she says, looking smug. "You're better at playing with balls than me. Guess you've had more practice."

She glances down at my crotch, then strolls toward her side of the field, leaving me laughing.

"Killer moves," Javier says when I return to the group. "Told you your presence distracts Jo."

"Nah," I say. "She's only watching me to make sure I'm having a good time. My first game and all. I just know how to rile her."

And she knew today would be a blast for me.

CHAPTER
Eight

Callahan

A couple of hours later, we're at Jolene's bar, nearing the end of our post-game drinks. Easy banter and jokes pass between our diminishing group. I'm more relaxed than I've felt in ages. Loose and happy as I sip my beer and enjoy the company.

Jolene pats my shoulder. "You should stretch when you get home. Losing so badly can tense your muscles."

Yeah, my team lost in the end. As predicted, Jolene has been lording her win over us like a ruthless queen.

I cross my arms and ignore her. Responding to Jo's taunts only eggs her on.

"No one likes you when you're like this," Javier tells her.

He's on the opposite side of our table with Lennon and Delilah—the last stragglers hanging out after our match. They all grumble their agreement. Even Lennon, who was on Jolene's team.

"When I'm like what?" she asks innocently.

The replies come swift and decisive.

"Intolerable."

"Insufferable."

"A poor winner."

I don't contribute to their rapid-fire jabs. There are better ways to end Jolene's poor sportsmanship. I lean across the table, speaking quietly to the group, like she can't hear me from six inches away. "We should have a league flower."

Delilah squints at me. "Why would we have a league flower?"

"It would be nice," I say. "A friendship symbol for all the camaraderie."

"Are we also making friendship bracelets and braiding each other's hair?" Lennon asks, clueless to the groundwork I'm laying.

Jolene, however, is very attuned to me and my odd flower suggestion. Her dark eyes narrow even more. I'm thoroughly enjoying the lead-up to what will invariably be her explosive reaction.

"We don't need flowers or bracelets or braided hair," she says. "Just fresh air and after-match beers."

"Bracelets are actually a solid idea," I tell Lennon, edging her further out of the conversation. "We can weave our team flower into them."

"Yeah, okay. I'll play along." Lennon flicks his attention to Jo and back to me. "Do you have a specific flower in mind?"

I lean back and spread my thighs, overtaking Jo's space. "Daffodils."

"Oh no, you don't." She shoves at my side, barely making a dent. "There will be no daffodils."

"But you love daffodils," I say sweetly, like I don't know she's insanely allergic and will spend the entire soccer game sneezing her face off.

She scrunches her nose, like it's already irritated. "You're a pest."

"Because I want your favorite flower to be our league symbol?"

"Because you have a death wish. If you stick a daffodil near me during soccer, I'll hide ants in your gym bag."

My insides shrivel. She knows how much ants bother me. Those tiny insects can disappear into unknown places.

"I wonder if you're still ticklish under your knee," I murmur, leaning forward.

"Nope." She attempts to barricade me from her legs. "Not even a little."

"Liar."

All she says is, "Ants."

That's it. I dart my hand forward, reaching for her horrendously ticklish knees. She goes into full panic mode and kicks at me, but her chair tips back and teeters.

Laughing, I anchor my hand on her thigh and right the wobbly chair. "Careful there, Daniels."

"You're the one about to get an ant invasion, Bower."

"So you *do* want me to fill your apartment with daffodils?"

"Try it." Her grin leans toward ferocious.

Mine is pure enjoyment. "I just might. Also…" I drop my voice, needing to tell her how much this afternoon has meant to me. "I can't thank you enough for including me today. I had a great time."

Her face goes soft. "I'm so happy. I knew you'd love it. It's a fun crew."

More than fun. This is the calmest I've felt since I returned to Windfall. The need to check my schedule and keep busy hasn't struck. My muscles are well worked but loose. Except my facial muscles, which are sore from grinning.

"I've played in this league for a couple years," she says, matching my quiet tone. "Not religiously, but whenever I can make it." She fits her hand under mine and links our fingers. "Today's the most fun I've had out there."

My heart seems to move—heavy thumping as it travels from my chest to my palm, where we're connected. I swear I feel hers in her hand too. A continuation of mine, like we're one being fused together as she watches me and I watch her and everything around us fades, and for the life of me, I can't pull away.

A throat clears.

Delilah, Javier, and Lennon are staring at us with mixed expressions of curiosity. I don't like it.

I release Jo's hand and fold mine unassumingly on my lap. "The ant thing and daffodils were inside jokes," I say, attempting to explain our antics and close proximity.

"Right. Jokes." Lennon looks smug as his penetrating attention fixes on me. "Callahan has so many *secret* inside jokes."

"Most friends have inside jokes," I say in my calmest voice.

Friends do nice things for each other too, like invite them to soccer. Trash-talk each other until they crack up. Taunt them with ant torture, but the urge to lean back toward Jo hits. To press my hand to hers again. Eavesdrop on her pulse as our hearts synchronize.

I bite down on my molars.

"Jolene," someone calls from our right. I don't recognize the woman, but she smiles at Jo. "I heard you and Jake are back together. So nice to hear."

The woman waves and leaves, and I nearly bite through my *tongue.*

The past couple of days, when at work with Jake, I've avoided discussing Jolene. He hasn't brought her up either, but my rumor-spreading has apparently taken on a life of its own. Or maybe he and Jo *are* already back together. And all I've done today is stoke my dangerous feelings for her, when I damn well know they can't go anywhere.

My phone buzzes. One glance shows a group Bower chat helmed by Jake.

Jake: Family meeting at the Barrel on Thursday.
We need to plan something for Mom's
homecoming.

Instead of replying, I abruptly stand and mumble excuses about having to leave. I'm stoked to make Mom's return to Windfall the best it can be. I appreciate Jake taking the reins as always, putting his family front of mind. Selflessness I need to emulate. Soccer with Jo was clearly too soon. I need to keep our friendship contained and our hands very far apart.

Avoiding her eyes, I head for the exit, walking as quickly as my long legs will take me.

CHAPTER
Nine

Jolene

I have a Callahan Bower addiction. Every time he smiles, a little zip travels up my spine. When he laughs, dopamine floods my brain, and my mind chants *more, more, more*. Unfortunately, when he blows me off with awkward exits, my high crashes and burns. As it should.

"Why is Cal leaving like his ass is on fire?" Delilah asks, watching the bar doors slam shut after him.

"He likes dramatic exits," Lennon says, but he slides a curious glance at me. "Or he reached his fun quota for the day and couldn't handle more. I haven't seen him that happy since before our lives imploded."

Heat rises to my cheeks.

I can't thank you enough for including me today. I had a great time.

There was nothing intimate about Cal's quiet confession before he tore out of here. But the way he said it? With his generous mouth moving slowly, his deep voice gruff with emotion, and his huge, callused hand splayed on my thigh? As far as my befuddled brain knew, he was saying *I can't live without you a second longer. Please be mine.*

Words I'll never—*and should never*—hear from my best friend.

"Hey, Jo. Sorry to interrupt." Sue-Ann, one of tonight's servers, crouches beside me, wearing a pained look I like to call Bar Bad News. "The stove is acting up again. I've already emailed Tim but haven't heard back. Hopefully he can make it out tomorrow."

My sigh is dredged from my toes. "I have his cell in my office. I'll text him too." I salute my friends and try to force a smile. "Duty calls."

I don't launch another dig about beating their sorry butts. Any lingering lightness from today fizzles as I try to put out the endless fires that pop up around here.

I close my office door and sit at my desk. The framed photo by my computer takes the edge off my stress—Aunt Becca and me, our arms slung around each other, my gold track-and-field ribbon clutched in my hand. The photo was the first decorative item she put in here. Beside it is the framed note she left me after she passed. It reads simply, *Great things happen when you dream big.*

The Barrel House was Aunt Becca's dream. Every time I look at the two side-by-side frames, I remember how much she loved this place and me, even if the office smells like the inside of a deep fryer. *Don't you love the deep fryer!* Aunt Becca used to say. *Everyone loves fried everything!* She adored every inch of this place, even that gross fryer.

I click on my emails to find Tim's number. An unpleasant message has my stomach dropping to the floor.

Letter of Resignation.

I open Jonathan's message—my best bartender who shows up early, stays late, and never complains about his shifts—as helplessness drains the last of my good mood. No matter how often I service equipment or try to boost staff morale with prank contests and monthly flag-football afternoons, stuff still breaks. Staff still quit. *First World problems.* I get it. But stress is stress, and Cal's abrupt dismissals lately have weakened my usual armor.

"How did you do it?" I ask the photograph on my desk. "How did this place not drain your energy?"

The only reply I get is a serving of my own guilt. Aunt Becca left me this bar as a gift. I'm a spoiled brat who needs to be more thankful—and more honest with myself. I do love the happy customers and fun theme nights we host. Pressure is part of any job.

I text Tim about the stove, then reply to Jonathan, wishing him the best. Apparently, he's starting a massage therapy course —an aspiration that's news to me, which feels shitty. I'm not close enough with my staff to know their interests. Or close enough with anyone, really. Having Callahan back has been an awakening of sorts. Realization that I've shied away from deeper relationships since he vanished twelve years ago.

A knock sounds at my door. I cringe, praying no one walks in here with another Bar Bad News face.

"Come in," I call.

The door opens and...I nearly give myself whiplash with my exaggerated double take.

"Larkin?" I say, pretty sure Larkin Gray is standing in my office, but I haven't seen a strand of her beachy blond hair since high school.

She gives me a timid wave. "Sorry for the surprise. Sue-Ann was busy and said it was okay if I came back. But if it's not cool, I can go. Come back later, or not at all if you'd rather not talk to me."

I blink at her, downright floored. I get why she's asking if I'd like her to leave. According to Windfall's gaggle of gossips, Jake cheated on me with her, after which I broke up with him and her family moved out of town. Like the rest of Windfall, she probably assumes I believed the rumors and lashed out at my boyfriend. I just can't imagine why she's here, of all places, facing me after all this time.

"I have no issues talking to you, Larkin. Jake told me nothing happened between you two, and I believed him. You were probably more harmed by those rumors than me. I'm sorry if you went through a tough time."

"Wow, thank you." She tips her head, assessing me as intensely as I'm watching her. "But if you knew the rumors were false, why'd you break up with him after that night?"

This conversation is veering too close to dangerous territory. Callahan territory—the man at the center of that erratic time of my life. The last thing I need is to exhume the *why* of those angst-filled days. Already, my default setting around Cal is *supress years of pining so I don't puke my feelings all over the guy's perfectly handsome face.*

"As much as I'd love to chat," I say, "I have some work to do. What brings you by?"

She rocks on her heels, then flashes me a disarming smile. "I'm a great waitress and an even better bartender."

I actually laugh. "I certainly like your confidence."

She smiles wider, her dimples sinking into her cheeks. She's even prettier than I remember. Tall with blue-green eyes. Thick lashes. Smooth, light skin, and a scar beside her nose that reminds you imperfections add to a person's beauty. Her air of confidence is new, though.

"I'm also good under pressure and could sell sand to a camel," she says. "I'm reliable and patient and have no issues working extra shifts. Except Mondays. That's the one day I have other commitments. I'm moving back to Windfall shortly and have worked in restaurants and bars since I was a teenager. If you're willing to give me a chance, I would absolutely love to work here." She blows out a breath. "I promise I won't let you down."

If all staff I interviewed came with this level of salesmanship and hustle, the Barrel House would print money. "Consider yourself hired."

She beams. "Really?"

"Your timing couldn't be better. I just lost a bartender and need to fill the gap. Today was turning into a nightmare, so thanks for giving me a reprieve."

"Sorry today's been rough, but thank you. This bar has a great vibe. Can't wait to be part of the team."

I smile easier. When things aren't falling apart, the bar really is great. It's a welcoming place where people come to relax and have fun, even though it hasn't been as busy lately.

"Happy to have you," I tell Larkin and pass her my card. "Email me what day you can start. I'll shoot a schedule over to you."

She takes the card and spins it in her hand, looking hesitant for the first time since walking in here. "I saw you when I came in—with Cal at that table. I'm glad you two are finally together."

"I'm not *with* Cal," I practically shout. "Why would you think I'm with Cal? He just moved back, and we're just reconnecting. As friends. Because we've only ever just been friends."

Just. Just. Just.

Might as well advertise my blatant feelings in Windfall's next issue of *The Jangler*.

Larkin holds up her hands, as though keeping a rabid animal at bay. "Sorry. You two were so close growing up, and the way you looked at the table..." She lifts her shoulders. "I assumed you and he—"

"You assumed wrong," I cut in. The words are so forceful my back gives an unforgiving twinge.

Another side effect of working at the bar has been developing intermittent back pain from lugging beer kegs. I grip the chair's armrests, close my eyes, and breathe slowly for the count of ten.

The pain recedes. The room goes quiet. Hopefully Larkin left, taking her painful questions with her.

I peel my eyes open.

Larkin hasn't left. She's seated across from me, leaning on the desk, her blue-green eyes full of compassion. "You have feelings for Cal, but he doesn't feel the same?"

No. That's the only word that should be careening inside my brain. I've never, not once, told a soul about my Cal Crush—the all-consuming longing that had me on the verge of pain during high school. The same anxious yearning that had me stumbling over myself while playing soccer when the guy *lifted the hem of his freaking T-shirt.*

Thanks, Captain America, for blinding me with your lethal abs.

Honestly. A move like that should be illegal. Ten years in prison for taunting me with chiseled perfection.

Cal was big before he vanished. He returned to Windfall a mountain and is as fun and sweet as ever, and here Larkin is, bluntly asking if I have feelings for him. A truth even I find appalling. What kind of woman would have dated the brother of the guy she truly wanted?

"Don't be ridiculous," I tell her. "We've always just been friends."

Just. Just. Just.

Maybe I'll have that written on my tombstone.

Larkin picks up the New York snow globe from my desk and gives it a shake. Cal bought me the globe when I was sick and had to miss a family trip to the Big Apple. I stayed home at my aunt's instead, sad and frustrated. But Cal surprised me with the globe and baked a batch of salted pretzels, because I'd been looking forward to trying those from street vendors. The pretzels were horrible, but I ate every bite.

I ate up every ounce of affection from Cal, then and now.

Larkin watches the fake snow fall, an intense expression

clouding her eyes. "If Cal's anything like his asshole oldest brother, probably best to dodge that bullet anyway."

Defensiveness rises in me. Jake has been making overtures since his return. I have no interest in revisiting that relationship, but he's a sweet man I cared deeply about. "All the Bowers are good guys, including Jake."

"Nothing about Jake Bower is good," she all but spits.

Okay, then... "I thought nothing happened between you two."

"Nothing did happen," she says vehemently. "I swear. But he made me a promise that night, which he broke. And—" Her throat works, several rough swallows as she pulls herself together. "Let's just say I hope I don't see much of him when I move back."

"Good luck in this minuscule town," I mumble, still horrified she ferreted out my true Cal feelings in a matter of seconds. At least I didn't admit the truth, but what if other folks read me as easily as Larkin and sense how much I like him? What if a nosy gossip-spreader says something to Cal and he starts stonewalling me again? As hard as some days are, wanting a man who doesn't want me back, losing him again would be unbearable.

Less time with him for a bit is what I need. The past week has worsened my Callahan Bower addiction. Detox is necessary. A stretch of time when his disarming smile and rumbly laugh aren't nearby. Then I'll see him in measured doses until I quit fantasizing about feeling his wide mouth slanting over mine.

CHAPTER

Ten

Callahan

I'm back at the Barrel House, the scene of my last crime—enjoying Jolene so much I forgot my brother was in love with her. My stomach simultaneously grumbles and dips.

After working all day with Jake on the Rosen kitchen reno, I zipped over to the Liangs' and dug the holes for their fence posts. Dinner got forgotten. My family meeting about Mom starts in precisely two minutes. While I'm eager to plan her return to Windfall, I'm both hungry and apprehensive about seeing Jolene at her bar again. I've had two days to obsess over my heart's synchronized reaction to her. My deduction: I got carried away. A man doesn't share a heartbeat with a woman after hanging out a few times. It had simply been so long since I'd had easy fun with someone, and my natural banter with Jo turned my brain fuzzy.

Seeing her again will be absolutely fine. We'll be nothing but casual friends who used to know every detail about each other. A friend I'll help out from the sidelines as I've always done.

With one minute left to spare, I hop out of my truck and strut inside.

Instinctively, my eyes zip to the bar. I don't see Jolene. As per recent reconnaissance, trying to figure out why she's stressed about work, Sandra learned Jo works Tuesdays through Sundays. Monday is her only day off. I also know she acts as her own bouncer, tactfully escorting drunk customers out when they've had one too many. She runs a monthly prank contest with her staff to make work fun. Neither Sandra nor I have figured out why Jo has been frustrated with the bar, but I've learned her schedule. If she's not on the floor, she must be working in the back.

My four brothers are gathered around a table, talking together and grinning. Except Desmond. He only smiles around Sadie and Max and generally prefers grunts. When he spots me, he points to the empty seat between him and Jake. At least I'm not sitting next to Lennon or E, who would no doubt get up in my business.

One second after I join them, Jake scowls at me. "You look exhausted."

"I'm fine." But my stomach grumbles loudly.

Sighing, he gestures at my traitorous midsection. "You haven't eaten."

"I was busy."

"Honest to God," he mumbles, while waving to get a server's attention. "Is this what happens when you live alone? You don't eat or sleep? You need to take better care of yourself."

"Give it a rest, Jake," Desmond says, looking as pissed off as usual. "Cal can handle himself."

"Yeah," Lennon tells Jake, but his mirth suggests he's about to get snarky. "You're just upset your little boy's all grown up and living out of the nest."

E snorts out a laugh. Jake lifts his middle finger.

A waitress comes to our table and does a not-so-subtle

perusal of our group. "The crew all agrees that having the Bowers back in Windfall is a boon for the town. You've improved the views considerably."

The other servers are openly ogling our table, causing my brothers to lift their square chins and puff up their broad chests. The server's open appreciation lands on me, and I shift uncomfortably. From my recent recon efforts to understand Jolene's work woes, I've done a thorough analysis of her employees. This woman is Sue-Ann Hinkley. She recently moved to Windfall, owns a cute golden retriever named Sam, and raised no red flags.

I take in her soft curves, displayed in a jean skirt and fitted T-shirt. She has long blond hair plaited in braids. Her dusting of freckles is sweet and attractive. I wait for my body to respond. To show a hint of interest, but it's like the power to my libido's been shut off.

"Where's Jolene tonight?" I ask.

Sympathy blankets her features. "She had to deal with something at her apartment."

I go rigid and shoot a look at Jake. "What's up with Jo?"

He shrugs. "Haven't seen her since the broccoli thing." To Sue-Ann, he says, "Can we get a plate of nachos for my brother, who works too much to eat?"

"And fries," E adds.

"And a few orders of chicken wings." Lennon grins at her. "We're all growing boys."

I'd laugh at the joke, but my mind is too busy puzzling out more Jolene drama. I haven't seen her since soccer and beers. I assumed she and Jake were officially a couple or had at least been spending time together. More romantic dinners. Hanging out at his pad. Sleepovers where *they don't sleep*. Jake and I work together, but we've been busy, and I've steadfastly avoided the topic of their reunion. I was sure they'd be inseparable by now.

"You had dinner with her, though," I say to Jake when Sue-

Ann's gone. "After the festival? Have you seen her since? Did she say anything about her apartment?"

He drums his thumb on the table and bounces his heel. Jake only gets twitchy when he's upset or frustrated. "She couldn't make it for dinner that night. Even made her favorite burgers, but she said no. Since then, I keep missing her when I call."

I frown. The Jolene I know doesn't like burgers. She says it's mystery meat that could be made of eyeballs. That strange inconsistency aside, when I was here with Jo two days ago, a customer congratulated her on reuniting with Jake. My rumors have clearly circulated widely. I have no doubt Jake and she have both heard often that the other is pining for them or that they're already a couple. If Jolene is avoiding Jake in the face of that gossip, I need to figure out why before pushing harder at their reunion.

At least I've made progress helping Lennon with his wiring issues.

"How's the house?" I ask Lennon. "Still cooking on your camp stove and doing takeout?"

"Funny you should ask." He stares at me for an unnerving beat. "I was in Sugar and Sips the other morning, and Dean of Dean Electric happened to be there too. He asked about my renovations—specifically, if I needed any help with the wiring."

At least that plan is chugging along smoothly. "That's awfully nice of him."

"I thought the same. I also thought his offer was odd since he's got jobs lined up until the fall." Lennon's staring becomes more of a judgmental scowl.

I shrug, secretly pleased my efforts were fruitful. I bartered with Dean so he'd fit in the work. In return, I'll be helping him build a toolshed. "I was buddies with him in high school. Guess he just cares."

I take a long pull on my beer. Something to fill my stomach until the food arrives and a way to avoid Lennon's watchfulness.

"Mom should be here in four or five weeks," Jake says, getting to the reason we're here. "She said she didn't want a fuss, but I think she deserves a fuss."

"A party," E says, nodding. "Something with her old friends. The quilting crew would be in."

I give him a thumbs-up. "Love the idea."

"Agreed," Jake says.

Lennon spins his beer bottle. "I vote for a surprise. Maggie's an event-planning guru. I could rope her in to help."

"Books," Desmond says while rubbing the side of his neck. "Mom loves reading. We could get a welcome-home cake in the shape of a book. I can make it with Max and Sadie. Maybe Delilah can help?" He focuses his thick-lashed eyes on E.

E cocks his head. "Since when does Mom love reading?"

"I don't know." Desmond reverts to his usual glower. "It was a guess."

Lennon perks up like an attentive prairie dog. "Didn't sound like a guess to me. That kind of evasiveness indicates there's something you don't want us to know."

Desmond's nostrils flare. "*That* kind of statement indicates you want to swallow your teeth."

"No teeth will be swallowed," I say, even though I sense we've just scratched the surface of teasing Des. The guy is too easy to rile.

Lennon nudges E with his elbow. "Do you think Des used to steal these alleged books Mom loves to read?"

"Questionable." E's face goes red the way it does when he's about to diss one of us. "I assumed his bad tattoos caused a rare blood disorder that made it hard to focus on words. I doubt he can read."

Lennon snickers. "Excellent point. He—"

"Whatever. Fuck it, fine," Des snarls. "Mom and I have a book club. We read the same books and discuss them. Happy?"

"Oh, I'm fucking ecstatic." Lennon's face lights up like a

Fourth of July picnic. "Do you serve tea sandwiches on little doilies at your adorable book club?"

E cracks up. Des growls.

"Quit the jokes." Jake's stern tone silences the table: Captain Mode engaged. "The book cake sounds great. I'm sure Delilah would love to help. E and Lennon, you two make a list of who to invite and start asking. If we make books the theme, Cal and I can build her a special bookcase for her house."

We share a round of grunts and nods.

E holds up his beer. "To the best woman we know. We'll make sure her return to Windfall is memorable."

We raise our beers and drink to Chelsea Bower, a woman who's endured more than her share.

"Make way for the food!" Sue-Ann returns, hands full of nachos and wings.

My stomach rumbles, and saliva pools in my mouth. Fuck, I really am hungry, but I don't let on how famished I am. No need to give Jake more reason to coddle me.

Just as Sue-Ann reaches our table, her attention darts to the front door. "Jo! How bad is it?"

One glance at Jolene's ashen face, and I'm shoving my chair back, taking long strides to reach her. "What happened?"

She rubs her eyes, while hunching awkwardly. "My apartment's fucked."

"Fucked how?"

"Flooded. Whole place is trashed, along with half my stuff. I just…" She glances around the bar, bleary-eyed, like she doesn't recognize her own business. "I can't catch a break."

In seconds, Jolene is surrounded by Bower boys, all of us ready to do battle in her honor.

Jake steps closest to her and runs his hand down her arm. "What's wrong?"

She flinches, but I can't tell if it's from Jake or if she's just extra upset, and her stiff stance looks uncomfortable. "A pipe burst in my place, and it'll take weeks to clean up. My sister's living at my folks' with her kids, so I can't crash there. Delilah said I can sleep on the couch, as did Sue-Ann, but my back's been sore from carrying kegs. Couch sleeping would do me in." She touches her back reflexively, still standing at an odd angle.

Jake lowers his head to catch her eye. "You can stay with me. My place is—"

"Small and dirty," Lennon says swiftly. He's wearing his smug expression, the scheming glint that never fails to have me on edge. "She just said she can't sleep on the couch, and no one wants to stay in your pigpen. My place is half in shambles since Mags and I started renovating it. But"—he smacks my back —"Callahan has a large two-bedroom. Tons of space. Excessively clean. You can commandeer his place."

Jo's eyes widen like it's the worst idea she's ever heard. Probably because she doesn't understand why I'm so hot and cold with her. Jake is staring daggers at Lennon. I have half a mind to jam my elbow into our conniving brother's ribs. I can barely speak to Jo in public without getting worked up. Living with her is out of the question.

"I'd rather not." Jo swallows slowly and won't even look me in the eye. "I don't want to put anyone out. I'll just get a blow-up mattress. Live in the bar office while I sort things out."

"No." The word is out before I realize I've opened my mouth. Nothing hurts me more than seeing Jolene frustrated and upset. Her back is clearly sore. Blow-up mattresses suck. I give her a reassuring nod, while my insides swirl into a cyclone of uncertainty. "Lennon's right. My place is plenty big. You can stay there as long as you need."

She nibbles her lip, glancing at Jake, who's suddenly looking less annoyed. Her attention slowly slides back at me. "You're sure?"

That this is the worst idea ever? "Absolutely."

"Okay," she says, but she doesn't look relieved. If anything, her brows furrow deeper. "I have stuff to catch up on here. I'll come over later."

I nod as she trudges toward her office, still cradling her back. I think she mumbles something like, "Lady Luck frigging hates me."

The guys return to the greasy food at our table. All but Jake, who's intent on me. "This is actually good."

"What's good?"

"You living with Jo. You'll be in close quarters. You can get me some intel. Help me figure out the best way to convince her I'm not the guy she thinks."

He's right. Jolene seems standoffish with him when he acts more than friendly. Probably because of why they broke up, even though Sandra's been trying to rewrite that false-cheating history for me. But if those old rumors *are* why Jo is avoiding Jake and acting odd with him, I simply have to make her understand that Jake never broke her trust back then.

"Consider me your wingman," I tell him forcefully. "I'll get the lay of the land from Jo, figure out how you can win her over."

I glance at the piles of food on the table, our brothers busy digging in. My stomach turns. Soon, Jolene will be at my house. Living in the room beside mine. Nothing but a thin wall between us while I play matchmaker. My goddamn body better behave, or rooming with Jolene will be as fun as spending another decade in witness protection.

CHAPTER
Eleven

Callahan

I add a folded blue blanket to the end of the bed in my guest room. Then I snatch it off. Then I refold it and put it back on. Then I remove it again and shove my hand through my hair.

This pretty much sums up my last two hours.

Jolene will be here soon. My home is as tidy as always. The open living area is painted a soft gray. A blue-gray backsplash highlights the stainless-steel appliances and mottled gray countertop. I bought a dark gray couch and love seat, along with decorative throw pillows in shades of blue, gray, and white. I even have several black-and-white photographs on the wall, highlighting architecture and life in the early twentieth century. Details and decor I like.

Tonight, I've uselessly rearranged most things fifty times.

A knock at my door turns my stomach into a cement mixer. "Goddamn Lennon," I grumble.

I don't know what his deal is. When Desmond was terrified to face Sadie, Lennon orchestrated it so Des was stuck working with her. He pushed E to return to Windfall and face Delilah, when we still weren't allowed to tell people about WITSEC and why we'd disappeared. Now he's been in my face, asking unnerving questions, shoving Jo into me on bench seats and into my spare bedroom, like he thinks he's cupid incarnate, ensuring his brothers all find love.

Except he's matching Jolene with the wrong brother.

Inhaling deeply through my nose, I replace the stupid blanket on the end of the guest bed and stalk to my door, unsure why I'm practically stomping. I yank the door open and freeze. Jolene is standing slightly hunched under the weight of a bag, a pained look on her face.

"Let me take that." I lift the bag from her shoulder, hating how she winces. "Go sit on the couch. Is the rest in your car?"

She's wearing the same white T-shirt and jeans from work, but they look more wrinkled. She nods and rubs her eyes. "I'd normally yell at you for assuming a woman can't handle moving a few bags, but your couch is calling my name."

She walks stiffly toward the living area.

I drop her bag and beat her there, placing a cushion behind her back as she sits. "This okay?"

Her soft sigh hits me in the solar plexus. "Yeah, thanks."

She sighs again, and my body heats uncomfortably.

"I'll grab your stuff and be back shortly." I hightail it out of there and give myself a mental slap.

My body shouldn't react to a goddamn sigh. The woman is in pain. The last thing she needs is me getting all worked up over her breathy sounds. I mean, honestly. Have I not matured past my sex-obsessed fourteen-year-old self who got turned on by a girl blinking in my direction?

Her apartment better be repaired swiftly.

Although I could carry her two remaining bags in one trip, I drag it out into two. Upon my first return, Jo is leaning her head on the couch back with her eyes closed, but her hands are fisted at her sides. It takes all my willpower not to sit beside her and pull her into a reassuring hug. After my second trip, Jo is on her feet, poking around my living area.

My attention darts to my open bedroom door. I doubt she'd have gone in there. She certainly wouldn't have opened my closet door or taken out the shoebox of memories I've kept since we were kids—the one item I took with me when we were shoved into WITSEC. I really should trash those relics.

She stops in front of the Berenice Abbott photograph by the kitchen and cocks her head.

"It's a print," I say, but my voice, for some unfathomable reason, comes out hoarse. "Manhattan in the late thirties."

"I love how it looks like a slice of life with the horse and the old cars. And the looming bridge in the back is amazing."

"I actually bought the prints in Houston," I admit, "but never framed them or put them up."

She glances at me over her shoulder. "Why?"

I shrug, not used to being asked personal questions. I didn't invite close relationships during WITSEC. I'm the listener of my family, not the talker—the one who asks questions and offers concerned advice. I don't burden others or lash out.

When I don't elaborate, she raises an eyebrow and says, "Callahan," in that way of hers.

I huff out a half laugh. She won't let this lie, so I think back to buying my first photography print. How drawn I was to the Ezra Stoller image with its play of lights and darks, the sharp angles, the flow of the softer lines, like the building was caught in transition. A living, breathing creature that could morph before my eyes. "I didn't hang them because I liked them too much."

She squints at me. "Isn't that usually why people *do* hang art?"

"Sure, but I didn't want Houston to be my home. Didn't want to give it the kind of permanence that comes with beautiful art.

These pieces"—I gesture at my meager collection, allowing the truth of my choices to settle—"were too interesting. Too fascinating to be part of my one-dimensional life. Hanging them didn't feel right."

Her eyes glass over. "I hate what you went through. I'm still so sick about it."

I cross my arms and chew the inside of my lower lip. "What's done is done. There's no undoing the past. My future is brighter now."

Her penetrating gaze sweeps over my face. "How do you do that?"

"What?"

"Always look at the bright side of things?"

"Do I?"

"You know you do."

I scratch my nose, feeling exposed. "I've had tough times. Days when I couldn't find the silver lining."

WITSEC was a zinger of toughness. As was hurting Jo and Jake with my jealousy. I also hated when those two would be locked in his room. I couldn't stay home those days without wanting to punch the wall.

Most of the time, though, I pushed through. Focused on the good. My family. My friends. "The bright side is easy to see when it doesn't all revolve around me. Seeing my brothers happy now—in love with their girlfriends and rebuilding their lives—that's my silver lining."

"Your happiness is important too. Finding love of your own." Her voice has quieted, the hum of the fridge the only sound in the room. She swallows slowly and steps closer, looking almost nervous. "Are you seeing anyone?"

"No." The word is a low baritone that reverberates in my chest. I don't know why it feels like the room is tilting or why my clothes are so damn tight. "I've dated here and there, but like with all of us, the effort felt off with our fake identities."

This conversation also feels off. It's not like Jo and I didn't discuss dating and crushes when we were young and inseparable. Before she started seeing Jake, at least. In my place, like this, quiet and older, the discussion feels heavier.

She licks her lips, a slow drag of her tongue that has the tightness in my clothes worsening. Her dark eyes settle on my mouth. *Blood.* I suddenly taste blood from biting my lip so hard, which she must have noticed.

"Jake," I force out. "He asked me to tell you he's free for dinner tomorrow. Wants to take you out."

She opens her mouth, looks like she's about to speak. Abruptly, she turns her back to me and resumes studying the photograph. "I'm glad you put your art up here. You have great taste."

"That's my favorite piece," I say, pleased she ignored the Jake prompt. There was no dinner invite. Mentioning him was a panic move. If Jo is still sore about the cheating rumors, more finesse is needed. I don't have the mental energy to pull strings tonight.

Taking her lead, I join her by the photograph. "I actually find the people in this more interesting than the architecture. I like wondering what those men on the street are talking about." If they were shooting the shit about a friend's gambling debt or the drudgeries of factory work or the Wall Street Crash of 1929.

When I purchased the photograph, something about the snapshot of life reminded me that everyone has a story. Mine sucked for ten years, but woes are woes. No one goes through life in a bubble of perfect happiness.

She leans forward, studying the slightly out-of-focus figures. "That's obviously Joe and Floyd. They're arguing over who should make their next batch of moonshine."

Relaxing my stance, I grin. She's playing our inventing-stories game. "Maybel is on those stairs near them, giving them hell for playing their swing music too loud last night."

"Nope." She shakes her head. "She's pissed Floyd took her sister on a date and never called again. Now she's debating lighting a match near his hair, which is coated in pomade."

I chuckle, enjoying the moment. Our easy banter returned. "You need help unpacking?" I ask. "Is your back okay?"

"I'll be fine. Back's tight but better than this morning. Once I take my muscle relaxants and sleep in a comfy bed, I should be okay. And, Cal." She faces me and *damn*, those eyes. Big and soft and achingly beautiful. "Thanks again for letting me stay. It hopefully won't be too long, but it's hugely appreciated. You made a really bad day a lot better."

"However long is fine," I say gruffly.

CHAPTER
Twelve

Callahan

The next night, I eat dinner alone, surrounded by evidence of Jolene. After living with Jake, I should be used to messiness, but her cowboy boots are kicked haphazardly by the front door. A pair of socks, of all things, are on my coffee table. A shirt of hers is tossed over the back of my couch. It hasn't even been twenty-four hours, and already, she's not picking up after herself.

Annoyance tenses my neck, but I don't touch her things. She'll have to learn to live tidier while here. Unfortunately, as I eat, my attention keeps darting to each carelessly tossed item. Her bedroom door is closed. If I had to guess, it's chaos in there.

After tidying the kitchen, I relent and clean up after Jo, grumbling under my breath as I stack her discarded socks on her now-folded shirt. I debate going to bed early afterward. I'm exhausted from my long day. Jolene leaves the bar late. It would be easy to avoid her, but what if she hasn't eaten yet? She probably leaves work exhausted too. Cooking is a pain when you're tired.

I prep some food, just in case—cut-up veggies that can sit in the fridge if not needed. I yawn afterward, debate finally heading to bed. For some reason, I grab my biography on Cesar Chavez and sink into the couch, where I read until my eyes feel heavy.

———

"Cal?" A soft voice breaches my consciousness. A hand sifts through the side of my hair. "You should sleep in your bed. You'll wake up stiff out here."

Jolene. I don't open my eyes yet. The feel of her hand in my hair is too good. And yeah, if she keeps doing that, something will definitely wake up *stiff*.

"What time is it?" I ask, my voice a quiet rumble as I move my book off my chest.

"Late."

I finally open my eyes, and Jolene is gazing down at me in a way that makes my stomach clench. "You okay? How's your back?"

"Better, thanks. And seriously, you should go to bed. I always get home late. Your days are long. I don't want you waiting up for me."

"I wasn't waiting up," I say. She raises an eyebrow, not bothering to call my bluff. "I didn't want you to come home and have to tiptoe around," I admit.

"Please don't worry about me. You need your sleep."

I quirk my lips. "Are you telling me I look like shit?"

She rolls her eyes. "Go to sleep, Cal."

I stand and head to the kitchen instead. "Did you eat dinner?"

"Not really, but I'm fine. Please, just go to bed. You get up way earlier than me."

Ignoring her, I pull out the veggies I cut up and the sauces needed for a simple stir-fry. "I'll whip something up for you. Do whatever you need to unwind. I'll get this going."

She doesn't reply. No noises indicate she's headed to her room. I turn, and Jolene looks like she's about to cry.

"Hey," I say, hurrying over to her. I cup her cheek. "What's wrong?"

"I'm just not used to anyone taking care of me."

My heart squeezes. The person who cared for her most was her aunt, who's now gone. And Jo doesn't know how much I've done for her the past twelve years. She can't ever know.

I shrug, like putting her first tonight is an afterthought. "We're roommates, Jo. Friends who help each other out."

I run my thumb down her cheek. Probably a non-friend gesture. She closes her eyes, turning into my gentle touch, then she spins away and says quickly, "I'll change and be right out."

Half an hour later, Jo and I are at my small dinner table while she eats my stir-fry of onions, peppers, broccoli, and bok choy, the veggies glistening with my usual concoction of black bean sauce, rice wine, and brown sugar.

"Did you go to cooking school?" She points her fork at her plate. "This is really freaking good."

I focus on sipping my water. Not on the pleased puff of my chest. "You know I cooked growing up. Helped my mother feed her impatient brood."

"Yeah, but...are you sure you'd call that cooking? Pretty sure I recall a pizza that could be used as a Frisbee."

We actually did that. Ran outside, cracking up, tossing my overcooked pizza back and forth until our hands were a mess and it fell apart. "Not my fault. The timer I set didn't work."

"And that day you made cookies with salt instead of sugar?"

"Honest mistake. And worth it. Remember when Lennon grabbed one without knowing?"

"Oh my God." She clutches her chest. "His face was priceless."

"Horror movie worthy. Actually," I say as a wonderful idea hits. "We should—"

"—ask Delilah to set him up?"

I guess Jolene can still read my mind. "She could bake something at her shop with salt instead of sugar and slip it to him."

"While we're there, of course." Her eyes dance. "We'd have to video his reaction."

We high-five, the two of us grinning like we're teenagers setting our first booby trap.

"Your brothers are the best, by the way. And although you *did* cook well growing up, you didn't cook like this." She takes another bite, savoring as she swallows.

I shrug. "Twelve years is a long time. Had to eat every day."

"You also didn't keep your college apartment this spotless." Her attention passes over the hardwood floor I sweep daily, my kitchen counter already cleaned from cooking, the small pile of her neatly folded clothes. "Jake said something about cleaning rules when you lived together."

"Yeah, well." I dust flecks of salt off the table, uncomfortable sharing truths under Jolene's steady stare, but we'll be stuck in close quarters for a while. If I stay quiet, she'll just say my name in that *Callahan* way. "We all had our coping mechanisms during WITSEC. One of mine was cleaning."

"Because it was something you could control?"

"I never thought of it like that. Assumed it was more of a distraction. But yeah, that probably played a part. What about you? How have you changed the past twelve years?"

She finishes her last bite of stir-fry and gives me a full-teeth grin. "Sadly, my tendency to be on the messy side of life has gotten worse. I'm a one-person hurricane, which I should maybe have mentioned before moving in."

I give her my best glower. "Guess you'll be changing those ways."

She bats her lashes. "Or you'll be relaxing your cleaning rules?"

This woman. As charming as Jo is, even she can't curb my fastidiousness. "Don't make my place messy, Jolene."

"But messy is so much more fun, *Callahan*." Her sweet tone has an edge to it I can't decipher. And yeah, my body thrums at the word *messy* dropping from her lips. The sentiment conjures images of clothes scattered on the floor, sheets askew, tangled limbs.

Chaos in my ordered world.

I shove my chair back and gather her plate and cutlery in a brusque clatter. Jolene tries to take over cleaning, but I only let her help. I fill the dishwasher while she washes the wok by hand. I grab a towel for drying, still too curious for my own good.

"You evaded," I say as she hands me the wet wok. "Name one thing that's changed about you the past decade."

She nibbles her lip and presses her thumb deeper into the soapy sponge. "I was so insecure growing up. So worried about what people thought of me, always assuming the worst. I'm more confident now, sure in who I am. But I also think I live my life scared in a way I never used to."

I place the dry wok down and lean my hip into the counter. "Scared of what?"

"I don't know."

"Yes, you do."

"Someone's pushy."

"Someone's avoiding her feelings."

She laughs. "At least this hasn't changed."

She doesn't need to explain what "this" is. Our banter and challenging conversations. Our need to pull out each other's innermost worries. "Why do you live scared?" I ask gently.

She focuses on the sudsy water in the sink. "Because I know what it's like to lose."

"Lose what?"

"*You*, Cal," she says more angrily. Her dark eyes shoot to me. "You and Jake. Aunt Becca when she passed away. And I actually did try to start a small cooking business. When I imagined myself a chef, I decided to make ready-to-eat meals for the elderly. Cook more interesting foods for them than those awful frozen meal services, but it tanked. I wasn't good at the marketing, and the planning got away from me. I lost a ton of cash in the process. So, yeah. I like things easy. The path of least resistance. Change scares me as an adult, because change in my life has always been bad."

Well, fuck. I grab Jo by the shoulders and pull her into my chest. "I'm sorry my disappearance hurt so much."

"It's not your fault."

"I know, but I'm still sorry. And starting that business was brave, even if it didn't work out."

"Maybe." She sags deeper into me, squeezing her arms around my waist. "But change still scares me. Including the changes between us."

A surge of guilt floods me.

Acting hot and cold with Jo has hurt her, and I need to do better. Whatever happens from here on out, I can't continue sabotaging our friendship. I'll help reunite her with Jake. Undo the damage I caused between them. But I'll also do this—hug my best friend when she's sad. Answer her tough questions and ask my own. Be each other's support.

Maybe I'll get past my attraction to her in the process. I mean, I'm hugging her, holding her tight to my body, not even getting worked up. Just enjoying her lightning-storm scent, the tenderness of being with my closest friend.

She gives me a tighter squeeze, then slinks out of my grip and adjusts her white T-shirt. "Going forward, don't worry about me for food while I'm here. This was hugely appreciated, but I mostly eat at the bar."

"Ownership perks."

"There have to be some," she says, no longer sounding comforted. She returns to the dishes, giving me her back. "Did I tell you I still have our Cool List?"

"Seriously?"

"It was luckily in my desk drawer and didn't get ruined by the flood. Figured, since you lost all your old stuff when you went into witness protection, I'd bring it over. A memento from the old days."

My gaze snaps to my bedroom door, to the closet edge I can see from this angle. I have a shoebox full of our mementos, but I don't mention it. An uneasy feeling has me tugging the back of my hair. "Yeah, we had to leave Windfall quickly. Didn't get to take much. I'd love to see the list, though."

"It's in an envelope in the top left drawer in my room. If you grab it, I'll finish up here."

My room. Not sure I'll get used to the idea of living with Jolene. Or to having someone back in my life who forces me to open up about tough topics.

I head to the guest room, happy to have some space between us. Don't fully understand why I didn't tell her about my shoebox of memories.

Two steps inside, I nearly trip over an empty bag and curse.

Jo wasn't joking about being a one-person hurricane. A messy pile of clothes covers part of the bed, half the dresser drawers are hanging open, cowboy boots and shoes are strewn by the wall, and her toiletry bag is partly spilled on top of the dresser.

"Give me patience," I mutter to myself and step over the bag that nearly sent me sprawling.

Since most dresser drawers are open, it's not hard to spot the envelope in the top one. It's beside her stack of T-shirts, but a tease of light green pokes out from the middle, looking incredibly familiar. Unable to resist checking, I lift the other shirts, and yeah. It's the green shirt with the leprechaun on it that I bought for her sixteenth birthday, because she was born on St. Patrick's Day. Whenever she wore it, she insisted on speaking in an Irish accent, cracking me up.

The fact that she still has it sends a wave of sentimentality through me.

Breathing through my deluge of memories, I pull out the envelope and close the top drawer. And nearly swallow my tongue.

Vibrator.

There's a pink pleasure device in the second drawer, tucked in with lacy underwear. Heat suffuses my face, my chest, *my groin*. Why the hell does she need a vibrator for a temporary living arrangement? Does she use it that regularly? Does she plan to use it while she's *here*? In the room right beside me? Will I hear the *sounds* she makes?

And hell, now I'm imagining her spread out on the striped gray duvet, wearing one of these lacy nothings, pushing the fabric aside, rubbing that pink pleasure toy all over her wet pussy while…

Mayday. SOS. Someone, *please*, bleach my overstimulated brain.

That compassionate hug was important and special, and I value my friendship with Jolene more than I can say, but I was not built for this. Maybe a different guy could handle living with an off-limits woman he finds unbearably attractive. I'm no longer sure I'm that strong of a man.

Flushed and overheated, I shove that drawer shut and strut for the door.

"Hey, did you—" Jolene slams into me, and I'm suddenly wet.

She's wet.

She must have been carrying a glass of water, because her white T-shirt is now drenched, and Jesus H. Christ, what the hell did I ever do to deserve this? Breast. Nipple. I see the contours of it all, and I can't unsee the sultry images I conjured a moment ago—vibrator, spread legs, my best friend licking her lips as she gives me an X-rated show.

"Need to change," I blurt and storm by her for the safety of my room.

I must have been delusional. Off my goddamn rocker. That's the only reason I could have believed I'm equipped to survive living with Jolene Daniels.

CHAPTER
Thirteen

Callahan

I, Callahan Bower, am a busy man. *Go, go, go* is my motto. Renovation work with Jake, where I push myself so hard we barely have time to talk. Porch building, fence building, reno planning. I also usurped the project to build Mom a welcome-back-to-Windfall bookcase, telling Jake I didn't need assistance.

I've been insanely productive the past week, leaving zero time to lounge around at home and enjoy the photographs on my wall. Or to run into Jolene.

My new roommate has the opposite schedule from mine. She leaves for the bar around midday, works until one or two a.m., then sleeps in late. I'm out of the house well before she's awake. I'm so exhausted from all my work that I pass out before she steps in the front door. The one Monday she had off, I spent the day and evening with Des and Sadie and Max. If it weren't for the chaotic mess in my once-tidy home, I'd barely know she was living with me.

I pull off my hat, wipe my forehead, and squint at the sun. Based on its height in the sky, must be getting near quitting time. A whistle comes from behind me. I turn in time to catch my flying water bottle. Jake lifts his in salute. Grateful, I take a deep gulp.

"Time to call it," he says, joining me. "We'll finish the rough-in work tomorrow. You have enough wood for the framing?"

I glance at the stack beside the table saw. "We're good. Have you coordinated with the plumber?"

He nods. "They'll send someone first thing next week."

I take another swig of water, the smell of wood chips still sharp in my nose. This is usually the point when I rush around so fast, Jake doesn't have time to ask me about Jo or push for intel on how to win her over. That conversation would lead to me actually having to *talk* to her, which is a no-go. The second I think of Jolene, all I picture is that vibrator and her see-through shirt molded to her full breasts. Facing her right now is a one-way ticket to Trouble.

Unfortunately, Jake isn't working as efficiently as usual. We're tidying my work area, storing everything in the Rosens' garage, but he's carrying smaller loads, dragging his steps.

When he starts uselessly aligning our wood pile, I stop and cross my arms. "What's up?"

He scratches his chest and scuffs his boot over the garage floor. "How has Jolene been?"

And here we are. At the conversation I've been avoiding. "Haven't seen much of her. Our schedules are pretty different."

He removes his hat and rakes his hand through his disheveled hair. "That's probably why I haven't heard from her much either. But I was thinking…"

A squirrel zooms by the open garage. We watch it while Jake gathers whatever thoughts are making him nervous, and I mentally kick myself for letting him down. The Jake I know doesn't do awkward. He helmed our family for the past twelve years, barking orders as needed. He pushed me to take hold of this career I love. Yet here he is, struggling to discuss his feelings about Jo, because I've erected a barrier between us.

"You were thinking," I prod. I'm a brother before anything else. It's time I remember that.

"Just…" More hair-tugging. "I get that Jo's busy. So am I. But this feels more like avoidance. Do you think she's still pissed about those cheating rumors? Is that why she keeps putting me off?"

"Could be." Although I'm no longer sure.

Jolene seems uninterested in discussing Jake or hanging out with him. Those ancient cheating rumors could be the cause, or she doesn't look at him that way any longer. For some reason, I haven't pushed her and asked. Jake, however, is an open book. My brother still has strong feelings for Jo.

"Next time I see Jo," I say, "I'll bring those old rumors up. Remind her the cheating didn't happen."

He nods a bunch, his focus kind of distant. "Maybe see what kind of date she's into. Recreating our burger nights doesn't seem to be doing the trick. She used to love the drive-in. Maybe see if that's something she still loves."

Frowning, I dust my hands on my dirty jeans. From what I remember, Jolene loved movies but hated the drive-in. She found the action around her too distracting to enjoy the main event. And the burger thing is still baffling. Unless I don't know Jo as well as I thought I did.

"I'll nose around." I slap Jake's shoulder and give it a squeeze.

———

Four hours later, after working on the Elroys' deck and then Mom's shelving unit, which Lennon is storing in the barn on his property, I turn the doorknob to my duplex and hold my breath.

I do this every time I come home, wondering if Jolene happened to leave work early.

I inch the door open, my pulse ticking in my ears.

A quick scan shows she's not here, but I groan. *Chaos.*

There's no other way to describe the state of my home. A sweatshirt is tossed over my love seat. Six pairs of shoes are scattered near-ish to the entryway. Water glasses are all over the place, because Jo takes a sip out of one, then forgets it or decides she needs another. For some reason, she can never remember to put recycling in the recycling bin. The pièce de résistance is her open bedroom door, revealing dirty laundry and a towel on the floor.

A towel she probably used after showering and dropped while still wet.

I'm annoyed about the mess, but I stare at the towel, feeling antsy. I picture Jolene pulling it off the rod, using it to rub her wet body, the generous contours of her breasts, the hard points of her nipples. Although that assumes she's turned on. Maybe she masturbated in the shower. Her vibrator could be waterproof. She might use it in there. Moan and shake as she comes on a battery-operated piece of metal.

My eyes cut to our shared bathroom, cluttered with her ten million feminine products.

Swallowing becomes an effort.

Clacking my teeth together, I march into my place and tidy up more forcefully than necessary. I'm not sure why I bother. Living with Jo is like living in a time loop. No matter how many glasses I wash or shoes and boots I line up neatly, it all reverts to lawlessness by the morning. As does my traitorous mind. My only saving grace is working myself so hard I'm too zonked out to dream.

Instead of making a proper meal, I toss together a quick turkey sandwich. It's not what I want to eat. I actually miss cooking. The hobby used to calm and interest me—playing with different recipes, experimenting with new ingredients—but my jam-packed schedule and long days haven't left much time for creativity.

I read while I scarf down my sandwich, barely breathing as I chew. I refuse to look toward Jo's room and *the towel*. I finally get into my biography on Cesar Chavez, but it doesn't take long for my eyelids to droop.

Exhausted, I wash up, strip down to my briefs, and crawl into bed. Where I unceremoniously pass out.

———

A *clang* jolts me awake.

It's dark through my window. My clock glows with 2:10 a.m. I blink the sleep from my eyes, see light streaming in from under my closed door.

Another *clang* sounds, followed by Jolene's aggravated "Just open already."

I should go out there, see what she's struggling with. Follow through on my promise to Jake and talk him up to her. Find out if she actually likes drive-in movies. But the shower turns on, as does my vivid imagination. *Jolene. Wet. Breasts. Nipples.*

I squeeze my eyes shut, bite the inside of my cheek. I count my breaths and try to get back to sleep. Ten guesses on how that's going.

I force my eyes wide and stare at the darkened ceiling, willing my pulse to calm the fuck down. She's showering because she's dirty from work. It's a normal, everyday activity. Old people shower. Prisoners shower. *Everyone* showers, and there's nothing sexy about it. Unfortunately, my thickening cock finds the simple sound of falling water pretty fucking sexy.

Groaning, I dig the heels of my palms into my eyes. Give them a hard rub, because I refuse to rub anything else. I will not jack off to my brother's ex and current love interest. I haven't touched myself since she moved in here and plan to uphold that record.

Instead, I focus on my worst mistake. The reason I need to be a better man.

The weeks when I morphed into my evil twin.

Jake and Jo had been together for two years. I was away at college but drove home most weekends. I was often a third wheel with them back then, tagging along on their nights out, feeling tense as they'd flirt and hold hands.

Then Jake went to visit a friend at school in New York.

It was just Jo and me. Like old times. We traipsed through my family's property, laughing about the adventuring we used to do.

Then she looked at me and said, "Let's go to our tree house."

We hadn't been there in ages, and my heart tripped over itself as we jogged toward it. Jo launched herself up the ladder like the bruiser she used to be. So fast, she stumbled on a rung. I jumped up after her, wrapped my arm around her trim waist. My face was almost pressed into her back, her signature scent all around me. *Lightning storm in a spring meadow.*

"I've got you," I murmured.

"Do you?" she asked quietly. She covered my hand with hers, and her stomach tightened.

Her body's reaction was for sure from the near fall, but I frowned at her vulnerable question. "I've always got your back."

She made a soft sigh I couldn't decipher, but my body hardened at the breathy sound.

Once inside our tree house, I tried to tame myself. Flexed my hands and bit down on my cheek. We lay next to each other, as was our way growing up—arms and thighs pressed together in the small space—and I gradually relaxed.

"I feel lost," she said quietly.

"Pretty sure we're on my family's property. North Carolina. Windfall, to be exact."

She elbowed my side. "With my life, smartass. My future. So many of my friends have a five-year plan. They set off for college, knew exactly what they wanted to do. I'm happy in Windfall, love living here, but the rest…"

"You feel like you have no direction?"

She nodded with a sigh.

"That's not a bad thing, Jo. I'm at college, but I don't have direction. I'm going through the motions, getting a general degree. Biding my time until I work out what I want to do."

"Not knowing doesn't bother you?"

"Some days, sure. I feel antsy at times. Considered accounting like my father but hate the idea of the repetitive work. Investment banking or consulting is a possibility, a job where I can work with numbers in a more creative way. But nothing feels right yet. I don't want to jump into something because it's easy."

"At least you know you're good with planning and numbers. All I know is I want to work with people and don't want to be confined to a desk job, but I'm not good at anything specific."

"Sassing people is specific."

She pinched my upper arm. "Say that again, Bower."

I chuckled. "You're a confident woman who will excel at whatever she chooses, Jo. Unless it involves being cool. Your childhood loser status will never be forgotten."

We laughed about our lame Cool List, talked more about our uncertain futures. Discussed our love of Windfall, how much I missed it when away at school. What I didn't say was how much I missed *her*. My best friend I didn't see as much, the one who was in love with my brother.

After a while, we breathed quietly. Jo shifted, and the backs of our hands brushed—the tiniest touch, but my body crackled to life. The telltale zing she always inspired.

"I've missed you," she said, mimicking my thoughts, her voice slightly shaky. "A lot."

"You see me when I'm home, and you have Jake."

"It's not the same." She linked her fingers with mine, shifted her attention to my profile. "Not the way I thought it would be."

I didn't know if she was talking about how our friendship had become strained—thinned with my distance and less time together—or that her relationship with Jake wasn't what she'd imagined.

Feeling out of my depth, I fitted our fingers more firmly together, rolled my head to look directly at her. Our eyes connected, and I swore I saw desire in her searching gaze. The first glimpse of interest in all our years as friends. Unless I was reading her wrong. But her lips parted. Mine became achingly parched. Her chest rose faster as her eyes dropped to my mouth, and a rush of heat flooded my abdomen, driving lower.

Her phone suddenly buzzed.

She startled. Sat up quickly, yanked her hand away, and turned her back to me. "It's Jake."

Her sudden stiffness should have clued me into the fact that I didn't stand a chance with Jo, but my mind wouldn't quit spinning over her words. *It's not the same. Not the way I thought it would be.* Did Jake not make her happy the way she'd hoped? Did she maybe like me? Had she wanted to kiss *me* just then?

For the first time since she started dating Jake, I wondered if Jo and I were meant to be.

At which point I morphed into my evil twin.

Our night ended abruptly. Jo said she needed to get home, but my thoughts kept running. Sprinting. Turning over her words and the tight clench of her stomach under my arm on the stairs. The sexy way she parted her lips while eyeing mine.

So I devised a plan.

Next time I was in town, we all attended a house party. I made sure they invited Larkin Gray, who notoriously drank too much. When Larkin was as messy as predicted, I sought Jake out.

"You're sober, right?" I asked him, attempting to keep my voice neutral while my nerves circled a racetrack.

"Since you told me I'm the DD before we left, I think you know the answer to that question."

"Right, cool." Not cool was the way my hands shook. "So yeah, Larkin is a mess, and I told her you'd take her home."

He darted a look at Jo, who was laughing with a group of girls. "Jo's not ready to go, and I barely know Larkin."

"I don't think Larkin should be here any longer." I gestured to her sprawled on the couch, looking sleepy and kind of sad. Or maybe angry. I didn't know why Larkin would be sad or angry. She was simply a pawn in my plan. "Seriously," I added when Jake didn't reply. "You should take Larkin home before some guy decides to drag her upstairs. I'll walk Jo home later."

As expected, Jake straightened—the Bower protector taking care of others when needed, even back then. "Tell Jo I'll call her later."

He marched over to Larkin, talked quietly with her for a bit, then finally led her out of the house.

The next day, I started rumors they hooked up.

The kindled gossip wasn't overt, as per my style. I let it be known they left the party together, suggested his truck was parked outside of Larkin's house. I didn't say for how long, just that it was there. At the time, Larkin had a reputation for stealing boyfriends. Before long, the town was aflutter with speculation. At one point, I heard Larkin had been knocked up by Jake and that Jake had given her ten orgasms in one night.

Jake vehemently denied anything happened between them, but I let the rumors build and grow. Never once assuaged Jolene's worries. Next thing I knew, she broke up with Jake. Jake got quiet and sullen. Instead of swooping in like I'd planned, I descended into despair. Hated myself for hurting my brother. Couldn't imagine going out with Jo when Jake was so upset about losing her. And Jo was acting weird around me, twitchy and quiet.

Two weeks later, my family and I got shoved into witness protection, and Jake took care of us all, clueless to what I'd done.

Now I'm lying in my bed, trying not to jack off to the sounds of his ex—*and current crush*—while she's showering.

The water shuts off. My imagination does not.

Jolene. Wet. Breasts. Nipples.

I picture her grabbing another clean towel, bending over and rubbing a path up her legs. My hips twitch. I picture her reaching the juncture of her thighs, rubbing herself a little harder. One of my hands falls to my chest, the calluses of my fingers rough on the hard muscle. I picture her biting her lip and dropping the towel. I press the heel of my hand harder between my pecs and flatten my palm, fighting the pull to drag my fingers down over my abs, into the band of my briefs, where they'll curl around…*nope.*

I flex my legs so hard I'm sure I'll get a Charley horse, and I strain my ears.

The bathroom door opens.

Feet pad across the floor.

More movement, seemingly everywhere.

Her door does its usual creak, then snicks shut.

I sit up and wipe my damp hand down my face. Even the horrible memories of hurting Jake and Jo didn't help douse my arousal. I need a better distraction. Something to tire me out and put me back to sleep.

Cesar Chavez.

That's what I need. There's nothing sexy about the labor leader and civil-rights activist, but my book on Chavez is in my living room. I can't go out there while Jo's around. The only words careening through my head are still *Jolene. Wet. Breasts. Nipples.*

Nighttime is clearly a no-go for me and my Jo sanity. I need to drop in at the Barrel House for lunch soon, prod about Jake then. Daytime hours are infinitely safer.

Unfortunately, if I want to sleep, I need that non-sexy book.

I wait another few seconds, straining my ears. When I don't hear more from Jo, I hurry out of my room. The kitchen light is still on. I beeline for the end table where I left the book, except my book isn't alone on the end table.

It's lying next to a bra.

Not just any bra. This bra is lacy and sensual and *dark purple*, and I choke on a moan.

Is this what I need to contend with now? Jolene's bras and underwear tossed all over the place? Wasn't ten years of witness protection enough suffering?

"Oh, shoot. Cal."

I swivel, my heart pounding like a jackhammer. "Jo."

That's it. One word. Because *hell*.

My best friend is wearing a tiny tank top and barely there sleep shorts, no bra in sight...unless you count the lacy purple number on my end table. Her attention isn't on my face either. Her brown eyes are the darkest I've ever seen them, intense and molten, tracing a pattern over my naked chest, down my abs, all the way to the cotton attempting to contain my very attentive penis.

CHAPTER
Fourteen

Callahan

I snatch my book from the end table and hold it over my crotch. "I thought you were in bed."

Jo darts her focus to the ceiling. "I thought you were asleep."

We avoid eye contact, looking everywhere but at each other. Except I'm not that strong. I glance at her again, unable to resist a snapshot of the way her tank's soft cotton tents over her pointed nipples. Her eyes flick to me too, do another dip down my chest. Abruptly, she looks at the floor.

I stare at the couch and clear my throat. "I woke up and was having trouble getting back to sleep. Thought reading might help."

"Because I woke you?"

"It's nothing. The book will help."

Slowly, I force myself to be a grown fucking adult and face her more fully. She glances at the book, which is barricading my uncooperative erection, and...is her chest rising faster? Her cheeks are definitely pink, but she was rushing around before and just had a hot shower.

"I'm kind of wired too," she says and crosses her arms. The move presses her breasts together and up, taking another year off my life. "I usually need time to decompress from work. I also get sick of wearing these contraptions." Sheepish, she slips her bra from the table. "Sorry for leaving my stuff around. I need to get better with that."

"It's fine." It's not. Her mess annoys me, and if Jo and I are living together, I need to be more honest. "Your tidiness is actually awful. Coming home is like walking into a war zone."

She sputters out a laugh. "Tell me how you really feel."

I grin. "I just did."

"Right, well." She glances at the shoe collection I tidied that is already a renewed mess. "I am pretty awful to live with."

"You are."

"I'll work on getting better."

"I'd appreciate it."

She rocks on her heels, and I notice her toes. They're small and cute, her toenails painted a pretty pink. *I like that.*

"What?"

I jerk my head up. "What?"

"You said, 'I like that.'"

"Did I?" Now I can't even think things without saying them out loud. "Your offer to clean more. I like that you're willing to try."

Jesus Christ. Someone, please, drop a meteor on my head.

She squints at me and nibbles her lip, then her attention slips back down my body. She doesn't glance away quickly this time. Her gaze lingers, her lips falling open on a puff of air.

Fuck. Me.

Desire grips me by the balls, but she swallows and lifts her eyes, her expression bland, like any heat I saw was imagined. Thank God. It's bad enough that I can't control my thoughts of

4 HINTS YOU LOVE YOUR BEST FRIEND   103

her. If the chemical reaction between us was mutual and *she* decided to act on it, I might become the World's Worst Brother.

"I was coming out to pour myself a glass of scotch," she says. "And to have something small to eat. I bought some food today since your fridge was getting pretty bare. If you open that jar of pickles, I'll make up for my mess by making you a great snack. You look like you could use a drink too."

No, I should say. Goodnight. See you in the daylight when I'm not a minute from jacking off to thoughts of you.

"Scotch sounds great," I say instead. The wrong choice, but hell if I know what I'm doing anymore. "I'll put on some clothes. And maybe"—I gesture at her general self—"you should too."

"Right. Yeah." Her cheeks flame red, and she ducks her head, being painfully cute in her embarrassment.

We disappear into our respective bedrooms, where I aggressively shove on sweats and a T-shirt, practically tearing a hole in the cotton. A few deep breaths later, I emerge from my room one hundred percent in control.

Jazz tunes croon from Jolene's Bluetooth speaker. She's tucked into the corner of the couch, also wearing sweatpants, but her shirt is still a problem. She's not wearing her hides-nothing tank top. She swapped that torture device for the larger green leprechaun shirt I bought her, and a blanket of warmth cocoons my chest.

"Guess this is normal for you," I say as I sit on my love seat, facing her. "Getting home late, being wired for a while." I lift the tumbler of scotch she poured for me and take an appreciative sip.

"Nature of the job." Using her foot, she nudges the jar of pickles toward me on the coffee table. "If you want that snack, I need you to open this."

I lift my scotch on the rocks. "After you poured me this complicated drink? I'm surprised you have the energy."

"Watch the sarcasm, Bower," she says. "I know where you sleep."

"You mean in this slum that used to resemble a clean home?"

Her lips twitch. "If you wake up with a mustache and horns doodled on your face with permanent marker, I swear it wasn't me."

"Do that, Daniels, and you'll be out of the running for Roommate of the Year."

"If your only other roommate has been Jake, pretty sure I win anyway."

I smile into my drink. "He has a father complex. Always ragging on me to take better care of myself."

"You should, you know."

"I should what?" Placing my glass down, I grab the pickle jar and muscle the top open. I hold it out to Jo, but her attention is on my arm.

"Take better care of yourself," she says, delayed, like her mind was elsewhere. She blinks and takes the pickles. "Work less. I'm assuming there's hardly any food here because you haven't had time to cook or shop. I hear how early you leave in the morning. Townsfolk have mentioned how late you work. If you're not careful, you'll burn yourself out."

Or I'll work less and won't be tired enough to pass out without dreaming of Jo. "I miss having the time to cook, but I love what I do—the physical aspect and helping people improve their homes. Townsfolk should mind their own business."

"Tell me about it," she mutters, heading for the kitchen. "Every five minutes, someone's mentioning Jake to me—how much he misses me or how badly they feel about those ridiculous rumors from eons ago."

She sets up a cutting board and knife, grabs mayo, sundried tomatoes, and prosciutto from the fridge. She starts cutting the pickles and swaying to her jazz tunes, like she didn't just say something shocking. Because *hell*. If she thinks those cheating rumors are ridiculous, she might suspect I'm the cause of them.

"You know Jake didn't cheat on you?" I ask tentatively, watching her from the couch.

"Of course Jake didn't cheat on me. This gossip-hungry town turned a kindness he did into a reality show."

"Then why'd you break up with him?" I'm relieved she doesn't suspect my involvement, but I'm seriously in the dark.

Her back is to me. Still, there's no missing the tension in her body as she pauses mid-slice of a pickle. "I realized some stuff."

"What stuff?" I plant my elbows on my thighs and tip my body forward. I was positive she broke up with Jake because of the rumors I spread. *I'm* the catalyst that shattered their love.

Nothing else made sense at the time.

She finishes her precise pickle cutting and starts on the sundried tomatoes. Without answering me, she builds tiny stacks, placing the pickle rounds on the outsides, with mayo and tomatoes and prosciutto stacked in between.

Finally, she sighs. "I really thought Jake was what I wanted. Or, more to the point, I *wanted* to want him. To love him and slot into that easy life, but it was a safe relationship when the rest of my life was up in the air. We both only loved the idea of each other."

"Jake's love was real."

She shrugs, staying quiet.

I open my mouth, ready to push. Ask more. Do my brotherly duty and nudge her toward Jake, but she just said she hadn't loved Jake like I assumed. That Jake wasn't what she really wanted back then. He was definitely less thoughtful when he was younger, more selfish. Her reticence to date him now might be linked to the way he was. That history doesn't mean she wouldn't fall for the caring, stalwart man he's become.

Or I'm trying to fit a square peg into a round hole.

As badly as I want to see Jake happy, I couldn't, in good

conscience, manipulate Jolene into dating him. Not if she isn't open to the idea.

I knock back a bigger swallow of scotch, breathe through the burn in my chest as I let these thoughts percolate.

She places her mini pickle stacks on a plate, organizing them equidistant from one another, then presents me with her platter. "Your orgasmic snack, as promised. Pickle sandwiches!"

Great. Now she's tossing around words like *orgasmic*.

Blocking that word from my subconscious, I pop one of her creations into my mouth, and...*wow*. Savory, tangy, and salty flavors explode on my tongue. "You're definitely my favorite roommate."

"Even though I turn your home into a war zone?"

She turns my brain and body into a war zone, but I admit the truth. "You'll always be my favorite, Jo."

Her cheeks pink as she places the platter on the coffee table. "At least *you're* enjoying the arrangement. I'm stuck living in all this"—she scrunches her nose and shivers—"*cleanliness*."

"Sorry, I take that back. You're a nightmare." I pop a second snack into my mouth, groaning as I swallow. "Also, you can't call these sandwiches."

She folds her arms. "Why can't I call them sandwiches?"

"Sandwiches have to have bread."

"*Sandwiches* are when items are enclosed between two outer things that hold those inner items together. In this case, *pickles*."

"Nope." I shake my head. "Gotta be bread. But these pickle stacks are *delicious*."

I reach for another, but she pulls the plate away. "Care to amend that statement?"

I debate pushing the point. I don't actually think a sandwich has to be made with bread. I'm all for inventive cooking and language play, but I've missed jousting with Jolene. Teasing her and riling her up. Not worth it when my stomach suffers.

I offer a small bow. "Apologies. Your pickle *sandwiches* are the best things I've eaten in ages."

"Apology accepted." She relaxes into the couch, devouring two pickle sandwiches in quick succession. We both reach for another at the same time and laugh.

"If your cooking business failed," I say as I swallow another bite, "it can't be because of the food quality."

"The food was good. The business end of things is where I fell apart."

"Not with the Barrel. It seems to be doing well."

A crease sinks between her brows. She takes her scotch in hand and runs her finger over the rim.

"Jo?" I lean toward her, delicious snacks forgotten. "Are you struggling with the business?"

"I'd rather not talk about it, if that's okay. This is my downtime."

I get that, but she's evading. Work is bothering her, and she won't tell me why. "What about your back? You seem to be moving better. It's hurting less?"

"Way less, thanks." She shoots me a soft smile. "It flares up at times, then settles. I do exercises to keep it in check. See a chiropractor monthly. That was just a bad spell."

"Well, if you need help with anything, you'll let me know, right?"

"You're letting me stay here, Cal. I think you're doing enough."

"I don't like seeing you hurt or stressed."

"Okay." Mischief laces into her tone. "I would be significantly less stressed if you got home from work at a reasonable hour on Mondays and cooked with me."

Such a schemer, trying to look after me by making me look after her. "My work hours are fine."

"If you say so, but you said you missed cooking. If you're

home this Monday for dinner, I could come up with something fun for us to make together."

I debate making plans with Desmond's family again. Keeping myself busy and away from Jolene. I run my tongue over my teeth, catch a whiff of her lightning-storm scent, and let out a gusty breath. "I'd love to cook with you Monday."

CHAPTER
Fifteen

Callahan

The next night, I come home late and sore. I probably shouldn't have worked out at the crack of dawn this morning. I knew my day would be long. But I was awake. Jolene was asleep in the room next to mine, and my uncooperative mind was imagining *things*. Leaving my home seemed like the smart option.

As expected, when I walk back in my door tonight, the space is disorderly. In addition to Jo's usual bedlam is a pile of hair elastics strewn over my coffee table. Like she was counting them and got an emergency call and had to leave in the middle of the diligent work.

"Give me patience," I mumble as I gather the elastics and try to find an empty inch of space on her dresser. Anywhere to store the haphazard pile in her room. Not an easy feat. Her discarded clothes practically need their own zip code.

A pebble of annoyance knocks around the base of my skull, but I laugh under my breath. Never thought I'd find messiness in my home amusing, but that's Jo for you. The loophole to my quirks.

A quick shower later, I towel my hair and trudge to the kitchen, hungry and exhausted. The idea of cooking pains me. Takeout won't be quick enough. I don't feel right eating the groceries Jo bought, but I should have some cheddar hanging around. A slab of cheese on bread with a few condiments is as good as tonight's dinner will get.

I yank open my fridge and freeze.

A Tupperware container is on the top shelf, with a note attached to the front.

In case you're too tired to cook.

Falling. That's the only way to describe this unfamiliar sensation. My stomach is hovering above me, while the rest of my body tips over an edge I can't see. There's a smaller line written underneath her note. I read it and chuckle.

I hope you like live maggots.

Smiling, I pull out the Tupperware and lift the lid. Jolene made me a stew of some kind, no live maggots in sight. The meal looks hearty and plentiful. Like she knew exactly what would hit the spot.

I take off her note, careful not to crease it, and strut to my bedroom. There's no hesitation in my movements. I pull open my closet door and drag out the old shoebox from under my duffel bag.

I don't go through my Jolene mementos like I used to when we were apart. I refrain from running my fingers over our *Simon Says* ticket stub, remembering how we snuck into the R-rated movie and spent most of the show hiding behind our hands, daring each other to watch the gore. I don't smile at the skull-shaped rock from our adventuring days. She called it Edwin and claimed it held magic spells.

I place Jo's note on top of our keepsakes and seal it inside, feeling less like I'm tipping over a cliff. More like I've landed on soft ground.

I eat her food afterward, savoring every bite, so damn thankful she cooked for me. I finish with a happy sigh, nearing food-coma status, but I don't lie down and pass out the way my body is demanding. I grab chocolate chips from my pantry and melt them over a double boiler. Next, I pull out the strawberries she bought.

I don't love using ingredients she purchased, but it'll have to do for tonight. When the chocolate is perfect, I dip the strawberries in the silky sauce and line them neatly on a plate.

At the broccoli festival, Jolene mentioned she loved strawberries dipped in chocolate. Hopefully she appreciates the surprise.

I leave the plate in the fridge where her Tupperware was and place a handwritten note beside it.

CHAPTER
Sixteen

Jolene

I leave my office and check the bar's kitchen like I always do at the end of the night. Make sure the stove is off, along with the lights in the walk-in fridge and freezer, but I frown at a stray bottle cap on the prep counter. A possible sign my chef is drinking at work again.

"If you don't get out here soon," Larkin calls from the bar, "I'll drink your wine and make you pay me for it."

Laughing under my breath, I join her out front. It's just us, as usual lately. She's fastidious about the bar area, polishing glasses until they shine, prepping mixes for inventive cocktail specials she's been offering.

I sit on the stool beside hers and take a grateful sip. "I think Mark might be drinking during his shifts."

She swirls her wineglass and brings it to her nose for a sniff. "Has that been an issue in the past?"

"At times. He started slacking off last fall, coming in late. Got heavy-handed with the salt and sometimes forgot to place orders. But he was one of Aunt Becca's first hires. She always went on about how much she loved him. I talked to him back then, and he sorted himself out, but he's been coming in a bit late again. I don't know, could be nothing."

"Or it could be something. I'll keep on eye on him and let you know if anything seems off. And what do you think about offering a rose-petal-infused gin cocktail for the summer? I'd like to experiment with some ideas."

Of course she would. "You're good at this, you know."

She slants me a look. "At what?"

"Bartending and dealing with people. Creative thinking and talking me off the ledge when our fridge breaks and we have to haul ice from the basement until we can get it fixed."

Today's super-fun bar drama.

She shrugs like she's not affected by my compliment—typical stoic Larkin—but her cheeks pink. "It's in my blood."

"Your family was in the bar business?"

A shadow crosses her eyes. "Sort of. So, the rose gin drink —you're in?"

"I'm in," I say, following her change-of-topic lead. Family is a subject she refuses to discuss.

"Awesome. We could launch it during a lunch with live music. Try to bring in more of a day crowd since it's been kind of slow."

I make a noncommittal sound. "Aunt Becca preferred keeping lunch low-key. Wanted it to be a place where people could come for quiet conversation during the day."

Larkin taps her fingers on the bar, studying my profile in a way that has me feeling exposed. "You don't seem happy with the bar."

"I'm happy," I say automatically. It's the proper response and not a full lie. I don't hate work. There are elements I enjoy, and I don't feel right discussing my frustrations with a staff member, no matter how close Larkin and I have become. "This place was my aunt's vision," I add. "Her baby. She wanted it run a certain way. It's important to me to live up to her expectations, even if it's not as busy as it was."

"But sometimes you need to change with the times. Give the place a boost."

"There's been a bit of a downturn," I agree. "And I've had ideas on how to revamp things." Renovating the kitchen by bringing it into the bar area, letting people watch food preparation, maybe hold cooking classes. Minimize deep-fried items. Introduce ethnic flavors.

Then I think about my one entrepreneurial effort—tasty meals for the elderly. How excited I was about the venture. How hard I worked at it. How hard that business tanked, sinking my savings and my dreams. With my track record, changing the bar could end in bankruptcy and killing Aunt Becca's legacy.

"It's daunting when all the pressure is on me," I say, talking around the subject. "There's risk with change, and nights have been steady enough. Plus, I don't have the time to plan and implement new stuff. I'm okay with how things are running."

Her lips turn down, but she nods. "If you ever want to bounce ideas around, just let me know."

"If *you* ever want to gush about the guys you're dating, just let me know." I nudge her elbow and wink. Prodding Larkin is way more entertaining than discussing my bar stress.

She rolls her eyes. "When will you quit pestering me about dating?"

"When you start dating."

She huffs out a sigh, then perks up. "How about this." She faces me, looking smug. "I'll start dating when you admit you like Cal."

I nearly snort out my sip of wine and turn away, reaching for a napkin. A lame attempt to hide my likely panicked expression.

This isn't the first time Larkin has asked me about Cal. Or the eighth. Every time he comes up, because I *maybe* bring him up more than I should—how nice it is that he's letting me crash in his spare room, the fun soccer game we played together, how easily he moved around his kitchen that one night he cooked for me, the dinner I made him before today's shift—she gets this smug look and launches another you-like-Cal bomb.

I prepare to offer my usual *we're just friends* retort, but a knot forms in my throat. My nose stings the way it does when I get upset.

Every night, I stare at Cal's closed door for a moment and feel a jab of pain. The hot, breath-stealing kind. I swear it's getting worse, not better, along with my guilt for pining after Jake's brother. All these uncomfortable feelings seem to be building to a sharp point that will soon slice me in half.

"Yes," I whisper to the bar top. The shaky word falls out in a whoosh. I turn to Larkin, needing to purge more of it. All of it. "I have feelings for Cal, but he doesn't feel the same."

"Oh, honey." There's no judgment in her kind expression. No censure for wanting my ex's brother. "Have you ever told him?"

"God, no. It took months for him to call me back after I learned about witness protection. Weeks for him to hang out with me after he moved home. He's only letting me stay at his place because I had nowhere else to go. And Cal has *never* shown an ounce of interest in me. Which is for the best since my history with Jake would make everything a complicated mess."

Her face pinches. "Jake is a selfish asshole, who only thinks about himself. I wouldn't worry too much about hurting him."

"Jake's a good guy," I say emphatically. It's the same line I use whenever she attacks his character, which is often. To say I'm dying to know what happened between them is an understatement. "Hurting Jake would hurt me, and it would devastate Cal. So, yes, it *would* all be a disaster if Cal had feelings for me, which he clearly doesn't. He keeps talking Jake up to me, like he wants us back together."

She makes a disgruntled sound and taps her nails on her

wineglass. "From an outsider's point of view, meaning *my* point of view, Cal was in love with you when you guys were younger. Mooned over you constantly. I'd be shocked if he didn't have feelings that ran deep—at least back then. Maybe he only sees you as a friend now. Maybe I'm wrong and he didn't crush on you as teens. Or maybe he's terrified to like you because of *Jake*." She spits out his name like it's poison. "Cal might shut down on you because he likes you too much and doesn't want to hurt his brother."

I replay how often he dodged me when he first moved back to Windfall. How weird he acts at times, like when he barricaded himself in his room after he got our Cool List and we collided in my room. He's barely at home, which might be normal for him with how much he works, or he's avoiding me.

Fear of his feelings could provoke those behaviors, but an interested guy wouldn't push me to date his brother. Cal certainly didn't fight for me or suggest he was interested when we were young and inseparable.

"Avoiding your feelings won't make them go away," Larkin says. "So, my offer still stands—if you tell Cal you have it bad for him, I'll go on a date."

"First"—I lift my index finger—"you asked me to admit to *you* that I like Cal, not to tell him. Second"—another finger—"I'm not fifteen. I don't *have it bad* for a guy."

"First," Larkin says, mimicking me with her raised finger, "I changed my mind on the bet. You definitely have to tell him, so deal with it. Second, you totally *have it so bad.* Unless there's another reason you've been stress-eating the greasiest food on the menu every night, followed by an ice-cream chaser."

I scowl at her. "Shaming a woman for eating is a low blow."

"If you want to just blow Cal, that still counts."

I snort out a laugh. "Jesus, Lark."

"Don't tell me you haven't pictured it. I saw him from a

distance before I barged into your office that first night. That man is all brawn."

My face is suddenly on fire, the memory of catching him mostly naked burning a path up my chest. "I saw him in his briefs the other day," I whisper, as though speaking too loudly will strike me down with lightning. "Like, without his shirt."

"And you're just sharing this detail *now*? What kind of friend are you?"

I duck my head, embarrassed. My vibrator has been overused since that night. "His body isn't human."

"That good?"

"Oh my God" is all I can say.

Chiseled doesn't begin to describe Callahan's body. The man should be bronzed and mounted on a pedestal—a sculpture for the world to enjoy. Smooth rock. Hard lines and shadows. Slashed hip bones. Thick thighs. His obvious erection that night nearly did me in, jutting to the side, bigger than I imagined.

And I have imagined.

"We should talk more about you starting to date," I say, feeling like I'm stuck in a sauna. "Or maybe tell me why you hate Jake so much."

She stares into her wineglass and doesn't speak, but she looks more sad than angry at his mention this time. Almost on the verge of tears.

"It's late," she says quietly and offers me a weak smile. "Think I'll head home."

———

An hour later, I walk into Cal's duplex, tired as usual but also wired. That's the thing about bar work. It drains you but leaves you keyed up. His door is closed. No noise drifts out. I quietly kick off my shoes and place my purse on the couch. I change into something more comfortable, then head to the kitchen for a snack.

The space is spotless, as usual, which has my attention whipping to the coffee table. I went on a rampage before work, annoyed that I couldn't find any hair elastics. Those things live in the land of lone socks and pens, stolen by elves who love fucking with us humans. I went through all my pockets and drawers, found some missing ones, proud of the mound I collected on Cal's coffee table. But I don't remember putting them away.

The table is clean now, and I wince.

Cal was probably cursing me earlier, grumbling about my hurricane ways. Hopefully the stew I made him was apology enough. Or he didn't eat it. He might have been annoyed with me and can't wait for me to leave his home and isn't sure how to tell me because he's too sweet.

Swallowing through my tightening throat, I open the fridge and blink.

Cal's portion of stew is gone. In its place is a plate of chocolate-covered strawberries. But...they're probably not for me, right? Someone must have given them to him, and these are the leftovers. Maybe Delilah had samples for him to try.

A small piece of paper catches my eye—a folded note beside the plate.

Feeling like a hummingbird is trapped in my belly, I open the note and read.

If you want more of my homemade goodies, I suggest not breeding hair elastics on my coffee table.

Forget a lone hummingbird. A flock of them erupts, fluttering through me. I know for a fact Cal's been working extra-long hours. Townsfolk have gossiped about his busy schedule. Jake has mentioned it a few times, but Cal took the time to make me a treat.

Was he excited for me to see his surprise? Did he make these because he remembered I love chocolate-covered strawberries?

Or my conversation with Larkin has me reading too much into everything.

I lift one from the plate and bite into it slowly, trying to picture the look on Cal's face when dipping them into the chocolate sauce, but I quickly shake my head. He's just being his generous self. Reading into his actions is a dangerous path I don't need to follow. But I should cook again for him tomorrow. Return his thoughtfulness since that's all this is. Two friends leaving each other tasty gifts.

CHAPTER
Seventeen

Callahan

I jiggle my key impatiently in the lock, then shove my door open. I don't take stock of Jolene's unruly mess. I don't remove my boots or unpack the groceries I bought. I march for the fridge and yank on the handle, smiling the second I see another Tupperware container.

It's not normal how excited I was to get home—this burbling anticipation pushing my foot harder onto the gas pedal. It's just food. Jolene is grateful I've let her crash in my place. This is her way of thanking me. I'm getting worked up over a simple kindness.

Still, I snatch the note and read greedily, laughing by the time I get to the end.

*This recipe is from that Middle Eastern cookbook my
dad got. It's one of my favorites.
PS: I was clipping my nails. Super sorry if some landed
in here.*

She's too damn cute for her own good.

I store the note in my shoebox with the others, then shower off the day's grime. As much as I want to scarf down her delicious meal, I eat more slowly, picturing Jo mixing together the cumin, coriander, and cardamom teasing my tongue. It feels special that she used a recipe from the book I sent her dad, that she's sharing something she loves with me.

The second I'm done, I get cooking. Jolene loves mint and chocolate together. At least she used to. I whip up a batch of mint chocolate Rice Krispies treats, grinning as I write her a note.

*Contains healthy, organic ingredients. Not suitable for
those with an allergy to cleanliness. FYI—cleaning is
that thing people do when they pick up after themselves
and put recycling in the recycling bin.*

CHAPTER
Eighteen

Jolene

Callahan should be an illegal substance. His face is a study in brute masculinity. His body belongs on the cover of a men's fitness magazine. His generous heart overflows with kindness, and he loves to challenge me by prodding my competitive nature.

Now he's playing cute food games with me.

Yesterday, I made him a pot of chicken soup, hoping each spoonful felt like a hug. The note I left him read:

I've been told chicken soup is good for the soul. And for curing men of mansplaining.

He retaliated by leaving me a mini pickle sandwich, similar to the snacks I made him after I saw the guy practically naked. His answering note read:

Soup ingested. Not sure it worked. Can't resist reiterating that this is a pickle SNACK. Without the bread, it can't be a sandwich.

Such a smartass.

Today, I'm upping my game. Or, more specifically, my "mansplaining" revenge.

Callahan loves Delilah's homemade cinnamon buns, as he should. They're little pieces of sugary heaven. I buy one of those beauties and take it home, then proceed to eat the entire thing except one tiny bite.

I place the sad leftover in the pretty pink box and affix my note to the outside.

For the guy who makes his roommate feel welcome.

I have no doubt his sweet tooth will jolt awake at the sight of a Sugar and Sips box. He'll be salivating before he opens the lid, only to find my leftover crumbs at the bottom, along with a smaller note.

Guess you're not that guy.

I laugh to myself as I close the box and arrange it neatly in the fridge. Now I just have to plan a fun menu for the two of us to cook tomorrow night for our first joint Monday night meal. And somehow keep my heart from getting carried away with this sweet man.

CHAPTER
Nineteen

Callahan

Jolene has had me chuckling to myself all day. Not sure how she manages it. We haven't spoken in person for five days. But here I am, replaying her cinnamon-bun stunt, probably with a goofy smile on my face as I hop in my truck and press the ignition, checking the time on my phone for the tenth time in the last half hour.

It's Monday. It's been Monday since I woke up this morning. Not a revelation, but tonight's the night Jo and I are finally cooking *together*, as per her suggestion. I swear the clock has been ticking backward. *Not* because I'm excited to get home and move around her in the kitchen as we tease each other in person. I'm simply curious what menu she has planned.

A knock on my window makes me jump. Jake motions at me to roll it down.

I comply and lift the brim of my ball cap. "What's up?"

"I spoke to Jo the other day. Seems like she's been crazy busy with work." He looks down at something in his hands I can't see, then he shoves an envelope through the window. "Can you give this to her for me?"

The idea of reaching for it makes my frown muscles kick in. "Why don't you drop it over yourself?"

"It's nothing big. Just a note asking her out to the drive-in next Monday."

Since Jo admitted she never loved Jake, I've thought hard on my cupid efforts. Analyzed the way she's acted around him, and her reactions when he's been mentioned.

My unfortunate hypothesis: Jo isn't currently open to dating Jake.

I haven't told him as much. Our disappearance hurt Jolene, and their history is apparently rife with miscommunication. It doesn't mean the people they are now wouldn't click. Jake is handsome and kind and would treat her like gold. If he shows her how much he's changed, he might win her over. But that outcome isn't certain, and Jolene's happiness is too important to me to push her into a situation she doesn't want.

As such, I've decided to step away from my match-making endeavors. Jolene will tell Jake she's not interested in her own time or Jake will change her mind and win her over. Either way, I won't be involved. Leaving the outcome to chance has me edgy, but if I push one way or the other, one of the two most important people in my life will be unhappy.

Now Jake is giving me an envelope, shoving me back exactly where I don't want to be—between my brother and my best friend.

I grab the envelope and force a calm smile. "I'll give it to her tonight."

He crosses his arms and fidgets. "She's doing okay?"

"Work seems to be stressing her, but she's good. Not that I've seen her much lately."

I don't mention that we've been leaving each other food and notes, or that we're cooking dinner together tonight. I mean, we're just roommates. If I lived with Javier or Ben, I wouldn't wax on about our dinner menus and evening schedule. Still, the unsaid words ferment in my gut, turning into something unpleasant.

Jake nods and struts to his truck.

I quickly drop the note onto my passenger seat, like holding it any longer would burn my skin.

My drive home is chaotic. Every time I think about walking into my place to find Jo at the counter prepping for our planned meal, I press harder on the gas. When I glance at the note, my stomach twists and I ease my foot off.

Fast. Slow. Heart racing but beating erratically.

By the time I park at the curb, I'm off-balance. I look at the small duplex where I live. The upper half of the cute green home is mine. I can't see through the curtained windows, but Jo's truck is on the street. She's inside organizing or chopping or cooking—doing something for the night she planned for us. Friends doing nice *friend* stuff.

For some idiotic reason, I snatch up my phone and call E.

"You okay?" he asks when he answers.

"What happened to a basic hello?"

"We're Bowers. We only call when something's wrong."

The sad truth of our lives. I massage my brow, attempting to untangle the ten thousand thoughts spinning through my head. "Jake is trying to get back together with Jo," I say, my voice unpleasantly rough.

"Yeah…" E answers slowly.

"And Jo doesn't seem keen on trying again."

"Agreed."

I glance at the envelope on my passenger seat. "Should I tell him she's not interested"—*should I light this letter on fire and dump the ashes in the trash*—"or should I let it all play out?"

"Are you asking for your sake or for Jake's?"

"This has nothing to do with me. I'm worried about Jake and Jo."

He huffs out an annoyed sound. "As long as I've known you, Cal, which is twenty-nine mostly fucked-up years, your greatest and worst trait has been the same."

"Which is what?" I ask the question guardedly, dreading the answer. E is intuitive and sensitive and digs deeper than the rest of our family—sees below our posturing into the heart of our worries. I'm suddenly not so sure calling him was a smart move.

He lets out a long breath. "You, Callahan, put other people before yourself."

I squint at my dashboard. "What's bad about that?"

"You don't take care of yourself."

"Sure I do. Making people happy makes me happy."

"Are you really happy, though?"

I look at the windows of my home again, and the strangest urge to bust through the door strikes. To run up the stairs and check that Jo is actually inside.

"This call isn't helping," I say, my tone harder than usual. "But I appreciate the input," I add quickly. "It's always nice to talk."

I never end conversations with my family on a bad note. Life is too unpredictable to live with regrets. Which, I guess, answers my question. I need to do as Jake requested and give Jolene his letter. Otherwise I might live another twelve years, worrying my involvement in their relationship wrecked their chance at love.

I tuck Jake's envelope into my back pocket and get out of my truck. I jog up my stairs, mentally preparing myself for Jo's usual chaotic war zone. When I open the door, my jaw nearly hits the floor.

Clean.

My home is so startlingly clean I could serve the president a five-course dinner on my hardwood floor. Jolene is in the kitchen, paying me no mind, soft jazz tunes playing as she grabs ingredients from the fridge.

"I must've walked into the wrong duplex," I say, impressed by the sparse shoe collection neatly lined by the door.

"Right?" She spins and plants her hand on her hip. "Something had to be done. I live with such a *slob*. Had to clean up after the guy."

I raise an eyebrow, trying not to laugh. "A slob?"

"You should see the way he leaves the bathroom." She shudders. "Grooming products everywhere."

"Sounds like he's a horrible roommate."

She gives a dramatic eye roll. "The worst."

The worst is how cute she is when she's being cheeky. "I bet he leaves water glasses all over the place too, tosses his underwear on the couch. Hasn't figured out where the recycling is yet."

She cringes. "He's not *that* bad."

"Oh, he is. He even leaves small bites of cinnamon rolls in the fridge."

"Heathen," she says, miming her horror.

"Agreed. And..." I glance at her bedroom door, which is closed. If I know Jolene, the madness from our shared living area has exploded in there. "I wonder if all parts of my home are tidied," I say as I strut for her door.

She pulls some impressive sprinting move and gets to the door before me. She swings her arms out, barricading entry. "You don't have permission to enter my room."

"Is there something wrong with your room?"

"Nope. No. Nothing."

"So it's as tidy as the living area?"

Her lips twitch. "It's incredibly tidy."

I should walk away. Let Jo have this moment. She *did* clean our shared space. She planned a dinner for us to cook, but messing with her is too much fun. I know exactly how to get her to move.

I twist my face into a horrified expression and shout, "Mouse!"

She squeaks and flings herself onto the couch, scanning the floor frantically. "Where?"

"Nowhere," I say, grinning.

I open her bedroom door and laugh. I should be horrified at the sight. The shoes normally cluttering the entryway are scattered on her floor, and the rest of the space looks like a teenager tossed their dirty laundry willy-nilly, but the space is so Jo.

"I can't believe I fell for that." She punches lightly at my back. "Move, you big oaf. That area is private."

Amused, I turn and catch her wrist before she smacks me again. "Guess you still have a fear of mice."

She scrunches her nose and studies the floor. "Those beady eyes are evil."

"But you're fine with snakes and beetles and bugs."

"Snakes and beetles and bugs are cool."

Chuckling, I release her hand. "I'll never understand you."

"The feeling is mutual," she says, no longer sounding cheeky or afraid. Her voice has a weight to it I can't parse. "Ready to cook?" she adds, reverting to upbeat.

I've been pathetically ready all day. "Are we making burgers?"

She curls her lip. "Ground meat is a mystery concoction of mashed eyeballs, lips, and ass. We're making fish tacos."

Her dislike of burgers is as I remembered, yet Jake seems to think she loves them. The awareness has me second-guessing giving her his letter, but I told Jake I'd pass it along. Best to do it after dinner, though, once we've had a chance to relax from our days. "Tacos sound great. One of my favorite food groups."

I take a quick shower, even though showering since living

with Jo is anything but simple. The feminine smells are mostly to blame. What man wouldn't take a minute to pop open her pink shampoo bottle and breathe in the spring scent? Aromatherapy is a thing, and I swear the sweet, flowery notes kind of calm me. At least I thought ahead and brought in a clean T-shirt and sweats. There's no need to dart past Jo in nothing but a towel.

Hair still wet, but feeling more human, I join Jo in the kitchen and survey the veggies on the counter. "Everything looks like it was cut by one of those infomercial kitchen gadgets."

She holds up her chef knife. "Because I'm exceptional with one of these. How was work this week?"

"We're making solid progress on the Rosens' kitchen. Hit a snag with one of the measurements, but I was able to fix it. And you should see the Liangs' puppy. Cutest damn thing." I smile, picturing those huge floppy ears. "Chases me around while I try to build their fence. And the Elroy deck is in the early stages but coming along nicely."

She tilts her head. "You love what you do."

I think about why I started construction—Jake pushing me to vent my anger and frustration through manual labor. But that's not why I still do it. "I like how tangible construction is. Real materials building real things. I get satisfaction with the end result and how happy people are with my work. Feels good to make a difference in a person's life, even if it's building a deck for family barbecues. And I get to use numbers and my planning skills."

"I love that for you."

I duck my head, more affected by the sentiment than feels warranted. I shift my focus to our food. "What do you need me doing, chef?"

She points her knife to an unlabeled jar. "The flour needs a tablespoon of my secret spice mix, then you can batter and fry the fish. Also," she says, pinning me with a serious look, "as happy as I am that you love your work, you're still doing too much."

I lift the spice jar and give it a sniff, ignoring her comment. "I smell cumin and something else I can't pinpoint."

"Way to dodge the topic, and don't ask what's in the mix. The recipe was my aunt's. It goes to the grave with me."

"I'm sure she'd love that you're using it, and that you're doing a great job with the bar."

She slumps slightly. "Can we not talk about the bar? I'm enjoying having a night off."

"Jo." I gently take her shoulders and turn her toward me. "What's going on with work? Something's clearly upsetting you."

She places her knife on the counter and stares at it a moment. "It's not what I thought it would be. Or it is, and *I'm* not what I thought I would be? Day revenues haven't been great, but I'm doing well enough financially. My aunt would be thrilled to see me running this business she created, but..."

"But?" I prod when she doesn't go on.

She shrugs a shoulder. "I don't know. I think I'm just having a bad run lately. Staffing issues keep popping up. Equipment is breaking all the time—like our fridge a few days ago. Javier's been too busy to fix it, so we're using ice buckets for beer, lugging that back and forth from the chest freezer in the basement. Some days I seriously dread walking in the front door." She gives another defeated shrug. "It's just exhausting at times, but I really am lucky to have it. It's all good."

No, it's not. Jolene sounds stuck. "The night you moved in, you mentioned that you live your life scared these days. That the traumas and setbacks you've dealt with have left you afraid to rock the boat. Is that part of the reason you've stayed with the bar until now? You're scared to strike out on your own and fail?"

"Jeez. Way to make me sound embarrassingly pathetic."

I cross my arms and stand so close to her she has to crank her neck back to look up at me. "Jolene Cynthia Daniels, you're as far from pathetic as a person gets. You're the girl who picked up snakes with your bare hands and pranked Lennon by making orange juice with Kraft powdered cheese just to watch him drop the cup and retch."

She laughs so hard, she tips her head into my chest. "I did do that, didn't I?"

I run my hand down her back, laughing with her. "You also walked up to Lane Ternent when he said rude things about Delilah and told him the only way he'd get laid is if he crawled up a chicken's butt and waited."

She laughs harder, the two of us shaking until we're wiping tears from our eyes.

"Lane was an asshole and deserved it," she says as she catches her breath.

"He was, although the mooning prank was satisfying."

Abruptly, her face sobers. "Prank? I thought his shorts just got caught on his bike."

I scratch the back of my neck, wincing. "I maybe put glue on his bicycle seat for knocking your books to the ground?"

"But we'd only just met back then. Why would you do that?"

The same reason I do most things. "I didn't like that you were upset."

She blinks at me, as though seeing my face clearly for the first time. "Are there other things you've done for me I don't know about?"

About a hundred and one over the past twenty-two years. "Nope."

She scrutinizes me so long I feel antsy, then she sighs. "All that stuff you mentioned was things I did when I was younger. That's not who I am now."

"Bullshit."

"Not bullshit."

"*Total* bullshit," I say with more force. "You cared for your aunt when she was sick, going there every day, no matter how busy you were. You're a boss who holds a monthly prank contest to make work fun for your staff. When customers are too drunk, you don't make a scene and throw them out. You escort them outside, cracking jokes, so it looks like you're just hanging out. I also heard you once told a table of bikers to quit making your server uncomfortable with their come-ons. So yeah, you're still smart and strong and ballsy and hilarious, and goddamn gorgeous. You're the type of woman men look at and think, *I'm not good enough for her.* So don't you dare go thinking you're any less for having fears or insecurities."

And...shit.

I'm breathing hard, unsure how those truths tumbled out.

Jo's chest is mimicking mine, rising and falling deeply, her eyes turning into twin pools of...wonder? Confusion? *Affection?* "How do you know about me taking care of my aunt and that other work stuff?"

Too much. I said too damn much. "Windfall is the size of an ant farm. Gossip is this town's gospel." I shuffle back a step, then two, my face overheating with each twitchy move. "Forgot about a call I need to make for work. I'll be back in a sec."

I strut for my room and shut my door. Place my head on the wood and try to remember how to breathe, while I berate myself for being so goddamn obvious.

I may as well have blurted that I was in love with her before WITSEC and that I think about her way too much now—ask about her, watch out for her, work to make her life better.

A fact I can't seem to change.

I grab my phone from my dresser and call Javier.

"Cal," he says in greeting. "What's up?"

"Jolene's fridge at the Barrel is broken. Can you get over there tomorrow to fix it?"

"Ah, shit. She called about that, but I'm in the weeds. Hoping I can get out there Friday or next week."

Which would leave Jolene frustrated and stressed for at least another four days, likely more. "Do you still need help remodeling your bathroom?"

"It looks like something from the set of *That '70s Show*. Simone complains about it whenever she stays over."

"I can start tomorrow—do two nights a week in the evenings with you, and Sundays instead of soccer. Get it done in a month or two, depending on the work."

"Dude, that would be awesome."

"Under one condition."

He laughs. "I'll shuffle some stuff around, get to Jo's bar tomorrow."

My shoulders drop a fraction. "Don't tell her I called you."

His lingering pause has my shoulders hitching back up. "You don't want her to know she has a guardian angel?"

"Depends. Do you want your new girlfriend to know that you came in your jeans the first time you tried to have sex?"

"Harsh, man," he says, more amused than irritated. "Super harsh."

"I believe we have a deal, then."

It's a short-term fix. I think Jo would be happier if she didn't have the pressure of the bar—running it the way her aunt wanted, feeling tied to it out of guilt. Without that shackle, she might push herself outside of her comfort zone, challenge herself to do something she loves more. I'll have to think on how to help extricate her from the Barrel, without her feeling like she's failed her aunt. Maybe there's a loophole in her lease agreement I can use.

For now, I need to get back into my kitchen, where I won't blurt more truths Jolene shouldn't know.

CHAPTER
Twenty

Jolene

Keeping my eyes on Cal's closed door, I snatch up my phone and dial Larkin's number. I'm not sure she'll be home. Monday is her "personal" day. The one day a week she can't work and falls off the grid, but I'm on the verge of freaking out.

"Hey, Jo," she answers, sounding tired and kind of sad. Gunshots blast in the background. Hopefully it's her TV. "You're not at work on your day off, are you?"

"God, no." Six days a week is already too much. "I'm at home, cooking dinner with Cal, and..." I glance at his closed door.

"And?"

"I think he maybe likes me the way I like him," I whisper. Honestly. Could I sound more like a lovestruck teen passing notes?

"Wow. Okay. An opening like that takes precedence over watching Jason Statham blow things up." Another flurry of gunshots echoes, followed by an explosion that quickly diminishes. "You have my undivided attention and better not skimp on the juicy parts. Also, I told you so."

She definitely did. "He said stuff about me, Lark."

"Define stuff."

"Really nice stuff. And he did this thing for me when we were kids—"

"Let me stop you there, Jo. Remember when I turned off a great action movie in exchange for juicy gossip? Descriptions like *stuff* and *thing* don't cut it."

I muffle an unhinged laugh. I glance back at Cal's door. It's still closed. My pulse is punching faster than the bullet spray in her movie.

I lower my voice and press my hand over my vibrating chest. "He pulled a mooning prank on a kid when we first met. Apparently, he orchestrated that scene to avenge my honor. I asked if he'd done other things like that for me over the years. He said no, but I know Cal. I'm pretty sure he was lying."

She *hmmmm*s for a few beats. "I'd have to agree. He seems like the sneaky type."

"He does?"

"No one's that nice all the time. Guys that hot and sweet usually have a dark side."

Jaded—that's the best way to describe Larkin when guys come up. She's ignored my prodding to date. She barely goes out at all, except for today—the Mondays she can't work. Tuesdays, she always seems super down, kind of like how she sounded when she answered the phone. I feel badly for making this call all about me. "How was your day today?"

She sighs. "Long and hard."

"I'm here if you want to talk about it."

"It's just family stuff."

Larkin continues to be a tough nut to crack, but I don't push. Eventually, I hope she'll open up to me about Mondays and her past when she's ready.

"Back to Cal," she says, "what else did his fine self say?"

"He seems to be keeping tabs on me at work," I whisper as I walk a few paces farther from his closed door. "Like, he knows about my routine when customers need to be cut off and that biker incident the other day. Or maybe that's just Windfall's gossip river flowing in his direction."

"Or he's keeping tabs on you because he can't stop thinking about you."

The soft spots on my heart contract. Those tender places have been there for twelve years, never fully healed from Cal's disappearance. They've worsened lately. Unbearable pressure when we're close and I imagine us as more and realize it will never happen. But: *You're the type of woman men look at and think, I'm not good enough for her.*

"Lark," I whisper hesitantly.

"Yeah?"

"He called me *gorgeous*. Said I was funny and strong and insinuated I'm too good for him."

Her gusty breath fills our silence. "I take back what I said. Cal is clearly the exception to the rule. He's hot and sweet *and* doesn't have a dark side. That man has it bad for you."

"Or he was just being kind. I was frustrated when he said it. He could've been trying to lift my mood."

"Sure, but you two have been doling out some serious foreplay this week."

"I haven't seen him all week."

"*The food*, Jo. The cute notes. That's Seduction 101."

Flutters spiral through my belly at the reminder. Chocolate-covered strawberries. Rice Krispies squares. Sweet treats a boyfriend might leave, but our provocative notes were plain fun. "The food stuff wasn't seduction. That was just us being us."

"If you say so, but what he said tonight—is that the kind of thing he's said in the past? Calling you gorgeous and the other sweet compliments? Because that sounds like crushing territory.

But you know Cal better than anyone. Did it *feel* like he was humoring you?"

For better or for worse, I do know the ins and outs of Callahan Bower. His fear of ants is adorably hilarious. *They're just so tiny,* he used to say. *They can crawl in anywhere.* He hates the sound of cutlery scraping a dinner plate. He failed his driver's license test the first time he took it and didn't tell anyone but me. He overheats easily, even when the temperature's not swelteringly hot. He has a sexy birthmark on his lower back, just above his underwear line.

I have a catalogue of Callahan Knowledge, filed and saved and listed in categories.

Things Callahan Loves.

Things Callahan Hates.

Things Callahan Shared Only with Me.

Things about Callahan I Wish I Didn't Know.

The last category is the worst. It's filed in my bruised heart— the in-between place where secret feelings get stuck, bound by history and truths never shared.

"No," I say so quietly I have to repeat the word. "No, he's never said such intimate things to me before. And the way he spoke was so intense, like he was purging himself of secrets. I think he has feelings for me, but what if I'm wrong?"

"Tests."

"What?"

"Run tests. Push his limits. Flirt more openly and see how he reacts."

Right. Yeah. Killer idea. Unleashing the feelings I keep contained won't bite me in the butt. The other day, I actually stuck my face in his freaking pillow to steal an inhale of the man's scent. But honestly, he smells so good. A new, spicy smell —woodsy and Mountain Manly—and it's everywhere in his home. One whiff kicks my Cal dopamine addiction into overdrive.

"Flirting overtly could backfire," I say. "I'm already so preoccupied with him. If I'm wrong, it could ruin our friendship. There's no way I could handle that."

"Then be subtle about it. Friends flirt all the time. Try some covert tests, which I'm sure he'll pass. Then you can finally jump his bones and ride him into the sunset."

I snort and cover my mouth with my hand. I cannot handle that visual right now. Not when Callahan is saying romantic things about me. Fact is, it's never just been about attraction with Cal. I love the man he is—sweet, considerate, funny. I like the woman I am around him—honest, witty, and at ease. I've always been my best self with him, while secretly wishing I'd one day lie on his chest knowing he was mine to hold.

Now I'm dying to know how his massive body would feel pressing me into the mattress, those heavy thighs pushing between mine, his work-roughened hands dragging over my hips as he—

"Do you need a minute?" Cal says.

Um. *Yeah.* More like fifty. Or an ice bucket dumped over my head.

Cal is standing by his open door, looking calm and collected. I'm a minute from grabbing my vibrator to relieve this unrelenting ache.

"Talk to you later," I tell Larkin and try to act cool.

I cross my arms and strike an unnatural hip-out pose. Cal squints at me. I try to tame my lascivious thoughts and quit picturing all that maleness under his clothes. *Easy peasy, lemon squeezy.* I'm certainly not letting my wanton gaze travel down his thin T-shirt to the sweatpants that sit *just so* on his narrow hips. Nope.

I'm now Scientist Jolene doing science stuff. I'm about to take Larkin's potentially dangerous advice and test if Callahan Bower also has a dopamine addiction to me.

CHAPTER
Twenty~One

Callahan

Jolene is acting weird. We've been moving around each other in my small kitchen, cooking together, and she's been clumsy. A trait I don't associate with Jo. Every so often, she stumbles over her feet and grabs my biceps, which flex in response. She whispers small *sorry*s, while I have to physically restrain myself from locking my arm around her waist and pulling her closer.

There's only one reason she's this off-kilter—my word vomit earlier made her uncomfortable. And I don't have a rewind button.

"Is it possible to do this without my fingers turning into a gluey mess?" I drop the last piece of fish into the hot oil, keeping my hands clear of Jo.

"It is," she says as she turns the tap on for me. "But it takes actual skill."

Always a ballbuster, but this is our comfort zone. Barbed banter. Friendly bickering. Instead of sticking my hands under the water to get clean, I wipe them on her shoulders.

"Hey!" She jumps back, sputtering out a laugh. "What was that for?"

"Guess I clean my hands as well as I batter fish."

She digs a spoonful of avocado crema out of her dish and angles it like a slingshot. "Any last words?"

"Fish," I say, holding up my hands in surrender. "You need to flip the fish, and I'm not sure I'd forgive you for wasting that crema."

She looks at her spoon with pride. "It is pretty epic, but I need a second opinion."

"Happy to be your guinea pig." I turn to wash my hands. By the time I swivel back, the fish is flipped and she's holding out a spoonful of crema for me. I reach to grab the utensil, but she holds the spoon higher, like she wants to feed me herself.

Swallowing is suddenly an effort.

I dip my head for a taste, unable to tear my eyes from hers as she slips the spoon past my lips.

"Good?" she asks, breathy.

I should focus on the avocado and lime lighting up my taste buds, but all I picture is her finger sliding inside my mouth instead of the spoon, a swirl of my tongue as I suck on her skin and murmur *so fucking good*.

Her eyes flare, like she knows exactly what I'm imagining. Like she planned to create this moment of intimacy. Does she *know* she's driving me mad?

"Needs more heat," I say roughly, pulling back.

She licks her lips while eyeing my mouth. "I can do heat."

I'm not sure either of us is still talking about the food. She spins away from me, moving deftly. She checks the frying fish, adds hot sauce to the crema, then takes the bowl to the table, as though I imagined the innuendo in our exchange.

"Mind taking out the fish while I put on a clean shirt?" she asks, heading toward her room.

"Already on it." I remove the golden fillets and give my head a hard shake.

Even if Jolene isn't into Jake, my attraction to her is moot. I wouldn't hit on a woman a friend wanted, let alone betray one of my brothers. There's no point analyzing her actions or mine.

She returns still wearing her jean shorts, but her new white T-shirt is fitted and shorter, revealing a tease of smooth abdomen. I clench my jaw.

She leans against the fridge, hands tucked in her front pockets. "Thanks for cooking with me tonight."

"I was looking forward to it all day," I admit, feeling my face heat. "Any word from your landlord on when your apartment will be ready?"

"Might be another month. The workers he hired can only fit the job in when they have lulls."

"Is that why you cleaned my place?" I side-eye her and raise my eyebrows. Having this impossible situation drag on isn't ideal, but I'm still happier knowing Jo has somewhere comfortable to stay. "You're trying to ingratiate yourself to me?"

She bows dramatically. "Guilty as charged."

More relaxed around each other, we work in tandem, grabbing plates, taco shells, slaw, napkins, while reminiscing about an actual food fight we had growing up—squirting each other with ketchup and mustard at one of her aunt's barbecues. We eat. We laugh. We talk about how much our lives have changed and the stories we'll never forget. My unwelcome attraction aside, I honestly don't remember the last time I've felt so content in someone else's company. Jokes mixed with easy conversation. History that creates deeper comfort.

And we make good food together.

"That was fantastic," I say, finishing my last bite. "Best fish tacos I've ever had."

Jo basks in my compliment. "Better than Casero in Ruby Grove?"

"Their fish batter wasn't this crispy, which is obviously my cooking prowess."

"Or it's the recipe," she says with a wink and knocks her foot into mine under the table.

She doesn't pull her foot away. Instead, she lets her knee fall out and hit mine, studying me with a curious expression, while I try to keep my body's reaction in check.

"I'm on cleanup duty," I blurt as I stand. Movement is good. Blood circulation.

"*We're* on cleanup duty. But do you mind if we do it later?" she asks hesitantly.

"You have something else planned?"

She fiddles with her napkin. "It's my one night off, and it's nice out. I was thinking of going for a walk."

Disappointment settles in my gut, which is ridiculous. This isn't a date. Jolene can do whatever she wants, even if it doesn't involve me. *Especially* if it doesn't involve me.

"Of course you should go. Gotta make the most of your free time. I'll clean without you." I lean down to pick up her plate.

She puts her hand on my wrist. "*With you*, Cal. I'd love to go for a walk with you."

My stomach spins faster than my circular saw, fuzzing up my brain. "Sure. Walk sounds good."

———

We leave as my neighbor walks up the steps to the lower half of our duplex. Anika is wearing her nursing scrubs and looks as tired as I often feel. "Long shift?" I ask her.

"Long but good. I have a date with a glass of wine and frozen pizza to look forward to. And thanks for fixing my cupboard for me. Works like a charm now."

"Thanks for paying me in homemade salsa. Stuff is addictive."

With a kind goodnight to Anika, Jo and I head out at a leisurely pace, sharing the sidewalk on this warm May evening. The sky is clear and still light. The huge hickories flash their foliage as we pass the Victorian-style homes standing pretty and proud.

Joan Christie waves as she gathers her mail. Two houses down, little Meryl and her twin brother, Rhys, chase each other around their front yard.

"Cal!" Avett calls from his door. He's an old friend of E's and a great neighbor, who's made a name for himself as a competent vet. "Thanks for fixing the back door. Huge help."

I salute him. "Thanks for helping when I moved in."

"Come for dinner soon."

"Sure," I say, relaxing into my stride.

"What's with the big smile?" Jo asks.

I chuckle, not realizing I have a lazy grin on my face. "It's this place. How much I missed Windfall."

"Which part did you miss most?"

"The feeling here, I think. Houston is huge and packed with people, and I had my family and work, but I always felt alone there. Here..." I try to parse the contentment this town brings me, the way it settles my soul. "I'm not sure how to describe it."

"Like you're wrapped up in goodness? Like you're living in a big hug? Like you have a place where you belong?"

"Yeah," I say, sneaking a look at her tender expression. "That's exactly it." I can always count on Jo to put my feelings into words. "Are you volunteering to help with the Yard Goat Gallery's reopening?"

"Of course. Will your brothers be there again?"

I nod. "Javier and his girlfriend too. Ben, obviously, and probably half the town. Guess that's the community hug you were talking about?"

"Everyone knows your business here, but they go out of their way to help when needed."

At least this part of my life is improving. No more cartel hit men lording threats over my family. No more hiding and fake names. Lots of work to keep me busy and employed.

"Did you ever consider leaving town?" I ask.

"Never. I mean, I'd like to travel more one day. Visit Mexico, but not the resorts and touristy areas. The smaller towns. Somewhere with markets I can explore." She gazes longingly at the sky, like photos of her imagined travels are displayed above us. "I'd love to learn more about the food and culture."

"Everything comes back to food for you."

"Unexpected, right? But Windfall is my home—the people and mountains and charm. I feel so lucky to have grown up here."

I nod, understanding exactly what she means, but there's a pull to brush my hand against hers. To link our fingers. Stroll hand in hand like a couple on this beautiful night.

"I won't be able to make it to soccer for a bit," I say, remembering my call with Javier—bartering to get Jo's bar fridge fixed. "A work commitment came up. Hopefully I'll be back at it again soon."

Jolene makes a huffy sound as she walks. Her hand *does* brush this time, and she doesn't pull away. I let our fingers touch again, because I'm clearly losing my mind.

Slowly, she fits her small hand into mine and gives it a squeeze. "Is it because I wiped the grass with your ass last game?"

I bark out a laugh. "Your humility is astounding."

"It's strategy. Bragging gets into my opponents' heads."

Her fingers threaded through mine have the same effect. "If that's the strategy, you're a shoo-in for MVP."

"I hope there's a trophy."

"I'll make sure the inscription reads: In commemoration of the poorest winner."

She elbows my side playfully, then slows her stride. "Did you not enjoy the game?"

"No, no." I stop and face her, unable to release her hand. "Like I said at the bar, I loved the game. Can't remember the last time I've had that much fun."

"Then why are you working when you could be playing?"

Because Jolene's happiness comes before my own.

I think ahead, my little white lie developing as I reply. "I made a promise to someone before you invited me, didn't realize the timing would conflict. Hopefully it won't be for too long, and I can hop back in."

"Please tell me you're at least planning to go to the Spring Fair in a couple weeks. Word has it Mrs. Moon's new secret pie recipe will blow Aaron Rothman's out of the water. And he does *not* take losing well."

Gotta love the dramatics in this town. "I'll do my best, but it depends on work."

She gives her head a shake. "It's not good for you."

"What isn't?"

"Working too much. I see how tired you are, Cal. How run-down. I'm worried about you."

Now she sounds like Jake, ragging on me to slow down. Unfortunately, slow isn't a speed I understand. "I'm good, but I appreciate you thinking about me."

She takes a step closer. Drags her thumb down the back of my hand, sending a shiver up my spine. "I think about you a lot."

Well...*hell.*

Not only does a snap of heat jolt up my thighs, but my heart has decided to test how hard it can beat against my chest, and the primal man in me *wants.*

I want to lean over Jolene, sift my fingers through her soft brown hair, tilt her lips up to mine. Finally kiss this woman who's been a fixture in my life for twenty-two years, no matter how far I've been from her. I want to taste those words on her tongue—*I think about you a lot.* Test them for their truth and share mine—*I think about you always.*

I want to give her so much pleasure she shakes for days. I want to share more walks with her, cook with her, show up at her bar and help out just to make her life easier, lie in bed with her for hours talking, our legs tangled, until our eyelids drag us into sleep.

I *want* to use that fucking vibrator on her and watch her body bloom as she cries out my name, and I'm starting to think she maybe wants me too. Real this time, not imagined. Her little flirtations tonight. Her worry for me. The way she's holding my hand so damn tight. And I want that too—her heart and every inch of her soul, because this clearly isn't just attraction for me, as I've hoped and wished. She's everything I want...and everything I can't have.

A familiar surge of guilt builds in my chest, spreading at an alarming rate. I drop Jo's hand and reach into my back pocket for the letter I damn near forgot about. "This is for you."

Tentatively, she takes Jake's envelope. Her eyes flick up to mine, and *fuck.* The look on her face nearly flattens me—hope, affection, and a hint of longing...because there's no writing on the envelope. She probably thinks this letter is from me. The heat under her intense expression is the look of a woman who's been harboring strong feelings for a man.

My fingers twitch to yank that note back. To tell Jake that Jolene isn't interested, but she's opening the flap, sneaking me a shy smile as she goes.

I think my ribs just spontaneously cracked.

She opens the note and frowns. Her eyes scan the page. There's no missing her flattening lips and the slump in her posture. "You're giving me a note from Jake."

"He gave it to me at work today, asked me to pass it along."

She stares at the letter. Hard. Then she struts ahead, so fast I have to jog to catch up with her.

"He still has feelings for you," I force out, stating the obvious.

"No, he doesn't."

"I know my brother, Jo. He wants you back." There's no denying those facts, or how much I hate relaying them to her. Fucking *despise* this conversation and how hot and frustrated I feel.

She huffs out an impatient noise. "Jake wants me because he wants to reclaim his past. Put everything back the way it was, but so much time has passed. He doesn't even know me now."

"And you don't know him. He's not the cocky guy who walked a golden path when we were younger. He knows hardship now—what it's like to lose everything. He's one of the best people I know. A thoughtful guy who'd lay down his life for those he loves. Maybe you should give him a chance."

She stops abruptly. "Is that what you want? For me to go out with your brother?"

Her tone is rock hard, her eyes narrowed and searching. The beauty mark on her cheek is as sexy as ever, but her full lips are pressed into an angry line.

I'm angry too. Furious at the situation, but my family has been to hell and back. My brothers are everything to me, which means there's only one possible answer to her horrible question. "I want my brother to have the happiness he deserves. If he wants you, then yes, seeing you two together would make me happy. As long as it's what you want."

She stares at me a beat, her chin trembling ever so slightly. A hot poker stabs at my gut.

She firms her jaw and hits a quick stride. "Jake's note says he wants to take me to a drive-in movie. I hate the drive-in."

"So why does he think you love it?"

"Because I was so insecure when we dated."

I rub my brow, confused and irritable. "You said that a bit ago—that you were insecure in high school, but all I ever saw was a confident girl who grew out of her awkwardness. You made friends with everyone."

"By being fake, Cal. If girls wanted to sit around and talk about makeup and clothes, which bored me to tears, I'd play along to fit in. If someone offered me a smoke, I'd do it, even though I hated smoking. That first year of high school, without you there, I was on the verge of tears most days. So, I took our Cool List to heart, like a fucking wild animal who adapts to survive, and that out-of-touch feeling didn't go away for a long time."

"I wish I'd known." Wish I'd been there for her when she needed me.

"Yeah, well." Her posture stiffens. "You were different in high school too—a foot taller, making friends, flirting with all the girls."

"What was I supposed to do? A few weeks into my freshman year, you kept ditching me to spend time with Blake Offerman." Football player. Bigger than me and infuriatingly good-looking.

"Because you told me you were hot for Angela Bernardini, never mind what the girls in the locker room said about you."

I lost my virginity to Angela Bernardini in a basement bathroom with little fanfare and tequila on our breaths. I barely remember that night, let alone what lies traveled along Windfall's gossip train, but I know exactly why I pursued Angela. "You were into Blake before I ever asked Angela out. I had to make new friends and survive socially, just like you."

She crumples Jake's note into a ball, strutting faster. "It doesn't matter. None of this matters. Fact is, Jake doesn't know me now, and he didn't know me back then. Anything he liked, I pretended to love. Drive-ins. His favorite foods, like ground beef everything. R&B music. I became one of those girls who takes on the personality of a guy, because I thought that's what I needed to do to be liked. And you went away to school, only came home on weekends. I was feeling out of sorts and lonely. I thought being with Jake would fill that void, and it did for a bit. I cared about him a lot, but it was never true love for me. In the end, we weren't compatible."

We're practically speed walking now, Jolene setting the pace, me hustling to keep up, physically and mentally.

I had no idea she struggled socially in high school until recently. I certainly didn't know she put on airs with Jake, played a role to please him. And she's rewriting our history.

If Jolene dated Blake Offerman because I talked about Angela, then she was jealous in high school. As was I—of every guy she glanced at. Of every crush she had. But we were both insecure teenagers and didn't do anything about our feelings. Now we're adults, barely scratching the surface of our misunderstandings, but my brother wants his ex-girlfriend back.

Jo stops walking and closes her eyes on an exhale. "I think I'd like to finish this walk on my own, if you don't mind."

"Sure," I murmur, my aggravation replaced by a helplessness that weighs me down. I shove my hands into my pockets, roll a loose thread through my fingers. "I'll clean up from dinner. Thanks for planning such a great meal." I force myself to turn away from her, but I swivel back. "Jo?"

"Yeah?" Her brow is lifted, her expression sad but also hopeful.

"I'm sorry." For being too scared as a teen to ask her out. For not being able to pursue her now. Even thinking about holding her hand before has me feeling like a traitor to my brother. "I won't push about Jake again. I'll tell him you're not interested."

"Please don't talk to him about me. I'll tell him myself."

I nod and work my jaw, wanting to say something else. The perfect words to erase this strain between us. A magic phrase to transport us back to joking about her messy bedroom or her pickle "sandwiches," no impossible feelings between us.

At a loss, I turn and walk toward my place, refusing to glance over my shoulder, but I swear I feel Jo's eyes on me as my heart tries to race back to her.

CHAPTER
Twenty-Two

Callahan

I knock out my last chest presses on the gym bench, grunting through the pain. It takes all my strength to heave the weighted bar to its stand, another few deep breaths before I can lift myself to sitting.

The twenty-four-hour gym is mostly empty this early on a Sunday. Exactly how I like it. Quiet time to push my body and blank my mind, but the second my pulse ebbs, this week's torturous mantra fills my head—*traitor, traitor, traitor.* Followed succinctly by *Jolene, Jolene, I wish you were mine, Jolene.*

Pretty sure there's a song like that.

I grab my towel and gym bag, shower and change into my work T-shirt and jeans, then head to Lennon's property. I park at his old barn. Practically leap from my truck and jog inside. Mom's partially finished bookcase is waiting where I left it. A gift I'm thrilled to work on for her, and a desperately needed outlet for me.

I get to work right away, cutting the plugs for the screw

holes, sawing any overhangs. I methodically sand the shelves. Steady motion and smooth strokes, only pausing to chug water and wipe the sweat dripping into my eyes.

My phone chimes, notifying me that this portion of my jam-packed morning is done. If I hadn't bartered with Javier to help renovate his bathroom, I'd be gearing up for a fun soccer match. But helping Jo's business is worth it. Especially when playing sports with her would only exacerbate my pathetic pining.

Bleary-eyed from today's heat and exercise, I leave Lennon's property, glancing briefly at his rural home. He's probably still in bed at this hour, cuddled up with Maggie, but there's a blanket and two empty wineglasses on his porch. Remnants of their evening last night, likely.

Envy slams into me.

I'm so damn happy for him. For all my brothers who are as in love as I hoped they'd be, but I'm starting to realize my heart is so full of Jo—adventurer Jo, tree house Jo, late-night-talk Jo, messy-in-my-home Jo, cooking-for-each-other Jo—I'm not sure there's room for anyone else. In time, I'll grow out of these intense feelings. At least, I better fucking grow out of them.

Unfortunately, that growth won't happen while she's living in my house. And until I help her navigate the larger issue she's having with the bar.

Maybe this will be the last thing I do for her. Help her climb out of the rut she's in, then step back. Stay occasional friends. Make room for another woman in my thoughts and heart.

I park on Javier's street and text Sandra, who's been looking into the lease at Jo's bar for me.

> Me: Did your contact at the lawyer's office come through?

As usual, dots bounce with an immediate reply.

> Sandra: Reading her file as we text.

Me: And? Any loopholes in her lease?

Sandra: She doesn't have a lease.

I frown at her message, wondering if that was an autocorrected reply.

Me: What do you mean?

Sandra: It's the opposite of having one.

I shake my head. As clever and discreet as Sandra is, she makes me work for her intel.

Me: Specifics, please.

Sandra: Her lease ran out. She's friends with her landlady. They have a lady's agreement now.

Me: What's a lady's agreement?

Sandra: The same thing as a gentleman's agreement, but with ladies.

I chuckle. Of course it is.

Me: Verbal and nonbinding?

Sandra: Jolene can close the bar any time she wants, no lease repercussions.

An unlikely outcome. From what I've sensed about Jo, guilt and obligation would trump her need to strike out on her own. She confessed she dreads going into work, then quickly covered the admission with a defeated *it's all good*. For her to make real change in her life—challenge herself, find a career she enjoys instead of one she feels stuck in—she might need a bigger push.

> Me: With the lady's agreement, if the building is sold, would the new owner be able to evict her and take over the space?

> Sandra: Yes.

I tap my thumb on my phone, spinning through that possibility. I'd have to find a buyer. Someone who wants to open their own business. Not too difficult, but I can't put those wheels in motion unless I'm one hundred percent sure Jolene wants out of the bar but is too loyal to her late aunt to make the move.

Letting those thoughts ruminate, I drag my tired ass out of my truck and walk up to Javier's new home. There's bathroom remodeling to be done and my end of a deal to uphold.

The second Javier opens his front door, his eyes widen. "You look like hell."

"Do you use charming lines like that on your girlfriend?"

"Do you think I'm an idiot? But seriously, man. You look like you haven't slept in a week."

More like the six days since my heated exchange with Jo on our after-dinner walk. We haven't seen each other since that night. Neither of us has left food and cute notes in the fridge either. Absence that seems to scream loudly when I walk in my door.

Forcing a smile, I slap Javier's arm and push into his new house. "I've been busy with work and extra projects, including the deal I made with a guy who can't remodel his bathroom on his own."

"I assumed a pretty brunette with a wicked sense of humor was to blame."

I catch my boot on the floor and stumble, righting myself quickly. "Nope."

Javier chuckles behind me. "Sure, friend. We'll go with *nope*."

I'm not sure when I lost the ability to camouflage my true feelings with placid smiles and congenial words. A shortcoming that'll bite me in the ass next time I see Jo, or if Jake ever brings her up with me.

I don't have concrete evidence that Jo has spoken to him about his overtures, explained she's not interested, but he hasn't brought her up since he gave me that letter, and he's been extra down. Introverted and broody. I assume Jo told him they didn't have a future, and I've been a shitty brother. I haven't asked him what's wrong or tried to cheer him up. Avoidance has become my brutal coping mechanism. And apparently denial with Javier.

We get to work demoing his bathroom, starting with the bathtub and tiling. Physical work that has me sweating all over again. It's even hotter in here than in Lennon's barn, the AC in this old house pumping sluggishly.

"I'm thinking of asking Simone to move in," Javier says during a break. He spins his water bottle back and forth.

"Wow." I drag my forearm across my brow and put down my hammer. I've met Simone once and found her fun and kind. Makes me happy for him. "Things are serious, then?"

"Things are great," he says. He's not as sweaty as me, but his ratty old T-shirt and jeans are dusty from our work. And he looks sickeningly in love. "The only downside is she lives an hour away in Ruby Grove, but I'm not sure she's ready for this next step."

"Based on that goofy grin on your face, I'd guess Simone will say yes, but I get the nerves. Putting your heart on the line isn't easy."

He rubs the back of his neck. "I swear I'm still seventeen around her sometimes. Insecure and shit." He kicks my foot. "What about you?"

"What about me?"

"Your guardian angel routine with Jo. Is there more than friendship there?"

My overheating body twitches unpleasantly. "She's my brother's ex."

"Not what I asked."

I glance in the mirror we haven't removed yet. My hair is damp from the heat and work, stubble covers my usually shaved jaw, and the bruises under my eyes give me an edge I'm not used to seeing. Like I've morphed into my grumpy brother, Desmond, and will soon only speak in grunts and glares.

"Jake still has feelings for her," I say. "He's been trying to get her on a date since we got back."

"Does trying imply failing?"

I give a jerky nod. "She's not interested in him that way anymore."

"And she's living with you, in the bedroom next to yours, every night, right?"

With a fucking vibrator in her drawer and shower towels on her floor. "Your point?"

He leans his shoulder into the wall and drags his hand through his sweaty dark hair. "In high school, I always wondered why you two never got together. I mean, she was a year older and way out of your league back then, but when she'd hang out with us, you two always seemed so connected. Inside jokes, like at the Barrel after soccer. Sharing a look and cracking up without uttering a word. You acted like more of a couple than the couples I knew."

I debate picking the hammer back up and dropping it on my foot. An injury to escape this conversation. "Still don't hear a point being made."

Shaking his head, he picks up a chunk of tile and tosses it into the hallway. "Between Jake and witness protection, your history is on the fucked-up side of complicated, but I'd hate for you to go through life always wondering what-if where Jo is concerned. If you have feelings for her, you should talk to Jake about it. Be honest and upfront. If nothing else, I know he wants to see you happy."

"I am happy," I say, attempting to smile, but my jaw seems to be made of cement.

Javier laughs. "Always the same schtick with you, man."

"What schtick?"

"Giving everyone else the oxygen mask on a nosediving plane, even when you're one short."

Forget trying to smile. My underused frown muscles slam into high gear.

His jab reminds me too much of E's comments the other week. *Your greatest and worst trait has always been the same. You put other people before yourself.* I understand that my need for control got intense during WITSEC, but caring about others isn't a bad thing.

On the brink of overheating, I grab my T-shirt by the back of the neck and try to yank it off, but it's damp and sweaty and gets caught in my hair.

"Javier! You guys up there?"

"Yeah, babe. I'll meet you at the top of the stairs. We have shit everywhere."

Javier didn't mention Simone coming over, but she's obviously here. Not that I can see her through my half-off T-shirt. I wrestle with the stupid cotton, pulling at it aggressively as Javier's advice ricochets through my mind. *Talk to Jake about it. Be honest and upfront.*

I could've used that advice fourteen years ago, when Jake and Jo worked together at Markers Construction.

Jake would bring her home some days, the two of them laughing as they'd walk in the door. She'd sit beside me at dinner but would flash him the occasional smile, and I'd be ready to spit nails. He'd grin, going on about the cute way Jolene slipped in mud at a construction site or about how funny she was. She'd laugh, and I'd practically grind my molars to dust.

I knew I was into Jo by then. She'd graduated, and I was still in high school, but we hung out tons. Grabbed shakes at the Smash Shack, stargazed at Bear Lake, spent hours in our tree house, talking about how disconnected I felt from my father and that I secretly listened to Madonna. She'd talk about how she felt closer to her aunt than her mother and her fear of eating peanut butter in public, because it would stick to the roof of her mouth. The deep stuff. The silly stuff. The small and big of our lives until I knew I was soul-deep in love with my best friend.

Even worse, I'd convinced myself she came to dinner after work with Jake so she could see *me*.

Finally, one day, I decided I'd had enough. I needed to tell Jolene how I felt about her. Confess how much I loved her wit and jokes and competitiveness. That I wanted to take her on a date. Kiss her. Make her the happiest she'd ever been.

I sat on my bed, rehearsing lines, beyond nervous but also excited. *Finally*, we'd be together the way I imagined. Finally, I'd be able to breathe without a hitch in my heart.

I picked up the phone to call her, anxious and shaky, but Jake barged into my room.

"You look like you're gonna puke," he said.

I shrugged and dropped the phone, trying to pretend I wasn't sweating over the girl I secretly loved. "I'm fine."

"Cool, so—is it okay if I ask Jolene out?"

"What?" I shouted the question and nearly punched my oldest brother in the face.

"Jolene. I was thinking of asking her out."

"You're twenty-three."

"And Mom and Dad are six years apart. Jolene's nineteen. It's only four years. And she's different from the girls my age, easier to be around. And we have tons in common." He smirked and waggled his eyebrows. "She's also hot."

"But—" *She's mine*, I almost blurted. Followed by, *Over my dead body*. Except I replayed some of our recent dinners, recalled

Jolene smiling at Jake, laughing at his antics, like she was reenacting our Cool List—laugh at everyone's stupid jokes.

Realization pulled the rug out from under me.

Jake and Jo spent tons of time together at work without me, driving to our house, maybe other nights I didn't know about. Jake wouldn't ask her out if he wasn't sure she'd say yes, which left only one conclusion: Jolene liked Jake back.

She'd been spending time with me, staying for dinner, to get to him.

"If she's into you," I told Jake, keeping my tone even while my chest caved, "go for it. I don't care if you ask her out."

"Thanks, man." Jake punched my shoulder and left the room, unaware he'd started me down a path of jealousy so consuming I eventually schemed to break him and Jolene up.

Now Javier's telling me to finally be honest with Jake, like hurting my brother and possibly causing a rift between us is a walk in the park.

I hold my sweaty shirt in my fist, relieved it's off, but no less overheated.

Javier and his girlfriend step into the partly demolished bathroom. I give her a tired wave. "Good to see you, Simone."

"Callahan. So good to see you too." Her grin is kind of manic, her eyes bouncing between me and the walls, finally landing on Javier. "Great job on the demoing. And, um, I just wanted to let you know we should leave soon. So meet me downstairs when you're ready?" Her attention darts to my chest. She giggles uncharacteristically, blushes, then looks pointedly at Javier. "Love you, babe."

The second she's gone, Javier rounds on me. "Dude, what the fuck?"

I glance around, trying to figure out why he's pissed. "What the fuck *what*?"

"You can't do shit like that."

"Like what?"

He gestures angrily at me. "Take your shirt off in my house."

I glance down at my chest, worried there's something gross on me. "Why?"

"*Why?* Jesus Christ. Your muscles have their own muscles. If you set the bar that high, the rest of us don't stand a chance. You practically blinded Simone with your ten-pack and potent masculinity. I still have to ask her to move in."

My face heats as I recall Jo seeing me in my boxers, how awkward she was too. I shouldn't smile, shouldn't enjoy the notion of her being turned on by me.

"Get that smug smile off your face," Javier mutters. "We need to go, and you need to put on a shirt."

"Go where?"

"You volunteered to help with the Yard Goat Gallery opening, didn't you?"

"Fuck." I drag my hand down my face, unsure how I dropped the ball on that commitment. "Must have forgotten to put it in my phone. I'll head home and shower. Meet you there."

"With some fucking clothes on, right?"

Chuckling, I punch his shoulder as I leave, but Jo said she'd be helping at the opening too. Jake will also be there, along with Meddling Lennon and Too-Intuitive E. If Des shows up, I'll be surrounding by my invasive family while I attempt to suppress my feelings for Jolene.

Guess I'm about to find out if the glass-half-full, congenial guy I used to be still exists under all this churning angst.

CHAPTER
Twenty-Three

Callahan

The Yard Goat Gallery looks miles better than the day after the storm. The sun is out. The fallen tree and debris are cleared away from the front lawn. Two men are hanging the new gallery sign, while other volunteers carry in canvases and merchandise for the art supply store.

Ben and Javier join me, the three of us surveying the progress with crossed arms.

"Looks good. And glad to see you started the carving," I tell Ben, awed by the tree stump he's transformed into art. The bear is partially done, carved so its upper body and front paws are lunging from the trunk. Even without the finer details finished, the animal looks like it's about to break into a run. "No clue how you do that."

"The wood speaks to me." He runs his hand over his shaved head. "Can't thank you enough for doing the drywalling in the gallery."

"When did you fit that in?" Javier asks, looking pointedly at the smudges under my eyes.

"When I had time," I say vaguely. Early mornings before I even hit the gym.

"Cal!" Sue-Ann Hinkley, the cute server from the Barrel, flutters her fingers at me. "I have some reno work needed at home, if you have time."

"Don't think I can fit it in right now. I'll keep it in mind for future."

"Whenever is good." Her fair skin is either sunburned or she's blushing up a storm. She leans toward Simone and Ben's girlfriend, Kiyana, the three of them whispering and laughing together.

"Hello, Callahan." Ms. Osorio, formerly Principal Osorio, stops in front of us and does this weird eyelash-batting thing. "When you're free, I could use my kitchen repainted. Day or night. I'm ready when you are."

She walks off with a hip sway that has me wanting to cover my eyes. Mrs. Cho, who just celebrated her ninety-fifth birthday with a cake at Delilah's coffee shop, leans on her walker and waves at me. Then she winks.

"What's going on?" I ask, exceedingly uncomfortable.

Javier purses his lips and shakes his head. "Told you taking off your shirt was a mistake."

"How does everyone know I took off my shirt?"

Ben cocks his head at me. "This is Windfall, man. Everyone knows everything. Now all the ladies in town want you working in their homes."

"But the only people there were Javier and Simone." As ravenous for gossip as this town is, even I'm surprised by this level of rumor-spreading.

Ben huffs. "Simone is your weak link. She called Kiyana and told her you were at Javier's and ripped off your shirt with one hand, right down the middle, like some kind of sexy non-green hulk. Now she wants me to reenact the move. So, fuck you very much."

"The bar," Javier says, shaking his head as they strut away from me. "Lower the goddamn bar for the rest of us."

More women send flirty smiles my way. I attempt to hunch and make myself less visible—not easy at six-foot-two. I beeline for the gallery, hoping fewer gossip hens are inside. The interior is bustling with volunteers. Artwork is being rehung and supplies set up for the store's reopening, everyone chatting and smiling as they work.

Unfortunately, E and Lennon are here with Delilah and Maggie, the group of them putting together the pamphlet display—a collection of advertisements to promote Windfall's tourist activities. If rumors are spreading about me, they'll be insufferable.

I turn on my heel.

"Heard you stripped at Javier's," Maggie calls before I get far.

Grudgingly, I face her and wrestle my calm expression in place. "Nonsense rumors, as you well know."

She fits a stack of Stallard Winery rack cards into the pamphlet display, a hint of mischief in her suppressed grin. "Not what I heard. Do you charge extra for that service? Like, does it cost more or less than the construction end of your work?"

An uncontrollable blush heats my cheeks. "Hilarious. How's your kitchen wiring, by the way? Did Dean get it sorted?"

Their wiring issue is an excellent diversion, and I haven't had time to talk to Dean lately, make sure the work has been done.

"He hasn't made it out," Lennon says. "Got too busy with his other jobs. What I don't get," he adds before I can ask for more details, "is why you took off your pants in front of Simone."

I freeze. "I didn't take off my pants."

"I get the shirt," he goes on, facing E now, amusement

written across his smug face. "But peeling down to his briefs is pushing it."

"Definitely over the line," E agrees, giving me a judging look.

"I didn't take off my pants," I say more forcefully.

"I heard his jeans were those Velcro kind strippers peel off with one yank." Delilah eyes me from my work boots to my what-the-heck-is-happening face. "Apparently he blasted music from his phone, something kinky by—"

"I didn't take off my pants!" I shout.

A hammer clatters to the floor.

All eyes in the gallery snap to me.

I attempt to smile at my audience and dip my head. "No pants came off, folks. Just a shirt, because it was hot. Not that it matters or should be of interest to anyone. Best if we all get back to work."

The volunteers slowly resume their activities. I swivel away from my brothers, attempting to control the flush burning my neck, and nearly walk into Jolene. She's in her cutest country outfit—cowboy boots, shredded jean shorts, sexy yellow button-up tank top that ties at her slim waist. I muffle my forlorn groan.

She raises her eyebrow. "So you took off your pants, huh?"

"*Shirt.* It was my shirt." I rub at my blazing neck. "I was working and hot, and now I'm apparently a stripper with Velcro pants that rip off."

"I also heard you had a threesome with Simone and Javier."

Forget a flushed neck. Every inch of me must be burning red. "Please tell me you're joking."

"You know this town, Cal. Gossip is its oxygen."

I squeeze my eyes shut and mumble a curse. Maybe I spoke too soon about missing Windfall so much.

"Also," Jo says more quietly, "I heard you and I were making out on your street the other night."

My eyes fly open, my heart gunning for my throat. "What?"

She shrugs like it's no big deal. "People saw us walking. Maybe saw us holding hands."

"But we didn't kiss," I say vehemently.

She flinches. "Wow. Say it with a bit more disgust next time. Don't want any of my ego to remain intact."

Ah, shit. The way she's blinking rapidly? The slight hunch of her shoulders, which are usually pulled back, relaying confidence? I am such an asshole.

"Jo." I guide her to a quieter area, flexing my fingers, which are dying to spread along the small of her back. "No part of me is disgusted by you."

"It's fine, Cal. We're just friends, right?"

"We are."

"And the idea of kissing me grosses you out."

How the hell can she think I'm not dying to crush her to the wall right now? Feel her body molded to mine as I lick my tongue into her sassy mouth?

I'm pretty sure Jolene is as torn up over me as I am over her. All her signs lately point to interest. The other night, we basically admitted we crushed on each other in high school. I assumed the feelings I've been fighting have been as easy to read, but she recently admitted how insecure she'd been when we were teens. Self-doubt that maybe still infects her life. My reaction to our kissing rumor could have made her feel unattractive and badly about herself.

Instinctively, I move. Crowd in closer to her, drop my voice even lower, needing her to understand. To see herself the way I see her. "The idea of kissing you, Jo, doesn't gross me out. It's the exact opposite."

She frowns and drops her gaze. "You don't mean that."

"Don't tell me what I do and don't mean. I was reacting to the idea of everyone thinking we were kissing. Not how I'd feel if I had my mouth on you."

Her eyes snap up to mine, a swirl of heat growing in their

depths. Her eyelashes flutter. "Does that mean you *want* to kiss me?"

"We can't talk about this," I say, feeling like all eyes are still on me. Jo's eyes, in particular, haven't budged. We're having some sort of staring contest, neither of us looking away, tension coiling as she assesses my sincerity. The question I refuse to answer: *Hell yes, I want to kiss you.*

More than kiss. I want to devour her. Here. Now. Twelve years ago.

Her mouth softens, and she shrugs a shoulder. "Just so you know, I'm not disgusted by you either."

I smile at my boots, can barely handle looking at her beautiful face. I have no clue how we can flip from a dangerous conversation to joking on a dime. "Glad the feeling's mutual."

"Are you, though?"

I blow out a rough breath, trying to keep up with this unplanned talk. My brothers are sneaking periodic looks our way. Other townsfolk join the glance-a-thon, probably trying to read our lips, while the word *kiss* loops in my mind.

I've never had true intimacy with a partner, felt deeply connected to a woman while in bed. But Jo? The idea of having her like that, knowing the exact way to thrust or touch or lick to break each other apart so completely that—

Nope. I blink hard, try to kill my fantasies.

But what if Javier's advice about facing Jake is on point? Based on Jake's despondency this week, Jolene seems to have told him she's not interested in dating him. If I confessed that I've never felt about anyone the way I feel about Jo, would he understand? If I admitted that not a day goes by without me imagining an impossible future with his ex, would he give me his blessing?

"Cal?" Jo is watching me intently, running a finger over her clavicle. So fucking sexy. "It feels like something is happening here."

I'm not sure exactly what she's implying. If she's admitting her feelings or sensing mine. Not that it matters. I try to get my head right. Try to end this too-intimate conversation. Problem is, I feel regret building already. A tangled web of what-ifs that might prevent me from ever truly finding love, when the woman I'm facing already owns my heart.

Pulse revving faster than my chainsaw, I swallow hard. "Can we hit pause on this talk? I have more I'd like to say, but not here. I have to—"

"Jo!" A nearby woman waves at us, interrupting either the best or worst words I've ever uttered. *I have to talk to Jake. Tell him I'm in love with you.*

Then hope like hell Jolene feels the same.

Her focus has shifted to the woman who called out her name. She's beautiful, with olive skin, blond hair, and striking eyes. She's also impressively tall and strangely familiar.

"Is that Larkin Gray?" I ask, surprised.

The girl I used to break up Jake and Jo. The epicenter of the rumors I spread. I'd heard she'd moved back to town, but seeing her still shocks me. I hate what I did to her all those years ago.

"Yep." Jo gives her a kind wave. "I hired her at the Barrel. We've actually been hanging out a lot."

"Why?" I ask, my tone harder than intended.

"Because she's nice and fun and I like her." Jo cocks her head. "I told you, I *know* Jake didn't hook up with her."

But she doesn't know I wanted her so badly I hurt her and Jake and Larkin without batting an eye.

"Isn't this gallery amazing?" Larkin steps between us, taking in the stained-glass art a man is installing.

Jolene's eyes are more intense, still locked on me. "We'll finish this conversation later, right?"

I nod and manage to smile at Larkin. "Welcome back to Windfall."

"Same to you." She openly checks me out and smirks. "I see

why all the women in this town want you doing their renovations."

Instinctively, I glance at Jolene. She's no longer looking at me. She's frowning at her cowboy boots, like she's upset.

"The gossip junkies of this town like to invent stories," I tell Larkin, but my words are for Jolene. I don't want her thinking I'm the kind of man who'd lap up that attention. "I have no intention of renovating any of *their* homes."

From the corner of my eye, I see Jo's shoulders soften.

"They'll no doubt be disappointed," Larkin says, then her expression turns strangely bitter. "Or maybe they'll hire Jake. I bet he'd promise them a show, then go back on his word. Take their money and run."

I wince at her angry tone. Guess those false rumors I spread still piss her off, and she assumed Jake was the cause. "Jake is honorable and would do no such thing. *Or strip*," I add. "Neither of us does any stripping."

"Speak of the devil," she mutters, glaring over my shoulder.

I spin, and there's my brother, walking into the gallery. He nods at E and Lennon and smiles. I relax a fraction. I haven't seen him smile this week at work. By the looks of his lighter expression, maybe he's finally getting over Jo's letdown.

He scans the room, waves at one of the volunteers. Then he sees me. With Jolene. Not an odd occurrence, but he seems to freeze. Gradually, his expression darkens. He spins abruptly and stalks from the building.

The kiss. He must've heard the rumor about Jo and me kissing, and he's furious and upset, and I can't let him go without apologizing. More bullshit rumors I need to squash.

I jog outside, searching for him. He's halfway to the parking lot, walking at a clipped pace. By the time I reach him, he's at his truck, already opening the door.

"Jake, wait. We need to talk."

He doesn't release the door handle or face me. "Now's not a good time. We'll talk later."

I place my hand on the door and ease it shut, forcing him to face me. "We should talk now."

He rounds on me, stepping into my space, his eyes on the wild side of unhinged. A look I haven't seen on Jake since the early days of WITSEC. "I can't right now, okay? My head's in a bad place and—"

"I didn't kiss Jo," I blurt, but hell. Jake never loses it like this.

His dark eyes are still hard, his attention flicking to the gallery and back. He heaves out a gusty sigh. "Of course you didn't kiss Jo. Fucking rumors in this town are brutal. I'd never believe that bullshit."

Because he would never believe I'd betray him.

Because he trusts me implicitly.

Because we're a family who's been through hell and back, and we'd rather die than see one another hurt.

Guilt is a mudslide in my gut. The conversation I wanted to broach with him—Jolene, how deep I'm in with her, that I'm dying to find out if she's as into me too—gets buried under all that rubble.

"I'm pretty sure Jo spoke to you about her feelings," I say. "That she doesn't feel the same as you. If you're upset and need to talk, I'm here for you. Always."

He digs the toe of his boot into the parking lot's loose gravel. "I'm not up for talking right now. Need some time on my own. Thanks, though. Always appreciated."

He hops into his truck, leaving me in a cloud of dust and misery.

Based on that stilted talk, there's no future for Jo and me. Not if my brother is this torn up over her rejection. My only option is to kill any and all fantasies I've been nursing. Quit imagining impossible things. Which means, I need to get Jolene out of my home, especially if I want to salvage our friendship.

4 HINTS YOU LOVE YOUR BEST FRIEND   171

Pacing an edgy line, I call Sandra, who picks up swiftly. "What do you need?"

"Jolene's current landlord from her apartment—I need his contact information."

"Is he slacking off on getting the repair work done?"

"No, but I can speed up the process."

Offer cheap labor he can't refuse. Work in the later evenings after his other crew is gone. Get Jo's flooded apartment in tip-top shape, so she can move out of my home and hopefully out of my heart.

"And Dean of Dean Electric," I say. "I need him to make room for a job at Lennon's house. I bartered with him, offered to help build his toolshed, but he hasn't reached out to me or Lennon. We need to delay one of his jobs so he can fit Lennon's in." Get those wires fixed before they cause damage.

"Leave it with me."

I try to absorb Sandra's confidence. Try to believe everything will be okay. With my family. With Jolene. But I'm having a hell of a time seeing the bright side lately.

CHAPTER
Twenty-Four

Callahan

Kitchen renovating is usually my favorite type of work. I thrive on the precision of it. Exact measurements that allow a cabinet to sit flush or a fridge to slide in perfectly. When focus and attention to detail are in play, everything works out as it should.

Today, I'm moving as efficiently as a run-down Chevy.

"I need a beer tonight," Jake says as he walks in from building the kitchen cabinets outside. "We should head to a bar outside of Windfall. Change of scenery."

"Sure," I say, knowing full well there will be no beers. The only thing I'm doing tonight is working on Jolene's damaged apartment. If I tell Jake as much, he'll get on my case. It's much easier to beg off beers later. Claim tiredness instead of having a night out.

Jake frowns at the wood boards in my hands. "Those are two-by-sixes."

"They are."

He gestures at the wall. "The windows are four-feet-nine-inches. You need two-by-eights."

I blink at the wood, and *hell*. How did I mess that up? Even worse, I don't have the right size here for the work needed to be done. "Must have gotten this job mixed up with another. I'll reorder and work on the cabinets with you."

Jake blocks my way, forcing me to put the wood down. "How many other jobs are you doing?"

"You know—the Elroy deck and the Liang fence."

"And Javier's bathroom."

"Sure."

"And Mom's bookshelf you insisted on doing yourself."

"That's a one-person job."

I don't mention my new nightly activity at Jolene's apartment. An extra four hours of work added to my busy days.

Jake studies my eyes, his lips firming into a commandeering line. "Ever since WITSEC, you've had issues slowing down. You worked too much in Houston. Barely stopped to breathe then, but not like this."

"I didn't work too much in Houston."

He cocks an eyebrow. "I don't think you've sat down for more than an hour in twelve years. If you weren't working, you were at the gym or going for a run. You don't know how to relax."

"*You* don't know what you're talking about. I cook and read."

In small bursts, and not recently, but still. My focus is single-minded these days. The past two weeks, I've barely had time to blink, let alone crack open my Chavez biography. I spend as little time in my home as possible. I sleep so hard I don't hear Jolene at all.

Yesterday, on her day off, I worked fourteen hours and got home after she'd closed her bedroom door. We haven't resurrected our food and note exchanges either, but she has texted me—daily messages since I almost confessed my feelings at the Yard Goat Gallery, to which I've replied vaguely.

> Jolene: Can we make a time to talk?

> Me: Busy with work.

———

> Jolene: We didn't finish our conversation.

> Me: We will eventually.

———

> Jolene: Are you avoiding me?

> Me: Just trying to focus on my job.

———

> Jolene: If you don't slow down, you'll work yourself to death.

> Me: Physical activity helps with longevity.

———

> Jolene: Keep this up, and I'll eventually wake you up at night or corner you at work.

> Me: I need my beauty sleep. And construction sites are dangerous.

I have become a pathetic sidestepper. A terrified man who chooses avoidance over facing the woman I can't have.

"I'm fine," I tell Jake. "Keeping busy keeps me happy."

A muscle worms in his jaw. "Denial keeps you happy."

"What does that mean?"

"You're afraid to stop for five seconds and feel."

"I stop plenty. Feel plenty." It's not like I don't eat or drink or take bathroom breaks. I felt enough during WITSEC to tip the scales at Fort Knox.

"Sure," he says, but his sarcastic tone indicates he thinks I'm full of shit. He tucks his thumb into his tool belt and scuffs his boot over the floor. "Has Jo been okay recently?"

The change in conversation causes me mental whiplash. Or maybe it's hearing Jo's name. "I wouldn't know."

"You live with her."

"Like I've said, our schedules are completely opposite. I never see her." Or kiss her, like I've been dreaming about and the town seems to think has already occurred.

His jaw pops again. It's a Bower trait. Our strong jaws never fail to show signs of irritation or anger. More proof his feelings for Jolene aren't as dormant as she thinks.

He looks about to speak his mind, but Omar Turner walks into our workspace. He's a slight Black man with thick glasses and an air of intelligence. Good thing, because he's one of the town's building inspectors, but I completely forgot he was coming today.

First, I forgot about helping with the Yard Goat's reopening. Then the window header screw-up. Now this.

"I'm a bit early," Omar says, surveying our work. "Hope that's okay."

"Happy to have you," Jake says, dragging his penetrating gaze off me. "We've got one window left to frame. It was supposed to be done today, but we had a small setback. Rest is done and ready for drywall. With your approval, of course."

Omar nods and readies his clipboard. "If I have questions, I'll holler."

Jake heads outside to work on the kitchen cabinets.

My phone buzzes. At the sight of Sandra's name, I step into the hallway and answer.

"We have a problem," she says without preamble.

I tighten my grip on the phone. "With Lennon's electrical work or Jolene's lease?"

"The electrical work."

"You weren't able to delay one of Dean's jobs?"

"A job has been delayed. There is now a biologist trying to ascertain why an endangered bog turtle is on the land where they're building townhomes by Corner Creek."

"How did you get a bog turtle on the site?"

"Do I ask you how you do your job?"

As usual, Sandra excels at putting me in my place. "If you got the work delayed, what's the issue?"

"Dean had an appointment with a building inspector that day. When she asked Dean where he was heading instead, he told her there was work to be done at Lennon's. But Lennon never applied for a building permit. Apparently, he got busy with his adventure programs and forgot."

Fucking hell. "Did they put a stop to his reno work?"

"All of it. Some has to be redone now, and there's a fine."

I curse again and tear off my hat, wiping at the sweat on my brow. Another heaping of guilt slides into my stomach.

Lennon should've acquired a permit, but if I hadn't interfered, the inspector wouldn't have known about his renovation work. He wouldn't have a fine and more work ahead of him. "I have Omar here now. Maybe I can do damage control."

"Worth a shot. On a positive note, I have my eye on a buyer interested in purchasing the building where Jolene has her bar. They would be opening a brewpub."

"That's good," I say distractedly. I have wood-ordering mistakes to fix. Jo's apartment to get sorted, so she can move home. More Lennon issues to tackle. "We can't move on that yet. I need to get a better read on Jo first." Which would involve actually speaking with her.

We hang up, and I drag my hand down my face. I need more hours in my day.

I head back to Omar and tip up my ball cap. "You know about Lennon's permit issue?"

"Your brother decided he didn't need to follow the rules."

"It was an oversight, not a flagrant rebuff of the system. He did all his permits properly when building his adventure camp. He simply got busy and forgot this time."

"Rules are still rules."

"One hundred percent. We've just had it rough, Omar. A real hard time for a bunch of years. I hate to see Lennon have a setback like this when it wasn't done maliciously."

Omar taps his pen on his clipboard with even, clipped strikes. "I'll see what I can do to soften the repercussions, but not a nail gets hammered until he gets his permits."

"Appreciated and agreed."

He turns to resume his inspection but swivels back. "Almost forgot. I saw Jolene earlier. Had lunch at the Barrel and mentioned I was coming out here. She said to tell you to call her. Specifically, that she's tired of chasing you."

This is not a good sign. Up until now, she hasn't woken me up at night or searched me out at work, as per her threats. Likely because Jake is here, and she knows I need sleep. If I avoid her much longer, she might come through and trap me in an unwanted situation.

"Thanks," I say with a forced smile. "I'll be sure to reach out."

Omar gets to work, checking the room's framing and plumbing. I grab the wood boards I need to replace and head into the sunshine.

Jake glances at me. Gives me a penetrating stare that has my crew neck feeling too tight. He resumes working on the cabinets. I deposit the wood boards and help him with the construction. We hit that easy stride we share when we're focused and productive. He doesn't badger me more about overworking or about Jo. He seems stuck in his head too, his brow puckered as he readies to use the table saw.

Abruptly, he straightens. "Are you and Jo fighting?"

The sun's rays drill through my skull. "Why would you ask that?"

"I was by the door when Omar mentioned she's asking after you. Why else would you be avoiding her calls?"

"It's nothing," I say, lying like the liar I've become.

"Yeah, but—"

Our phones buzz.

We share a concerned glance. If our phones buzz in tandem, it's always our family group chat. Furious messages about our father, usually. Life-altering bombs dropped on our heads.

We snatch our respective phones…and my tensed shoulders lower. Just Mom's welcome home party.

> E: We need to finalize details for Mom's party.
>
> Lennon: I thought we decided that Desmond's hosting a tea party so they can talk about their book crushes?
>
> Desmond: Fuck off.
>
> E: Meeting tonight at the Barrel at 8.

Nope. The last place I can be is at the Barrel. I can't exist in Jolene's orbit right now. I'm close to getting her apartment fixed up. If I put in enough hours during the next few nights, she can move out. Then I'll finally meet with her. Talk about the relationship we most certainly cannot have. I'll be able to escape to my quiet home after. Her chaotic self will no longer be there to tempt me.

Me: I'm busy tonight.

Jake's message pops up right after mine.

Jake: Can't make it.

I glance up at him. "Why can't you make it?"

"Because I can't," he says, terse. "Why can't you?"

He's been extra broody since I saw him at the Yard Goat, but he told me he wasn't up for talking. I've respected his silence. Haven't prodded him about his feelings.

Maybe that was the wrong move. "I have plans, but you said before you were hankering for a beer. Are you avoiding the Barrel because Jolene's there? Is that why you wanted to go somewhere out of town? Are things weird with you guys now?"

"I don't know, Cal. Are things weird with *you* and Jo right now?" Irritation sharpens his cheekbones.

Jake is sidestepping, like me. We're just a couple of anxious evaders, hoping we can outrun our feelings. "I'm here, Jake, whenever you need to talk."

"Talking won't help," he says, dropping his gaze. "Some things can only be fixed with time. Or not at all," he mumbles under his breath and gets back to work.

It feels like a nail gun has shot through my sternum.

I knew Jake would be upset if Jo didn't reciprocate his feelings, but he's hurting more than I expected. Worryingly so. Even after I sabotaged his relationship, and Jo broke up with him, he was down and distracted, but not this forlorn. I'll have to find a way to reach him. Coax him to open up, and make sure he never learns how close I was to irrevocably breaking his trust.

I join him at the cabinets, both of us hammering and sawing with a little more muscle in our moves. Omar signs off on our permit. I order the proper wood for the window header. We grunt goodbye at each other, Jake driving to some bar that isn't the Barrel for a drink, while I head to Jo's apartment to pick up where the landlord's construction crew left off, so I can hurry up her departure from my home.

CHAPTER
Twenty-Five

Callahan

A bunch of hours later, I screw in the final sections of drywall, blinking when the board blurs in and out of focus. I stop and swallow hard. Fight the urge to close my eyes.

If the daytime crew working here wasn't balancing several jobs, Jo's apartment would have been ready by now. As it stands, her place and the damaged ceiling in the apartment below have turned into a tedious repair job. Taping compound still needs to be applied to the drywall seams. Then sanding, priming, and painting. New carpeting and trim laid down.

I put my drill on the floor, looking around for the taping compound. Good luck with that. Furniture is piled haphazardly and covered with cloths. Tools and supplies are carelessly spread out. I nearly trip and fall over a random saw that could cut someone and do real damage.

"Goddamn lazy construction crews," I grumble as I move the saw, wondering what other dangerous obstacles are around. This place makes Jolene's room look like a pristine army barracks.

Unable to find the compound, I trudge to the bedroom, hoping it's stashed in there.

"Callahan?"

I straighten and freeze. It's nearing two a.m., and that was a woman's voice. *Jolene's* voice, if I had to hypothesize. Guess she got tired of my evading, and *I'm* too tired to do anything but step in the doorway and sigh at the sight of her. "Hey, Jo."

Her dark eyes do a sweep of my disheveled self, passing over my stubbled jaw and likely red-rimmed eyes. "What the hell are you doing?"

"Drywalling?" I say it like a question. Like I'm not even sure what I'm doing any longer.

"Why are you drywalling at two in the morning?"

"The crew your landlord hired can barely fit this job in." I rub my bleary eyes. "Told him I'd do what I can to speed things along."

"Why?"

"*Why?*" I swear my brain is functioning in slow motion, words clanging around for purchase.

"Yes, *why?*" she says. "Why are you working yourself to death, when I have a place to stay? Or is that the issue? You don't want me in your home anymore?"

"Can we have this conversation later?" When I'm not a minute from falling asleep on my feet.

"Oh, like during the day when I call you and you refuse to answer? Or how about when I pass messages through Omar and you ignore them? Are *those* the times we're going to talk?"

"Yes?" Her sarcasm is switched to high, but my brain is definitely stuck in quicksand.

"You're infuriating, you know that?"

"I know."

"You've been avoiding me since the Yard Goat."

"I have."

She lets out a cute growl. "Stop being so...*honest.* I'm mad at you and need to yell at you, but you're making it really freaking hard when you're not fighting back and you're one second away from face-planting in this mess."

I sway on my feet, proving her right.

Worried I *will* hit the floor, I lean my shoulder into the doorjamb. I don't have the energy to sidestep the subject any longer. "I'm sorry."

She sags forward and rubs the space between her brows. "At the Yard Goat, you asked if we could hit pause on our talk. You mentioned that you had more you'd like to discuss. What did you want to say?"

I'm in love with you. I wanted to talk to Jake and ask for his blessing to finally take you out. Truths that will only hurt us more now. "Nothing important. Nothing worth talking about at this hour."

She makes a huffy sound and stares at the mess on the floor, then she skewers me with intense eyes that nearly blow me through the wall. "I don't believe you, and I'm exhausted from keeping my feelings inside. I'm barely sleeping these days and can't seem to move forward, because the truth of the matter is I'm crazy about you."

She breathes faster, her brutal honesty carving off pieces of my heart. "I think you feel the same, but you're scared to hurt Jake and your family. And I get it. *I'm* scared of it all. But Jake knows I'm not interested. When I spoke to him about him and me, he actually agreed that he was living in the past, not acting on current feelings. We *joked* about the end of our relationship before WITSEC and that we're not really compatible."

"No." I shake my head emphatically. "He told you what you wanted to hear. Fact is, he's devastated. Haven't seen him this rough in a while, and I won't contribute to his pain."

"Because you *do* feel the same about me?"

I blow out a pained breath. Can't admit what she wants. If I tell her how consumed I am by her voice, her laugh, her stupid mess in my home, I won't be able to shove those feelings back down.

I stay quiet, bite down on my tongue.

Her nostrils flare. "I guess I'm reading you wrong, then. You're not dying to know what it's like to kiss me. To be with each other and finally unleash *years* of pent-up attraction. I guess my feelings are one-sided."

Goddamn it.

I'm suddenly very awake...and turned on. She's not playing fair. None of this feels fair. Jolene and I wouldn't simply connect. We'd be a New Year's Eve fireworks display. A Thunderbirds airfield show, blasting through the sky, wild and in sync, but...

Talking won't help. Some things can only be fixed with time. Or not at all.

Jake obviously put on a brave face when Jolene let him down. I won't hammer the nail in his coffin. Lying is the only way to end this now, and hopefully salvage our friendship later. "My feelings don't matter, Jo. I won't hurt Jake or my family. What we're feeling is only attraction anyway. Nothing more, nothing deeper. I'm working here to get you out of my place as soon as possible. Then we can go back to being friends without all this...stuff."

"Only attraction," she murmurs, her expression shell-shocked. She blinks as her attention jumps over the cluttered room. "I am *such* an idiot."

A rush of red rises to her cheeks. Glossiness sheens her chestnut eyes. *Upset.* I've upset the one woman I'd give my life for, and there's not a damn thing I can do about it.

"I really thought you felt the same. Was so sure, but..." She breathes harder, more red rising to her face. "I'm so sorry, Cal. I never should've said anything. I'm moving out. To the couch at the Barrel. It'll be easier for us both."

"Jo." That's all I have. Her whispered name on my lips. No heartfelt words to bridge this gaping divide.

With one last pained look at me, she spins and rushes toward the door, through the chaotic mess of this unkempt place.

"Careful," I call, feeling gutted. Anxious. Not well.

Why the hell did no one clean up this floor? Why didn't *I*?

She doesn't slow down. Her moves are jerky, and her foot catches on something, pitching her forward. She gasps, flinging out her arms to brace herself.

"Jo!" I yell as I lunge for her. I'm not fast enough.

Her head hits a piece of covered furniture. A sharp *thwack* that has my gut plummeting as she sails toward the floor.

CHAPTER
Twenty-Six

Callahan

"Jolene. *Jo.*" I leap over strewn equipment, my knees slamming into the floor as I crash to her side. "Jo, honey. You're okay. *Please be okay. Please open your eyes.*"

She's not moving. She's utterly limp as I brush the hair from her forehead, trying to assess her injuries without jostling her body. There's blood. A red gash on her shin that has sandpaper scraping down my throat. She hasn't moved. Not a blink or a moan. "Fuck."

I fumble for my phone, my heart hurtling off a cliff. I clamp my jaw, start dialing for an ambulance. She groans before I finish.

"Jolene, baby." I drop my phone and brush my hand over her cheek. "Where does it hurt? Can you move?"

She adjusts her body and winces. "My back."

"You hurt your back?"

"I think someone is stabbing it with a hot poker."

"A flat person is stuck under your back, jabbing it with a hot poker?" My joke comes out half croaked with relief, but she hit her head when she fell. Passing out isn't good.

"It's either a flat person," she says on a strained breath, "or my pride dislodged from my body on my way down and is intent on drilling a hole through my spine."

"If you were being attacked by your pride, Jolene, you'd be in a coma right now. And we're going to the hospital."

I help her to sitting. She sways and presses her hand to her forehead. "I'm fine. No hospital. And are you implying that my pride is strong enough to kill me?"

"I'm stating that you're often stubborn and willful. Headstrong, like a feisty Chihuahua who'd rather chase a squirrel than stop for traffic. Or in this case, go to the hospital."

"Now I'm a dog?"

I'm not sure how we started bantering after that horrible argument and her fall, but I latch on to the familiar jousting, hoping it distracts her from her pain. "You're a cute but determined dog, who's choosing getting hit by a car over caution."

"Are you always this sweet when your friends have near-death experiences?"

"I am when they need medical care. The hospital is happening, Jo."

"Bossy," she mumbles.

"Worried," I counter. "You hit your head hard enough to knock yourself out. And you're bleeding."

I place my hand on her ankle, below the cut on her shin. She stares at the blood like she's surprised it's there. "It's not that bad," she says.

"What's your name?" I ask, steadying my other hand on her back.

"Is this a trick question?"

"Head injuries are no joke."

"Jolene Cynthia Daniels," she says, dragging out each syllable.

I almost smile at her defiant nature. "Where are you right now?"

She stares at me with pursed lips. "In my apartment, because you're here when you shouldn't be, at too-late o'clock, because you're working yourself to death so you can get me out of your house as quickly as possible."

Blunt as ever and hitting me where it hurts. "Definitely a Chihuahua, but with rabies."

"I'm vicious now?"

"Terrifying."

Except I'm the scared one. My heart hasn't recovered from seeing her fall, watching her black out. I lead her toward the door, but she's hunched and her steps are stiff. "I'm gonna pick you up, carry you to the car," I say.

"I can walk fine." But she tenses and hisses out a breath, proving herself wrong.

"Denial doesn't become you, Jolene."

"I'm barely hurt," she says with a lift of her obstinate chin. An actress gunning for an award. She takes a small step forward, but she slumps. "I might need that carry."

Thankful, I bend down. "Put your arms around my neck."

She complies. Wraps her arms around my neck as I gently lift her into my arms. A reluctant sigh pushes from my chest. Having Jo in my arms feels good.

I tuck one arm under her legs, hold her closer than is decent. Take measured steps, wishing I'd cleaned that room so she hadn't fallen. That I'd told Jake I had feelings for her fourteen years ago, when he first wanted to ask her out. That my family hadn't endured hell, and I hadn't missed twelve years with my best friend.

I press my chin to the side of her head. "Hopefully the hospital won't be too busy. You'll get checked out quick."

"Cal."

The way she says my name—furtive but also on the edge of desperate—has me stopping outside her building. "Is something wrong?"

"I really don't want to go to the hospital. It's late. I'm tired from working all day and embarrassed about…everything. You're being sweet and caring, but I really just want to go to sleep. I'll move out tomorrow, if that's okay. For now, I just want to pretend this night never happened."

She's talking about our fight. Her heartfelt confession. My brutal dismissal of us.

I stroke my hand down her arm, press my lips to her hair. Hate that my rejection has cut another scar on her heart. For most of my life, I've worked to keep Jolene happy. Ensure she thrives and succeeds. All my return to Windfall has done is cause her pain.

"The neighbor in the other half of my duplex is a nurse," I say as I head to my truck. "I'll call her. If she's home and willing to look at you, I'll forgo the hospital. If she's not, we're heading to emergency."

Because I love you, I don't say. *I hate seeing you upset and hurt and will hurl myself into traffic if it means saving you pain.*

She nods and presses her face into my chest. Inhales deeply, I think. Maybe I have a lightning-storm scent too. A surge of electrical force that sparks near Jolene. Crackling voltage when the words I can't speak scrape against my throat.

CHAPTER
Twenty-Seven

Callahan

I carefully place Jo on her bed and prop her up with pillows. "Is there still a flat man jabbing pokers into your back?"

"He's more of a lumpy gnome who got stuck under me," she says.

I mock glower. "Those lumpy gnomes are what's wrong with this world."

"Their big, poky hats should be banned."

"Their huge noses stick where they shouldn't."

"You're ridiculous," she says, wincing as she laughs, but a slew of affection gathers in her dark eyes. My fellow adventurer's eyes. My best friend's eyes, with a hint of *I wish we were more.*

I drop my gaze. Cup her calf and frown at the dried blood on her gash. "This needs cleaning."

"Cal."

My gaze draws a slow path up Jolene's reclined body. Along her legs, her jean skirt, her rumpled tank top, her slender neck, and the perfect bow of her mouth—soft lips, full but not too full, slightly pursed. Jo's lips always carry a hint of thought. Like she's spinning a question she's not ready to voice.

"Yeah?" I say quietly.

She opens her mouth, then closes it and frowns. "Nothing."

A knock sounds on my front door, cutting me off from prodding. "Be right back."

I hurry to the front door and yank it open. "I'm sorry for calling so late," I tell Anika right away. "Jo's had a rough night and didn't want to go to the hospital, and I was worried about her. She hit her head hard. Passed out for a few seconds. I probably should've—"

"Callahan." Anika is tall and broad, strong from her CrossFit workouts. She always exudes confidence. In one steady word, she manages to calm me. "I'm happy to look at her. If I have any concerns, she'll have to go to the hospital, but Jolene has taken care of my father when he's had one too many at her bar. Escorted him out and saved him embarrassment. We pull together in this town."

The giant hug that is Windfall.

I nod and step back, ushering her toward Jo's room.

"Heard your head decided to get in a fight with a floor," Anika says as she brandishes a flashlight from the small bag she brought.

Jo smiles warmly. "It was a poorly concealed coffee table, and I lost."

"I'm sure the coffee table looks worse." Anika crouches in front of her. "How about I check those eyes of yours?"

I wait in the living room while Anika takes care of Jo. I pace an edgy line. Try to hear what's going on, but their words are too quiet. I pace faster while I tug at my disheveled hair, picturing her falling over and over, worry frothing in my gut. By the time Anika comes out, I'm surprised I have hair left in my head.

"You look exhausted, Cal." Anika is in the living area, watching me with concern.

I fit on a smile. "Long day. How is she?"

"I cleaned and bandaged her shin, and her pupils are responding well. She's not dizzy and doesn't exhibit any memory loss, but she has a headache. If you can keep an eye on her for the rest of the night, that would be best. Make sure she doesn't develop signs of nausea or ringing in her ears. Slurred speech or confusion are signs of a concussion too. If any of that happens, take her to the hospital."

Concern worms through my stomach. "Should I wake her hourly? They do that for possible concussions, right?"

"Old myth," she says, brushing her bangs out of her eyes. "Sleeping is good for healing. But stay with her in case she wakes up and doesn't feel well."

Right. Sure. Stay in Jolene's room. No problem at all.

"Of course," I say, unsure when my life turned into a torture chamber. Actually, that's not true. It's been twelve years of turmoil and strife. Why should this be any different?

I walk Anika to the door, dragging out my impending doom. "If you need anything fixed in your place, you know where to find me."

"Don't you worry, Callahan. I'll be cashing in." She waves at me with her flashlight. "Make sure you get some sleep too."

While in Jolene's room? I'd have better luck sleeping in an erupting volcano.

CHAPTER
Twenty~Eight

Callahan

When I was sixteen, I was in a car accident. Mom was driving. She'd picked me up from football practice. We'd grabbed Lennon from a tutoring session and E from his friend Avett's. E and Lennon were goofing off in the back seat, ragging on each other about who had to take out the garbage when we got home. Mom usually took our arguing in stride, but she was distant that day, seemed distracted and snippy.

"I'll take out the garbage," I told my brothers, just to shut them up and give Mom some peace.

She smiled at me. A tired smile.

Then a car slammed into the driver's side.

My head swam as my heart rate shot through the roof. "Mom." I reached over, grabbed her shoulder with a shaky hand. "Are you okay?"

She blinked. Didn't seem to recognize me. Then she said, "Yeah. Yes, I think so." Her eyes shot to the rearview mirror. "Lennon? E?"

They didn't reply. Something in my chest ruptured. I tried to turn, but my seat belt locked me in place. My throat wouldn't work. Fear like I'd never known had me tearing at my buckle as I thought, *they're hurt. My brothers are trapped, maybe bleeding. Maybe worse.*

When I finally got the belt undone, I whipped around to find E and Lennon grinning, shushing each other in a silent pact to terrify the living shit out of me.

"Assholes, the both of you," I muttered while my pulse pounded in my head.

Lennon laughed, but E's face pinched. "Sorry, Cal. That wasn't nice."

He looked chagrined, and I waved him off. Got out and helped Mom deal with the driver who'd hit us. Kept her calm and made sure everyone was really, truly okay. The car was too damaged to drive. Word got around town, as word did, and a friend of Mom's drove us home. We went inside. Ate dinner that Mrs. Moon had dropped off and Desmond heated.

Jokes abounded as usual. Even Mom jumped in to tell Des about Lennon and E's horrible prank. I didn't join in the fun, just poked at my food. Could barely eat, let alone act as though I hadn't had the life scared out of me.

"You okay?" Desmond asked as E and Lennon started clearing the table.

"Fine. Just tired."

Not fine. Not tired. But I didn't know how to explain what was wrong. Mom wasn't hurt. E and Lennon were healthy and as obnoxious as ever. All that got damaged was a car.

The second we were done, I jogged to my tree house and hid inside, too shaken up to do much else besides stare at the wall. Heat burned the backs of my eyes. Tightness suffocated my chest.

"Cal?" Jolene's voice penetrated my fortress, followed by her head poking through the door. "You okay? I heard about the accident."

I shook my head—*no, I'm not okay*. I bit my cheek. Tried to find my equilibrium, but I kept picturing our smashed car, and my eyes burned hotter. I didn't want to cry, but a swirl of emotion spun through me until biting my cheek didn't help.

"Oh, Callahan." Jolene climbed all the way in and wrapped her arms around me, hugged me so tight I thought she'd break a rib. "It's okay. Let it out. It must've been so scary."

I gulped out a sob. An embarrassing sound as the stressful day rushed out of me. "Fuck. I don't know what's wrong with me." I gathered myself, rubbed my eyes and nose. "They're all fine."

She hooked her arm through mine and rested her head on my shoulder. "You love your family, and something really bad could've happened today. Of course you're upset."

I nodded and leaned my head on hers, breathing easily for the first time since that car slammed into us. "Thanks for coming over," I said.

"There's nowhere in the world I'd rather be."

Because we were best friends. Because if one of us was hurting, the other was always there to offer a shoulder when needed. Friends before anything else. Like right now.

I stretch my jaw, wipe my dampening palms down my jeans, and step into Jo's doorway.

She's under the covers, wearing her green leprechaun T-shirt. A piece of our history.

I clear my throat. "How's the patient?"

She tucks the covers tighter under her arms. "Embarrassed and will hopefully pass out shortly. Anika gave me something for my headache, and I took a muscle relaxant for my back."

"There's nothing to be embarrassed about, Jo. The apartment's a disaster zone. Anyone could've fallen."

She shakes her head, her mouth puckering slightly—trapped words knotting the corners—but she doesn't speak.

I drag in a breath, readying to explain what I'll be doing for the rest of the evening. She was my shoulder growing up. I'll be hers always. "I'm going to sleep in here tonight."

Her tired eyes widen. "You're...what?"

"Anika," I say, as if that explains everything, including the uncomfortable tingling taking root at the base of my spine. Miniature lightning strikes. Static electricity near Jo. "Anika said to keep an eye on you, and..." I glance at the floor, where I should sleep. Lay out a blanket and pillow by the wall, but what if Jo gets up and is disoriented? What if she *does* have a concussion and confusion hits and I don't hear or feel her and she takes another spill getting up?

"Your bed," I say.

"What?" she says again, her voice sounding as panicked as my thoughts.

Panic that seems to be draining my IQ. I'm a college graduate, for God's sake. An avid reader, when I find the time. Where the hell are my words?

"Anika," I start again, "said to keep an eye on you, in case you wake up and feel dizzy or confused. I could sleep on the floor, but if you get up and don't remember I'm here and you stumble out of bed, you could hurt yourself. If I'm on the bed, I'll feel you move."

"You'll feel me move," she says, sounding less frazzled, but her eyelids drift lower and huskiness weaves into her tone.

Hell, do I want to *feel her move*. With me. Under me. Over me. The two of us locked in a seductive rhythm I have no doubt would singe my skin. I slow my next blink, search for my control. The brother I am, first and foremost. The best friend Jolene deserves.

"It's settled," I say and give a sharp nod. "I'll shower and be back here shortly. Hopefully you'll be asleep by then."

She doesn't answer. Just watches me intently as I strut for the door and the coldest shower I can handle.

CHAPTER
Twenty~Nine

Callahan

Jolene is asleep when I return in my T-shirt and briefs. I leave the door open, allowing a bit of light in from the living room, in case she wakes up disoriented. The soft glow makes her face look younger. Her fanned eyelashes rest delicately on her cheeks.

I'm suddenly not tired at all.

I could watch a sleeping Jolene all night. Subscribe to this station. Marvel at the soft parting of her lips, the way her haphazard hair decorates her pillow, knowing my best friend is safe and protected with me near, like our early days in the tree house.

Maybe sleeping in her bed won't be so tough after all.

Quietly, I lift the sheets and slide under, shifting on my side to face her. As run-down as I am, I doubt I'll sleep a minute. This might be the only time I ever share a bed with Jo as an adult.

Contentment sinks through me as I watch her. A peace I haven't felt in a long while.

I feel myself smile, basking in a fantasy I shouldn't indulge—

Jolene and me sleeping like this every night, but not quite like this. Her head on my chest. My leg slung over hers, my hands drawing soothing patterns on her back as we talk into the night. We fall asleep together. Wake up together. Cook breakfast. Go for a walk in town. Play soccer. Hang out with friends and come home to her chaos, where I'll tease her for being a human hurricane and she'll needle me for working too hard and we'll make love like we have all the time in the world, then do it all over again the next day.

"Cal?" Jo's eyes flutter open, and I feel exposed. Caught.

"Didn't mean to wake you," I whisper.

She licks her lips, like they're parched.

"Are you thirsty?" I ask. "I can get you water."

I start to get up, but she places her hand on my arm. "I'm really sorry."

The heaviness in her voice stops me, as does her imploring glance. "It's okay, you weren't snoring that loudly."

She smiles at my joke but still looks sad. "About my apartment, the things I said."

"Please don't apologize," I say, wishing I could redo that whole conversation. "Whatever you felt—whatever you *feel*—is real and valid. There's nothing to be embarrassed about."

"It's not that." She shakes her head and worries her lip. "I mean, *it is*. I'm embarrassed about blurting out my heart, but I'm also kind of appalled with myself. You…" She pushes her hand in between mine. A tender hand sandwich as we lie on our sides, facing each other. "All you do is think and worry about others, but all I've been thinking about since the Yard Goat is *me*. What *I* want. What *I'm* feeling. I let my imagination run away with me, assuming you felt the same as me, and I'm scared I ruined everything now. That I'll lose you as a friend. I can't lose you, Cal."

"You won't lose me. Ever." But her confession hurts more than heals. She ran away from me and fell because I lied. She might have a concussion because I wasn't strong enough to tell her how I truly feel. What if my continued silence festers and grows and really does dissolve the rest of our relationship?

I drag in a ragged breath, suddenly realizing I haven't been breathing. "Jolene..."

"Yeah?"

"I..." Can't speak. My shoulders are bunched up. Clammy sweat grips the back of my neck.

"Cal." She squeezes my hands tighter. "What is it?"

"You're not wrong," I say in a rush. "Your imagination, what you said about my feelings—none of it was wrong."

She inhales sharply, more tears gathering in her eyes. "I wasn't?"

I shake my head. "I'm an asshole. Haven't handled this well. I pushed you away when I first moved back, avoided you since the Yard Goat. Everything's been so intense, but my fear of hurting Jake is just as strong. It all messed with my head. I should've been more honest with you from the start."

She shifts closer. "If you'd been more honest, what would you have said?"

"You really want to know?" Better question...can we handle airing more truth?

"I do."

"Why?"

"I don't like living with unknowns—questioning myself and my feelings because I'm getting mixed signals. I don't trust that this isn't a dream."

All I've given her are mixed signals. Smoke signals. Unattainable messages that disperse into the sky, their meaning lost to the clouds. "Some signals are better left in the dark."

"Not always."

"In this case, yeah."

Her attention moves over my face, drops to my lips, then detours to my eyes. "I think about you too much. All the time, without fully understanding how we wound up here. I want to understand so I can move on."

"Chihuahua with masochistic tendencies," I say, pinching the meaty part of her palm. "Poking bruises doesn't help them heal."

She pinches me right back. "My particular breed of Chihuahua is protective and loyal, as long as I understand my environment."

As long as she understands me.

I haven't given Jo a hell of a lot to work with in the understanding department. I haven't trusted her enough to share my hard truths. Maybe blunt honesty will show us a way out of this.

"Okay," I say slowly, trying to sift through the threads of our friendship and recent heartache. My brother at the center of it all. But our story started well before she said yes to dating Jake. "You sure about this?" I ask. "Once things are said, they can't be unsaid."

"I'm sure."

I'm not, but hell if I know a better solution to moving past this painful situation.

"Okay," I say again, taking a fortifying breath. "If I was honest with you when I was a stupid seventeen-year-old boy, I'd have asked you out before Jake ever had the chance."

She stills, doesn't blink. Just holds my hands tighter.

"When I didn't have the guts to tell you how I felt," I go on, committed now, for better or for worse, "and he came and asked me if I'd mind if he asked you out, I should've said yes. *Yes, I fucking minded.* I should've admitted then and there that I was in love with you and wouldn't be able to handle seeing you two together. But I didn't. I was insecure and didn't think you felt the same. So I fucked that up, and I didn't learn from that mistake.

"The second we got out of WITSEC," I continue, focusing on our linked hands, talking faster—a mudslide of unstable history crashing over me, "I should've called you and told you I missed you so badly my stomach ached for twelve years. That I have regrets about my youth and us, and life's too short for regrets. If I was honest, I wouldn't have tried to set you and Jake back up. I'd have shown up at your door and asked you on a date and tried to make up for being a stupid coward of a kid."

I can't meet her eyes, but I can't stop talking. *Truthing.* Hanging every heart-wrenching piece of myself out in the wind. "I'd have told you I want to get to know you now—the smart, funny, gorgeous, ballbusting woman you've become. I'd have told you I'm falling for you all over again. That I'm not sure how I'll ever meet a woman who makes me feel as whole and alive and happy as I do when I'm with you. And then, after baring my soul, I'd have remembered myself—who I am and what my family's been through. I'd have told you my brother and family mean the world to me."

My throat is a gravel road, every brutal truth driving over the roughness. I lift my focus from our linked hands, and my eyes clash with Jo's. There's no other way to describe the vibrations that reverberate through me, the shock in her tortured expression.

A one-way street I can't reverse on.

"I'd have told you, Jo, that the thought of hurting Jake in a way that could cause a permanent rift between him and me is my own version of hell. Then I'd have admitted my one dying truth when it comes to you." The hard fact I can't ignore. "I'm in love with you, Jolene Cynthia Daniels, but sometimes love isn't as important as duty."

There's no warning for her tears. No slow, glassy start and eventual spillover. Tears push from her dark eyes so forcefully, I drag her into my chest.

"You asked," I say as I stroke her hair, unable to control the way either of us trembles.

"It's not fair."

"Agreed."

We don't speak again, just cling to each other as my eyes start to burn too. Threaten to leak onto her hair. One night of no-holds-barred honesty, that's what she wanted. What *I* wanted. Then we can return to being friends. Best friends who might always wonder *what if*, but we won't live with doubts and questions.

Gradually, her body softens, emotional exhaustion and muscle relaxants doing their work.

I'm wiped, too, but also stunned. Shocked I confessed all that heartache, overwhelmed that Jolene is in my arms, under the covers, our bodies tucked together for comfort. But comfort eludes me. She fidgets and settles, wraps her arm around my back. Her breaths even out, but my eyes burn hotter. A sea of regrets pushing to the surface.

"I love you too," she mumbles into my shirt, surprising me by being awake. Gutting me a thousand times over. "The bar drains me. It's all so hard on my own," she says, her words running together in a kind of slur. "Wish it was out of my hands. Then you came back, and it didn't matter as much. *Nothing.* Nothing matters as much as"—she fists her hands into my T-shirt—"*you.* How *you* make me feel. Stupid fucking feelings. I've loved you most of my life, even when you were gone. More then, I think. Missing and missing. Now I have to let you go again."

"No." I lock her against me. Try to stem the pain pouring out of her. Too much damn pain. "We're friends, Jo. Always. Best friends who will get through this together."

"Life." She shakes her head and blows out a long breath. "Life is a fucking asshole."

E used to say the same thing. Blame the machinations of life for being torn away from Delilah and upending our worlds. Unfortunately, in that case, our degenerate father can take all the blame. In this case, there's no one to blame but me. I should've pursued Jolene when I had the chance.

Her body goes slack, her breathing turning deeper. I stroke

her hair, frustrated in a way I've never felt. Furious at our circumstances. But at least one good thing came out of Jo's pain meds and loosening tongue. *The bar drains me. It's all so hard. Wish it was out of my hands.*

I no longer have to wonder if guilt is what's keeping her there. She's running the Barrel out of familial responsibility and duty. Not because she loves it or even likes her work. And I know Jo. She won't make a change unless she doesn't have a choice in the matter.

Something concrete in her life I can fix.

I'll talk with Sandra tomorrow, get moving on the buyer she mentioned. They'll take over the space, lift this weight from Jo's shoulders. She'll finally be able to pursue cooking like she secretly wants—with a little help from me when I line up a new job for her—and I'll breathe a bit easier.

I kiss the top of her head. She doesn't stir, and my eyelids droop.

I'm suddenly as tired as the dead. Too drained to plot or relive tonight's messy confessions. My body drapes more heavily over Jo, everything drifting away except for the constant ache in my chest.

CHAPTER
Thirty

Callahan

Heat. Slick skin. Damp cotton. A warm heart beating against mine.

I blink. Confused, unsure where I am. Then it hits.

Jolene's bed.

Light filters through her window. Her bedside clock reads 8:27 a.m. I should be at work with Jake soon, but I'm tangled together with Jo, and she's moving.

No, not moving.

She's *roaming*.

Her hands are gliding over my bare back, under my shirt. And hell. I'm as hard as Sheetrock. So fucking hard for her, my erection pressed into her thigh as I grapple with my control.

"Jo," I say. One barely croaked syllable. "How are you feeling?"

Way to go, Cal, resorting to small talk instead of addressing the erection in the room.

"Frustrated," she says. "But fine." Her lips hover at my neck, barely brushing over the straining tendons. "I want…"

She doesn't finish, and she's not the only one who *wants*. Her hot breath on my skin has my eyes nearly rolling into the back of my head. "What do you want?" I whisper.

"To know."

"Know what?"

A full press of her mouth to my neck. "What your lips taste like. I know we can't be together. But what you said last night and how it made me feel…" She trembles against me. "Just once. Just one kiss. I want to know your taste before I let you go."

"Just once?" I hear myself saying. I am certifiable. Maybe I fell and hit my head too.

"Just once." Her tongue flicks over my collarbone.

I hiss through my teeth. My hands find her hips and dig in. "Just once," I repeat, because I need this too. To be selfish for a spell. One small taste. Then I'll be the good brother. A stand-up guy. Look out for Jake the way he always looks out for us.

But we need utter honesty, or this can't happen.

"One kiss won't work anything out of our systems," I say, as my hands roam too. Around her back and into her hair.

"I know." Her thigh pushes between mine. "It'll make it worse, but I need to know."

I grunt. I am nothing but pumping blood and too-big feelings crammed behind my ribs. Her fingers massage my back. I anchor her against my thigh, and *Jesus*. She's wet. Her sleep shorts are riding up and rubbing against my quad.

"Please," she murmurs, and I'm done thinking and worrying and waiting. A lifetime of pining for Jolene Daniels.

I dip my head as I surge over her, capturing her lips with mine. The second we connect, the electrical force between us ignites. Sparks up my spine. Static crackling through my limbs. Currents of energy surging through my heart. She groans into my mouth, grips my hair and gets more demanding, our tongues slipping into a seductive slide.

More voltage strikes my sternum, exploding through my body as tenderness burns the backs of my eyes. *Love.* I love this woman so damn much.

I didn't know kissing could be like this, short-circuit my brain while filling my heart. I think her name—*Jo. My sweet Jolene* —but I can't speak. I can only kiss her more deeply, breathe her oxygen as we move against each other, again and again, our bodies grinding to the rhythm of our mouths. Pushing. Pulling. Searching for an answer to this impossible situation until her legs are latched around my waist. My hand is fused to her hip, my aching cock notched against the hot center of her.

My cock pulses. Her hips jerk.

Our lips are still connected, but we're not kissing now. I don't move a fucking inch. It would be so easy to tear off my briefs, strip her naked. Learn the full glory of the woman under me. *Just once. Just a kiss.*

I pull my head back slightly. Enough to see her face. I pant out a desperate sound. Tears cling to her lashes. An encyclopedia of unsaid words splays across her face, that mysterious beauty mark the punctuation to her turmoil.

Our on-edge bodies stay flush, but I cup her cheek. "I wish..."

"Me too." She drags her thumb over my bottom lip. "If I was ruined for other men before, I'm destroyed now."

I drop my head into her palm, like a cat needing affection. "Told you once wouldn't help."

She shifts her hips, making the situation in my briefs unbearable. "Still worth it."

"For some asinine reason, I agree."

We stare at each other. I nip the tips of her fingers, can't bring myself to separate our bodies. And maybe I shouldn't. This is the type of connection that has hope burning bright through every crack in my heart. Our hips press harder, like we're speaking through movement. Testing how far we're willing to take this. *Just once. Just a kiss.*

The barest friction turns my body haywire. Our chests pump hard, and I can't stop. Don't want to. I never want to leave this room or lose the addictive feeling of Jolene pressed up against me.

My phone rings.

For sure Jake. Work.

I blink, rattled. Suddenly furious at myself for letting this get out of hand.

"That'll be Jake," I say, pulling away, trying to get out of the sheets, still so turned on it hurts to move.

"Cal," Jo says, pausing my rising panic. "We didn't do anything wrong. Jake and I aren't together. All we did was kiss. Please don't push me away. I'm sorry if I made things worse."

She's right. Sort of. Maybe not. And that was more than a kiss.

I scrub at my face. "I wanted that kiss as much as you did, so don't you dare apologize. I promise I won't push you away again, but I need to get to work and get my head on straight. I'm not feeling great about myself right now."

"Okay," she says, her voice so small it breaks me.

I hurry to the phone, so Jake doesn't worry about me and where I am. So he doesn't wonder if I was breaking his trust and ruining our relationship by choosing a woman over him.

CHAPTER
Thirty-One

Callahan

The second I get to work, Jake takes one glance at me and looks ready to spit nails. "Do you even sleep anymore? Jesus, Cal. You look like you've been hit by a truck."

He's not wrong. I caught a glimpse of my face in the mirror this morning—the dark circles under my eyes and stress lines sunken into my skin. I'm tanned from my outdoor work, but I looked drawn. Or maybe terrified. I'm certainly furious with myself for betraying Jake. I'm wrecked that I'll never kiss Jolene again, feel the hungry swipe of her tongue, her hands pulling at my back—Jolene as desperate for me as I am for her.

Nah. I definitely looked *shattered*.

"Had a rough night," I tell Jake and glance around the in-progress kitchen reno like I've never been here before. Like I've never seen walls and nails and tools. Like I can't figure out how I'm walking and talking when my heart is dragging behind me.

"Cal." Jake takes the tool belt from my hand and drops it on the floor, forcing me to face him. "What the fuck is up with you?"

He has brown eyes, like me. We're both tall and built, with big biceps and veined forearms from our physical job and gym workouts. We have callused hands and small scars from occasional work accidents, like the time I sliced my elbow on a jagged piece of pipe and bled all over the room. Our insides, however, are nothing alike.

Where I stay positive through action—plotting, planning, taking chance out of circumstance—Jake is a worrier. Hard eyes. Firmed mouth. Thick shoulders shoved back, like the platoon leader he tries to be, wrangling his brothers so we don't fall off any more cliffs.

At this precise moment, he looks ready to sit on me until I tell him why I'm a mess.

"Jolene," I say. The source of all my angst. Except she's not to blame for my nonsensical behavior. No one's responsible for my present circumstances but me. "She got hurt last night."

He startles and swallows hard. "Is she okay?"

Right there—that worried tone, the concern widening his eyes. He still loves her.

Asshole, table for one, please.

"Yeah, she's fine. Fell and hit her head. My neighbor checked her out, and I stayed with her last night to make sure she didn't wake up confused or show signs of a concussion."

"And she's okay?" he asks again. The worrier worrying, but there's no missing the way his voice softens too. Worrying with a side of heartache.

"She hurt her back, but she'll be fine." Or she's feeling as gutted as me, and she's not okay.

I rub my eyes. I swear there's grit in them. Some must have leaked down my throat too.

Jake makes a growly sound I'm not used to. I open my eyes, and he's glowering at me.

"You and I…" He points to me then to himself. "We're taking the day off and going to Sugar and Sips."

"No, we're not. We're working." I plan to hammer and saw until I can't feel anything but the burn of my muscles.

He snarls, looking concerningly like Desmond. He shoves me to get walking toward the door. Forget looking like Desmond. He's a cranky ship captain walking his mutinous crew member toward the plank.

We don't speak as we trudge to our respective trucks. I follow him into town. Catch him glancing in his rearview mirror, checking that I haven't tried to shake him. We don't speak when I get out and shut my door. My feet move by muscle memory as I walk toward my doom, otherwise known as an inquisition from my oldest brother.

He won't let my behavior slide. He'll stare at me until I crack. But I won't just crack. The secrets inside me are knocking around, growing bigger. Scarier. *I kissed the woman you love. I've loved her most of my life. I tried to split you two up before WITSEC and broke your heart.*

Someone pass me a paper bag, stat.

Jake turns, likely sensing my instinct to flee, and points toward Delilah's coffee shop. "Get in there."

Yep. He's going to stare a hole through my head.

Once inside, the pretty pastel decor does zilch to calm my rioting nerves. The space is warm and inviting as always, half full with laptop workers and chatting friends. Sandra and her immovable perm are in their usual stakeout position, where she can eavesdrop to her heart's content. The chalkboard menus are decorated with summery doodles. The air smells like melting sugar. I should relax, breathe more steadily. I'm a gas leak too close to an open flame.

"Hey, guys!" Delilah beams her usual smile from behind the coffee counter. "Shouldn't you be working now?"

"Yeah." E sidles up to us, his brown eyes darting from Jake to me. "You're always working at this hour."

As is he, but he's usually in here, where he can work on his illustrations close to Delilah. Also, he's not my only family in this pretty shop. Apparently, this day *can* get worse.

Desmond and Lennon are converging on us from a corner table, where they were likely discussing the adventure programs they run together. A vein in my forehead throbs. Nothing good happens when all my brothers get their briefs in a bunch. Three pairs of squinting eyes are darting between Jake and me.

Desmond crosses his arms. "Why aren't you two working?"

"Cal needs a break," Jake says, not beating around the bush. "He and I are gonna have a talk."

"Count me in," Lennon says way too eagerly. "I'm an excellent listener."

"Meddler," E corrects. "He's an excellent *meddler*."

Don't I know it—shoving me toward Jo on benches, getting up in my business about her.

I attempt not to grind my teeth.

Lennon hooks his thumb toward Sandra, who's sitting at a far table, conspicuous as ever. "If there's a meddler competition, Sandra wins, hands down. Last week she told me not to let Mrs. Ward from Ruby Grove sign her son up for my mountain bike program, like she runs our business."

Jake studies Sandra, who hasn't once looked our way. She's just an ordinary woman with a pointy nose and bad perm, who happens to work for me. "Did you let the kid sign up?" he asks.

"Of course not." Lennon squints at Jake like he's lost his marbles. "Sandra *knows* things."

More to the point, *I* know things.

Lennon and Desmond have worked their butts off building their adventure programs, but new businesses are tricky. Windfall is the Town of Wagging Tongues. One negative comment can sink you faster than the *Titanic*. So I asked Sandra to get the lay of the Kid Land. Suss out which little shits in Windfall and neighboring Ruby Grove are troublemakers.

I'm not privy to Sandra's methods—whom she speaks with, the leads she follows—but I pay her to keep an eye on my brothers, sit nearby at Sugar and Sips, listen for problems they haven't shared with me. When she heard them mention Mrs. Ward, or maybe she hacked into Lennon's computer and saw the kid's name—if I don't know, it's not my problem—she quickly told Lennon not to sign the kid up. Possible catastrophe averted.

"I think she's clairvoyant," E says, eyeing her with suspicion. "Her intel verges on creepy."

Lennon nods, then his hipster smirk shifts to me. "If she's clairvoyant, we should ask her why Jake and Cal are here to have a mysterious talk, when they should be working."

"We *are* working," I say, keeping my face relaxed. I am cool and collected. Not one of my feathers is ruffled. "Jake and I are here to talk about work, so you can all go back to painting your nails and gossiping about Sandra and *The Bachelorette*."

Lennon cracks a joke about Desmond loving reality TV, which he hates, but I don't listen to his barked reply. I need an escape route before this conversation returns to me. I could sneak through Delilah's kitchen, then out through the back door. Or go to the bathroom, slip out the window, then tell Jake I felt sick and left.

Yep. That's the ticket.

Humming in time to the music playing, I retreat from our circle and head innocently toward the bathrooms.

A few feet from freedom, Lennon steps in front of me. "Going somewhere?"

I gesture to the bathrooms. "Is this high school? Do I need a hall pass to use the lavatory?"

"No. You need to explain why I had a surprise visit from a building inspector the other day."

"You had a visit from an inspector?" I ask innocently, going for quietly concerned.

"I did," he says, getting up in my face. "She showed up with Dean, and I've been wondering ever since how Dean suddenly had time to work on my wiring, when he'd already told me he couldn't fit me in."

Continuing with my dumb act, I say, "Huh. That's odd."

"You're the only odd thing here," Lennon says, not buying my naïve routine. "The only reason I can figure that Dean decided to help me and inadvertently alerted the inspector to my lack of permit, comes back to you since you two were friends back in the day. I also know you were a secret vigilante growing up, avenging us if we were wronged. So, I'll ask again, did you do something covert to try to help me fix my wiring issue?"

I almost attempt another round of playing innocent, but my nerves are shot. This conversation is draining my fortitude and needs to end. "Yes, fine. I did it. I got Dean to work on your place."

"By doing deeds with the devil?"

"By doing what needed to be done."

"And now I owe extra cash and have to pause my renovations."

I huff. "I'm not the one who didn't apply for work permits."

"Not my finest move," he says, sounding annoyed with himself. "I've been busy, and it slipped my mind. But you need to quit it with the interfering. I know you mean well, but my life isn't your responsibility. You made this worse for me, not better. I need you to promise you'll quit meddling in our lives."

Agreeing should be easy. I just have to give him my word, then I'm free to shimmy out the bathroom window. But I think back to the first week of witness protection, how utterly bewildered I was. Learning all the lies Dad told, clueless to the guillotine he'd rigged over our heads. Never once did I suspect he was laundering money, cozying up with a drug cartel, sending us on a collision course with disaster.

That's when I vowed to protect my family at all costs. I would monitor their lives more closely. Never have to watch E sob into his knees again, begging to contact Delilah, heaving so hard he puked. I wouldn't have to witness Desmond punch walls with bloody knuckles and scream himself raw, missing Sadie and the life that was torn from him. Lennon turned despondent during WITSEC. Jake shoved his wants and needs into a lockbox and hurt himself taking care of his messed-up family.

Nope. Never happening again. Not on my diligent watch.

So, I look at Lennon, give him my most serene expression, and say, "I won't meddle in your lives again." *Unless I have to*, I don't add.

He folds his arms and taps his fingers on his elbow. "Such a liar, but back to Jolene."

"We weren't talking about Jolene."

"We're always talking about Jolene. I heard about her accident. She okay?"

Probably not since I kissed her to the clouds and back, then left her as quickly as humanly possible. "She seemed better this morning."

I drop my eyes. Can't risk Lennon sussing out how deep I'm in with her.

"For once in your life, Cal, can you be honest?"

I force my focus up and don't like what I see. Serious Lennon is worse than Meddling Lennon. "I'm honest."

"Not with yourself. Or with Jake. Or Jolene. I've been beating around this triangular bush, waiting for you to admit how much you like her, and I'm tired of waiting."

My face heats. I *was* brutally honest with Jo last night. Look where that got us. "You know damn well—"

He shoves his hand in front of my face. "Before you say anything about Jake, I'm pretty sure he's not really into her. There's other stuff going on with him."

A stone drops through the sudden quiet of my mind. Jake has seemed off lately. More intensely off than I expected, even with Jolene's rejection. "What stuff?"

"Don't know, and it's not the subject at hand. You killing yourself by keeping away from Jo is the issue. I saw you two together at soccer, having a blast. At the Barrel, joking around. You're both so fucking into each other, and you're not willing to do anything about it. You need to be honest with Jake. Talk to him about your feelings. He wants what's best for you."

"How is hurting Jake best for me?" I keep my voice down, but honestly. Does Lennon want to ruin our family again? "What good will come out of telling him?"

"Gee, I don't know." He taps his chin dramatically. "You might finally take a breath and be happy."

"Thanks for the sarcasm."

"Thrilled to deliver it." He plants his hand on my shoulder. "Your fear is driving you, nothing else. It's why you do secret deeds you shouldn't for me and everyone else. You think if you control everything, then nothing bad will happen to us. But news flash—you're not omnipotent. Bad stuff will happen to Jake and Jolene. To me when I do absent-minded shit like forget building permits, and there's nothing you can do about it. But there's one thing you can control." He knocks his fist into my chest. "Your Jolene-obsessed heart. Take control of your life. Finally go after what you want."

He stalks back to the group, and I waver on my feet. Should I take his advice? Tell Jake how I feel about Jo? Admit the lies I told when he first asked permission to date her and confess that I kissed the woman he wants? Or do I keep him happy and keep my betraying mouth shut?

"Cal." Jake interrupts my mental gymnastics and points to a table. "Let's sit and talk."

I'm back on that wooden plank, following my captain's orders, shark-infested waters surrounding me as I'm pushed toward a fate I can't evade.

CHAPTER
Thirty-Two

Callahan

Jake likes making direct eye contact. It's his thing. He thinks intensive staring allows him to read our moods and lies. Normally, I'm excellent at presenting a neutral front. *Nothing to see here, move along.* There's no way I'm neutral at this juncture.

Our brothers have all left. Jake probably kicked them out so he could have my undivided attention. Force me to spill my guts.

He doesn't start with pleasantries. "We're not leaving here until you tell me what's going on."

"It's nothing," I say. The comment is a cursory admission that something *is* off. Pretending I'm fine won't cut the mustard. His eye contact is extra laser focused this morning. "I'm dealing with the issue."

"Clearly not." He turns his laser beams to high. "I know you, Cal. Lived with you for most of your life. I've been giving you space, hoping you'll come to me when you're ready, but I'm done waiting. Something is eating at you. You haven't worked yourself this hard since the early days of WITSEC. I want to know why."

Guilt is a termite burrowing through me. Eating into my organs, my bones.

My hands turn damp.

"Cal," he says more insistently, "you better speak the fuck up. You're scaring me."

The bell above the door jingles. Mrs. Jackson walks in and waves at Delilah. Two teens are huddled on the comfy yellow chairs by the far window, laughing as they look at their phones. It's nice to see happy faces, but all I feel is tired. Exhaustion so thick my jaw finally loosens.

"I broke up you and Jo," I say. Not the confession I expected to blurt. A confession, nonetheless. Jo may have said my scheme wasn't why she ended things with Jake. Still, I was a catalyst, and my intentions were malicious.

I work my jaw and brace myself. Wait for Jake to explode.

His laser beams become extra glary. "What do you mean, you broke us up?"

"Before WITSEC, I was jealous and started that rumor about you and Larkin Gray."

He shifts back in his seat, blinks so slowly he looks like a confused robot. "You're the one who told me to take Larkin home that night. Said she didn't have another ride."

"I did."

His next blinks are faster. Angry pops of his eyelids. "So... what? You planned it all? Put that whole fucking mess in motion?"

That's me. Traitor with a capital T. I don't look down. I let him see how gutted and sorry I am. "I did, yes."

"Why the fuck would you do that, Callahan?"

"Because..." There's no stopping this runaway train. The conductor filtering my words has officially jumped out of the moving vehicle. "I was in love with Jo," I say quietly.

"Jesus Christ." Jake tears his eyes away from mine and glares at the windows. He looks stuck in his head, like he's replaying the memories of that fateful night—me nudging him to take Larkin home, telling him I'd see to Jolene, while I planned to weasel my way into the cracks I'd created and make Jolene mine. Except I didn't weasel far. I was too devastated by the damage I'd caused to do anything but cut Jo out of my life.

"I'm sorry, Jake. You have every right to be furious with me. Hate me. What I did was horrible."

He's back to staring, but this is no staring I know. His lips are trembling. *Incensed* trembling—like his emotions are too volatile to keep still. "You have no idea what you did, Callahan."

"Trust me, I do." But his voice has a scary edge I've never heard.

"No." He plants his elbows on the table, practically hissing. "*You don't know*, Cal. You have no fucking clue what you caused."

My hands shake with remorse. I squeeze them into fists, try to swallow.

"I asked you," he goes on, voice hard as nails. "Made sure I asked if it was okay if I took her out. Thought you maybe liked her, *so I asked*. You said it was fine."

I shrug, helpless and nauseated. "I was insecure. Didn't think she liked me back. I should've spoken up then, but I fucked up instead."

"And now?" His jaw bunches into knots. "Do you still have feelings for her now?"

We're well past laser beams. He's a high-powered telescope peering into my soul, searching for my secrets. I squeeze my fists tighter. The action doesn't help my shaking. Lennon's advice stabs at me too. *Take control of your life. Finally go after what you want.*

An avalanche of turmoil starts, punctuated by this morning's memories—Jolene's mouth on mine, her fingers, hungry and insistent, digging into my back. The mind-bending snap of desire when I settled between her thighs.

Jolene's quiet, *If I was ruined for other men before, I'm destroyed now.*

Ominous tingling overtakes my neck and scalp. The cracks in me widen, all my secrets clamoring to get out. I look at Jake, my selfless brother who's taken care of me and our family, and I utter the worst words known to man. "Yes, I still have feelings for Jo."

He flinches, like he's been punched. "For how long?"

"I don't know."

Fire shoots from his eyes. "*How long,* Cal?"

I try to find saliva. There's nothing left. No way to swallow the truth I've unleashed, and I'm suddenly mad. Furious at myself for leading us down this path. I deserve every bit of Jake's fury. "Since the first day I met her, okay? I was in love with her back then, was torn up over her during WITSEC, and have been sick with wanting her since I came back. And I kissed her this morning. So there's that too. I'm a fucking asshole. A shitty brother. I promised I'd help you win her back, and all I've done is lie and hurt you both."

Puking up a lung is probably a thing. It's on the verge of happening as I stare at Jake's reddening face, the tight press of his lips as he tries not to erupt. He's internally erupting, though.

Bulging eyes. Pumping chest. Purpling skin.

The bell above the door jingles. I glance that way—anywhere but at my brother, whom I've irreparably hurt—and guess who just walked in? Jolene and Larkin. Because this moment isn't calamitous enough. They're probably here to grab a delicious coffee in this delightful shop, clueless to the devastation I just caused. If they knew what I orchestrated all those years ago, they'd hate me too.

Jake makes a pained sound that ups my torture. The sight of

Jo is no doubt driving my stake further into his heart. Also? My traitorous body decides it's a good time to ping to life.

Needy lips.

Insistent fingers.

If I was ruined for other men before, I'm destroyed now.

I whip back to Jake, try to think this through. Get us back to the close brothers I need us to be. "I told her we can't happen. She knows. *I know.* It was just a blip this morning. We were both tired and overwhelmed from her accident and weren't thinking clearly. But I *am* thinking now, Jake. Jolene will only ever be a friend to me. You come first from now on."

He's not even looking at me. His hardwired focus is on Jo, and he looks beyond distraught. Equal parts mad and...*fearful* almost?

His furious attention snaps to me, zero forgiveness in his hard eyes. "You have no fucking clue what you did."

He scrapes back his chair and storms from the shop, abandoning me on this shark-surrounded ship. He doesn't need to walk me off this plank. I'll walk myself right quick.

Jolene comes over. She reaches forward, like she wants to place her hand on my shoulder, but she falters. Must be the tortured expression on my face. "Are you okay, Cal?"

I shake my head.

Frowning, she glances at the shop's door. "Why did Jake storm out of here like his ass was on fire?"

You have no fucking clue what you did. I slump into my chair, rub my eyes. "I've lost him."

"What do you mean, *lost him?*"

I blink at Jo, no longer attuned to my body's reaction in her presence. There's a boulder on my chest. Air is barely pushing past. How do I live without my brother in my life?

"Cal," she says and gently touches my shoulder, "what just happened?"

"I told him about this morning." My voice sounds strange to

my ears. Distant. "About my feelings for you. The kiss. He, of course, hates me now."

Her hand shoots to her mouth. "Why didn't you talk to me first? We could've done it together."

"There's no together," I say, my tone as lifeless as I feel. "You saw Jake tear out of here. There's no coming back from this. He won't forgive me, and he shouldn't." *You have no fucking clue what you did.* "I broke his trust and his heart."

"It doesn't make sense," she says, shaking her head and watching the closed door. "He was okay when I spoke to him the other day. I told him I wasn't interested in dating him, and he wasn't mad or upset."

I fling my arm toward the door. "Did that man look okay to you? Like a guy who isn't torn up over losing you to his brother?"

"First"—she leans into my space—"you don't *have me*, Callahan. No man has me. I'm my own woman, who chooses which man she cares about, and that man happens to be you. Although that status is questionable at the moment. Yes, he looked furious and upset, but I'm telling you, it's not because of me."

She's wrong. Jake doesn't get this livid or rattled. He doesn't tear off without finishing conversations. He took one look at Jo and practically ran out of here.

"I'll sleep on E's floor until your place is ready," I tell her as my stomach churns. "Once you've moved back in to your apartment, we'll see about trying to salvage our friendship. Until then, I think we both need space."

"Space." She rears back, clearly unimpressed with my solution.

I give a helpless shrug.

"Didn't you promise you wouldn't push me away again?"

"That was before I broke my brother's heart. I need to be there for him. Find a way to make this better."

A muscle below her eye twitches. "Fucking men," she mumbles and returns to Larkin, who's presumably been watching this car crash with glee. "I need to speak to Jake," Jolene tells her. "Whatever you wanted to talk about, can we do it later at work?"

"Sure, of course," Larkin says. "Do what you need to do."

Jo shoots me a look I can't decipher and leaves to find Jake. I don't know why she's bothering to chase him. He'll only hate me more.

Larkin saunters up to my table and crosses her arms. "Your brother is a fucking asshole."

I bristle. "He is no such thing."

"Oh, he is." Her face pinches, like she just tasted expired milk. "He has a knack for ruining lives. A talent he seems to be extending to you and Jo. My advice is to cut him out and get on with living. No good comes from Jake Bower."

She marches up to the counter, looking furious. The guilt termites living under my skin take a few more bites. I assumed Larkin shrugged off the rumors I spread. Dealt with the backlash and moved on. Apparently, she still hates Jake with vigor, and I'm an even bigger bastard than I assumed.

My phone chimes. I pull it from my pocket, but the device shakes in my unsteady grip. It's a reminder to pick up the extra wood I ordered for the Liang fence—this afternoon's scheduled project. The one I need to work on before meeting Javier for his bathroom reno, after which I planned to tackle more of Jolene's apartment.

Since Jake and I are clearly not working today, I can contact E before then, ask to sleep on his couch. Find Jake once he's cooled down and grovel my ass off.

Who needs sleep, anyway?

My phone chimes again, this time with a text from Sandra, even though she's sitting nearby. I glance at her. She doesn't look my way, just pretends I'm not here. When the rest of my life goes to shit, I can at least count on Sandra's staunch professionalism.

> **Sandra:** Buyer for Jolene's building is on the hook.

> **Me:** Lock them down.

> **Sandra:** You're not thinking clearly.

I frown at her message. Tiredness aside, my objectives are crystal clear. I have to win back Jake's trust, an uphill climb with no end in sight. Jolene and I will revert to being non-kissing friends. Since that outcome will hurt her, I'll do whatever I can to improve her life.

> **Me:** I'm as clear as a bell. She told me last night she wants out of the bar. Go ahead with the purchase.

> **Sandra:** I'm not talking about the building. You're not thinking clearly.

> **Me:** About what?

> **Sandra:** Jolene and Jake. You have the facts wrong.

I almost jump up from my chair, storm over, and confront Sandra. Demand to know what nonsense she's spouting, but we're in a public place. Delilah is behind the counter. One hint that I know Sandra more than casually, and our cover is blown.

> **Me:** What facts?

> **Sandra:** There are as many sides to a story as there are people.

Me: Did you read that in a fortune cookie?

Sandra: I read people. You're not thinking clearly.

Me: Then clarify things for me.

Sandra: Knowledge is best learned when discovered by oneself.

She definitely got that nugget from a fortune cookie. She's also an excellent spy, and her hints have trepidation creeping up my spine.

I try to catch her eye. She continues ignoring me. Gathers her belongings and leaves without a glance or text to shed light on her unsettling clues.

I'm more unbalanced than ever. Jake. Jolene. Lennon's prodding. Larkin's cutting words. Sandra's vague hints that I'm not seeing the forest for the trees, and I'm so fucking tired. Too overwhelmed to think clearly.

I stand and march for the door. I need to get moving, but the idea of working has me feeling sicker. I can't go home. Even if Jolene's not there, too much of her perfect chaos is in my space. I could go for a hike or head to Bear Lake. Stare at the water until the knots in my brain unwind. But there's only one location that's ever been my safe place.

My fortress away from the world.

I have no clue if it's still there. If it is, using it would be trespassing. Still, I find myself walking then practically jogging, hoping like hell the tree house Jo and I built still exists.

CHAPTER
Thirty-Three

Jolene

Leave it to Callahan Bower to shock the breath out of me. I thought this morning was the first and last time I'd ever taste his lips. I thought he'd bury our kiss and never mention it again. Then he goes and confesses it all to Jake, like he maybe wants to find a way through this mess together? Or this was his form of penance. Now he'll be so remorseful, the remains of our friendship will be scorched to dust.

I search Main Street for Jake, sure I'm too late to find him. He tore out of Sugar and Sips so fast, he's likely long gone by now, but I spot his parked truck, with the man sitting inside.

I jog over and knock on his window.

He startles, then glances at me. And...*God*. He doesn't just look upset. He looks like a man shaken to his core.

My heart gives an uncomfortable pinch.

Maybe Cal was right. Maybe Jake's acceptance of my rejection was a show for me. Maybe he's actually been torn up over it, forcing his emotions down, and I had no clue. I might not have romantic feelings for him. Our relationship was more surface than deep and loving, but he's a good man. A friend I care for deeply. My part in his devastation hurts to think about.

I circle to the other side, open the passenger door, and slide into his truck. The air feels thick with heartache.

"I'm sorry," I say on a heavy exhale. "When we talked the other day, I didn't mention Cal because I was sure he didn't feel the way I feel. I was positive it would never be an issue. Then last night and this morning happened, and there's obviously no going back from here. So I need to be one hundred percent honest." I angle toward Jake, bite my lip at how torn up he seems. "I love Callahan. I think I have for most of my life."

He stares hard out the front windshield. "Even when you were with me?"

"In a way, but more like he's always been a part of me. An organ that makes me function properly. But when I was with you, I was *with* you. I didn't spend that time pining for Cal. But then you and I started to drift apart. I know you felt that too—that we weren't all that compatible in the end. Or maybe from the start."

He sighs at the truck's roof. "I did."

His admission eases a bit of my remorse. "The other day, when I told you I only wanted to stay friends, you agreed it was for the best. You said the *idea* of getting back together was what drove your interest, not any real feelings. Was that true, or were you putting on an act, pretending you were fine?"

"Jolene." He hangs his head and massages his brow. "When I moved back to Windfall and saw you, it was like time froze. Or more like I could rewind time? Pick up where we left off and erase the hell of my past twelve years. It was a false emotion and fleeting. So, yeah—I meant everything I said the other day. I was wrong to pursue you. I'm not mad that you're in love with someone else. I *am* shocked it's Cal, but I'm not angry with you."

"But you're angry with Cal? That's why you ran out on him?"

A muscle in his jaw bunches. "This isn't about you and Cal. Not really. Don't get me wrong. Seeing you two together would be…strange. It'll take some getting used to. But I didn't tear out of there because of that."

"Then what? Why are you so upset?"

He grips his steering wheel, twisting his hands around the rim. "The night those cheating rumors started, something happened with Larkin."

Hurt instantly rises. Anger at Larkin, not him. My feelings for Jake are too watered-down to get mad at our ancient history, but Larkin has become a friend. My closest friend outside of Cal. She sat there and lied to me, telling me they never hooked up. "I'm honestly floored. I believed you when you said nothing happened, and Larkin assured me you two didn't hook up."

He shakes his head quickly. "We didn't. It was nothing like that, except…"

"Except?"

"If I'm honest, since today seems to be an honesty bloodbath"—he runs his tongue over his teeth—"I wanted to. Larkin and I talked a lot that night, and I felt something for her, which made me feel awful and guilty, but I didn't act on it. Something else happened that night, something I don't want to discuss now or probably ever. Larkin has every right to despise me, and I'm a little furious with my brother right now for setting all that in motion."

I face forward, relieved but also concerned. I'm worried for Jake and Larkin and whatever it is they went through. I'm terrified there's too much baggage between Cal and me for him to give us a true shot, and Jake's last comment means Cal's guilt could be even worse.

If Jake's upset with Cal for putting him on that collision course with Larkin, then he thinks Cal's the one who started the cheating rumors. As did I, back in the day. Or maybe *wished* is the better word. I selfishly hoped he'd orchestrated that debacle because he loved me as much as I loved him. Then everything got too messy on my end. He pushed me away, and I no longer trusted my Callahan intuition. But a lot has happened since then.

"Did Cal arrange it so you had to take Larkin home, and then he started the cheating gossip?"

"Ah, fuck." Jake knocks his head into his headrest.

"I take it that's a yes?"

"Yeah," he says, sounding drained. "Probably shouldn't have said anything, although fuck that. *Yes*, Cal planned that whole fiasco. He wanted you, but was likely too guilt-ridden afterward to do anything about it. And now Larkin—" He clams up and his jaw pulses. "You don't sound surprised," he says, switching topics. "Did you know Cal orchestrated it all?"

"I had a feeling, yeah. I was planning to end things with us anyway, and I was thinking about Cal a lot. I assumed when we were over, Cal and I might finally have a chance together, but I realized afterward that I wouldn't have been able to handle it. The idea of dating him right after dating you, *if* he was interested, felt wrong. And he got really distant anyway. Would barely speak to me."

"Then we went into witness protection," Jake finishes. The kind of plotline you'd see on TV. "What about now?" he asks, still looking out the window. "You two obviously have strong feelings for each other. Does the idea of dating Cal still feel wrong?"

Jake's dashboard is dusty. I trace a slow line through it, a divider between then and now. "Twelve years is a long time. We've all changed, and what happened with you and me seems distant now. Like two different people in a different life. With our history, dating Cal isn't ideal. I don't want to create awkwardness with you or your family, but the idea of being with him doesn't feel wrong anymore. It feels terrifyingly *right*."

He nods as my admission lingers. "All I want in the end is for my family to be happy. For Cal to take a breath and look after himself."

"Does that mean you're okay if he and I get together?"

He rolls his head toward me, a kind smile spreading over his face. "I love you, Jo. Not romantically, but as a friend. And I love the hell out of my brother. If you'll make him happy, then yeah." He pats my thigh. "I'm okay with it."

"I never meant for this to happen," I say, my voice sounding watery as I grip his hand. "You know that, right?" Dating brothers is a stress I don't need or want, but staying away from Callahan is agony.

He shrugs. "The heart wants what the heart wants."

"You'll meet someone." A man this kind and undeniably handsome won't stay single in Windfall long. "But she'll have to be pretty amazing to deserve you."

He huffs out a sad laugh. "I need some time to process all of this, but you should get out of here and find Cal. Go make my brother happy."

I nod, barely able to contain the swirl of excitement spinning through me. Today is *not* going as I expected. "If he's not at work with you, where would he go? Home?"

"Doubt it. Right now, he's berating himself for hurting me, while also trying to forget you. There's too much of you around his place to do that."

My heart hitches. Cal must be wrecked right now. Barely holding it together, clueless to the fact that we finally have a chance to be everything we both want.

"I have to find him, Jake. I have to—"

A loud knock makes me jump.

Sandra is at the window, patiently waiting for us to roll it down.

Jake turns on his truck and complies.

"Callahan was seen driving toward his childhood home," she says bluntly. "You can find him there."

She spins and marches off.

Jake watches her warily. "How did she know we needed to find him?"

"Don't question the ways of Sandra," I say as I push the door open, my heart racing faster than I can move.

"Are you sure she's right?" he calls. "Why would Cal go to our old house?"

"He's not going to your house. I know where to find him."

He'll be at our tree house. His safe place when we were kids, because he's likely falling apart at the seams. I need to get to him. Be there for him. Tell him he never has to hold back from kissing me again, and hope his guilt doesn't keep him from letting me in.

CHAPTER
Thirty-Four

Callahan

Coming here was a bad idea. I'm parked on an old grass-covered farm road, the one that led to my family's dilapidated barn, and I've been here for a while. I don't remember the last time I've sat idly with nothing to do except think.

Only slivers of our house are visible from here, but I see my family playing football in the fields. My brothers and me ganging up on Desmond when wrestling in the yard. Adventuring with Jolene, chasing butterflies and pretending they were faeries.

I see the first day we drove to this place—our new home in a new town—and how I gripped my seat belt, shaky and nervous, terrified to start school. I see myself driving home in a rush the day we celebrated Des getting into Duke Law. I was so damn happy for him then. Proud of my smart, determined brother. I see Jake slinging his arm around me at our campfire, telling me I'm his favorite brother so I'd give him the last marshmallow to roast.

I see the last day we were driven away from here in a US Marshal van, E's pained sobs echoing in the small space, Desmond growing eerily quiet. Lennon was unable to quit shaking. Jake's jaw was so tight I was sure it would crack. Dad was already at the Safesite, leaving Mom alone with us, nearing hyperventilation herself.

Then there was me.

I barely moved on that fateful drive. Gravel crunched under the van's tires as my family's misery grew thick and stifling, my stomach twisting so forcefully I thought I'd puke, but all I did was stare ahead of me, helpless and in shock.

Tingling spreads below my jaw now and down my throat. Uncomfortable heat suffuses my face. I shove my door open and start moving. Running. Heading to the one place filled with only good memories. Jolene memories.

Please be there. Please don't be broken like everything else.

I run faster, like I'm being chased. A deluge of history barreling down on me. Then I spot it. The tree house is too far to tell if it's falling apart like me or if it's still usable. The simple walls protrude from the old oak tree, claiming its place at the edge of the forest. I push my legs harder. Air rushes my face, but it doesn't cool me down. The closer I get, the faster my heart pounds.

The ladder going up looks intact. More than intact, actually. It looks like it's been rebuilt with sturdy steps. I grip the first rung and pull myself up. Barely recall moving my feet or arms, but I'm suddenly in here. My place—*our* place. I lean my back into the wall and sink down to my ass. Pull my knees to my chest and drop my head, trying to drag in slower breaths.

Everything burns. Like I'm roasting on a spit, my molecules moving under my skin.

"Callahan!"

I blink, sure I'm hearing things. "Jo?" I say, but it comes out as a quiet croak.

She's not here. I must be dreaming. Imagining a world where I'm allowed to love her.

"Callahan." This time her voice is closer, like she's climbing toward the tree house.

I tilt my head and see her mirage. Or is that really her? Jolene, Savior of my Serenity?

I rub my eyes, which feel gritty.

"Oh, Cal." She rushes to my side and wraps her arms around my shoulders. "It's okay. *You're* okay. I'm here, and I'm not going anywhere."

Nothing is okay, but I cling to her and shove my face into her neck, hugging her as those memories continue bombarding me. I don't recall the last time I gave myself permission to relive those days. Don't remember the last time I slowed down long enough to feel. This place, though. These walls. This woman. It's like I'm safe enough here to finally let go.

Slowly, I pull my face out of her neck. "You found me."

She rubs a reassuring hand down my back. "I'll always find you, Cal. You're stuck with me."

I take deeper breaths and wipe a tear tracking her cheek. "It kills me that I hurt Jake. Not sure he'll forgive me. Not sure I'll forgive myself. And you…" I look at this woman whom I love with all my heart, feel a piece of it tear off and wither. "I'm not sure how I'll live without you."

More tears trail her cheeks, but she smiles. A trembling smile I don't fully understand. "You don't have to live without me. We don't have to pretend anymore."

I shake my head vehemently. "But Jake—"

"I spoke to Jake," she cuts in, "before coming here. He's not upset about us. Not really, at least. He's upset about Larkin."

I blink at her. Nothing she said makes sense. "He ran out on me. Told me I had no clue what I'd done, like I ruined his life."

"Cal." She threads our fingers together, keeping us close.

"The night you schemed to break up Jake and me by using Larkin, something else happened between them."

"Jake told you I planned that?" My pulse stumbles back into a jog.

"He did."

"And you don't hate me?"

She blinks at me like I'm clueless. "I knew back then, Cal. At least, I was pretty sure that's what happened. The rumors made it easier to break up with Jake, which I'd been planning to do anyway. And I was so sure you and I would finally be together. But I realized being with you so soon after Jake wasn't right, and you pushed me away. But none of that's why Jake ran out of Sugar and Sips. He's not mad about losing me now or even about you and me dating. I think he broke a promise to Larkin or something. Hurt her in a way neither of them will explain. *That's* why he's so upset. He's angry with you for putting in motion whatever went down."

I think back to seeing Jake at the Yard Goat Gallery recently. He took one look at me and Jo, and his good mood plummeted. He tore out of there and wouldn't talk to me. Larkin had been with us then, standing right between us. Then today at Sugar and Sips. I assumed seeing Jo walk in was the final blow to Jake's heart after my miserable confessions, but Larkin had come in too. That was when Jake said, *You have no fucking clue what you did.*

"What could have happened between them to upset him this much?"

"Wish I knew. But, Cal, Jake isn't mad about the idea of us. He actually gave us his blessing."

"He did?" She nods, but it's not enough. Today has been a whirlwind. I pull our linked hands to my chest, want her to feel how fast my heart is racing. Proof my body is linked to her every word. "Could he have been telling you what you wanted to hear?"

"No." She shakes her head firmly. "We had an honest conversation. He said seeing us together might be awkward for a bit, but more than anything, he wants you to be happy."

It's still not enough. I'm scared to believe her. Terrified to let myself finally imagine having Jolene in my arms whenever I want. "He could be lying."

"He's not."

"You might realize dating me doesn't feel right in the end, like when we were younger. You might regret trying."

"Well, let me dispel that worry for you." She wraps her arms around my neck, getting even closer. "I love you, you big dope. I've loved you as long as I've known you. Sometimes just as my best friend. Sometimes as more. But since you've been back, those feelings have multiplied. They've grown so big I can barely concentrate some days, and seeing you half naked did *not* help. So you don't have to worry about me having second thoughts. Jake is okay with us dating. The only question left to ask is...are you okay with this? Or will you always feel guilty about our history?"

No way in hell, if it means I get to have this woman.

I kiss her hard. Dive right in, capturing her lips before either of us can change our minds. I move in closer, deep and hungry, on the edge of desperate. She moans. My answering grunt is savage.

How did I end up worthy of Jolene's love?

My hands are in her hair while she grips my shoulders, breathing hard.

I press my forehead to hers and murmur, "Yes and no."

"Yes and no?"

"Yes, I'm okay with this—with *us*. No, I won't feel guilty about being with you. Not if Jake is okay with it. Something this right can't be wrong."

We both smile, and I gather her closer, pulling her between my legs with her back flush against my chest. My arms are latched around my best friend, probably too tight. For the first time since barging in here, my chest doesn't feel like it's vibrating. I'm calm enough to look at my surroundings.

Whoever fixed up the stairs also redid the interior. This smaller side is sparse, the walls painted a deep red. A shimmery curtain divides the space.

Curious, I lean forward, tug it aside, and freeze.

"So...um, this place looks different." There's a mirror on the ceiling with a small plush cushion below. Bars have been installed on the wall, and handcuffs and a riding crop are in the far corner. "Are we in a sex room?"

She snorts, her ear closest to me burning pink. "I believe we are."

"Oh my God." I bury my face in her neck and laugh, the two of us shaking and losing it together. Could this day get any wilder? "Who owns this home now?"

"New couple from Raleigh. They're only up on weekends. Apparently, they have a kinky sex life."

I'll say. There are large beads and a collection of different-shaped vibrators in a basket, which has me thinking about Jolene's vibrator and the not-so-subtle comment she said a moment ago. "What were you saying before about seeing me half naked?"

She leans her head back and noses my neck. "You have to know your body drives me wild. Half the women in this town want you doing their *renovations*."

I chuckle, still can't believe I can breathe her in like this—lightning storm and fresh spring growth. A new beginning, no more guilt holding me back. "The only woman I plan to do renovations for is you, Daniels. But I don't want you to move out." I lean over and drop a kiss on her beauty mark. "I want you to keep living with me."

She tips her head up, suddenly bashful. "We're not even officially dating."

I rub my nose against hers. "We're already doing it—living together. Why quit now?"

"In separate rooms?"

"No fucking way."

She melts into me. "Yeah, okay. But…"

"But?"

"I need you to promise me something, Cal."

The serious note in her tone has me tensing. "Anything, Jo. Ask, and it's yours."

"No more schemes. No interfering in my life. I understand what drove you to start that Larkin rumor, but it wasn't cool. You pulled that prank on Lane Ternent eons ago and have likely done other deeds over the years to avenge me or help me in some way. While the sentiment behind the meddling is sweet, I'm not a damsel in distress. I don't need saving. I don't want you working on my apartment without telling me. Next time, if you're worried about something or about me, start a conversation about the situation. Talk to me about it, but don't take over and cut me out. I need to make my own mistakes and find my own solutions. Most of the time, you're meddling because of *your* issues and concerns, not mine."

Yep, I'm definitely tense.

I'd wager tasking Sandra with extricating Jo from the Barrel House—having the building sold and Jo evicted to chase her true dreams—counts as meddling. And she's right. My actions aren't selfless. I interfered to make myself feel better after hurting her. Lennon was spot-on too, berating me for messing up his renovations. Jake is furious with me for setting him and Larkin on a mysterious collision course. I need to learn to let life unfold naturally.

"I promise," I tell her. The second I'm back in my truck, I'll tell Sandra our work together is done. "I won't meddle in your life again. Or anyone's. It won't be easy for me, but I'm realizing I'm making most things worse."

"Thank you. Boyfriend," she adds with a quirk of her lips.

I smile. "Can't believe this is real."

"Neither can I." She runs her thumb over my knuckles. "Are you still feeling out of sorts? You were pretty shaken up when I got here."

I take stock of my body. The too-tight, rushing feeling has left my chest. Memories aren't crashing into my present. "I'm better. Calmer."

"Was it just Jake? Worry over causing a rift with him?"

"Partly. I was pretty devastated over the idea of losing you too, but it's also the history of this place. My old home and Windfall in general."

"I'd be shocked if all that pain didn't affect you."

"Yeah, but...Jake said something to me the other day. Told me I haven't stopped moving since WITSEC, that I've been worse again since returning here. I brushed him off. Didn't want to pick apart my actions, but I think maybe he's right. I think I've been scared to stop and feel. Like I'm living in a house of cards— one wrong move and it'll all come toppling down."

She traces the crew neck of my T-shirt. "Do you think you're ready to slow down now? Feel whatever it is you're feeling instead of bottling it up?"

I nod. "It's time. I know it's time." To let go of my scheming and planning. To slow the fuck down. "Might mean I have some tough days, but I'll maybe call you when that happens? If that's okay with you. You have this way of calming me."

A galaxy of affection fills her eyes. "You better have me on speed dial."

We stare at each other a moment. Connected without uttering a word, then we kiss sweet and slow, adjusting to get better access. But something digs into my back.

I reach behind me and pull out a...strap-on dildo?

Jo chokes on a laugh, cracking up so hard she's crying. I'm

right there with her, laughing until my stomach hurts and I'm wiping at my eyes. Yeah, today has been wild.

"Can we go home?" I ask, amazed I'm allowed to say that. *Home*. With Jolene.

"Home sounds perfect. Do you want to stop for food or anything on the way?"

"I'm barely holding my head upright at the moment. All I want to do is crawl into bed with you and sleep."

"Kinky," she says, giving me a cheeky wink.

I kiss her temple but feel a new rush of nerves. Jo and I have never discussed sex. I don't know what she likes and doesn't like. Compatibility goes beyond emotional connection. "I'm not a sex-room kind of guy, Jo. Is that okay with you?"

The only way to describe her expression is *enamored*. "I'm okay with whoever you are. And I'm not a sex-room kind of woman, so no worries there."

I exhale as a bubble of anticipation rises. Soon, when I sleep off this stress-packed day, I get to explore her. Take my time with her. Show Jolene Daniels, Savior of My Serenity, exactly what kind of lover and boyfriend I can be.

CHAPTER
Thirty-Five

Callahan

I wake up in my room. I'm in my bed—the space that used to plague me, knowing Jolene was on the other side of the wall. Now she's locked against my chest, probably too forcefully.

"You're a furnace," she says against my neck.

I run my hand down her back, slowly waking up. "Is that bad?"

She shakes her head. "I like it. How long did we sleep?"

I blink at my clock. "Jesus. Five hours. Don't you have to be at work?"

"I texted Larkin when I got here. She offered to cover for me tonight."

"Sounds like she's been a good employee and friend."

I keep stroking Jo's back. She's tracing shapes on mine. We're both in T-shirts. She's in her sleep shorts. I'm in my briefs, and the hard length of me is very happily pressed to her thigh. Even better, we're still talking. Best friends to the core. Talking and tracing, shifting with anticipation, knowing we'll be doing a heck of a lot more than talking soon.

"I honestly don't know what I did without Larkin before I hired her," she says and kisses my neck. "Except she wanted to discuss something about the Barrel this morning. We got sidetracked by you and Jake. If she quits, I might lose my mind at the bar."

Sandra. The building. Instantly, I want to intervene. Give Jo the out she craves, but I already spoke with Sandra after leaving the tree house. Told her to back off from selling that real estate, and I promised Jo I'd do better. I *want* to do better.

I run my nose through her soft hair, press my lips to her forehead like it's the most natural thing in the world. "If there's an issue, let me know. We'll talk it out."

"I will." She nips my collarbone. I hiss out a strained breath. "Maybe she just wants to tell me she's crushing on someone at the bar and is worried about inter-coworker romances."

I drag my hands lower, slip them into the waist of her sleep shorts. I find the divots along her lower back and trace the crease in between. Her breath catches.

"Do you two gossip about men?" I ask with my mouth at her ear. "Did you tell her about your feelings for me?"

"There may have been some gushing. Especially after I saw you half naked." She slides her legs farther around my thigh and rubs against me.

And *fuck.* She's wet and hot. Too good to be true.

I push my hands farther down, take two glorious handfuls of her bare ass. I make a guttural sound I've never heard. "Want another viewing?"

"Yes." One syllable. A pant of breath.

"Only if I get one too." I'm more rested than I've felt in a while, recovered from this morning's shell-shocks. I'm taking an actual day off, but my muscles are coiled. Bunched with awareness of Jolene. She's everything I want in a partner—fun, witty, kind, caring. I can cry in front of her and not feel like less of a man. I can tease her. Laugh with her. This intensity between us might short-circuit me, but I don't care one bit.

Her hands are on my shirt before I can get to hers. She's pushing the cotton up and over my head. By the time it's off and tossed to the floor, Jo is leaning over me—a fucking gorgeous view. Cherry-ripe cheeks. Pretty eyelashes lowered. Full lips slightly open.

Her attention fixes on my torso. "Jesus, Cal. You don't even look real."

Heat suffuses my face, and I glance away from her. "It's just a body."

"Are you serious right now? You know you're spectacular, right?" When I don't reply, she brings her hand to my cheek. "Why are you embarrassed?"

I shrug, feeling oddly exposed. I place my hand on her hip. My palm looks huge on her. "Girls didn't look twice at me growing up. If anything, I was laughed at." Too-long arms. Lanky build. Confidence of a skittish cat. "Objectively, I know I'm fit. Attracting women hasn't been hard. Some insecurities never go away, I guess." I run my thumb over the soft fabric of her shorts. "I care a lot what you think of me."

She sighs. A soft sound I can't fully interpret. "Just when I thought I couldn't fall any harder for you."

She straddles my lap, taking control. *At your disposal, ma'am.* My cock is hard and insistent, pressed between her thighs. I hold her down harder, rub her a tiny bit.

"God." Her eyelids drift closed, then they snap back open. "Quit moving. You're distracting me from my perusal."

"Perusal?"

"I was surprised when I saw you shirtless—wasn't expecting much chest hair." She runs her fingers through the patch on my chest. "The rest of you is so smooth. I need to soak it all in."

"Do you like chest hair?"

"According to my body's reaction right now, I love it. And I really love this tempting trail." Her fingers dance down my chest, to the finer hairs leading toward my briefs.

I flex my fingers and tense my thighs, but I follow her orders and do *not* shift a muscle.

Before my eyes roll to the back of my head, she's on the move again, charting the contours of my pecs, the hard bumps of my abs, the V that is very sensitive right now. "Your hip bones are ridiculous, by the way. And these abs? You should be photographed for a fitness magazine. But…"

Unable to stay still, I rotate my hips the tiniest fraction and barely refrain from tearing off her underwear. "But?"

"If you decided to work out less and eat more, if you were softer under my hands, I wouldn't be any less attracted to you. The only thing about you that can't change is this." She presses her palm over my heart.

That's it. I'm done for. So far gone for this woman I may as well get her name tattooed on my forehead: Property of Jolene Daniels.

I pull her down, kiss her breathless. Hungry tongues. Nipping teeth. Moans shared as our tongues slide. "My turn," I murmur as I flip us around.

I fit myself between her thighs and place her hands above her head. "Don't move."

"That's my line."

"I'm too turned on to think of fresh material."

Smiling, she complies, arching her back slightly. I mentally add *seductress* to the list of things I fucking love about Jolene. I lift the edge of her top, unhurried, enjoying the slow reveal, like the rise of the sun over land, one gorgeous landmark exposed at a time—the gentle slope of her belly, the slight jut of her ribs, her lush breasts that pull a gusty breath from my lungs.

I toss her shirt over with mine, smiling at the goose bumps spreading over her skin.

"Can I move now?" she asks.

I shake my head. "I've waited a lifetime for this. Give a guy some time."

She sinks her teeth into her bottom lip, squirming a little. Unsure where to start, I place the back of my hand against the side of her breast, follow the contour. Barely brush my knuckles over her pert nipple. Her breath trembles.

"Are your nipples sensitive?" I ask. "Do you like attention there?"

"Yeah, but not too rough."

I use my thumb and forefinger this time, give her friction, but not too much. "Good?"

Her answering nod is jerky. Her arms are still above her head, but they're flexed, her hands squeezed in small fists. Her body is as on the brink as mine, and I fucking love it.

With my hips between her spread thighs, I rock forward, small thrusts, making sure I hit her clit through her sleep shorts. Her moan is a gift. I grin, still exploring her breasts, using my tongue this time. Sucking on her lightly, studying her every reaction—which moves make her arch more, breathe harder, squirm under me.

I spread my palms on her rib cage. "Sorry my hands are so rough. They feel brutish on your soft skin."

"I love it," she whispers.

"Yeah?"

She nods, and I love *this*. Open exploration. My unquenched need to please Jolene. Letting her guide me, show me, teach me. I drag my callused palms down. Her hips buck up, but I pause. Her sleep shorts have lowered over her left hip, revealing discoloration.

I trace the darker shapes of color. "What's this from?"

She wrinkles her nose. "Just a birthmark. Kind of ugly. I've always hated it."

"Jolene Daniels." I move down her body, hooking her shorts

as I go. "Your whole body could be covered in birthmarks, and I wouldn't be any less attracted to you. The only thing about you that can't change is your inside."

"You keep stealing my lines," she says on a happy sigh. "Again, all my blood is rushing south. Too turned on to think."

I wink at her and fling her shorts off the bed, and *hell*. Those tight, dark curls. Her fucking glorious body. I shift backward, press my palms to her thighs, and spread them apart to look my fill. "Goddamn, you're gorgeous."

"Um," she says softly.

Heart stuttering, I flick my eyes to hers. "Is this not okay?"

"I don't know. I feel weirdly exposed. I think I need to move my hands. Touch you."

I travel up her body, adjust us so we're both on our sides. She digs her fingers into my back, her lips plump and parted.

My rough hands don't abate. I massage her ass, her thighs, lick a path up her ear until she shudders. "This better?"

"Yeah. But I need you naked." Her thumbs are already in the waistband of my briefs, dragging them down. I lift my hips, but she can't reach too far, and the material bunches under my ass.

This part of fooling around has always been awkward for me. Briefs that get stuck. Bras that don't unfasten with ease. Stilted smiles or laughs that are more anxious than amused. With Jo, everything is different. She laughs and tips her head into my chest, shaking lightly. I chuckle with her, not caring in the least how unsmooth I am. We work together, wrestling the cotton off my impatient legs, and I get a little overwhelmed.

I think this is the true intimacy I've never experienced. The non-perfect parts of sex made perfect through comfort. Learning what we like and don't like. The fumbles. No worries or judgment. Every second with Jo is fun and exciting.

When I'm finally naked, I pull her flush and groan. "Do you have any idea how fucking good you feel?" Skin against skin.

Our thighs threaded together, and the way her intimate curls are pressed against the aching length of my cock.

"I have some idea," she says with a lick up my neck.

I kiss her again. Can't *stop* kissing her. Tasting her lips as I roam my hands over every inch of her skin. She reaches between us and grips me. Gives my dick a squeeze.

There's no controlling the buck of my hips, the animal sound that escapes me. "Goddamn, Jo."

She's a busy little thing, pushing me onto my back, working her way down my body. I stroke my hands through her hair, still overwhelmed. On fire. So fucking entranced by her all I can do is grunt my pleasure. Then her mouth is on me, kissing the length of my twitching cock. My blood turns to lava. Her tongue slides up a pulsing vein, and I drop my head back and curse.

"Jo, baby. You can't be down there long. This needs to last."

She pauses, brushes her lips lightly over my abdomen. "Say that again."

"This needs to last?" Each strained word is packed with gravel.

She tilts her head to meet my searching eyes. "Call me baby again."

"Baby," I murmur on a smile. More intimacy. So fucking much I can barely handle it. "You're tearing me apart, honey. Piece by piece."

Her eyes gloss over. With her focus locked on me, she takes the tip of my cock between her lips and sucks. I don't blink, even though fire is blasting through my veins. I refuse to get lost in sensation. I keep my eyes on my best friend's stunning face, her enraptured expression brimming with emotion, like she's as awed by this as me.

She alternates between small sucks of my cock and teasing tongue strokes. Pleasure nearly blinds me.

She lowers one of her hands, strokes my balls lightly. "Do you like this?"

Another buzz zips up my spine. "Not normally, but whatever you're doing, don't stop. It's fucking fantastic."

She hums. "What about when you're getting head? Do you like it tight and fast or slow and deep?"

Is she trying to murder me? Kill me with each seductive word? But I love that she wants to learn about me too. "The tip," I ground out. "Tight and fast just there, then—" She flicks me with her tongue, blurring my vision again and stealing my voice. "Fuck, Jo."

"You were saying?"

My laugh sounds half tortured. "Tight and fast on the tip, then slow and deep."

Another satisfied hum. "Delayed pleasure."

"It's all pleasure, baby. Every fucking second."

She follows my description with vigor, but the second she presses the head of my cock to the back of her throat, heat tears up my thighs. "Too good, baby." I cradle her head and ease her up. "I'm not coming in your mouth this time."

I kiss her hard. My new favorite hobby: kissing Jolene Daniels. Pretty sure I could come like this, with my tongue stroking hers, our greedy hands restless on each other. I flip her over, moving faster down her body, no longer stopping to explore. I am impatient. So fucking turned on and desperate to get my mouth on her. I clamp my hands on her thighs, spread her open, then remember her hesitancy earlier.

I look up. "Is this okay?"

She's lifted on her elbows, her pupils blown wide. "Yeah. It was the watching before, I think. I got self-conscious."

"Good, because I'm fucking *dying* to get my mouth on you."

I close my eyes, breathe in her musky scent. Lick a slow path up her pretty pussy. *A meal fit for a king.* She falls back on a moan and grips the sheets in desperate fists. I've never been so entranced during sex. So full of anticipation and excitement, the need to make Jo fall apart directing my every move. I watch each jerk of her hips, each spasm of her belly, cataloging her reactions, storing them for later as I lick and suck and use my fingers to take her higher.

"Fuck, Cal. *God.*" She pushes harder against my mouth. A final lurch, then she's shaking and fluttering around my fingers, and I truly do feel like a god. Capable of anything, because of the woman calling my name.

Her fingers dive into my hair. "*Now* I'm ruined for all other men."

"There will be no other men, Jo. Only me from now on."

"Yeah," she whispers. "Only us."

That sentiment hits me in the heart, adding to this whirlwind of emotion I can't contain.

I kiss her inner thigh, pay special attention to the discolored birthmark at her hip. "I want to be inside you. Unless it's too soon. We don't have to have sex today."

"I've waited a lifetime for you, Cal. I'm not waiting any longer."

I smile against her soft skin and give it a little nip. "Let me grab a condom."

She touches my forearm before I get far. "I'm on the pill, and I've been tested."

My cock pulses. So strongly, Jolene looks down at my flushed length and licks her lips.

Fuck, do I want to dive into her bare, have her be my first like that, but I'd never put Jolene at risk, even if the risk is minimal. "I've always worn protection and haven't been with anyone in a while, but I haven't been tested since. It'll be condoms until I get that sorted."

She sinks her teeth into her bottom lip and nods.

I fish a condom from my nightstand and settle back between her thighs. Go to tear the packet, but she takes it from me. Another usually awkward part about sex. Safety and precautions hitting pause on desire.

Jo quirks her lips. "This better be the extra-large variety."

I pinch her thigh lightly. "I'm not that big."

"Babe, you're the envy of dick pics everywhere. A card-carrying member of the Perfect Cock Club."

I laugh, deep and unchecked. I've never laughed while in bed with a woman. More firsts with Jo. "Say that again."

She quirks her eyebrow. "You're a card-carrying member of the Perfect Cock Club?"

I trace a slow line across her belly. "Call me *babe* again."

Her dark eyes shimmer. "Babe."

"Yeah, baby?"

Her laugh is full of tenderness. "This feels like a dream."

"I'd prefer not to wake up, then."

"Me too."

She strokes the length of my erection—body buzz number fifty—then lines the latex over the tip, looking so full of affection and excitement, I'm not sure I'll survive sex with Jo. She has a way of stripping away my layers. Exposing the soft center of me.

I'm completely at her mercy.

She slides the condom down, checking that it's secure.

I lean over her, needing our bodies touching as my tip finds her entrance. "I'm yours, Jo. Always have been. Always will be."

"Never leave me again," she says, and her eyes fill until tears spill over.

I kiss her cheek, wipe the wetness with my thumbs. Try to erase the hard parts of our history. Years we spent together reading the signals wrong, letting our insecurities dictate our lives. Me disappearing into WITSEC.

I press my lips to hers as I ease my hips forward—a slow and purposeful push while kissing, refusing to rush this moment, even though desire is pulling my muscles taut.

She makes the sweetest *ah* sound.

My rough noises mingle with her name on my lips, along with "Ah, fuck. Jolene. Perfect."

We're flush now. Hips fused, her knees digging into my sides. I thrust deeper, then go still, affected by everything—the emotion clogging my throat, being with Jo in this way. I frame her face with my hands and look her in the eye. "I love you, Jo. Kind of drowning in it over here."

Her inner walls pulse around me, and a deep flush blooms up her neck. She turns her head, kisses the center of my palm. "I knew I loved you, Cal. Knew what I felt for you was big, but I didn't know it would be like this."

"Scary big?"

"Are you talking about your cock again?"

I bark out a laugh and move, pull my hips back then sink into her tight heat. She gasps.

I grin. "You're gunning for a punishment, Daniels."

She moans and thrusts up, meeting my purposeful strokes. "Do your worst. I can take it."

Fuck yeah. She can.

I resume my new favorite hobby—kissing Jolene's smart mouth—a little rougher this time. I rotate my hips while locking us tight, grinding against her pelvis, getting so lost in her I'll need a map to find my kitchen afterward. Each drag out has my mind screaming *no*. Each push in has me murmuring words like *love* and *you* and *home*.

"I'm close," she pants in my ear, clawing at my back.

"Right there with you, baby."

I alter my angle the way she seems to like, push up into her, hitting the spot that makes her eyes go hazy and her inner walls clamp down.

"Fuck." One breathy word, then she's gone, convulsing around me. Tight squeezes that detonate through me. I come in a rush, chasing her pleasure, because that's my duty now. Following her. Ensuring her happiness before I take my own.

And *hell*. Either an earthquake is rocking Windfall, or Jolene just tilted my world.

The aftershocks are an experience of their own, stealing my vision and tremoring through my limbs. When my soul returns to my body, I run my nose up her cheek. "We'll need to repeat that."

"Often."

"Daily."

"Aim higher."

I laugh, cuddling her closer.

"I used to imagine," she says in my ear, trailing her fingers through my hair, "superheroes having sex."

I grin. "Your brain is weird."

"Our sex was superhero sex."

"We should trademark that."

"I'm still a little shell-shocked I get to have you," she says, her tone turning serious.

I drop small kisses on her eyelids. "You're stuck with me now."

My phone buzzes from my dresser, and I shoot my attention there. In the past, if my phone went off while with a woman, I wouldn't hesitate to drop what I was doing to grab it. The move always irritated the person, but my family history has made me dependent on the device. If something happened with one of my brothers, or if our father pulled another stunt, I couldn't wait to find out. The need to be there for them was too strong.

I kiss her again. "Is it okay if I grab that? If it's one of my brothers or Mom—"

"You don't have to explain, Cal. I know how important they are to you. Do whatever you need. I never want to come between you and your family."

I nod, loving her more by the second. I deal with the condom and come back into the room buck-ass naked. Jolene's eyes are on me. One hot look, and my spent cock takes notice.

I check my phone.

> Jake: I'm taking tomorrow off. Not because of you or Jo. Just need a breather. Be back the next day. We can talk at work then.

"Everything okay?" Jo asks. She's suddenly behind me, molding her soft breasts to my tense back. Her arms snake around my waist.

I press my hand over hers. "Jake's taking tomorrow off. Needs some time alone. Says it's not about us."

She runs her nose up my spine. "Based on my talk with him, I'd believe him. Whatever happened with Larkin, I think it was a big deal. Seems like he's dealing with a lot of guilt."

And I'm the one who toppled the first domino of that mystery.

Reluctantly, I move my hand from Jo's to tap out a reply.

> Me: If you need me, call. See you Friday.

I drop my phone back on my dresser and swivel in Jo's light hold. "Guess I'm working alone tomorrow," I say, running my hands through her hair.

"Or you could take the day off too. The Spring Fair starts tomorrow. I could play hooky, and we could go together. Larkin can cover for me again."

I run my hands down the smooth lines of her back, ending by tracing the divots above her ass. "I'd have to disappoint my clients. Let them know things are being delayed."

"Even though you have superpowers in bed, you're not indestructible. You need a break. They'll have to understand."

She massages my shoulders, looking up at me with such adoration I swear I'm dreaming. My cock thickens, letting me know I'm pretty darn awake.

"Okay," I say. "We'll take tomorrow off, but I'd rather not go to the fair, if that's okay. The town will go nuts at the sight of us.

I'd rather go somewhere quieter. I'll plan something else for us to do."

Her face lights up. "Like a surprise?"

"Exactly like a surprise, because I know my girl loves surprises." I kiss her and grab her ass, lifting her until she twines her legs around my waist.

"You're so strong," she says as I prop her back against the wall and claim her mouth. Hot, slow kissing. Our bodies cling and grind until I'm rock hard again, rubbing against her slickened clit.

"I'm gonna ruin you tonight," I murmur, "Fuck you over and over."

She digs her heels into my ass. "Not if I ruin you first."

I lick the corner of her sassy smile. "Good fucking luck on that."

CHAPTER
Thirty-Six

Callahan

My truck rocks as I drive down Windfall's country roads. Luke Bryan strums from the radio. The sun is bright through the windshield. The touchdown on this gorgeous day? I have Jolene's hand in mine.

She leans forward in her seat. "Are we heading to the quarry?"

"There's nothing romantic about a big old hole in the ground."

"But we *are* doing something romantic?"

Her tone is so cute, so bright and hopeful, I can't keep her in suspense. "We're going to Sugarhill Farm." The farm we visited often growing up, always ending with our fingers stained red and our stomachs full of sweet berry goodness.

"Really?"

"I wouldn't lie."

She gets quiet, and I glance at her pensive profile. "Is Sugarhill okay?"

"The farm is perfect. I just haven't been there since you." She lifts our linked hands and kisses my knuckles. "I've missed it."

I squeeze her hand. "Me too. Strawberry season is nearing its end, but the raspberries are out early this year. We're gathering dessert for our picnic."

"Careful there, Bower. If you set the bar this high, you're setting me up for disappointment in the future."

I huff, thinking about Javier's high-bar jabs and those ridiculous stripping rumors. "Why is everyone going on about me and bar setting? And anyway, this is me on low. You're not ready for my high bar yet."

"Someone's overconfident."

Or determined to make Jo the happiest she's ever been. "I know you. Know what you like. There might be a visit to a flea market in our future."

"Really?" Her voice pitches in excitement.

I chuckle. I have the perfect market in mind, where we'll invent stories about bets lost, wars won, family squabbles lasting generations. We'll look at pieces like they're the photographs on my wall. Stories locked in time, as Jolene and I give them new life while having a laugh.

"That is definitely a high bar," she says. "I haven't been to a market or antique store in ages."

"No time?" I ask, glancing at her.

She runs her nails down the side of my hand. "Like with Sugarhill, they reminded me too much of you. Going places filled with our history was hard."

I blow out a rough breath, wishing I could time travel. Rewrite those awful years. "I hate how hard our disappearance was on you."

"And on *you*. I've been thinking about that a lot lately—how devastated you must've been. And I heard about your half brothers, that your father dropped that bomb on you through his tell-all biography. Have you met them?"

I nod. Another shocking surprise from the man who ruined our lives, this one less unpleasant. "I don't talk with our father or see him, but I'm the intermediary with his wife. We've met the boys a few times. They're sweet kids, and I'm glad they know about us now. I don't trust that they won't need to lean on us in the future. We're not close, but I've made it clear they can reach out if needed."

The truck bumps over a pothole. Jolene releases my hand and threads her fingers through the back of my hair. "How did such a good, sweet man come from that piece of shit?"

Only Jo can make me smile while talking about Raymond S. Bower. "You can thank my mother and brothers for my goodness. She raised us right. Or maybe it was my best friend?" I nudge her thigh. "She kept my arrogance in check with her poor sportsmanship."

"Poor sports*woman*ship, but all I am is a proud winner."

"Or just plain obnoxious."

She flicks my ear. I flinch and rub the sting away, smiling.

We pass the sign to Sugarhill Farm and pull down the gravel road to the U-Pick area. I've come here with Jo a hundred times. Two best friends living the small-town life of fresh-grown foods, free time filled with outdoor activities. Nothing much has changed about the Clark family farm, including the large boards with cutouts for faces and painted strawberry bodies below, where tourists take pictures. But this is the first time I've helped Jolene from my truck, held her hand, stopped to kiss her softly because I simply could.

She hums against my lips. "I like Romantic Date Callahan."

"He likes you too."

"Callahan Bower? And is that..." I turn to find Gabby Clark blinking at us. "Hey, Jolene."

Jolene instantly drops my hand and steps away from me. She gives Gabby a small wave. "Beautiful day. Has it been busy? God, it's nice out, isn't it?"

4 HINTS YOU LOVE YOUR BEST FRIEND 259

I almost laugh at Jo's awkwardness. She's likely worried for me. I may not have been ready for the onslaught of Spring Fair gossip, but I don't want to hide my feelings for Jo. She deserves to be treated like the queen she is.

I wrap my arm around her and pull her into my side. "Gabby, great to see you."

Jo relaxes, settling her hand on my stomach. Gabby's eyes widen. I haven't seen Gabby since my return, but she's still tall and slim, her dark skin offset by her orange sun hat. Her family has owned this farm for generations. From what I've heard, she runs it with her brother now.

"I probably shouldn't make a thing of this," she says, gesturing to us, "but you two always made sense as a couple to me. Feels good to see you together."

"Real good," I say, brushing my hand down Jo's arm. Goose bumps travel in my wake. "Do we still pay after we pick?"

"You know the drill." She fans her hand toward the stacked containers. "There are a few tourists out there now, but it's quiet. Spring Fair is the place to be this week." She stares at us another beat, then shakes her head. "Have fun, you two."

"Our first public couple moment," Jo says, watching Gabby tidy a stack of hay bales. "Do you mind?"

"That people know we're together?" I swat her ass and nudge her toward the stacked buckets. "Not one bit. I just haven't talked to Jake yet. I'm still worried about hurting him. I'll feel better about full-town events once we've cleared the air between us in person. For now, we have a raspberry-picking competition to attend."

"Because you think you'll pick more than me?" She grabs two buckets and tosses one at my head. "Fat chance."

I catch it with one hand. "I know I will. Should we place a wager?"

She holds her bucket against her stomach, looking pensive. "If I win, you can't comment on my lack of tidiness for a month."

"Yeah, okay." I certainly won't tell her I don't mind her mess as much as I once did. Her hurricane ways don't need encouragement. "If I win," I say smugly, "you can't boast after a soccer win for a month."

She rolls her eyes. "That's lame, but fine. I don't need to boast. The knowledge of victory is enough for me." But her cheek twitches. Not rubbing everyone's faces in their losses will murder her.

"May the best roommate win," I say and hold out my hand.

We seal the wager with a shake, then she bolts ahead of me— sneaky woman—racing to the raspberry patch. Thankfully, my legs are longer. I overtake her quickly, then hear an "Ow."

Worried, I stop and whip around. Jo waves her fingers at me and darts by. Laughing, I take a sharp left, hoping the shortcut through the apple orchard is the same. *Bingo.*

"You're cheating!" she calls.

"It's called winning!" I holler back.

I beat her to the raspberry patch and have a handful of berries in my bucket before she starts picking. Over the next half hour, raspberries are pelted at my head. Jolene yanks my shorts down once, not far from an elderly couple. I almost drop my stash and have to hop around to pull them back up. I smear raspberry pulp onto her neck.

She body checks me away with a haughty "Act your age."

"Mentally, I'm still sixteen and obsessed with you."

That earns me a blush that matches the raspberries in her bucket.

When we're done, we stand over our buckets and peer inside.

"It's no big deal," she says, frowning at my larger haul. "Silent gloating is a thing. I can mess with people's heads quietly."

I wrap my arm around her, leading her to the exit. "I'll get you a stress ball. Something to squeeze when the urge to brag becomes too much." She pinches my side. I kiss the top of her head. "Ready for our picnic?"

She moons up at me. "Can't wait."

I drive us to Bear Lake, pleased only a couple of other trucks are here, but nerves spin through me. I brought more than food with me today. It's no big deal, a gift I think Jo will appreciate. Or more of an offering? My heart laid bare for her.

Trying to act casual, I haul my basket and a blanket out of my truck bed. "If you take this to our old spot, there's something else I need to grab."

"I love that we have a spot," she says and kisses the center of my chest.

I smile down at her and run my thumb over her bottom lip. "Spots, plural. Half of Windfall is filled with memories of you."

A stockpile of history I never forgot.

She steals another kiss, then carries the basket to our old spot —a secluded rock ledge on a quieter side of the lake, a bit higher from the ground—while I pull the bag I stashed from behind my seat.

When I join her, she has the blanket down. She's sitting on the ledge, her legs dangling over with her face lifted to the sun. I put my bag down and join her. We watch a couple swim lazily in the shallow area. Two women are lying on a blanket by the shore, sharing food and the occasional kiss. The surrounding trees sway in the slight breeze. A fish pops to the surface and disappears in a ring of water. We don't talk for a bit, just let the beauty of Bear Lake lull us. Tranquility I've sorely missed.

"So," I say, lifting my hand to brush back the stray hairs blowing across her face, "I brought something for you."

"If it's a poor loser medal, I'll pass."

Smiling through my nerves, I drag my bag closer and pull out a shoebox. *The* shoebox. The one thing I took with me when I was ripped away from my life.

Swallowing roughly, I hand it to her.

"What's this?" she says, scrunching her nose at the box. "Did you buy me shoes?"

I shake my head and wait. She slants me a questioning look, then slowly lifts the lid. She stares at the contents a moment. No reaction. The recent notes she wrote for me are on the top—our food flirting and fun cooking game. She picks one up, reads it, and bites her lip.

She moves those to the side and digs more purposefully through the box. Sifts through our old movie and concert tickets. Edwin, her skull-shaped rock. A stick she used to use as a wand to cast spells while adventuring. There are small notes she left me over the years, including her cute "You suck at football," written after I fumbled the ball, giving Jake's and her team the win.

She traces the bubbled curves of her writing. "You said you left Windfall without taking any of your stuff."

"No, I talked around the question—said I had to leave Windfall quickly, that I didn't get to take *much*. Truth is, this is the only thing I grabbed from my room. I had a feeling I wouldn't see you again, and I couldn't leave this behind."

"Oh, Cal." She carefully replaces the lid and runs her fingers over the closed top. "We lost so many years apart from each other. Not knowing or understanding..." She trails off, blinking out a tear.

"Hey." I tip her face to mine and brush her cheek dry. "We know now. Understand now. I wasn't comfortable sharing this with you before—letting you see how much you really meant to me. But I wanted to show you now. Put it all out there. I love you, Jolene. Plan to make you so damn happy you can barely stand it, while kicking your ass at berry picking."

Her watery laugh is full of fondness. "I love this box of history, and I love you." She presses her forehead to mine. "Even when you cheat at berry picking."

"There was no cheating," I say, with a tickle to her side.

"Also, Mom's homecoming surprise party is in two days. Will you come with me?"

She pulls back. "Are you sure? It's a special day. I don't want to make this uncomfortable for anyone."

"My family loves you, Jo. And they love me. They'll be happy we're there together, and I'll let Jake know ahead of time. If he's as okay with things as he says, he won't mind."

"Then, yes." She leans her head on my shoulder and runs her hand along my thigh. "I'd love to be there with you."

"It's settled, then." I twirl her hair around my finger, getting turned on by her proximity. The soft drags of her hand close to my suddenly aware cock. "Also, how do you feel about getting finger-fucked on this ledge out here?"

She sputters out a laugh. "Jesus, Cal. Who are you right now?"

I ease her away from the ledge. Adjust us so she's lying down and I'm on my side, protecting her from being seen. "Too blunt?"

She pushes her hands up my T-shirt, fondling my abs. My cock goes from aware to demanding. "Perfectly blunt. Dirty Talk Cal is as much fun as Romantic Date Cal."

"Wait until you meet Spoil You Rotten Cal. He has plans."

She beams up at me with so much trust and affection, my chest gets all locked up. Jammed with a landslide of feelings.

I trace a path up her soft thigh, under her skirt, and run my knuckles over her panties. I groan. "You're already wet for me."

"Seems to be a constant problem around you." She reaches between my legs, squeezing the hard ridge of my shaft.

Heat snaps up my legs, but I bat her hand away. "Just you right now. I want to take care of you."

"Only if I get to touch you after."

"Deal," I say as I push her underwear to the side and grunt again. "So fucking wet and perfect."

She clutches my forearm as I drag my thick fingers over her slit. The color on her cheeks deepens, and she tips her head back, giving me control. Her hips jerk. Her eyelids flutter. Her breasts push up on faster breaths. "Cal," she says on a pant.

"I know, baby." I crowd closer to her, addicted to the sight of Jolene getting off.

Her body coils tighter, her composure faltering with each flick of my finger. I don't blink. I thank the fucking stars that Jolene and I found our way to each other in this crazy life I've led. Never again will I have to know the agony of living without her.

CHAPTER
Thirty-Seven

Callahan

I'm at work before Jake, and I'm never at work before Jake. Granted, I'm usually coming from an early gym workout and have to haul ass to get here. I did a different kind of calisthenics this morning, involving Jolene, the shower, and her legs wrapped around my waist. I barely beat the clock afterward, but I did. And Jake's not here.

He's furious with me, my mind chants. *He can't stand to be around me right now. He won't forgive me for whatever trauma I caused.*

I stand in the driveway. Plant my fists on my hips as I think. He might be at home. Or at the lake. When talking about Windfall over the years, he often mused about Bear Lake— missing the tranquil spot and the clear water. If he's struggling, he could've gone there.

I head to my truck just as his blue Ford rolls down the street. He turns into the driveway, parks, and shoves his door open.

I wait, heart rattling a nervous tune.

Dark circles ring his eyes, and his face is drawn. "Why aren't you working on the cabinets?" he says, like today is any old day. Like I'm not in love with his ex-girlfriend.

Like I didn't monumentally fuck him over before WITSEC.

"Jake," I start and then take off my baseball cap. A sign of respect and seriousness. I cradle it against my nervous stomach. "Thank you for understanding about Jo and me."

He hooks his thumbs on his pockets, standing straight and stiff. "You're together, then?"

I try my hardest not to grin, fighting the happy feeling bubbling up from my goddamn toes. "Yeah. She's gonna stay living with me."

"Wow." He passes his hand over his mouth, revealing a surprising smirk. "You can let out that idiotic smile, Cal. I'm happy for you both. You deserve every good thing—as long as you're not doing this because of the excitement of being with someone off-limits. You have to be with her because she owns your fucking heart."

I swallow through the guilt that still lingers and remember how perfect the last couple of days have been. Raspberry picking. Sharing my shoebox of mementos. The utter comfort in our quiet moments. The intimacy and fun of sex with Jo. "I love her. More than I thought possible. She's the best thing to ever happen to me. But no matter what you say, I know this must be tough on you. Weird or awkward, at least. I'll do my best to make things comfortable when we're all together."

He nods. Glances at his boots as darkness tinges his expression. "I'm still furious at you. You caused a lot of damage with that Larkin stunt. A really bad string of events."

"I'm sorry, even though I know words don't help. I have no excuse for my behavior. Wish I could go back and punch myself, change what I did. But if there's anything I can do to help now and make amends, even if it's just being a sounding board for you to vent, please ask."

He rubs his sleep-deprived eyes. Lifts and lowers his ball cap. "Unfortunately, there's no talking through this. I'd just like to get to work."

He brushes past me, but I grab his arm. "But we're good? You forgive me?"

"Cal." He grips the back of my neck in a reassuring hold. "My family is everything to me. *You* are everything to me. I'm pissed and frustrated, and seeing Larkin around town isn't helping, but we're bound by more than blood. We've been through a shitstorm of hell, and the last thing I'll allow is a rift to form between us. Be with Jolene. Let yourself be happy. If I'm in my head and distant, don't take it personally. You might have set that stuff with Larkin in motion, but I made bad choices that night too. Those consequences are on me."

He pulls me into a hug, because we're huggers in this family. The crushing kind with back pounds and huge arms offering comfort.

"Thanks," I say as we pull apart. "I asked Jo to come to Mom's surprise party tomorrow. Hope that's okay."

He nods, then chews his lip. "Does Mom know about you two yet?"

I shake my head. "Thought I'd tell her in person."

"More surprises at her surprise party," he muses.

I scratch my neck. "You think she'll be upset?"

"Like me, all Mom wants is for her family to be happy. I'll make sure she knows I'm okay with things."

"Thanks," I say gruffly. "And I plan to slow down too. Not work as much." Spend time with Jolene instead of filling my days with endless distractions. Play soccer with her. Maybe lounge around on the odd vacation day, drag her to Bear Lake for more picnics *and finger-fucking*. Goddamn, yesterday was a stellar day.

Without warning, Jake plants his huge hand on my face and

shoves me back. "Get the fuck to work and keep that nauseating smile in check."

Not sure that's possible, but I feel lighter than I have in a lifetime. Especially when I think about stopping by the Barrel tonight to see Jo.

My phone buzzes before I get far. I frown at Sandra's name. After my talk with Jo, I thanked Sandra for her diligence over the years and ended our working relationship. I told her to terminate the deal selling the Barrel's building, and that I'm done trying to control everyone's happiness. If Sandra's messaging me now, she must have hit a snag.

Feeling uneasy, I tap her message.

> Sandra: The deal with the Barrel's building is going ahead.

> Me: I told you to kill it.

> Sandra: The wheels were already in motion. Francisca got it in her head that she wants to sell and use the money to buy a place in Florida.

I stare at the message as oxygen saws against my lungs. This can't happen. Jolene made it clear meddling in her life wasn't acceptable. *I* don't want to meddle any longer. And what the hell is so good about Florida, anyway? Windfall has mountains and charm and community. This town is all Francisca needs.

> Me: She can't sell now. I promised Jo I wouldn't interfere.

> Sandra: Avalanches only travel in one direction.

Here we go again with Sandra's fortune-cookie talk.

> Me: What does that mean?

Sandra: You asked me to push the first rock.

Shit. I drag my hand down my face, doing my best not to slam my phone on the ground. I don't make false promises to Jo. If this goes ahead and she finds out I intervened, she'll be understandably upset.

…Unless she doesn't find out.

I straighten and think. Fact is, Jolene doesn't want to be tied to the Barrel. If the land is sold and she's evicted, she'll actually be relieved. Before my promise not to interfere, I organized a possible job for her running one of the local food trucks, which I think she'll dig. And I did *try* to stop the avalanche. I listened and kiboshed all meddling. If there's nothing to be done at this point and Jo benefits anyway, what's the harm?

Just as quickly, my optimism plummets.

Not admitting what I did is a lie, no matter how I frame it in my mind. Even if Jo is eventually happy with the sale, I have to tell her what I did. Warn her about what's to come. Pray she understands my actions were borne of love.

My insides twist as I reply to Sandra.

Me: You did all you can. Thanks for your work over the years. I'll take it from here.

And hopefully not wind up devastated and alone.

CHAPTER
Thirty~Eight

Jolene

Most days, I walk into work with my shoulders heavy and steps slow. My mind is often muddled with bar issues that need fixing until I remind myself how much Aunt Becca loved this bar and me. How proud I am to carry on her legacy.

Today, I'm peppier than a one-woman cheer squad.

"Someone had a good morning." Larkin is filling a beer glass, while my other staff serve the meager lunch crowd gathered for their greasy favorites.

I don't scrunch my nose at the sight of deep-fried mozzarella sticks and deep-fried chicken wings and deep-fried mushroom caps on the few occupied tables. I drop my purse on the bar and grin at Larkin. There's a chance I look slightly deranged. "I had an excellent morning, if you must know. And an excellent night. An excellent couple of days, actually."

"*Really* excellent?" she says, lacing her words with innuendo.

"Excellent and beyond," I singsong. Cheer squad with a dash of crazed-woman-high-on-pheromones.

She laughs. "You sound like Buzz Lightyear after multiple orgasms."

"Well"—I lean forward on the bar and lower my voice—"I did have superhero sex. Multiple times, so..."

"I'm assuming Callahan Bower was wearing the cape?"

I melt to the side, resting my head on my hand. "All this pining and waiting, and he's better than anything I've ever imagined. Not just the sex, which is..." I bite my lip. There are no words to describe connecting with a person on that level. "He's so caring and sweet, which I already knew, but it's different now. So intense, but also easy."

"You're going to be unbearable for a while, aren't you?"

My cheeks already hurt from smiling. "Odds are high."

"Since you're in such a chipper mood, can we talk for a minute in your office? We're not super busy. I can slip away for a bit."

We aren't busy at all, really. The lunch crowd hasn't picked up lately. It looks even quieter than usual. The decrease in business should have stress lines creasing my forehead. Today, nothing can dent my good mood. Unless Larkin is about to quit.

Walking with a tad less cheer, I lead Larkin into my office. Her blond hair is tied into a neat braid, her expression distant, like she's spinning words in her head. The usual sarcastic glint she carries isn't anywhere in her blue-green eyes.

Instead of falling onto the couch for a casual chat, I round my desk and sit in my chair. Everything about Larkin reads, Serious Talk.

"Lay it on me," I say. There's no point beating around the bush. Larkin is a straightforward, honest woman. If she's quitting, I'll just have to work more. See Cal less.

A pin of disappointment pricks my happy balloon.

Larkin sits taller and nods. "I want to buy in to the bar."

"You...*what*?"

"Buy in to the bar. Be a partner with you. You've done an

amazing job giving the Barrel life. It's a staple in the community and a testament to your hard work. But it can be better. The food. The decor. Special events to liven up the lunch crowd. I have ideas—*lots* and lots of ideas. And I love working with you," she goes on, talking quickly. So confidently, I'm hanging on her every word. "I have funds saved and have spoken to the bank about a loan. I know changing the Barrel is a tough hurdle for you, but I also know you haven't been happy with it. Not truly. I think you want to keep it. Keep your aunt's legacy alive, but that doesn't have to be exclusive of you thriving. With a partner, all the pressure wouldn't be on you. I'd be here to share the burdens. Together, I think we can do great things."

She draws in a deep breath. I'm not sure I'm breathing at all.

My first reaction is *no*. I can't change this place. Not the food I hate. The atmosphere, which hasn't been pulling in as many customers lately. I can't change the Barrel because the Barrel is Aunt Becca. It's the last piece of her I have. She left it to me. I'm supposed to keep her dreams alive.

Great things happen when you dream big.

Her framed note looms large from my desk. Her dream. The Barrel. This casual gathering place she envisioned and built.

Or did I misinterpret her note?

Maybe she wanted this to be my jumping-off point, not my end goal. Maybe she wasn't referring to *her* dream continuing on through me. What if she wanted to inspire me to chase my own dreams instead?

"The regulars might not like changes," I say. Not an outright *No*. Not *Thanks, but I don't feel right changing this place.* "We could lose more business."

"We could." She nods. "But reward only comes with risk. And the Barrel House will still be the Barrel House. I'm not talking about a complete overhaul. Definitely a big menu shift and some other fixes. With your love of food, you'd have to help with that end of things. Hire a new chef who jives with the changes and doesn't forget to place meat and produce orders because he's drinking at work—which has been happening, by the way. And I was thinking we could make lunch fun for people. Like let people roll dice when paying their bills on a certain day—if they roll snake eyes or something, they get a discount. Families would eat that up."

I stare at Larkin, still shocked and overwhelmed, but seriously impressed. "*Everyone* would eat that up. Do you have more ideas like that?"

She taps her temple. "They're fighting for space."

I cover my mouth with my hand, glancing again at Aunt Becca's note. *Great things happen when you dream big.*

I've dreamed of revamping the menu for years, renovating the kitchen, but I always dismissed the ideas, afraid to fail. With Larkin's offer, those old dreams resurface. Along with new ones coming alive—having a contest for kids to be a sous chef for a day. Weekend fun for the whole family, not just the nighttime bar crowd. And like Larkin suggested, the pressure wouldn't all be on me. I'd have more time to make changes.

"Larkin," I say, my voice wobbly with excitement, "I kind of love this idea."

She clasps her hands at her chest. "You do?"

"To be clear, I'm terrified. Like, I'd be a bit of a stress case, but in a good way."

"Is that a yes? You want to join forces and take over this town?"

"Holy crap. Yes."

We grin at each other, then I'm up, hurrying around my desk to shake on the deal. But Larkin doesn't grab my hand. She drags me into a hug, and my excitement grows. This is the kind of business partner I want. A hugging agreement made, rather than a handshake.

"Where do we start?" I ask.

"With the contract. I have a lawyer who can get to work on it."

I knock her arm. "Look at you, all fancy with a lawyer at your fingertips."

Her smile slowly fades. She pulls her braid over her shoulder and hunches forward.

In all the time I've spent with Larkin, she's only exuded confidence. She's a strong woman who knows what she wants and chases it. "Did I say something wrong?"

She swallows hard, then brightens. "Nope. Just a rush of nerves, but the good kind."

I study her, unsure she's being honest. But I feel the nerves too. And the excitement. I can't wait to bounce bar ideas with Larkin, build a new business plan together, change the menu.

I inhale deeply and look at this old office with new eyes. Hopeful eyes. Dreamer eyes. *Holy crap* eyes.

I can't wait to celebrate this news with Cal.

CHAPTER
Thirty~Nine

Callahan

I'm a mess as I walk toward the Barrel. The prospect of seeing Jolene's gorgeous face light up with a smile has my adrenaline spiking, but nausea has joined my excitement.

Shortly, I'll be sharing my bad deed with the love of my life.

She'll be pissed I interfered with her job. She'll be furious I didn't discuss her options with her first. But she'll be relieved too…right? She'll find her feet quickly, take over that food truck, if it excites her. Or I'll help her brainstorm ways to chase the dreams she put on hold. Whatever she decides, she'll finally be doing what she wants.

Everything will work out just fine.

I push into the Barrel, and my heart decides to beat an ominous tune. The bar isn't busy, but I spot Maggie and her boss on stools. Lennon is at a table with Desmond and E. I feel another twinge of guilt that the Barrel will be turned into a brewpub when the new owners take over. Lots of people love this place, but change is good.

I spot Jo easily—a force field that lassos me in. She's behind the bar with Larkin, the two of them grinning like they're sharing the secret Pepsi recipe.

The urge to bite my tongue and let the chips fall without telling Jo my part in what's to come rises, but changing my controlling patterns means owning my choices. Jolene is the center of my goddamn world and deserves full honesty.

Her attention zips to me. I guess force fields know when they've got an object locked in orbit. The corner of her lips kicks up, and a pretty blush dusts her cheeks.

"Damn," I murmur, aching to have my hands on her. My mouth. A moment to remind us both how right we are together, no matter my stupid mistakes.

"If it isn't our cagey brother." Lennon steps in front of me, getting in the way of where I need to be. "What brings you by the Barrel? I thought you avoided this place."

"Only because you're here." I move to dodge him, but E and Desmond saunter up, boxing me in. Fucking great. "Is there a family meeting I wasn't informed about?"

"There is," E says. He flicks his attention to Jo, who's watching us with amusement I don't share. "The meeting is about you."

My three brothers cross their arms, going for intimidation.

They don't scare me. I mirror their poses and exude my calmest facade. "If this is about Jake and me at Sugar and Sips, we've worked out our differences. No need for any meeting."

Desmond grunts.

Lennon points at him. "What he said."

"He didn't say anything."

"We're here about you and Jo," Desmond says, using his out-loud voice. "We're tired of you hurting yourself to make everyone else happy. You and Jo should be together. We all know it. Have known it for a while, along with the fact that Jake isn't really into her. We plan to sit on him until he gets the message. She's the one for you."

"Wow, Des." E knocks his arm. "That was incredibly heartfelt. Didn't know you had it in you."

"It's the book-club books he reads with Mom," Lennon says. "They've softened him."

Des punches Lennon in the ribs. E snorts. I glance at Jo, and another wave of nerves rolls through me.

"Actually," Lennon says on a pained cough, "maybe Des should start a dating advice column in *The Jangler*. Dear Desmond has a ring to it."

E shoots up his hand. "I vote for Dating with Desmond."

Des gnashes his teeth. "You're all assholes. Can we get back to why we're here?"

I try to dodge them and get to Jo, but I don't see her with Larkin any longer, and Lennon plants his hand on my shoulder. "It's time to follow your heart," he says.

"This heart?" Jolene appears beside me and ducks under my arm, hugging me with a tap to my chest.

The heart in question beats double time. No matter my stress about our impending talk, I'm a mess for this woman. "Hey, baby." I kiss her head and breathe her in.

She plants an answering kiss between my pecs, the heat of her body calming me slightly. "I missed you."

"Me too," I murmur and brush a strand of hair out of her eyes.

A throat clears. My brothers are grinning at me. Except Desmond, who looks sour. He's probably pissed he doesn't get to sit on Jake and lay down the law.

Lennon dusts his hands, like he just lifted a load of wood. "Guess our services aren't needed."

"Is Jake okay with this?" E asks me, always the one to worry.

I nod. "Said it'll take getting used to, but we have his blessing.

His moods lately aren't because of Jo." I glance at the bar. Larkin is chatting with a customer, her braid gliding down her back as she laughs at something he said. "The source of his angst is right there."

All eyes swing to Larkin.

Sensing our collective attention, Larkin's lips pinch. "Keep your eyeballs to yourselves, Bowers. If you should be worrying about anything, it's your eyebrows."

E tilts his head, trying to look up and see his own face. "What's wrong with my eyebrows?"

Jolene's shoulders shake with amusement. "Word of advice— don't engage Larkin unless you enjoy public humiliation. She doesn't hold back."

"Interesting," Lennon murmurs. Then he focuses on Larkin. "We're just having a riveting conversation about Jake," he calls to her, lacking self-preservation. "You should join us."

The only way to describe Larkin's expression is feral. "I would, but I prefer a battle of wits. You're clearly unarmed."

Jolene and I laugh against each other.

Desmond's mouth tilts into a quarter smile. "I like her."

"Co-signed," Lennon says.

E huddles into our group. "Jake didn't actually hook up with her, did he?"

"Nope," Jolene says quickly. "Larkin despises Jake, and Jake is torn up over something about her. That's all I know. But if I knew more, I wouldn't tell you. Mind your own beeswax."

My brothers and I share a clipped nod. That's it. One small head movement and we know what we need to do: go into Bower Protective Mode. We'll do our best to suss out the issue and help Jake out, *without* me actively meddling.

"As fun as this catch-up has been," I say, "I'd like to spend a moment with my girlfriend alone." Tell Jo what I did. Help her plan what's next. Kiss her so good she'll be too breathless to get mad. "Can you spare a minute?" I ask her quietly.

"I actually wanted to talk to you, so your timing's perfect."

She takes my hand and leads me to her office as my brothers catcall us from behind. I lift my middle finger in reply. If we had a family crest, the middle-finger salute would be front and center.

"How are you?" Jo asks the second her door is closed. "Did your talk with Jake really go okay?"

I cup her cheeks and slant my mouth over hers, kissing her long and hard until she sags into me. "It was good." I sit on her couch and pull her into my lap. "He's still upset over whatever happened with Larkin, and I still feel like shit about it. But he reiterated what you said, about wanting what's best for me. Confirmed he was happy for us."

She places her hand over my heart. "Do you still feel guilty about it all? About our complicated history?"

I think about my angst the past couple of months, how hard I fought my attraction and feelings for Jo, along with my worry over Jake's reaction. "A little, if I'm honest. Might take more time for that to go away completely, but no way in hell will I waste another second hiding from the truth of my feelings." I press my hand over hers, let her eavesdrop on my heart all she wants. Hope she remembers the devotion when I say what needs saying. "What about you? Does any of this feel wrong to you now that you've come up for air?"

She curls in closer and shakes her head. "My relationship with Jake ended twelve years ago. I'll always care for him, but that was a different time in my life. I was different back then. I obviously wouldn't choose to date brothers, but being with you isn't really a choice. It's fate."

"I like that," I say, running my nose through her hair. If Jo is fate's reward for ten years of witness protection, I'll gladly accept. "I love you, Jo. So damn much. Couldn't wait to see you tonight and get my mouth on you, but I also have something we need to discuss."

"Okay, but..." She adjusts on my lap and beams at me.

"Something just happened with work, and I'm busting to tell you. Can I go first?"

Forget beaming. Her energy could power a rocket, and I'm suddenly less distraught.

If Jo is this excited about work, the "something" that has her glowing must be big, and I'm pretty sure I know what's lighting up my girl. Francisca must've told her she's selling the building, that the new buyer will be ending Jo's lease and turning the Barrel into a brewpub. Jo doesn't seem angry or sad. I don't sense any remorse over losing her aunt's place.

Clearly, the sale and eviction are exactly what she needed to free herself from duty and start fresh.

I run my hand down her back, so damn relieved. "Tell me all about what happened, and don't skimp on the details."

"Well," she says, her face flushed with excitement, "you know how Larkin wanted to speak with me the other morning? That's why we were at Sugar and Sips when everything went south with Jake."

"I do." But I'm not sure how this relates to Francisca selling the building. Maybe she knows the purchaser. "Go on."

Jo's shoulders hitch. "Turns out Larkin wants to be my partner."

Tingling overtakes the base of my skull. "Partner for a new venture?"

"Of course not. *Here*, at the Barrel." She shakes her head, like I'm a numbskull. What I am is on the verge of puking. "She's going to buy in. And we have plans, Cal. So many amazing plans already! Ways to liven up the place. Fun events to pull in more customers. We still need to finalize it with lawyers and stuff, but for the first time in forever, I'm excited to be here. I think this is exactly what Aunt Becca would have wanted for me and the bar."

Heat suffuses my face and neck. I try to swallow past the

knot of dread in my throat. "But you hate the bar. You've been so unhappy here."

"Sort of, but not fully. I think I was focusing on the negative with you."

"Because you're not happy here," I say again. She *can't* be happy here. Not with the news I have to share.

"No." She shakes her head, her brow pinched as she thinks. "Before you and Larkin came back to town, I didn't have a lot of close friends. I certainly couldn't bitch about work to my employees. Then I had you and could finally vent, so I probably made it sound worse than it was. But I do enjoy a lot about the bar—the customers, being a gathering place for the community. I just don't like the stress of all decisions landing on me. With Larkin, I'll have someone to share the burden."

I blink slowly, try to calm the tsunami gathering in my gut. "Partners can add stress. Having Larkin on board might not be as easy as you think."

Jo leans back and squints at me. "Why don't you sound happy about this? I thought you'd be thrilled for me."

I fucking should be. If I hadn't done what I did, I'd grab a bottle of champagne from the bar and spray the room with it. Congratulate her and Larkin and help them any way I could.

Instead, I'm a minute from hyperventilating. And I have to come clean.

Jo palms my cheek. For some reason, I barely feel it. "Are you okay, Cal? You look pale."

I try to speak, but my pulse revs and her desk phone rings.

"That's the bar calling," she says. "Give me a sec."

I nod, overheating to the point of pain. She stands and walks toward her phone. I tug on my T-shirt's crew neck. Try to drag in deeper breaths while I review what I need to say, words to soften the bomb that's about to blow up Jolene's plans. I've got nothing, and my vision turns spotty.

"Oh, sure," Jo says into the phone. "That's actually great timing. Send her back." She hangs up and turns to me. "So weird—my landlady's actually here, which is good, I guess. We need to hammer out a proper lease, and I can tell her about Larkin and me revamping the bar." She smiles at me, but concern drags her lips down. "You look flushed, Cal. Will you wait for me at the bar? Have a beer and rest a sec. We can chat about whatever you have going on after."

I'm about to ask her to put Francisca on hold. I don't want Jo to be blindsided, but there's a knock on the door, and the heat gripping my body worsens. My lungs constrict, squeezing so tight the spots in my vision worsen.

Francisca comes in. Jo says something, but it doesn't register. I swear, my lungs are nearing collapse, and this heat is melting my spine. I somehow make it through the door, mumble a vague hello to Francisca, then I'm rushing, hitting a near jog toward the exit. I bust outside and suck back air, but it's like breathing through a clogged straw.

Selling the bar wasn't a small screw-up that will be forgiven. Jolene's about to have her hopes and dreams shattered. Fated to be together or not, she'll never look at me the same again.

"Fuck." I need to think. Figure this out. Find a way to give Jo everything she wants, but the only concrete thoughts ricocheting through my head are *fuck, fuck, fuck.*

On the verge of hysteria, I grab my phone and pull up a group text with my brothers.

I enter five words and hit Send.

> Me: Help. Parking lot. Barrel House.

CHAPTER
Forty

Callahan

After I send that desperate text, I find a section of privacy and crouch by the building's back corner. I drop my head into my hands. Squeeze my eyes shut and focus on my chest rising and falling, forcing more air into my lungs. Scuffling registers. Boots running on gravel.

"Where is he?" one of my brothers calls. The concern sounds like E.

"Why can't I fucking see him?" The growly swear is definitely Des.

"Shit. He's here. Jesus, Cal. What happened?" Lennon's hipster shoes show up in my vision.

"Out of the way." Desmond's boots replace Lennon's. He crouches in front of me and lifts my chin. "You okay?"

I shake my head.

"I think it's a panic attack," Lennon says.

Desmond's expression gets extra intense. "You having trouble breathing?"

I nod.

"We got you, okay? Focus on my face. Nothing to worry about except that right now."

"Look at the ugly ink on his neck," E says, but his voice doesn't hold its usual humor.

I do as I'm told. Focus on the subpar lion on Desmond's neck until I breathe easier and the suffocating heat is less intense, then I sit my ass on the gravel.

The screech of tires cuts through the air. More running and cursing carries over.

Jake is suddenly standing over us, breathing hard. "What's wrong with Cal?"

Des is still crouched in front of me. E is gnawing his lip, looking upset.

Lennon isn't faring much better, but he points at my face. "He's having a panic attack."

Jake's focus darts between each of us. "Since when does he have panic attacks?"

"Since ten minutes ago," I manage. Or maybe since I visited my tree house the other day. Suppressing my emotions and interfering in people's lives isn't doing me any favors.

Jake squats beside Desmond and plants his hand on my shoulder. "How are you doing now?"

Breathing doesn't take as much effort. I'm still shaky but more in control. "Physically, better. Mentally is a shitshow, but not because of the panic stuff."

Jake watches me carefully, concern in his searching eyes. "You okay to talk this out? Or do you need time?"

I massage my brow. Time would be great, but I don't have that luxury. I finally stand, maneuvering so people coming in and out of the Barrel can't see us. "I did something I shouldn't have."

"Oh, here we fucking go." Lennon is already seething, pointing at my face. "You meddled, didn't you?"

"I did."

"Fucking knew you wouldn't stop." The skin around his beard reddens. "With Jolene, I assume?"

I slump. "Yeah."

"Told you that shit would bite you in the ass. But you just had to—"

Jake shoves his hand in Lennon's face. "Give him hell later. Cal, tell us what went down."

Lennon attempts to burst my head with his glaring. I deserve it, and my brothers deserve the full story of why I'm here, falling apart. I keep glancing forlornly at the wall, wishing I could see through the bar, into Jo's office. Be there for her when Francisca blindsides her with an eviction notice. How can I offer support when I'm the cause?

"I've always had this impulse to help," I say, rubbing the back of my still-hot neck. "Smooth issues over for the people close to me. But when WITSEC hit, that impulse became more of a need."

Jake resumes his role of Eye Contact Champion, staring me into submission. "So you did stuff to feel like you were more in control of your life?"

"Yeah, but I was also worried about all of you. About Jo and my friends back here. How everyone was coping." I spill the secrets I've kept, including some of the dealings I've done: buying into Ben's gallery to see him succeed, getting Javier a discount on his work equipment, helping Jo when she had car and roommate troubles, sending her gifts when tragedy struck, keeping an eye on each of my brothers as they moved back to Windfall.

"Let me get this straight," Lennon says, his bearded jaw firmed, "you're the reason my first date with Maggie came with flowers and free dessert at the restaurant?"

I nod and tense, waiting for him to smack me again.

He grins. "Thanks, man. Definitely earned me points."

E rocks on his heels. "You needed all the help you could get."

"Not me." Des puffs up his broad chest. "Unlike you assholes, I didn't need interfering. I won Sadie back all on my own."

"The shock of the century," Lennon mumbles.

"All well and good," Jake says. "But *how*? How'd you pull off that stuff from Houston? And how'd you keep your name out of everything?"

I shrug. "I have a shell company when necessary and a spy in town."

Jake's expression hardens. "What the fuck do you mean, *a spy*?"

My brothers crowd closer, eyes narrowing like they're one being working in sync. Their mission is to make me crack. They won't let this go, and the secret doesn't matter any longer. The faster I get this over with, the faster we can get to the fiasco at hand.

"Sandra, okay? I hired Sandra. Found her shortly after she moved to Windfall, and she's worked for me for years. She spied on you idiots as needed, but I've since cut ties with her. Unfortunately, the last issue I had her resolving has become a disaster. When Jo learns about it, she'll leave me and hate me forever. I royally fucked up."

"Fucking Sandra." E shakes his head, laughing to himself. "I knew she was a spy."

"We'll unpack that shock later," Lennon says, getting up in my space. "What did you do to Jo?"

I cross my arms and dig my toe into the gravel. "Sold her bar."

"What?!" my brothers shout in unison, except Jake, who's glaring at me.

"She hates it, okay? At least, I thought she did. We had talks about how much pressure she felt living up to her aunt's expectations. She has other dreams she hasn't chased, things I thought would make her happier, but I knew she wouldn't walk away. So I had the choice taken away from her." The building sold. Her business evicted. I confess it all, along with her latest bombshell that she hadn't shared *all* her feelings about the Barrel, the way people sometimes focus on the negative with their closest friends, ending with her and Larkin's planned partnership—a dream I've since killed.

"I don't know how to fix this," I say, breathing hard again. "I came here to tell her what I did, assuming she'd be mad but would be relieved in the end. When I saw how excited she was about revamping the business, the panic attack started and Francisca showed up. So Jo doesn't know what I did yet."

Jake grips my shoulders. It's his standard move, aside from forced eye contact. The vise that holds us all together. "You need to quit thinking you're everyone's guardian fucking angel."

"I know."

"You can't fix all our problems."

I try to hang my head, but his grip tightens, keeping me where I am. "Agreed," I say.

"And you will *not* lose Jo. We didn't go through hell for that to happen."

"That part's easy," E says but doesn't go on.

Des snarls at him. "Want to share with the rest of the class?"

"Simple. Someone else goes to Francisca and matches the brewpub offer or beats it. Francisca was close with Jo and her aunt. If she had a choice, I bet she'd choose the offer that allows Jo to keep the Barrel."

"And how are we supposed to find someone with that kind of cash on this short notice?" Jake asks, tossing up his arms. "Specifically, someone who doesn't want to operate the space with their own business."

My overheated skin cools. The overworked gears in my brain slow. Could salvaging Jo's business really be that simple? Was I so distraught, I couldn't come up with that basic answer?

"I actually have the cash," I say, desperately hopeful that I can fix this for her.

"How the fuck do you have that kind of cash?" Jake sounds furious all over again. He doesn't like being in the dark.

Lennon leans back, smug. "Must be the stripping he does on the side."

I lift my middle finger. Again.

Desmond's jaw pops. "Is it from Dad's book money? You invested it?"

"Some, yeah. Jake and I used part for our business, and I invested the rest." The cash our asshole father earned from his tell-all biography, given to us like it absolved him of his betrayal. At least some good came of that money. "The rest of my nest egg was from the WITSEC cash at the start. I played the stock market. Made good moves. Added earnings over the years and used it to pay Sandra. I have enough to get a mortgage on the bar."

Even if that plan works, E's solution would only solve part of my problem.

Lennon steps back from me. "If you can buy the building, why do you look like you're about to puke?"

"I can't keep this from Jo. Whatever happens, I have to tell her what I did, which means I'll lose her all over again." But it would be my fault this time, not my criminal father's. I look at my brothers, barely able to swallow. "I don't think I can love another woman like I love her. She's it for me."

E grips my arms, usurping Jake's oldest-brother move. "You're it for her too. She might need time to get over this, but Jolene knows you. She knows you have good intentions, even if you overstep. She loves you too much to walk away. Sorry," he adds to Jake with a wince.

E doesn't go on about the awkwardness of Jo and me in the wake of Jo and Jake. But yeah, my fucking family. Always on the complicated side of messed up.

Jake holds up his hands. "Don't worry about me. I'm tired of dealing with Cal's work mistakes. If he's with Jo, he's less likely to saw through his hand."

"Excellent older brother selflessness," Lennon says. "Does this mean we can crack jokes about Jolene choosing the brother packing more heat?"

Jake headlocks Lennon, dragging his upper body down. Desmond locks eyes with Jake. A shared smirk later, Des grabs the band of Lennon's exposed boxers and yanks them up in a wedgie. Lennon yowls. Jake and E laugh so hard they nearly fall over. I'm actually smiling on this debacle of a day, not shaking while descending into a panic attack.

Thank God for my immature family.

Unfortunately, when I head to my truck and the daunting tasks I have to face, my smile slips into a grimace. If Lennon's wrong, if Jo doesn't forgive me, I doubt family wedgies will make a dent in my devastation.

CHAPTER
Forty-One

Callahan

As I wait for Francisca outside of her house, someone calls my name and waves. I lift my hand and nod but don't bother checking who it is. The brightly painted homes and prettily lined trees barely register. Jolene has texted me. The messages are no doubt filled with anger over her meeting with Francisca, but I haven't read them. Seeing her devastation will siphon my meager fortitude. Instead, I focus on a swatch of grass while I spin over my offer—how I'll convince Francisca to sell me her building.

No big deal. Just a light conversation that'll alter the course of Jolene's life.

Francisca's blue sedan pulls up. She frowns at me through her windshield.

I wipe my damp palms on my jeans. Don't think I've ever been this nervous in my life.

"What brings you by, Cal?" Francisca's face is drawn, like she came from a stressful situation. Namely, killing Jolene's dreams.

I bite my cheek and get my head in this game. I may have hung up my meddling ways, but I'm good at swaying people with suggestive words.

"I'm here," I say, gathering my confidence, "to offer you peace of mind."

She squints at me. "Have you convinced my grandson to get a proper job and quit thinking his sock-puppet TikTok videos will be his ticket to fame?"

"Sadly, no. This is a business visit."

"Shame, but I'm all ears." She hikes her purse up her shoulder. "What can I do for you?"

I clasp my hands, going for casual kindness. "Sell me the Barrel's building."

She startles, then shakes her head. "Is that building on a secret oil deposit I don't know about? What's with everyone clamoring for it?"

"Jolene loves the bar," I say, avoiding the topic of her current buyer. Sharing my involvement in the development won't help my cause. "She must've been upset when you told her you planned to sell. She doesn't want to lose her business, and I'm guessing hurting her isn't sitting well with you."

Francisca deflates. The wrinkles by her mouth deepen. "Believe me, the last thing I want is to hurt that girl. Her aunt was a dear friend. The Barrel is a great establishment, but I have to think about my future. Plan for my retirement. I didn't realize how much I needed a change until I got that surprising offer."

Until I stuck my nose where it didn't belong.

"What if I told you I could match your current offer, but I wouldn't kick Jo out? You'd get the sale you're after, and no one would evict her—the peace of mind I mentioned. The Barrel and Rebecca's legacy would carry on. Jolene wouldn't be devasted to lose her livelihood. Would you sell the building to me instead of the current buyer?"

"Well, I…" She frowns, blinking at the asphalt. "I wish you'd come by sooner, Cal. I gave the buyer my word, which means something to me."

Nope. No. That answer is not acceptable.

"From what I gather, Jolene was upset when you told her about your plans, right?"

"She tried to put on a brave face, but...yes. I think I might have broken her poor heart."

Jesus. Of course Jolene forced kindness in the face of her shock. Of course her heart's been shattered into pieces. Might as well dig myself a grave now.

"If you sell me the building," I say more forcefully, "you can mend her heart, Francisca. Save a business that's been a staple in Windfall for years. I'll even increase the offer. How does an extra ten grand sound?" When she hesitates too long, I say, "Your grandson."

"My grandson?"

"I'll hire him. Teach him construction. Give him something to focus on besides sock puppets."

She juts out her hand. "Then you, my friend, have yourself a deal. But you can't back out. I'll want that last part in writing."

I shake her hand, somewhat concerned about her grandson's ability to wield a hammer, but hell. I'd hire a sloth if it meant saving Jolene's dreams.

We discuss a few more details, then I head to my truck and finally read Jo's text.

> Jolene: I got the worst news. Kind of falling apart here. Can you come back to the bar to talk?

Yep. My grave needs to be excavated. She's understandably upset, and I hate the part I played in hurting her. But I still have to tell her about my involvement in this debacle. Privacy is needed for that confession.

Me: I've gotten sidetracked. Can't make it back, but I'll wait up for you. We'll talk when you're home.

My gut churns as I hit Send. This might be the last time Jo texts me when she's upset and needs a friend.

CHAPTER
Forty~Two

Callahan

I've been pacing in my home for the better part of an hour, waiting for Jolene to walk in. It's late. Sleep is nowhere on my radar. My brothers have all messaged, telling me to update them when I can or call if needed. All I need right now is Jo and her forgiveness.

The front door rattles, and my pulse pounds in my ears.

Jolene pushes into *our* home—which might soon be *my* home —and *damn*, she's definitely devastated. Her lips are pressed tight. Worry lines are carved into her forehead. When she looks up and her red-rimmed eyes find mine, I debate joining a monastery. The isolated kind where I'm forced to live in silence and contemplate the bad deeds I've done.

"I lost the Barrel," she says, sad and quiet, walking toward me in a rush. Her arms are around my waist in seconds. She mashes her face into my chest and exhales, seeking comfort. I don't deserve to hold her soft body, but I fucking do. I try to absorb her anguish, refuse to pity myself. All that matters right now is Jo.

She sniffles and clings to me. "Francisca sold the building, and the person buying wants to open a brewpub. A fucking *brewpub*. A cookie-cutter cliché, which means I'm evicted. My plan with Larkin is bust. All the work I've done was for nothing. Why the hell didn't I make sure I had a secure lease?"

I hug her so hard I'm worried she can't breathe. "I'm so sorry, but it'll all be okay."

The sound she makes is a half sob, half growl. "I just…I don't understand. Everything was finally falling into place. Larkin and I were so excited. It felt like us working together was fate."

She said the same about the two of us. *Being with you isn't really a choice. It's fate.*

Then I went and ruined everything.

I kiss her head and rub her back. Try to show her how much I love her—forever, always. "Sit with me. There's something I need to tell you."

She lets me lead her and falls onto the couch with a heavy sigh.

I sit facing her and try to steady my pulse, but it feels like someone's in my chest, having a boxing match with my ribs. "The Barrel isn't being evicted from the premises," I say, taking her hands. "I put in an offer on the building tonight. Francisca accepted it, so no one's tossing you out. There won't be a brewpub. You and Larkin get to work together and turn the Barrel House into the coolest bar north of the equator."

Jolene doesn't whoop and cheer. She tilts her head and peers at me more intently. "What do you mean, you bought the building? Since when do you have that kind of cash? And why would you spend it on the Barrel?"

"I might not have gone into finance like I toyed with in college, but I'm good with money and numbers, and I don't live large. I knew the money would come in handy one day, and it has. I bought the building for *you*, Jo. So you can live out your dreams."

Her frown deepens. She gives her head a small shake. "But...how?"

"I spoke to Francisca, like I said. Offered her more than the other buyer."

"No, Cal." She pulls her hands out of mine and scoots back on the couch. "How'd you know this was happening? The only person I told was Larkin. If there was gossip about this beforehand, believe me, it would've trickled into the bar. Someone would've said something. So...how? How did you know the building was sold if I didn't tell you?"

Here it is. The moment I destroy Jolene's belief in fate and us. There's no softening what I've done. She already sees right through me and has created space between us on the couch. She senses that I did something unforgivable.

"I know," I say roughly, "because I arranged the sale of the building in the first place."

She sucks in a shocked breath and clutches her chest. "What?"

"You were so unhappy there. So stressed. When we talked about it, I got the feeling you were keeping it out of obligation to your aunt. Not because you truly wanted the bar. Then the night you fell and hit your head, we were in bed and you said the bar drains you. You *said* you wished it was out of your hands. And I wanted to help. Give you an easy out so you could finally chase your dreams, and I was really messed up from thinking we'd never be together. I thought helping you would make it hurt less."

"But you didn't ask me if that was what I truly wanted. You didn't say a damn thing to me about any of this."

"I know. What I did was—"

"*No*," she says, cutting me off. Angry tears shimmer in her eyes. "This is not okay, Cal. You had no right to interfere in my life that way, or at all. I told you I'm not a fairy-tale character who needs saving. I'm a real live person who has to fuck up on her own to learn. Or *not* learn. The point is that this is my life, and your meddling almost ruined my livelihood. And you promised you'd talk to me. You said if you had the urge to be a fixer and jump in without my consent, you'd tell me instead of acting rashly."

"I know, and I meant every word. I put the sale in motion before that talk. Right after, I tried to pull the plug on the deal, but things were already in play."

"And instead of coming to me and talking it out, you spent your hard-earned money on a building you had no intention of buying."

So this is what suffocating feels like. Being buried alive by your irrevocable actions. "I did it for *you*, Jo," I say, desperate. "I bought it for you."

"No, you didn't. You bought it so I'd forgive you. You bought it to absolve yourself of your guilt. You thought buying it would fix what you broke between us, which, in case you're wondering, was trust." She stands and sways slightly. She puts her hand on the couch arm to steady herself while more tears track her cheeks. "I need to go. I can't be here right now."

A whoosh roars in my ears. My heart has officially ruptured, but I can't let her go like this.

"You're right," I say as she grabs her purse, readying to leave our home. To leave *me*. I stand and take a step toward her. "I should've admitted what I'd done when we were in the tree house. Come clean and asked you what you wanted with the bar. My only excuse is I was scared, because I love you, Jolene. So much it's hard to breathe when we're apart. I was worried I'd lose you, which is a shitty excuse for my behavior. But I want to be clear about one thing."

I walk until I'm right beside her, hovering over her. "Part of the reason I help people is because it gives me a sense of control.

It's my nature to look out for others, but after what my father put us through, it became more of a weakness. An urgent need to protect those I love so I wouldn't have to watch that kind of suffering again. But I didn't buy that building to ease my guilt. I didn't buy it so you'd forgive me. My actions broke something between us. I know that now. Knew that when I went to Francisca today. This wasn't a last-ditch effort to make amends. I bought the building because I want you to be happy, even if it's without me."

She covers her mouth and hunches, hiding her face from me. Then she's moving, walking so quickly out the door she stumbles into a jog. I lurch after her and want to scream, *Stop! Please don't go.* But I have no right to ask her to stay.

I stand on my front steps, watching her drive away, as a wave of despair washes over me.

CHAPTER
Forty-Three

Jolene

"I don't understand," Larkin says, staring at me like I have six arms and four heads. Maybe I also look like a woman who has an actual beating heart. "How did we get the bar back after losing it, like, five hours ago?"

I'm standing in her doorway, unsure how I haven't sunken to the floor and landed on my butt. "Callahan bought the building from Francisca, *after* he schemed behind my back to sell the building and have me evicted."

She blinks for several slow beats. "We need wine. Yours will come with a straw."

"Two straws," I say, following her inside. Intravenous might be better. I'm not sure how I got here. I barely remember driving.

The second I sit on Larkin's couch, my eyes burn with tears.

She returns and puts a glass of wine in my hands. It doesn't have a straw, but the glass is nearly overflowing. "Don't skimp on details," she says. "I need to know how long I have to torture Cal before I kill him."

The thought of someone hurting Cal has my eyes spilling over. "This is so messed up," I whisper to my glass. *Thank you, wine, for not scheming behind my back.* I take a grateful sip, blinking to clear my vision. "Apparently Cal thought he'd swoop in like some knight in shining armor and save me from myself. He assumed I hated the bar and felt stuck there out of duty. Which, *fine*—a lot of days were a slog and I did feel stuck, and I probably harped on the negative too much around him." Stupid Callahan, being so damn easy to confide in. "But what kind of person plots to have his best friend *evicted*?"

Larkin scowls. "An evil one. He's probably plotting to hack into satellites next, black out the world."

"Or rig the stock market since he seems to have piles of cash he's using to buy our freaking building."

She taps her nails on her glass. "On a level from Captain Hook to Ursula, his type of evil hovers around Gaston."

"Gaston acted out of jealousy." Bringing a mob to kill the beast to get to his beloved Belle.

"And Callahan acts out of fear," Larkin says. "Volatile emotions cause irrational behavior."

They sure cause a landslide of damage. I cradle the wineglass and draw my knees up tight. "I'm not sure I can accept him buying a building for me. It's way too much, but I hate the idea of giving up on our business plan."

"Actually…" Larkin leans toward me. "We don't have to give up on our business plan, and we don't have to rely on Cal."

I squint at her. "What do you mean?"

"I didn't want to say anything before I spoke with my brother, Julian, but after Francisca dropped that bomb on us, I thought of the same solution as Cal."

"Julian wants to buy the building?"

"He lives in New York, does consulting work I don't fully understand for a crap ton of money. He's talked to me about investing in real estate in the past, and Windfall land value is getting hotter. So, I spoke with him about our issue. He seems really keen to buy the Barrel."

Her news gives me mental whiplash. One second, I'm down on my luck. Next, I have two people willing to invest in my future. "Would you feel good about him being our landlord?"

"No issues there. Julian and I have always gotten along. And, personally, I'd feel way better about him acquiring the building as an investment, rather than Cal doing it as an emotional reaction."

A huge weight lifts off my shoulders. "I completely agree and would have to thank Julian profusely. Hopefully Francisca is okay with the change."

Larkin nods, looking equally as relieved as I feel, but her expression sobers. "With that covered, let's circle back to Cal and how you're feeling about him."

Too many emotions fight for dominance, making me dizzy. "Do we have to?"

"Unfortunately, yes. As pissed as I am at him for his asinine scheming, you were *happy* with him, Jo. Like, fall-on-your-face in love."

Accurate and as painful as you'd imagine. I take another large sip of wine. "How do I trust him after this? He didn't just overstep. I feel violated and duped."

"If needed, I can help you hide his body."

I manage a laugh. Larkin continually passes the friend test with flying colors, but hurting Cal would hurt me. "How can I love someone so much and be so angry with him at the same time?"

She tucks her legs under her and swirls her glass. "Bowers have a special life-ruining gene. Clearly inherited from their father."

"Larkin."

"I know," she says, before I jump to Jake's defense. "*Jake is a good guy,*" she adds, mimicking my usual rebuttal, but she makes it sound like *Jake is a worthless piece of shit.* "Assuming Callahan truly wanted what's best for you and wasn't interfering to satisfy some weird hero complex this time, can you forgive him? Trust him moving forward?"

Isn't that the question of this awful night?

I roll the word *No* on my tongue. Taste it and wait for my reaction.

I am a strong woman. I don't need a man to fight my battles. I don't want a partner who makes assumptions and acts without consulting me. But the thought of never touching Cal again, never seeing him blush when I openly admire his body, never cooking with him or smashing raspberries into his face is, frankly, abhorrent. Losing him again would be like losing the ability to taste food.

But the words *Yes, I can trust him* don't come easily either.

Knocking sounds from Larkin's front door.

It's him, I instantly think. The assumption is followed by a leap of my heart, like the lovesick organ is answering Larkin's question without hesitation. But I don't move. If I can't verbalize a reply to Larkin, how can I face Cal?

"Stay here," she says, annoyed. "Guy can't give you ten minutes to untangle the mess he created. I'll tell him to go away."

She plunks her wineglass on her coffee table and marches to her door. From my angle, I can't see Callahan. All I hear is Larkin's sharp intake of breath. Followed by, "You have some fucking nerve showing up at my home."

Even with Larkin's offer to hide Cal's body, that level of fury is surprising. I hurry over, only to find Jake standing in her doorway. But this is no Jake I know. If someone pasted a picture of "remorse" in the dictionary, this would be it. Jake's hair is askew from restless fingers, his brow lined and drawn. His eyes are so apologetic they're twin pools of regret.

"I'm sorry," he tells Larkin in a plaintive croak. Definitely not the Jake I know.

She crosses her arms. "For *not* doing what you were supposed to do twelve years ago or for showing up now, when you know the sight of you makes me want to claw out your eyes?"

Jake winces like he's been slapped. "I'm sorry," he says again. "For everything, even though the words are useless. I know you don't want me here, but I need to talk to Jo." He glances past Larkin's rigid shoulder at me. "Please," he adds.

"Over my dead body," Larkin says. "Or, preferably, yours." With how tall and fit Larkin is, she should be our bar bouncer, and she isn't caving an inch to Jake's heartfelt pleas.

I'm not quite so immune. "It's okay, Lark. I'd like to talk to him. We'll go outside."

Jake nods at me and goes to turn, but he glances at Larkin again. His eyes do a slow sweep of her face, a hint of unexpected longing in his expression.

Maybe I was wrong about the word "remorse." He's the definition of *tortured*.

"You okay?" I ask Larkin before following him out.

"Never better," she mutters and marches back to the living area.

Feeling like I'm in my own brittle shell, I join Jake at his truck. Both of us lean against the hood. The night is quiet, most stars blotted out by clouds.

"I just came from Cal's," he says, but his attention keeps flicking to Larkin's closed door.

"He called you to come over, I guess? Told you I left."

"No." He shakes head and rubs his eyes. "I was on the street for a bit, parked outside. We knew he was planning to tell you everything tonight, and I figured you'd be upset and probably leave. I wanted to be there for him."

This is why I stayed with Jake as long as I did. He's a sweet man. "He's lucky to have you."

"No, Jo. He's not." His lips twist into a frown. "I knew he was into you when we were younger. That's why I asked him if I could take you out. I also expected him to pretend he didn't care, say it was okay to date you, because that's what Cal does. Puts everyone before himself, even if it kills him. And I let him do it. Convinced myself he didn't have feelings for you, even though, deep down, I knew he'd be hurt, because I was a selfish asshole back then."

He rubs at the creases on his brow. "Cal doesn't show emotion easily. He hides himself under smiles and polite talk. But I saw how jealous he was when I was with you. Watched him struggle to hold himself together when you were over. I know my brother and haven't always done right by him, but in all our fucked-up years, I've never seen him as upset as he was tonight. That includes witness protection."

My heart twists painfully.

Cal's as upset over losing me as I am over losing him, and I'm so mad. Angry at him for putting us both through this. For ruining the best thing that's ever happened to me. "He did this to himself," I say.

"He did, but for the right reasons. The last thing he ever wanted was to hurt you."

I lean my tailbone into the hard metal of Jake's truck, hoping the ache behind my breastbone eases. It doesn't. I don't want to be mad. I want to rise above, forgive and move forward with the man I love. It all seems so daunting.

"More than anything," I admit quietly, "I think I'm scared."

"Of what?"

"When your family disappeared, it wrecked me. I was so confused. Scared and worried about you all, but also angry and hurt. What happened tonight was a taste of that same agony, but worse. Like, completely suffocating. And Cal and I have only just started dating. I think I'm scared of getting in even deeper with him and losing him down the road. That kind of pain…" I force a swallow and shrug.

"Jolene." Jake moves in front of me and tips up my chin. "The fact that you love him so much you're scared to get hurt again says it all. That's real, honey. That's what the rest of us strive for. And you're not alone in those feelings. Cal fucking cried tonight when I was there. I haven't seen him shed a tear since that first week of WITSEC, and that was over you too. Holding a grudge over this will only hurt you both."

I press my hand over my mouth. "He was crying?"

"Pathetic, right?"

I instantly want to break into a run. Race back to Cal and soothe him, promise him we'll work through this. Be together forever. But what if I end up back here in a year or two? What if he's upset because his plan to "help" me went south and he's ashamed of his actions, not because he loves me as much as I love him?

"I accused him of being manipulative," I say tentatively. "Of buying the building to win me back and make himself feel better about interfering in my life. He said he already knew he'd lost me when he did that. That he only wants me to be happy, even if it's without him. Do you think he was being honest?"

Jake laughs under his breath. Laughs, like I'm not a freaking mess right now. "You lost a roommate five or so years ago, then the apartment building where you live now suddenly lowered the rent to an amount you could afford. Sandra mentioned it to Delilah, who mentioned it to you, right?"

I squint at him and lean away. "Should I be getting a restraining order? How the hell do you know all that?"

"Because that was Cal, Jo. Apparently, Sandra has worked for him for years. If she heard that someone he cares about was in a jam, she'd tell him. He used her to help out. Made some deal with your landlord to pay part of your rent. He helped get your truck fixed by flying parts halfway across the country. He sent your father a cookbook after his accident. Sent a donation and flowers when your aunt passed away, and has probably done a ton of other things he didn't share. He's been in your life, caring for you for twelve years, and never once told you about any of it. Why do you think that is?"

Because he didn't do those kindnesses to boost his ego or ease his guilt.

Because he only wanted to see me happy.

Because I was always in his heart, even when we were apart.

And he got my dad that cookbook? The one that changed my life?

Those are four huge hints that my best friend has always loved me—selflessly. Unflinchingly. No matter our physical distance or emotional road bumps, he has put me first.

"I shouldn't have run out on him like I did," I say, calculating how quickly I can drive back to his place.

Jake shakes his head. "Don't go back tonight. Let him stew over what he's done. That meddler needs to learn his lesson. But you should come to our mom's party tomorrow. We'd all love to have you there."

He has a point about the stewing, and I could use a breather. A night to sleep off today's roller coaster of emotions. I take Jake's hand. "After everything with you and me, how are you still so kind and sweet?"

"Like I told you, all I want is for my family to be happy. You're Cal's happy." His attention drifts back to Larkin's door, his expression back to tortured. "And I'm not that kind and sweet."

He leaves me, and I almost don't take his advice. My body is wound up, ready to spring back to Cal. Instead, I imagine how it will feel to surprise him tomorrow. How good it will feel to sink into his arms and tell him the only place I want to be in this world is with him.

CHAPTER
Forty~Four

Callahan

Once upon a time, forcing cheer was my superpower. I could exude outward calm and contentment, no matter how unhinged I was inside. Today, everyone around me is buzzing with happy excitement.

Mom will be here soon. She has no idea her new home is packed with old friends eager to surprise her. I'm tucked against a wall, like a dehydrated plant wilting in the corner.

Lennon comes over to me, his fifth time this morning. "This is Mom's surprise party. Please tell me you'll actually smile when she gets here."

I grunt my reply, but my cheek muscles shift downward.

"Did you swap bodies with Desmond?"

I don't even grunt this time. I can't muster the energy.

"Did Jo knock out your teeth? Is that why you can't move your mouth?"

"In a manner of speaking, yeah." Losing her knocked out a heck of a lot more than my ability to be congenial. Pretty sure my lungs are sewn half shut. My chest is packed with cement. If I don't get my shit together soon, I'll take one look at my mother and *cry*.

Surprise! Your thirty-two-year-old son is a fucking moron who lost the best thing in his life.

E zips over. He's checked on me seven times already. "We should give him a dunce cap. Tell Mom he's punished for jacking off in her oven mitt again."

"Jesus Christ." I duck, hoping no one heard this asshole. I was home alone that day, or so I'd thought. I'd just spent the afternoon playing catch with Jolene and was worked up, then Lennon busted into the kitchen and caught me in the act. "That was one time, and I grabbed the nearest thing to me."

"The one time that you were *caught*," Lennon says. "Maybe it's a fetish. Maybe it's a mommy complex and oven mitts get you excited."

I grumble under my breath. Can't teenage boys do idiotic things without it chasing them for eternity? Except, adult me is still doing idiotic things, and there's no escaping this fallout.

I work my jaw, focus on the wood floor. There's a divot I'd love to sand by hand. I could redo this whole floor. Work until I can't feel the ache in my chest any longer.

Jake's scuffed boots appear in my line of vision. It's his eighth visit to my sad corner, but this time, Lennon feels the need to fill him in on my masturbation embarrassment.

"Huh," Jake says. "I didn't know about Mom's mitt, but I did catch him slapping the salami on that camping trip to Hood Rock."

Again, I thought I was alone at the time, and I was fourteen, for fuck's sake. Jolene joined us for a family camping trip, and I snuck out at night to take the edge off. "Can you all leave me alone?"

"Nope." Des joins us for his tenth visit. He's been the most concerned today. Broodily silent as usual, but staying nearby. A gnarled but supportive tree, bringing me a glass of scotch to calm me, but my body doesn't thrive on alcohol. My body is parched from missing Jo. "You're stuck with us," he says.

Jake smacks me on the back. "Today's a new day."

My first day in hell, yeah. And Jake's optimism is getting under my skin.

With how concerned he was last night, showing up out of the blue, consoling me while I fell apart in front of my home, his spritely attitude pisses me off. Jolene hasn't called or texted or sought me out. She was probably waiting until I left the house, so she could move her stuff out without seeing me. I blow out an agonized breath.

"Jake," Mrs. Jackson calls and gives him a knowing wink. "Glad to hear you and Jo are finally back together, with one night to spare before your mother got home. She'll be so happy."

My molars lock and grind. Jealousy burns a path up my chest.

Before I know what I'm doing, I have Jake slammed to the wall, the front of his shirt in my fist. "Did you go after her last night? Told me some bullshit, then took advantage of her when she was upset?"

I'm Mount Vesuvius about to bury this place in ash, but my brothers don't intervene. They cross their arms, looking so amused I want to tackle them too.

Jake, the traitorous bastard, actually *smiles*. "Get yourself under control, Callahan. Don't say something you'll regret."

My only regret is not speaking my mind when he showed interest in Jolene fourteen years ago. "Were you with Jo last night?"

He leans into my face, not fighting back. "Yes."

If Mom's friends weren't here, I'd punch him. Knock out his teeth. Break his nose, because...*how*? How could he do this to me when he knows Jo is my world? I settle on jamming my forearm into his throat. "I won't forgive you for this."

"Christ, Cal." He yanks my arm off him and shoves me back. "Since when do you believe Windfall's gossip mill? Calm the fuck down so I can explain."

There's too much static in my head to calm down. Angst, regret, devastation.

"What's going on here?"

Jolene. The fight leaves me in a rush.

I whip around, and she's here, looking angry but gorgeous in a flowy yellow dress, her lips pink and glossy. Her eyes are twin lasers of irritation aimed at me, because I guess she's with Jake now, stepping in to defend my brother. The Bower who didn't scheme to get her business evicted.

Unable to handle seeing them together, I storm through Mom's back doors into her small yard. I pace for a while, trying to slow my breaths. It doesn't help. I crouch into a squat and drop my head into my hands. "Fuck."

Sometime later, I hear a soft "Cal." Jolene's voice is achingly tender. Her small hand splays on my back. "Jake came by last night to talk about you. To convince me to forgive *you.* People must've seen us outside by his truck. Whatever Mrs. Jackson said isn't true."

My heavy exhale is equal parts relief and cutting razor. Having her this close when I can't touch and kiss her is unbearable. Also, I'm an asshole. How could I have believed that ridiculous rumor?

She moves in front of me and holds out her hand. "Come sit with me for a sec?"

"Sure," I say. My voice sounds as rough as I feel. This will be her let-me-down-easy talk. The closure she needs. No matter how hard this is, I'll force myself to nod and smile and tell her everything will be okay. Offer to still be friends, even though I doubt I can handle that.

Following her lead, I wrap my hand around hers, get lost in

the feel of her soft skin one final time, how perfect her small fingers feel threaded with mine.

She leads me to one of the two loungers Jake bought recently. Lennon and E chipped in for the flowers decorating the yard, including Mom's favorite azaleas. Desmond and I hired someone to build a vegetable garden Mom will love to tend. She'll be happy here, I hope. More settled and at peace. That bit of knowledge eases the sting of losing Jo. Slightly.

Jo sits down and pulls me next to her. "Did you really think I'd jump into dating Jake again right after being with you?"

I shrug, not feeling like myself. "My brain's been on fire since yesterday. I'm not acting rationally. Feel kind of unhinged. I'll apologize to Jake after."

I pick at my cuticles, can't look at her gorgeous face.

She stills my fidgeting and dips her head, forcing eye contact. "I love you, Callahan Bower."

Everything in me goes deathly quiet. Thick silence as I pick through the meaning behind her words. Does she love me as a friend? As more? Is she forgiving me or cutting me loose? I alter our hands, wrapping my palm over hers, needing to feel her pulse. Eavesdrop on her true feelings—the frenzied beat mimics mine.

"Jo?" It's a plaintive question without words.

Is your pulse saying what I think it's saying?

Does your world not make sense without me either?

"I love you," she says again, intensely, and this time, I know. The vehemence in her words, the slight tremble in her voice—somehow, she's forgiven me. Somehow, I didn't lose her.

"I'm so fucking sorry." I press my forehead to hers, too relieved to believe this is happening. "I love you so much I can't think straight. Last night killed me. Didn't sleep for a minute."

"Me neither. I mean, I was upset with you, but not being with you was harder."

I kiss her softly, still worried she'll pull back. Push me away.

By some miracle, she doesn't. "I won't overstep again, swear to God."

"Just talk to me next time. If you're worried about me, say something. I need you to be there for me and listen. I don't need you to jump in and fight my battles."

I nod, holding her hands so goddamn tight. "I promise."

"And…" Her lips quirk. "Maybe tidy up after yourself once in a while. It's no fun living with a slob."

A relieved laugh moves through my still-sore chest. "No promises."

"Also," she says, her tone more serious, "Jake told me about the stuff you've done for me over the years. Some of it, at least— my apartment, my truck, the cookbook you sent my dad."

Maybe Jake won't be getting an apology after all. Maybe my interfering brother *will* lose teeth today. "Are you mad?"

"Callahan." She shakes her head, the softening of her mouth quelling my nerves. "Knowing you cared that much all these years blew me away. That you were with me, even when I didn't realize it, is overwhelming, but in a good way. Like, seriously romantic. So, no, I'm not mad. I'm grateful."

I release her hands, sift my fingers through her hair and tip her face up to mine. "I don't deserve you."

She brushes her nose against mine. "Yes, you do. We're a team. We won't always make the best plays. Sometimes we'll fumble, but we'll stick together. Forgive each other and move forward."

I kiss her, more deeply this time, not caring if the people inside can see us through the glass doors or that I'm getting worked up when I'll have to stand soon. Losing Jo for one day turned me into an erratic mess. Having her lips surrender to mine is an addiction I have no interest in kicking.

"About buying the building," she says quietly, "Larkin's brother offered to do the same. He's excited about the opportunity to invest in Windfall real estate. And as much as I appreciate you offering first, Larkin and I are more comfortable with him owning the Barrel. I don't mean that offensively. We just—"

"Jo," I say with a kiss to her ear, "whatever makes you happiest is what I want. But Francisca and I had a side deal going on—for me to take her grandson on as my apprentice. If she still wants that in the paperwork, please put it in."

She laughs and shakes her head. "Always an angle with you."

"Not anymore. From here on out, I'm nothing but a straight line." One that points steadfastly toward Jolene.

"That's settled, then." She lets out a happy sigh, but a hint of mischief sparks in her eyes. "Also, since we're back living together, I have one request."

"Anything."

"Can you promise not to masturbate in any of the oven mitts?"

I jerk back and glare at the windows. Of course my brothers are there, spying on us.

Lennon waves.

"He is so fucking dead," I grumble. "Can we just pretend he didn't share that story?"

"Should I also pretend you didn't jerk off in the woods on that camping trip we took with your family?"

"Jesus Christ. You were alone with them in there for, like, two minutes. What the hell else did they tell you?"

"Nothing much." She kisses my neck. "Unless you count the time you got a leech on your penis and ran around screaming that your dick was going to fall off."

I try to emulate Desmond's death glare and pierce the glass between myself and my idiot brothers, but I don't barge back inside to throw punches. My fingers are in Jo's hair. Our thighs are flush. I'm too happy to let their trash-talking dent my mood, but we can't stay out here forever. "You ready to face the world?" I ask her.

Nosy townsfolk.

My antagonizing brothers.

My mother, who will be here soon and doesn't know I'm dating Jake's ex.

She nods. "As long as I'm with you, I'm good."

"Same." I kiss her again, still awed that she's forgiven me.

We smile against each other, then I take her hand and head inside.

My brothers have paired off with the women they love. Maggie and Lennon are chatting with E and Delilah, the four of them sharing a laugh. Desmond, Sadie, and Max are at the kitchen table, putting final decorations on Mom's book-shaped cake. Des takes a dollop of icing and smears it on Sadie's nose. Max cracks up. Jake is by himself in the living room, watching them with a small smile on his face, then he turns to us.

Instinctively, I pull my hand out of Jo's. She twines her fingers together and looks down. We create space between us, which fucking kills me, but Jake admitted seeing us together would take getting used to. After all he's done for me, I don't want him to be uncomfortable.

"Sorry about the blowup," I tell him. "And thanks for talking to Jo last night." I glance at her, my hand twitching to splay on her hip. I bite down on my cheek.

"We appreciate how sweet you've been," Jo says. Her eyes dart to me, and she fidgets, like standing this close without touching is as painful for her.

"For fuck's sake," Jake says, gesturing angrily at us. "Just make out or something. Watching this display of awkwardness is worse than seeing you all over each other."

"No need to make out," I say, but I slip my arm around Jo and settle my hand on her hip. *This is where my hand is meant to be. On Jo, always.* "We'll be quietly affectionate, if that's okay."

He rolls his eyes and heads over to play with Max.

She nestles against me. "People are looking at us."

It's true. We have an audience of Windfallians trying to deduce why Jolene is wrapped around me, when most of them heard she was back together with Jake. "Does it bother you?"

She plants a kiss on my chest. "Nope. Let them talk. As long as it doesn't bother you."

"The only thing that bothers me right now is that you aren't naked."

"I don't think getting naked in front of everyone counts as quietly affectionate."

"Alone, Jolene." I drop my voice. "I wish we were *alone* and naked, but we'll save that for later. I plan to fuck you hard and fast. From behind, I think. Slam this angst out of us, then I'll take you so deep and slow we combust."

"God, Cal." Her cheeks burn red.

I brush my hand down the back of her pretty dress. "Too blunt?"

"Too hot. You just melted my underwear."

I chuckle and flex my thighs. Time to rein myself in and remember I have forever with Jo now. An eternity for slow sex and hard fucking and nights cooking and walking the streets, hand in hand, like the couple I've always imagined.

"Chelsea's driving down the street!" someone calls. "Should be here in a couple minutes."

I smile wider. *Mom.*

The quilting crew gathers, holding up a "Welcome Home" quilt they made together. Jo and I move to stand by the bookcase I built for Mom. I put a big red bow on it, and Des filled a few shelves with books. We have streamers up and that great book cake Max made with Des, Sadie, and Delilah. Most important, though, is us. Her five sons, finally finding fulfillment and happiness in the aftermath of our father's betrayal.

My eyes fall to Jake, standing on his own with crossed arms.

His brow is pinched into the broody expression he's worn lately, like he's lost in his head, replaying bad memories.

"You can't scheme to help him," Jo says, reading my mind.

"I know, but is his funk all because of Larkin? Is that really why he's been so down?"

Her attention lingers on his shadowed eyes. "When he came by last night, it was intense. He definitely fucked up with her, but I don't know how. And you're not going to interfere, right?"

"Nope. Definitely not." Unless Jake asks me to help. Which he might if I find a way to get him to open up. A definite possibility...

"I can hear your brain overworking." She pinches my side. "Quit it."

"Fuck. Yeah, I know." I breathe her in, fill my lungs with springtime storms. "What if I just tell you all my scheming ideas but don't act on them?"

"You can start a journal. We'll store it in your creepy shoebox shrine to me."

I smile. "I thought that was romantic."

"In a creepy stalker way, sure."

I chuckle and kiss the top of her head.

The room quiets. My nerves hit a happy buzz as the front door pushes open.

Everyone shouts, "Surprise!"

Chelsea Bower stops in her tracks, eyes wide with shock. Then she covers her huge smile with her hands. "Oh my God," she says, bewildered but clearly thrilled. "What is all this?"

Jake moves up to her first and clasps her shoulders. Commander Bower, reporting for duty. "This is for the best mother in the world. Welcome home, Ma. Living here hasn't been the same without you."

She's a fountain now, tears overflowing with joy. My brothers descend on her one by one. Hugs are shared. More happy tears fall. Mom can't stop covering her mouth or clutching her chest, saying *Oh my God* and *I had no idea* on repeat.

I don't leave Jolene's side. I'm not sure how Mom will take this news. She loved Jo growing up. She was thrilled when Jo stared dating Jake. Seeing her with a different son might not sit well.

Mom hugs Mrs. Jackson, the two of them laughing about Mom's abysmal quilting skills, then her gaze lands on me. Her assessing eyes slip to Jolene—to my possessive hold on her hip. She blinks and says something to Mrs. Jackson.

Jolene's so close I feel it when she tenses and breathes faster. She's nervous.

Mom leaves Mrs. Jackson and heads our way. Instead of going to Mom and hugging her the way I normally would, I hold Jolene closer, showing her my support.

"Welcome home, Ma," I say quietly.

She tips her head, giving me no clue to her thoughts. "Seems we have some catching up to do, if this looks like what I think it does."

I give Jo's hip a squeeze. "It does. Jo and I are together."

She worries her lip. "Is Jake okay with this?"

We glance over at him. He's got a drink in hand, standing with Lennon and Maggie, gesturing as he talks about something. He looks more relaxed now, in his element with the family. "He is."

Mom nods, then takes both of our hands in hers. "Don't tell Jake I said this, but you two always made more sense to me. Thrilled to have you back in the family, Jolene."

Mom kisses her cheek, and I can't play it cool any longer. I haul Mom in for the hug she calls my polar bear hug—big and soft and safe. That's all I've ever wanted for those I love. Safety and happiness.

She pats my back and whispers, "I'm so happy for you."

"I'm happy for me too."

She joins the party and *oohs* and *aahs* over the bookcase and her special cake. Max gives her a drawing of the family that makes Mom cry. My face hurts from grinning.

Jolene clinks her wineglass with mine. "You boys did a good thing for her."

"She deserves the world." I run my knuckles down Jo's arm. *Quietly affectionate.* "And so do you."

"I'll settle for more chocolate-covered strawberries."

"I was planning on chocolate-covered brussels sprouts, since you liked the chocolate broccoli so much."

Her answering smile is concerningly cheeky. "As long as you don't ejaculate on them."

"That was in a *mitt*, not in a—you know what, nope." I pop my jaw, then force a placid expression. "I won't indulge your teasing."

She laughs. "Razzing you at soccer is gonna be extra fun."

I attempt to glower, but the effort is useless. Everything with Jolene Daniels, Owner of My Heart, *is* extra fun.

CHAPTER
Forty~Five

FOUR MONTHS LATER

Callahan

I turn into the Barrel's gravel lot and, no word of a lie, can't find a parking space. It's a large lot. Even on their busiest nights, there are free spaces on the far end.

"Looks like the grand reopening is already a success," Jake calls from his driver's window as he pulls up beside me on the street.

"I had no doubt."

He snorts. "You were nervous as shit."

He's not wrong. Jolene's been restless lately, having trouble sleeping at night, worried their reopening wouldn't be as busy as they'd hoped. I could've schemed, ensured patrons came from far and wide to fill the place. I did no such thing. My new leaf has been turned over. Jolene has handled this venture on her own, and I'm proud as hell of her.

Jake and I both park down the street, then walk toward the bar together. He glances my way. "Did you get the kitchen shelves installed in time?"

"Barely, but it's done."

"And the countertops—you got the company to fix the sizing issue?"

"All sorted." What isn't sorted is how invested Jake's been in this renovation, when he was specifically asked not to be involved. "If you have other concerns, you can ask Larkin directly. See if she needs anything extra done around the place."

The edges of his jaw sharpen. "You know very fucking well I'm not welcome to work on the Barrel."

"She might have warmed toward you. I told her your connection got us that deal on the new kitchen flooring."

He glances at me hesitantly. "Yeah?"

"She did say, 'Then tear the fucking floor out,' but she didn't follow through on the demand." I slap his shoulder. "I'd say that's progress."

And I haven't interfered in their strained relationship once. No meddling. No texting Sandra to dig for dirt on why Larkin despises my brother so much she refused to let him help me with their renovations. My level of self-control has been astounding.

Jake picks up his speed and shoves the bar door open. A blast of music and happy voices smacks me in the face. The place is packed with regulars and a slew of newcomers. Larkin's been all over social media, drumming up buzz—a swarm of bees who will pollinate the Barrel House, ensuring it thrives. Pictures will be posted online during the night. The raucous crowd of friends and families will spread the word.

All because Larkin and Jo had a vision and followed through.

Our brothers and their better halves are hanging out by the railing around the dance floor, looking like they've had a few. Javier and Ben are playing pool. Larkin is behind the bar, helping the staff keep up with demand. Jake takes a long look at her, then swivels away, lats bunched as he marches toward our family. I don't join him. My eyes are fused to Jolene's stunning profile.

She's in the newly finished open kitchen, rushing around, her intense expression right at home among the gleaming stainless-steel and modernized appliances.

Aside from adding hand-painted sayings and art on the wall, Larkin and Jo decided to keep the rest of the Barrel House as is —to honor Rebecca's vision—but the kitchen was a complete redo. It's bright and airy now. There's enough space to hold classes, with a long counter where customers can watch the chefs work on the less grease-centric menu—house-made sausages with apple, cabbage, and caraway slaw. Crab and dill crostini. Thick burgers topped with bourbon bacon jam and grilled shishito peppers. My personal favorite is a platter of bar bites, including Jolene's famous pickle and prosciutto "sandwiches."

I strut toward the woman at the center of all that deliciousness, my heart pounding louder than the country tunes. It's always like this when I see Jo. Electric excitement. A shot of adrenaline through my sternum. Like I'm still shocked I'm allowed to touch her in public.

I pass through the staff entrance into the kitchen and hang back a moment, watching the master work. She's making notes on a menu, talking to her new chef, Emmanuel. The tall Haitian man towers over her, nodding in interest. He takes his pen and marks something on the page.

"Oh my God." Jo beams up at him. "That's perfect. Add it to next week's menu, with the vegan pork belly. This town won't know what hit it."

They high-five as a cook shouts, "Two burgers, one crab, and a chicken!"

Emmanuel moves into action, not missing a beat.

I slide to Jolene's side and drop my mouth to her ear. "Watching your brilliant mind in action is incredibly sexy."

She leans into me and sighs. "I missed you. It's weird not having you here every day working on stuff."

"I missed you too." I smooth my hand over her hip, guiding her to a quieter corner. "Maybe we should tear out the kitchen again. Redo it. I'll be at your beck and call night and day."

"Or," she says, breathier, "we could text each other when we're apart. Dirty promises about what we'll do when we see each other later."

"Tempting, but no." Just discussing dirty texts has me hungry for a taste of her. "I'm liable to accidentally saw off a finger."

The corners of her lips quirk. "No sexting, then. Wouldn't want to put a hitch in the finger-fucking."

My body burns hotter than her gas stove. "Someone's asking for trouble."

"Too blunt?" she asks, mimicking my deep voice and the line I often use.

I laugh and kiss her lips, then drop my voice to a whisper. "Only if you don't mind me bending you over your office desk and fucking you so hard the walls shake."

Her breath catches.

I chuckle and look through the cut-out window into the packed bar. "Rain check for another day?"

"Yes, please."

We watch Larkin shake up a fancy cocktail, entertaining the waiting customers with a show. Waitstaff hold trays high, pushing through the crowd to serve their tables with the new menu.

More pride fills me. "You've done it, Jo. Kept Rebecca's dream alive, while making it your own. Your aunt would be so happy."

She presses her hand over her heart and nods. "She would."

"And you?" I ask, facing her. "Are you happy?"

She links her hands behind my neck, giving me those warm eyes that never fail to slay me. "So happy."

I steal another kiss, deeper this time, clutching her tight.

She pulls away first, flushed and beautiful, and gives me a light shove. "Now get your hot ass out of my kitchen. I have work to do."

I laugh and wink at her, eager for later—the two of us in our home, clothes stripped off, no interruptions as I make Jolene shout my name.

Leaving her, I head toward my family, but a crash has me spinning around. Larkin is crouched low, her face pinched as she stares at a shattered glass. Not good.

Worried someone will hurt themselves, I head to the storage area, looking for a broom. By the time I'm back, Larkin is still crouched, and Jolene is with her. Neither of them is moving to clean.

"Did you cut yourself?" I ask Larkin, looking for blood.

She shakes her head and blows out a long breath. "Just embarrassed myself is all. An ex of mine showed up out of the blue."

I glance up. A slick guy with gelled hair is leaning on the bar, periodically glancing down at Larkin. He has a smug look about him I don't like. "Want me to have a word with the guy?"

"Definitely not. Like I told Jo, I can handle him. He just caught me by surprise."

I nod, feeling protective of Larkin. She's become Jolene's closest friend—a smart businesswoman, who's strong and feisty and loves putting my brothers in their places. But as per my new leaf, I will not intervene unless asked.

I help them clean the glass, then head to my family, who has overtaken a table. Lennon points to a beer and an empty chair. "Your throne awaits."

I lick my lips, parched for a refreshing sip, but Jake steps in my way and pulls me aside. "Is Larkin okay?"

"For a guy who claims not to care about Larkin, you're awfully invested in her emotional well-being." While secretly helping me source materials for her bar.

His nostrils flare. "Just answer the fucking question."

I glance back at Larkin. Her colorful bartending show is on hold. She's moving quickly, avoiding helping her ex, who's still intent on her. "An ex turned up, seems to be making her uncomfortable, but she said—"

Jake moves before I finish, on a mission for the slick guy, his hands balled into fists.

"What's with Jake's Terminator impression?" E asks.

"That's his impression of you right before you try to fight," Lennon says. "He'll trip and fall any minute."

E throws a crumpled napkin at Lennon's face, but Lennon karate chops the paper away.

Delilah nudges Maggie. "Who's the guy at the bar watching Larkin?"

"I don't know, but I know that look on Jake's face. He ran over there to protect her. He's definitely smitten."

"And about to get murdered by Larkin," Sadie says, wincing. "Whatever Jake just said to her did not go over well."

She's not wrong. Larkin is skilled at unleashing looks that could kill. Right now, her glare aimed at Jake is dialed up to hydrogen bomb levels.

Desmond grunts. His arm is latched around Sadie, but he kicks my boot. "Have you figured out the deal there?"

I hold up my hands. "Don't ask me. I don't meddle anymore."

Lennon snorts. "Likely story. But I might not be opposed to you getting the dirt on them. Jake clearly needs some help."

Abruptly, Jake swivels from the bar, looking like he might puke. He aims for the exit, rushing so fast he smacks into a server. Her tray nearly topples. Jake bumps into a table next, then stumbles into a jog toward the doors.

"Fucking hell," Desmond mutters.

"I've got this," I tell them, already up and hurrying after our brother.

Once outside, he's not hard to find. He's the frantic guy pacing in the parking lot, tearing at handfuls of his hair.

I step into his path. "What did you do?"

"The dumbest fucking thing I could've done." His pacing quickens, then he stops and shouts, "Fuck!" at the sky.

"Jake." I grip the back of his neck, not liking this one bit. Jake is the controlled brother. The stern guard who watches our backs. "Start talking before I go in there and ask Larkin what happened."

The fight drains out of him, along with the color from his face. "I told her ex I'm Larkin's fiancé."

"Why the hell would you do that?"

"Because I'm a moron."

"Clearly, but that explains nothing."

He slumps and rubs his jaw. "I went over there to make sure she was okay, and she was talking about a fiancé she has, which I know for a fact she doesn't, and he was being pushy. Asking why she doesn't have a ring. She started fumbling and getting anxious, and I—" He tosses up his hands, like he's raging at the sky. "I lost my ever-loving mind and said I was her fiancé."

I sputter out a half-choked laugh. Larkin can't look at Jake without turning a vengeful shade of red. She's the president, treasurer, and secretary of the I Hate Jake Bower club. "I'm guessing she didn't take that well."

"Depends if you consider Larkin digging her nails into my wrist until she drew blood well." He holds up his arm to show off red welts. "Then her ex inviting us to his wedding."

"But you said no, right? Made an excuse about being busy?"

"I panicked, okay? He was pissing me off and asked in a challenging way, like he knew we were lying, and I said yes before I could think straight."

I blink at my idiot brother. "Do you have a death wish?"

"Apparently," he mutters and curses the sky again.

"We could call our US Marshal handler," I say, amusement overtaking my shock. "Ask him to reinstate you in WITSEC."

He jabs my chest, no smile in sight. "This is your fault."

"How is this *my* fault?"

"You told me to drive Larkin home that night. Put this whole mess in motion."

"Care to tell me what exactly this mess is that I created? Because I'm on pins and fucking needles over the mystery."

He growls and bares his teeth.

Not bothering to reply, he blows past me, hops into his truck, and drives off in a screech of tires.

"Cal?" Jolene hurries to my side, watching the last of Jake's truck disappear. "What the heck is going on? Larkin tore into the kitchen and tossed a ladle across the room."

"A ladle?"

"It was the first thing she could grab."

Yep, Jake needs to relocate. "You won't believe what Jake did, and I need alcohol to bring you up to speed. But we'll save it for later. Tonight's about you and your booming business. Let's go in so I can tell anyone who will listen that the brilliant co-owner of this jam-packed bar is the love of my life."

She takes my hand, leading me back to the door. "You're my personal cheering squad."

"Damn straight."

She gives me a sweet smile over her shoulder, and I think for the millionth time how goddamn lucky I am that this woman is mine to love.

Epilogue

TWELVE YEARS AGO

Jake

Being the only sober person at a party blows. Cheers ring out from the beer-pong table, reminding me that tossing a ping-pong ball into a cup is only fun when you're three sheets to the wind. A chick bumps into me and laughs. Someone spills their drink on my boots without so much as a *sorry*, and if Katy Perry's "Firework" plays one more time, I might place an anonymous call to the cops. End this fucking misery.

"Isn't this party the *best*?" Jolene's words run into each other, her brown eyes glazed with happiness and beer. "I'm so glad we came."

"Yeah," I reply, annoyed with myself for my mood.

Even sober, I should be happy. I have a beautiful, sweet girlfriend at my side bopping to this awful song. Makers Construction just gave me a raise, and I love the carpentry work

I do. But I've felt out of sorts lately. Less in sync with Jolene. Distant from my brother Callahan, who's been acting weird too. Or maybe I've been the weird one, edgy for reasons I can't explain.

Maybe I'm too old for house parties—twenty-five going on ninety.

Jolene leans her head back and laughs. "I can't believe they're playing this song again."

Yep. That call to the cops might be happening. "They should force prisoners to listen to this song on repeat. Guaranteed no one would break the law again."

"Such a grump," Jo teases.

I make a grumbly sound.

She nudges me with her elbow. "We should dance."

"Hard pass."

"You used to dance with me."

"Katy Perry and I don't mesh."

Jolene's shoulders slump, and I immediately feel like a dick.

I used to dance with her at parties. We'd people watch and laugh and make out in dark corners. At the drive-in, she'd drape herself over me. If we went for burgers—Jo's favorite food—our legs would always be twined together under the table. Tonight, the only times we've touched are when Jo has poked me with her elbow.

I fold my arms, trying to figure out what's wrong with me. Or with us.

Jo bounces her knee to the music and sips her beer. Abruptly, she says, "I'm gonna go chat with Tvisha." She kisses my cheek and heads over to her friend.

I mentally picture myself anywhere but here.

Callahan joins me and awkwardly bobs his head to this painful song. "You're sober, right?"

Thanks to him, I am. "Since you told me I'm the DD before we left, I think you know the answer to that question."

"Right, cool." Cal twitches awkwardly and nearly drops his drink. Drunk *and* clumsy. "So, yeah, Larkin is a mess, and I told her you'd take her home."

I search out Jo first. She's laughing with Tvisha and another friend, looking way happier than she did standing next to me. "Jo's not ready to go, and I barely know Larkin."

"I don't think Larkin should be here any longer," Cal pushes, gesturing to the blonde sprawled on the couch.

I don't think I've exchanged more than a few words with Larkin, but I remember her from high school—two years below me and ostracized for hooking up with random guys. A double standard that's always bothered me. *Girls who like sex are sluts. Guys are high-fived.* I've seen her at the odd Windfall festival, usually with her much-younger brother, holding his hand protectively.

I look harder at her, notice a sheen in her eyes.

I may barely know Larkin, but I'd say that glassiness is only partly due to alcohol. She looks sad. Still, I don't answer Cal. I'm supposed to be here for Jo.

"Seriously," he says *again*. "You should take Larkin home before some guy decides to drag her upstairs. I'll walk Jo home later."

Imagining a woman being taken advantage of has my shoulders bunching. And he's right—guys are casting glances at Larkin. I don't know all of those dudes, but I know those predatory leers. Like Larkin is theirs to play with if they choose, all because she has some bullshit reputation.

"Tell Jo I'll call her later," I say, already walking over to Larkin. If something bad happened to her, I'd never forgive myself.

When I'm in front of her, her sad eyes flick to me. "What do you want?"

I crouch and force a smile. "I'm Jake Bower. I'm gonna take you home."

She blinks, that sadness morphing into something sharper. "Why would I get into a stranger's car?"

"I'm not a stranger. We went to school together."

"Right. Mr. Perfect Football Player. Too cool for the likes of me."

Sadly, she's not totally off the mark. I might not have trash-talked girls like Larkin, but I didn't go out of my way to befriend those deemed less cool. "I was a bit of a jerk in high school, but I like to think I've grown out of that bullshit, which we can discuss once you're in my truck. You're drunk and need someone to see you home."

"I'm not drunk," she says on a hiccup.

I raise my eyebrow.

"Fine, I'm *tipsy*. Still don't know why I should trust you."

"For one, I have a girlfriend. I'm not interested in hooking up."

"Having a girlfriend doesn't stop guys from being assholes."

Valid point. "Would it help if I told you my mother would have my hide if I didn't offer to help a woman who looked sad and drunk, while *actual* assholes eyed her like they had the God-given right to do as they pleased?"

I'm not sure why I feel so defensive. My voice has risen, and I've curled my hands into fists, like any guy who stepped close to Larkin would get a right hook to the jaw.

She stares at me for the duration of another agonizing "Firework" chorus, then rolls her eyes. "Fine. Lead me to your chariot."

Good thing she agreed. Tossing her over my shoulder was the next option.

I attempt to help her up, but she shrugs me off with a mumbled "So damn *chivalrous*."

I chuckle under my breath, thankful when we're out of that noisy house.

"I think my ears are bleeding," she says plaintively. "Fucking Katy Perry."

"I was seconds from waterboarding myself to end the misery."

She snorts. "A week of medieval rat torture would be better than listening to that song on repeat."

I glance at her profile, can't help noticing the cute slope of her nose. "What's medieval rat torture?"

She stops and faces me. Her blue-green eyes are no longer sad or sharp. *Villainous* is the only way to describe them. "They shoved rats in a cage and placed the cage over a victim's stomach. Then they agitated the rats by heating the cage until the rodents were frantic enough to gnaw through the person's stomach—anything to escape the fire. Death by rat gnawing," she adds with flair.

"You're disturbing," I say, twitching at the visual.

"But it's cool, right?"

"If you're a sadistic villain."

"Maybe *you* should be afraid of getting into a vehicle with *me*."

I laugh. "We should both text friends. Let them know our last known location." I pull out my phone to take a picture of her, but she sticks out her tongue and pulls a face. "Now I'm really scared," I add and snap the shot. I pretend to send the picture to someone, hoping it encourages her to actually tell a friend I'm taking her home. I want her to feel safe with me. "Your turn."

With a headshake, she pulls out her phone and takes her time lining up the shot. I watch while she fiddles with her phone. Use the seconds to examine the greenish flecks in her blue eyes, the thick sweep of her mascara-lined eyelashes. Her blond hair falls in layered strands around her face. Her cheeks are pink from blush or alcohol. A one-inch scar beside her nose gives her feminine features an edge, and the word *sexy* pops into my mind.

There's no denying Larkin Gray's appeal. To *other* guys.

"Sent," she says and pockets her phone. "My brother is at a friend's house on the other side of town. If you rat torture me, he now knows who you are, and you do *not* want my brother pissed at you."

"Isn't your brother, like, ten years younger than you?"

"Right, yeah." Her brow furrows and her nose twitches. "I just mean he's at a sleepover and he'll talk your ear off—worse than listening to Katy Perry. Because he's the only brother I have."

I side-eye her as I unlock the passenger side of my truck. I'm not sure what Larkin is hiding, but it doesn't take a genius to notice the ridiculousness of her reply.

I grab her elbow to help her step up into my truck, but she pauses. Larkin is a tall girl. Just under six feet, if I had to guess. The way we're standing, with her head tipped back as she gazes up at me, her lips are closer to mine than I'm used to.

"Thank you," she says softly. "Most guys I know aren't this nice."

"If guys aren't nice to you, you should tell them to fuck off."

Her answering smile is tight. "Easier said than done."

She glances down at her wrist. There's a faint bruise there I hadn't noticed, and anger has me seeing red. "Did someone hurt you, Larkin?"

She ducks her head and gets up into my truck, hiding her face from me. "It's nothing, and it's been handled."

I'm about to open my mouth and tell her any kind of bruise isn't nothing, but she grabs the door and slams it shut.

I don't know Larkin. We have zero relationship, but my mother made it a point to tell us often and forcefully that hurting a girl, even accidentally, was never acceptable—a too-firm grab, not listening if they said no for any reason at any moment, taking advantage when a girl was drunk and not of clear mind. Chelsea Bower has five sons, all of us tall and strong, and she drilled it into us that we have a responsibility to keep women safe and always treat them with respect. Or to step in if we see a girl in trouble.

To this day, the idea of a man hurting any woman has always infuriated me. How cruel and insecure does an asshole have to be to stoop that low?

And Larkin has a fucking bruise on her wrist.

By the time I'm in my front seat, my teeth hurt from clenching my jaw. Larkin is staring out her window. I shouldn't say anything more. She's not mine to look after or defend. Unfortunately, my mother did too good a job of baking in my protective gene.

"When you say the issue has been dealt with, what do you mean?"

"This isn't your concern, Jake."

"I'm making it my concern."

"So damn bossy," she mumbles, hunching farther away from me.

I stare out my windshield, debating my options. None of which are *let this go.* Larkin has no reason to trust me, unless I give her one.

"I broke in to my father's office last week."

She glances at me sharply. "Why?"

"There's something about him lately I don't trust. I mean, we've never been close, but he's been acting odd this year. More distant than usual. Traveling for work, when accountants like him don't normally leave their offices."

I have to support a client who's being audited, he told Mom.

I no longer live at home, but I'm there for family dinners. Mom didn't flinch when explaining why he wasn't around much lately, but I sure as hell took notice. I'd recently caught him in a lie. I'd called him at home to discuss a time-sensitive birthday gift for Mom—concert tickets to Kenny Chesney that needed to be purchased the next morning. Mom said Dad was working late. I called him at his office and he didn't answer, so I went by. He wasn't there.

Assuming he'd stepped out for something to eat, I waited for a while, but he never showed. The next day, when I asked how late he worked the night prior, he said he was at his office all evening.

At which point, I got really fucking mad.

Mom's lectures to watch out for women may have been meant for younger girls we met and dated. As far as I'm concerned, I would also protect my mother with my last breath.

"I think he's having an affair," I tell Larkin—pissed-off words I've never spoken aloud. "I didn't find anything in his office, but I can't shake this feeling that he's going to break my mother's heart."

"Have you talked to your brothers about it? Are they also suspicious?"

"I haven't told them. We're all pretty protective of Mom. If I'm off base, I don't want to rile them up."

"And what does Jolene think?"

"Haven't told her either." Which feels odd at the moment. I've debated discussing my concerns with Jo. I just...never do. "You're the only person I've told."

She huffs out an incredulous breath. "Well, that's weird."

"Is it, though?" I'm angry about her bruise and my suspicions about my father, but I force gentleness into my tone. "Feels easier sharing this thing that scares me with a virtual stranger. Someone who won't judge me or my family. Someone who isn't emotionally involved. Honestly, saying it out loud felt pretty damn good."

Her eyes roam over my face, more emotion softening her features. Then she scoffs. "Save your psychobabble for someone with a lower IQ. I see what you're doing, sharing bullshit so I'll do the same. So fucking lame."

She returns to staring out her window, and I sigh. "I wasn't lying, Larkin. I'm upset about my parents and haven't told anyone, but I get that whatever you're going through is tough. If you need to talk to someone at any point, you can come find me."

She doesn't answer.

At a loss, I turn my truck on and start driving. I ask where she wants to be dropped, and I get a one-word answer. I ask what she did during the day. She says, "Not much."

Her stonewalling is irritating, but telling someone about my dad *did* feel good. Those negative thoughts have been weighing me down for a while. Sooner rather than later, I'll need to confront my father or do more intense sleuthing. Head things off before they get worse. Maybe tell my brothers. Or just Callahan. He's the most level-headed.

"I have two half brothers," Larkin whispers suddenly.

We're a few blocks from her house, but I pull over and park at the curb, my heart knocking a faster beat. I don't say anything. Whatever she's sharing sounds personal. Pushing will only make her clam up.

She stares straight ahead and nibbles her lip. "My birth father is Otto Briggs."

That wakes me the fuck up. "*The* Otto Briggs who broke in to Malcolm Boyd's body shop and stole his cars?" The same lowlife who sold drugs to local kids.

"The one and only. Great DNA running through my veins."

"How come I've never heard that before?"

"He's not on my birth certificate and never lived with us. And my mother warned us no one in this town could know or we'd basically be crucified."

She's not wrong. As much as I love Windfall and wouldn't want to live anywhere else, the gossip junkies here aren't always kind. Having links to a man who sold drugs to underage kids would have been brutal. But she's telling me.

"When you said you messaged your brother that you're getting a ride with me, you meant Otto's son?"

She nods. "Hunter and I are really close. He lives in Ruby Grove, but he's visiting a friend in town tonight. He's a good guy and super protective of me—hates Otto and all the shit that comes with sharing that man's last name."

"I'm glad you have someone who's got your back."

"Yeah, but like with your family, his reactions can be intense." She runs her fingers over the bruise on her delicate wrist. "I never told him about Derek. They used to be friends. Things went south when Derek stiffed Hunter on some cash he owed. Hunter *warned* me the guy was bad news." Her voice quiets. "I should have listened."

My fury threatens to rise again, but I force it to settle. I take a deep breath and say, "Will you tell *me* about Derek?"

Her next swallow stutters down her neck. "We started dating about five months ago, and he was nice enough. A bit of a bad boy, but not, like, a bad *guy*. Things got serious fast. I was basically living there after a few months. Then a friend of his got out of jail, and they started hanging out more. Derek isn't a good drunk and was going on benders, during the day and stuff, staying out all hours. We fought way too often—verbally, not physically. Until Monday."

I don't say a thing. There's no way my tone will be kind or gentle. I grip the steering wheel and wait for her to go on.

"I decided to end things, went over to tell him and grab my stuff, which included my passport that I need for an upcoming road trip. He got mad and got…physical." She touches her neck, as though imagining his hands on her throat. "I got out of there with a swift knee to his nuts and told him to never contact me, but I didn't get my clothes or my passport, so I'm kind of screwed right now."

I look closer at her neck. The faintest bruise stains her smooth skin. "That fucking asshole."

"Isn't this supposed to be a safe space where you're not emotionally involved?"

She's right. It is. But there's no changing my nature. "Give me your phone."

"What?"

"Give me your phone. I'm putting my number in there. Your brother doesn't live close. If you ever hear from this prick again, or get caught in a bad situation with him, you're gonna call me."

"Why do you care? I'm the girl everyone calls a stupid slut."

This fucking town. "Your sexual history is nobody's business but your own. Anyone who makes you feel bad because of anything you've done isn't worth your time."

Her lips tip up into a sweet smile. "I hope Jolene knows how lucky she is to have you."

I blink at my lap, the same edginess I felt at the party returning tenfold. "Things are changing between us. I don't fully understand it. We have tons in common. She loves everything I love, even watching sports and going fishing. But things have been...strained lately."

"Have you talked with her about it?"

I shake my head, scrub my hand over my jaw. "Maybe we're just growing apart."

Or I need to make more of an effort. Do something nice for her. Break us out of this rut.

"Whatever you do," Larkin says, "honor yourself. If you love her, fight for her. If your feelings have changed, don't string her along. Women aren't dumb. My bet is she knows something's up."

I nod. Jolene is far from dumb. She's smart and sassy and sweet and hot. Everything I should want. But I look at Larkin— this girl I barely know—and I feel strangely connected to her. I'm not sure why telling her my secrets has been so easy. Why the mix of green and blue in her eyes seems to suck me in.

Larkin holds out her phone. "If the offer still stands, I'd

actually like your number. I'll feel safer if I have someone to call."

"Good," I say gruffly. I enter my digits into her phone and send myself a text. But I can do better than being a standby bouncer. "Is Derek home on Saturday nights?"

She curls her lip. "Doubtful. He's for sure wasted at that biker bar outside of town."

"How do you feel about a little breaking and entering?"

Her eyes spark. "What do you have in mind?"

"You need your passport and clothes, so we take back what's yours. If I'm with you, and he happens to come home, he won't be able to lay a finger on you." And I might get the chance to sink my fist into the asshole's face.

"Really?"

I turn my truck back on. "Consider me the Clyde to your Bonnie."

"Is that some crack because I'm the progeny of Otto Briggs?"

"You should be proud of the relation. Takes a strong woman to rise above her degenerate parent. Tell me where we're going."

I feel her attention on my profile as she explains that her ex lives in the house by the junkyard. After a beat, she says, "You, Jake Bower, weren't this kind and thoughtful during high school."

Busted. "I was an obnoxious jock."

"And brain-cell challenged. I remember something about you jumping off Amari Harper's roof into his pool, like you were an invincible superhero."

I smile at that wild memory. I honestly thought I had nine lives. "As idiotic as that was, it wasn't my fault. According to my mom, you can't grow balls and brains at the same time. That's why men take longer to mature."

She laughs, so hard tears leak from her eyes. "I like your mom."

"She's the best." Which has me angry all over again with my father.

I can't go to Mom about his possible affair until I have proof. And then what? I tell her and watch her fall apart? I don't tell her and live with the knowledge of his deceit? My stomach pitches and my palms turn damp. Maybe my instincts are off base. Maybe he really has been helping clients out of town. That office lie could have been a misunderstanding.

By the time I park outside a run-down bungalow near the junkyard, I'm freshly frustrated.

The lights in the house are off. There are no vehicles in the driveway. "Doesn't look like he's home."

"Based on his typical nights, he won't be home for another hour or so, and the neighbors on the other streets are super nice. I've always felt safe when walking to my mom's from here, but I wouldn't have had the guts to come on my own. So, thanks for doing this."

"Glad I could be here," I say, but I can't shake thoughts of my parents.

Larkin doesn't move to get out. She places her hand on my thigh. "You're worried about your mom."

"Am I that easy to read?"

"To me, you are. Which is kinda odd, considering we only officially met tonight."

Except I can somehow sense Larkin's troubles too. "If I'm right, this will crush her."

She leans closer and squeezes my leg. "Only a strong woman could raise you five boys and live to tell the tale. And she has you to lean on. Whatever happens, you'll all get through it."

The pressure on my chest eases. "Thanks. I needed to hear that, I think."

She smiles kindly, but her attention drops to my mouth. Instantly, heat swells in my groin. More than appreciation spreads through my sternum. Larkin's bottom lip is fuller than her top—the kind of plump lip that makes a man feel thirsty.

Suddenly, the pressure of her hand on my thigh becomes unbearably intense.

Neither of us moves. The air seems to thicken with unspoken tension, our chests rising in tandem, until we both lean forward, like we're magnetized. Drawn toward each other. And the urge to kiss Larkin slams into me. So forcefully, I jerk back and bang my head into my headrest.

"Passport," she says as she uselessly pats her hair. "I'll just run in and grab my bag and passport. Then I'll be out, and you can drive me home."

"No," I bark, hating my harsh tone. How unraveled I suddenly feel.

I don't wait for her reply. Just rev my engine and turn us around.

I feel fucking turned around.

I'm in a relationship. I love Jolene. At least, I used to. Maybe still do. And I was a millisecond away from kissing another woman.

What the hell is wrong with me?

Larkin braces her hand against the dash. "What do you mean, no? Why are we leaving?"

"This was a bad idea. You shouldn't be here. I'll take you to your mother's."

"But I want to get my stuff."

"And I said *no*." I need Larkin out of my truck. Away from me. Even now, I want to pull over. Drag her into my lap and claim her mouth.

I press my foot on the gas, driving faster than I should.

Larkin's confusion is palpable, as is her anger as she says, "Stop."

"I'm taking you home."

"And I want out."

"Not until you're safe."

"Yeah, well, I don't feel safe with you anymore, so stop the fucking truck!"

Her words are a punch to my gut.

I instantly pull over. Grip my steering wheel so hard my knuckles whiten. I'm not surprised Larkin is uncomfortable. I'm shaking with barely contained self-hatred. I nearly kissed her a second ago, even though I told her I'm not the type of asshole who'd cheat on his girlfriend. Maybe I'm more like my father than I thought.

I should say something. Apologize, convince Larkin to let me drive her home.

I stare out the windshield and inwardly fume.

"Oh my God," she suddenly says.

Her tone sounds so shocked, I glance at her. "What?"

Fury burns a blotchy path up her neck. "Did someone dare you to drive me home and hook up with the town slut? Is that what's going on here? You thought you'd get in my pants but chickened out last minute?"

Hell no, is what I should say. Tell her the truth. I wanted to kiss her a minute ago. I want to devour her now. But I'm on a date with my girlfriend tonight—the only woman I should be devouring. I need to get back to that party. See Jolene. Kiss *her*. Make things right with *her*.

Feeling ill, I shrug. "Just let me drive you home, okay?"

Larkin's glassy eyes widen. "I am *such* an idiot."

She leans away from me like I'm contagious. Quickly, she shoves her door open and nearly falls while scrambling out. She slams the door so hard my truck rattles.

I roll down the window, thinking of ways to backpedal and erase the hurt from Larkin's face. "You sure you're okay to walk home from here?" is my genius retort.

She lifts her middle finger. "Have a nice fucking life, Jake Bower."

I know this area. It's safe. I'm the one who doesn't feel safe near Larkin Gray, but I don't like leaving her like this. Still, I pull my truck out and speed away from her.

———

Larkin

"Unbelievable," I mutter as I watch Jake's truck peel away.

My asshole radar is clearly on the fritz. I mean, how did I miss the signs? How didn't I see the creep under Jake's sweet-talking? I actually believed that shit about his parents. His stress over his relationship with Jolene. His care for *me*.

The jerk should be nominated for an Academy Award, and I need a reality check.

I was nothing but a joke to Jake Bower. The target of a cruel trick—make the slut feel safe and worthwhile for a minute, then take what you want.

My next exhale sounds like a growl.

Lampposts light the large trees and small bungalows on this part of Birch Street. A cat struts on a front lawn, watching me—Lola, by the looks of her size and bushy tail. Hopefully she was out terrorizing the boys on the block.

"Men are such assholes," I tell her.

She mewls. I take that as an agreement, but I don't feel better.

I rub my eyes. Resist the urge to dig my nails into my cheeks. I am so *tired* of men using me. Of being physically weaker. Scared. Judged. A freaking damsel in distress, needing to be saved. It's time I find my backbone and take charge of my life.

What better time than the present?

Swallowing down tonight's humiliation, I turn and strut for Derek's home. I need my clothes and passport. Derek won't be home for ages, and I'm a strong, capable girl. The type of fierce woman who solves her own problems.

The last thing I need is Jake Bower to have my back.

———

What happens when Larkin's ex unexpectedly turns up drunk and discovers her near his house? Find out in Book Five, 7 Steps to Seducing Your Fake Fiancé.

Buy your copy today!

Author's Note

Thank you for reading Jolene and Callahan's story! I hope you loved them as much as I did. Fair warning: Jake and Larkin's happily ever after is more intense and has completely dismantled me. I can't wait for you to fall in love with them and revisit Windfall one last time.

Also By Kelly Siskind

Bower Boys Series:

50 Ways to Win Back Your Lover

10 Signs You Need to Grovel

6 Clues Your Nemesis Loves You

4 Hints You Love Your Best Friend

7 Steps to Seducing Your Fake Fiancé

One Wild Wish Series:

He's Going Down

Off-Limits Crush

36 Hour Date

Showmen Series:

New Orleans Rush

Don't Go Stealing My Heart

The Beat Match

The Knockout Rule

Over the Top Series:

My Perfect Mistake

A Fine Mess

Hooked on Trouble

Stand-Alone: Chasing Crazy

Visit Kelly's website and join her newsletter for great giveaways and never miss an update!

www.kellysiskind.com

About the Author

Kelly Siskind lives in charming northern Ontario. When she's not out hiking or skiing, you can find her, notepad in hand, scribbling down one of the many plot bunnies bouncing around in her head. She loves singing while driving, looks awful in yellow, and is known for spilling wine at parties.

Sign up for Kelly's newsletter: www.kellysiskind.com and never miss a giveaway, a free bonus scene, or the latest news on her books. And connect with her on Twitter and Instagram (@kellysiskind) or on Facebook and TikTok (@authorkellysiskind).

For giveaways and early peeks at new work, join Kelly's newsletter: www.kellysiskind.com

If you like to laugh and chat about books, join Kelly in her Facebook group, KELLY'S GANG.

Connect with Kelly on social media:
Twitter/KellySiskind
facebook/authorKellySiskind
Instagram/kellysiskind

CPSIA information can be obtained
at www.ICGtesting.com
Printed in the USA
BVHW042114140723
667266BV00002B/16